The Second Life
of Doctor Albin

The Second Life of Doctor Albin

by
Raoul Gineste

translated, annotated and introduced by
Brian Stableford

A Black Coat Press Book

Visit our website at www.blackcoatpress.com

ISBN 978-1-61227-467-6. First Printing. February 2016. Published by Black Coat Press, an imprint of Hollywood Comics.com, LLC, P.O. Box 17270, Encino, CA 91416. All rights reserved. Except for review purposes, no part of this book may be reproduced or transmitted in any form or by any means, electronic or mechanical, including photocopying, recording, or by any information storage and retrieval system, without permission in writing from the publisher. The stories and characters depicted in this novel are entirely fictional. Printed in the United States of America.

Introduction

La Seconde vie du docteur Albin by "Raoul Gineste," here translated as *The Second Life of Doctor Albin*, was originally published by the Librairie des Mathurins in 1902, and reprinted several times in rapid succession as it achieved a success that was, alas, to prove meteoric. It was the author's first novel, following two collections of poetry associated with the Félibrige—a movement launched in the 1850s by a group of Provençal writers desirous of reviving the Occitan language—although he published more poems in French than in Occitan, and was also been associated with the Parnassians.

Born in 1849 according to the Bibliothèque Nationale, 1852 according to other sources, "Gineste," whose real name was Adolphe Augier, came rather late to the Félibrige, and *La Seconde vie du docteur Albin* was a rather belated debut as a novelist, but the success of that first venture led him to follow it up with several more novels before his death in 1914, as well as a volume of mildly satirical reminiscences, *Soirs de Paris* [Parisian Evenings] (1903). As the subject-matter of the novel suggests, Augier had spent most of his life working as a physician in Paris, although he also frequented the Bohemian literary milieu of the Latin Quarter, being acquainted with Théodore Banville, José-Maria de Heredia, Charles Leconte de Lisle, Arthur Rimbaud and Paul Verlaine, among others; his memoir attests that he was well acquainted with the milieu of "café concerts" described in the novel. Seen in association with his second novel, *Le Nègre de Paris* [The Negro of Paris] (1903), *La Seconde vie du docteur Albin* also suggests that he might well have felt something of an outsider, if not an actual outcast, in all the sectors of Parisian society except for "Bohemia."

As a contribution to the tradition of *roman scientifique*, *La Seconde vie du docteur Albin* belongs to a set of fictions that explore the supposed psychology typical of scientists with considerable analytical intensity. The tradition in question had begun in the 1840s in the "*fantaisies scientifiques*" of S. Henry Berthoud, an archetypal exercise in that vein being the striking "Voyage au ciel" (1841; tr. as "A Heavenward Voyage"), which Berthoud followed up with such further examples as "Le Maître de temps" (1844; tr. as "The Master of the Weather") and "Le Second Soleil" (periodical publication uncertain; book version 1862; tr. as "The Second Sun").[1] That groundwork had been laid for some time before the phrase *roman scientifique*—used since the 18th century to refer to scientific theories considered too fanciful by the user—was adapted in the 1870s as a description of a kind of fiction, primarily with reference to the works of Jules Verne, whose fictional scientists closely resembled the model developed extensively by Berthoud in terms of their supposedly distinctive psychological quirks

In the same decade, however, the term was also adopted by a number of critics, led by Édouard Rod, to apply to the "Naturalist" fiction then being ardently promoted by Émile Zola and his followers, on the grounds that Zolaesque examination of human character was a quasi-scientific exercise, a kind of analytic psychology in itself. That label inevitably took on a particularly strong connotation when Zola and other writers in that vein focused their attention of protagonists who were scientists, as in Zola's *Le Docteur Pascal* (1893; tr. as *Doctor Pascal*). Whereas Zola and the first generation of Naturalists tended to focus on supposed hereditary and social determinants of character, the second generation, led by Paul Bourget's example, took far more inspiration from rapid developments in psychological theory, and their work became more probing as well as more clinical, in such determined analysis of the "scientific mind" as André Beaunier's *L'Homme qui a perdu son moi* (1911; tr. as *The Man Who Lost*

---

[1] Included in the collection *Martyrs of Science*, Black Coat Press, ISBN 978-1-61227-229-0.

Himself), which might conceivably have taken some inspiration from Raoul Gineste's quintessential account of self-loss.

One of the central planks of the model of the scientific mind—or, or more accurately of scientific genius—constructed by the early writers of *roman scientifique* who followed where Berthoud led is the notion that a true love of science is essentially incompatible with, and perhaps antithetical to, love between the sexes. It would almost be possible to write "the love of women," because almost all the scientists represented in *roman scientifique* are male, but there are female examples, like Geneviève Gasquin in Jean Richepin's *L'Aile* (1911)[2] and Jeanne Fortin in Félicien Champsaur's *Homo-Deus: Le Satyre invisible* (1924),[3] whose separation from amorous experience is even more dramatic. Moral tales such as René de Pont-Jest's "La Tête de Mimer" (1863)[4] make much of the supposed incompatibility in question, to the point, in that particular case, of representing the lure of science as a literal diabolical temptation, tragically freezing the heart against the author's preferred version of true love.

Many scientists featured in *roman scientifique* are, of course, married, but it is almost invariably taken for granted that they neglect their wives, often to the latter's chagrin, and always prioritize their work when any conflict of interest arises; sometimes, that neglect became an ironic central theme, as in "Le Microbe de Professeur Bakermann" (1890)[5] by "Charles Epheyre" (the physiologist Charles Richet). Often, the scientists of *roman scientifique* love their daughters far more, the love in question demanding a far less complex reciprocity. It is not necessarily the case that the typical genius of

---

[2] tr. as *The Wing*, Black Coat Press, ISBN 978-1-61227-053-1.

[3] tr. as "The Invisible Satyr" in *Homo Deus*, Black Coat Press, ISBN 978-1-61227-351-8.

[4] tr. as "Mimer's Head" in *The World Above the World*, Black Coat Press, ISBN 978-1-61227-002-9.

[5] tr. as "Professor Bakermann's Microbe" in *The Supreme Progress*, Black Coat Press, ISBN 978-1-935558-82-8.

roman scientifique does not love his wife—the protagonist of Berthoud's "Voyage au ciel," for instance, loves his wife very dearly and makes considerable sacrifices in her favor—but their love is invariably somehow unorthodox; its truth, when it is true, is not the same truth as that of the traditional poetic image of true love.

Although it is not the only feature of the psychology of scientific genius brought into close and intense focus in *La Seconde vie du docteur Albin*, the protagonist's involvements with sexual love are a leading feature of the plot, and perhaps the most interesting one. The novel provides what is perhaps the most searching analysis of that allegedly-perverse emotional involvement to be found in the genre, and, although it is not necessarily accurate—indeed, the fundamental model might be nothing more than a bizarre myth—it is certainly thorough, in terms of the detail of the protagonist's thought-processes. From a "poetic" viewpoint, its thoroughness might make it seem one of the most damning such analyses—René de Pont-Jest would probably have thought so—but Gineste was a scientist himself as well as a poet, and his attitude is far more balanced than some, infused with a genuine puzzlement and exploratory curiosity as well as a sense of inevitable tragedy.

Other repetitive themes of *roman scientifique* crop up in Gineste's novel in various ways, mostly marginally, and to draw up a full list here would constitute a spoiler in one vital instance, but the novel has other interesting features, and has the enormous advantage of setting up a genuinely intriguing situation, whose development maintains a considerable dramatic suspense throughout a long and complex series of events. That dramatic quality is exaggerated to the extent of relentless toying with the elements and clichés of melodrama: a play which is to some extent deliberate teasing but also has a considerable depth of sincere feeling. As in many melodramas, the plot makes use of outrageous coincidences, whose accumulation eventually reaches such proportions that the reader, like the protagonist, will surely come to the conclusion that they cannot be the product of chance, and that Dr. Albin's *alter egos* really are being actively pursued by a malevolent fate intent on punishing him for the sin that he initially considers to be venial, but whose cardinality he learns to his cost. The novel remains, however, conscientiously Naturalistic, even taking the trouble to include a digression arguing the nonsensicality of the idea of the supernatural.

The story's elements of speculative science remain stubbornly marginal; the two significant inventions made by the protagonist are only employed momentarily as inconsequential plot levers, and we are never told what Dr. Albin's theory of biological chemistry actually asserts, what it crucial flaw is, and how its repair might be effected; that absence is a trifle frustrating, although it is perhaps more honest than the more common science-fictional technique of filling such conceptual gaps with gobbledygook. The story could not refer to an actual theory—all the more so as it begins more than a quarter of a century before its publication date—so the one that it invokes is necessarily symbolic, and the author presumably felt that its symbolic quality made detailed information unnecessary as well as impractical. One consequence of the omission is that, in spite of the tight focus the narrative has on the protagonist's thought and feelings, the one thing we never overhear him thinking about is the science he loves so dearly—but all fiction of this kind is, and has to be, more interested in the side-effects of a true love of science rather than the object of the amour itself.

Some readers might feel that the absence from the narrative of any detailed scientific or pseudoscientific rhetoric is a flaw, others might think the same about its over-reliance on coincidence, and some might consider that its account of the protagonist's ten-year odyssey through hell on earth contains too many digressions, but none of these aspects of the text are mistakes, and they have their virtues as well as their irritating aspects. In sum, the book is a bold and original venture whose originality reflects considerable intellectual and literary acumen as well as a certain winning audacity—something the original readers responsible or its initial success evidently realized. It is certainly highly readable, and maintains its dramatic tension to the end.

This translation was made from the copy of the second printing of the Librairie des Mathurins edition reproduced on the Bibliothèque Nationale's *gallica* website.

Brian Stableford

Chapter I

The first event that troubled the quietude, so profound until then, of Dr. Albin, the illustrious author of *Biological Chemistry*, occurred in the spring of the year 18**. His only daughter, his adored Jeanne, whose beauty was emerging more radiantly every day from the uncertain forms of childhood, died of typhoid fever at the age of fifteen.

All the leading medical lights in Paris, combined with all knowledge and all devotion, were unable to avert the fatal conclusion. Intoxication, secret troubles or intellectual overexertion? What did it matter? The disease had defied all remedies; death, as if to affirm its invincible power, had struck, in his pride as a healer, in his future projects, and in his dearest affection, the man who had made a game of snatching away its prey.

So, the man whose miracles were proclaimed by renown, the artist of reliable diagnosis, the scientist always guided by logic and prudence, victorious in so many reputedly desperate cases, was unable to save from death the one being he loved with all his heart. The death that he had chased from so many dwellings had settled coldly that day, ironically and implacably, in his own hearth. Why?

He had not found himself in the presence of an incurable disease, a devastating attack, or an irredeemably worn-out organism. Is human science so uncertain that it becomes impotent just at the moment when it is most necessary?

For a long time, the desolate father had before his eyes the drawn features, the ashen lips, and the feverish and imploring gaze of the dying girl. For a long time, as if nursing a rancor against the science that had, so to speak, betrayed and abandoned him, he deserted the school and the amphitheater; then, begged by his admirers and those near to him, solicited by all wishes, he was finally seen—somber of expression, to be sure, with silver threads in his long black hair—to emerge

11

from his solitude, resume his chair and once again hold hundreds of young men from all over the world under the spell and authority of his instruction.

Should not the ardent and positive convictions of Dr. Albin have been above a personal tragedy? No, science was not responsible for his woe; the only true guilty party was him, who, to avoid too heavy a responsibility, had appealed to the enlightenment of others. Why that sentimental weakness? Why had he not cared for his poor Jeanne himself, and alone?

Briefly, the learned professor had thought that his wife, who was much younger than him, would help him to overcome his chagrin; but there were so many misunderstandings between them, so many points of friction, insignificant in appearance but in reality profound, so much divergences in the fashion of envisaging wellbeing, that he had quickly returned to his initial state of conjugal indifference. Madame Albin, a simultaneously worldly and pious Parisienne, an elegant doll who divided her time between the concerns of toilette and works of charity, a quintessential product of an honest but futile bourgeois education, was too distant from her husband for a catastrophe, terrible as it was, to be able to bring them together definitively.

Furthermore, a painful observation had come to offend his self-esteem. His favorite pupil, his protégé, the Dr. Larmezan he had once chosen for his daughter and received into his intimacy, was overtly courting his wife, and appeared to be paid in return. To what degree were they culpable? The certainty of their sin would only have caused him scorn, for the one who had betrayed his confidence and the other who had betrayed her duty. But there was in their attitude, replete with frankness, a kind of reproach for his blind indifference, and a kind of affirmation of the right to amour that wounded his vanity without rekindling the sentiments of old. Their apparent loyalty seemed to legitimate their passion, and the fear of ridicule, and the consciousness of his own faults, obliged him to suffer it.

Gradually resuming the noble occupations of his past life, therefore, he plunged more ardently than ever into the arduous studies that had edified his glorious reputation.

To crown his endeavors, he wanted, before dying, to leave the scientific world a general history of chemistry that would summarize all the doctrines of the past.

Previously, he had judged anterior efforts in accordance with more or less documentary accounts. His need to create, his overly exclusive admiration for the modern era, had caused him to neglect the treasures accumulated over so many centuries. Now that he had to attribute to everyone his just share of genius, he found himself obliged to return to the most distant sources. It was thus that he was led, logically and naturally, to undertake a profound study of the alchemists of the Middle Ages and the Renaissance.

Arrested to begin with by the symbolic language that hid their works from the intelligence of the vulgar, forced to comprehend and initiate himself into the occult sciences, he was soon astonished and seduced by the profundity of the vision of certain traditional theories. Those first endeavors, veritably conscientious, had the immediate result of causing him to abandon all prejudice. Soon, the corners of the veil were torn. Applying to the study of Alchemy the rectitude and power of modern experimentation, he embarked on a new and fecund path, the horizon broadened, unknown stars shone in his eyes, and inviolate formulae delivered their secrets to him.

Encouraged, he redoubled his efforts.

In the wing of the old princely town house that he had transformed into a laboratory, in the midst of alembics, furnaces, retorts and apparatus; among jars and bottles of every color and form; surrounded by anatomical preparations and folio volumes; equipped with his glass mask, interrogating with his anxious gaze the seething of his crucibles and the effervescence of his phials, he spent the greater part of his time discovering the laws and affinities that link inert and living matter.

His Great Work was not to transmute base matter into pure gold; it was the cell that he wanted to animate, and movement, the secret of God, that he wanted to learn.

That was the enthusiastic work that elevated his soul and scarred over his dolor—and it was that incessant and loyal search for the Truth that caused the second, irreparable, misfortune.

On the eighteenth of June 18**, a decisive experiment, repeated and concluded a hundred times, came to destroy from top to bottom the scientific scaffolding that had won him so much prestige and renown, Dr. Albin's *Biological Chemistry*, the capital work that had provoked so much polemic and caused his name to resound in all the universities of the world. The victorious doctrine that had provided the basis of present knowledge, in the name of which he had denied principles and broken opposition, the glorious monument that he had believed would be transmitted indestructibly to posterity, was built on a false—completely false—principle.[6]

Ingenious deductions, indisputably true relativities, had emerged from it, but the bronze colossus rested on feet of clay, and it was Dr. Albin himself, the creator of the false god, who had discovered it!

---

[6] Although we are not told what Dr. Albin's theory is, the hints dropped in this opening passage allow certain deductions. It is presumably a materialistic replacement for the theory of "vitalism"—the notion that living matter is essentially different from inert matter because it is possessed of a mysterious "vital spark"—which had been seemingly belied by the rapid development of organic chemistry in the second half of the 19th century. Albin's crucial experiments might have indicated the necessity of reintroducing some such crucial energetic factor, conceived in a new way. The author might or might not have been aware in 1902 of the thesis of "*élan vital*" [vital impulse] that Henri Bergson was developing for eventual publication in *Evolution créatrice* (1907; tr. as *Creative Evolution*).

Alternately dejected and enthused by that revelation, sometimes wanting to proclaim it and overturn his work, sometimes envisaging fearfully the inconveniences that would ensue, caught between his love of the Truth and his legitimate pride as a venerated scientist, arrested by the memory of ardent struggles and vanquished rivalries, pushed by the voice of his conscience, Dr. Albin was tossed for some time by cruel hesitations. Was there, after all, any first principle that was truly demonstrated? Were not all sciences based on hypotheses? Who could boast of having found the great X, the absolute? A chimera: what did the point of departure matter if the deductions were fecund, if humanity benefited therefrom?

Perhaps, a few months before, the illustrious professor would have clung to those sophisms. Perhaps a paltry but very human cause would have determined him to do so. But today, his beloved daughter was dead, his glory and his power could no longer serve to secure the happiness of his own flesh and blood. Ought he not to sacrifice to the Truth the work that he recognized as false and the reputation unjustly acquired?

Even though his dolor was of a purely intellectual order, it was even more poignant than the first; and the scientist, wounded in the heart, returning to the past, wondered fearfully whether, as Azaïs[7] claimed, the sum of our joys must be compensated by an equal sum of distress.

The son of a justly esteemed professor, Louis-Jacques Albin, laureate of the general competition at sixteen, intern at nineteen, graduate in physiology at twenty-five, was already almost famous at an age when so many others were still on the

---

[7] The philosopher Pierre Azaïs (1766-1845), author of *Des Compensations dans les destinées humaines* [Compensations in Human Destiny] (1809), which attempts to prove that there is a necessary and strict balance between happiness and misery; not only is that notion very prominent in the present text, but so is one of the principal corollaries that Azaïs drew from it: that inequality is natural and inevitable, and leads inevitably to revolutionary fanaticism.

benches. Fanatical about science, tenacious in study, although he undermined those qualities by virtue of a crazy avidity to know everything that prevented him from fixing his attention on the same subject for very long, he astonished the scientific world by his prodigious faculty of assimilation. Once, he would have been one of the encyclopedic doctors of the Middle Ages who gloried in knowing everything, and whom the Church hastened to deliver to the pyre.

Devoured by pride, inclined to ostentation, prompt to anger, but good, generous and trusting to the point of naivety, precious to his allies and faithful to his friends, launched in all societies, placed in favorable circumstances and on a road cleared of obstacles, nothing had been able to stop his triumphant march.

The skill, and above all the audacity, of his surgical operations had earned him is initial success. At thirty, gripped by a sudden enthusiasm for chemistry, he had let go of his worldly relations, published his *Research in the Physical and Chemical Phenomena of Life* and justified, by his personal endeavors, the fortune that the curious and his rivals attributed to paternal influence.

In the same epoch he became the son-in-law of a renowned professor, uniting two powerful parties. Three years later, the famous treatise on *Biological Chemistry* consecrated his nascent glory in spectacular fashion, and earned him, at the age of thirty-five, a chair in biology specially created for him.

Since then, the most incredible luck had not abandoned him for an instant. A surgeon in the hospitals, a brilliant clinician whose lectures foreign students flocked to hear, a member of the Institut, a dispenser of positions, a great elector of Academies, the commander of a multitude of medals, a député, even a minister in one of the ephemeral cabinets that are born and die of political intrigue: almost all the favors and titles that human ambition can desire had arrived as if natural and legitimate.

Was he not the man of an entire people: the peerless scholar, the personality that rival nations envied us, the famous author of *Biological Chemistry*? Was not the prestigious operator combined with a grandiloquent orator, a writer of clear and muscular style, and a musician that even artistes praised? Never had governmental and popular favor been more justified!

And all, or almost all, of that surprising fortune derived from a fortunate birth and a false theory that he had developed brilliantly. How could so much power and so much profit have emerged from a hazard, his birth, and an error, his work? It was necessary, for that to have happened, that the influence of the environment in which he had evolved had been singularly unjust and corrupt!

Outside of his spirit of intrigue and the manual dexterity of an operator, a talent of an inferior order compared with that of an executive or a worker, he had only been the expression of an ensemble; he did not owe his elevation to his own value. And yet that value existed; it was undeniable, a kind of genius; his discovery was the proof of it; why should he not destroy his past work? Was it not an advertisement, and indication of destiny? Ought he to remain the product of official mediocrity? Ought he to wait for the hour of justice to chime, for the contradictors driven into the shadows to take their revenge?

Yesterday, even today, anyone who had dared to oppose him would have almost have been reckoned a national enemy, but tomorrow? Someone else, perhaps a foreign rival, might be about to discover what he had just discovered, to attack the imposing false god, to bring its down irredeemably into the mud. Was it not better that he should at least have the honor of overturning himself?

In the first place, the thing seemed logical and easy; but numerous objections soon came to lay siege to his simultaneously proud and virtuous mind.

His combativeness had made his theories a veritable philosophical and scientific doctrine. A powerful political party had seen them as the confirmation of its anti-religious principles. The confession of his error would be seen, by those prejudiced men, as a shameful retreat, a treason. His most fervent supporters would refuse to follow him and would be in league against him. Then again, would it not be cruel to witness the collapse of his work, to deny the absolute affirmations of the day before, to be the butt of the scorn and mockery of his enemies, to ruin the publishers of the *Rational Encyclopedia* of which he had been the editorial director, to destroy the influence of numerous disciples or allies who had defended his ideas, to see his lectures deserted and his admirers disillusioned? That someone else might carry out the ingrate task in the name of Truth was one thing, but did he really have the right and the duty to do it himself?

If he had been able to build immediately, on the ruins of his *Biological Chemistry*, a new theory that would victoriously replace it, hesitation would not have been permissible; but the principle he had discovered, while destroying his work, was only as yet a point of departure; it would take years to crown the new edifice and acquire—legitimately, this time—an indisputable and more durable renown.

The eminent professor thus found himself facing a dilemma: either to live in a cowardly compromise, to continue publicly to teach the error while shamefully pursuing the truth in the shadows, at the risk of seeing a fortunate rival do what he did not have the strength to accomplish; or, to destroy himself, without delay, to his own detriment and that of his partisans, the work on which his reputation and power were based. The spirit of truth told him that the latter course was the only one worthy of a true scientist; his sentimentality and everything that attached him to the past persuaded him to keep quiet.

It was then that, seeking a middle way, his pride, an insatiable wild beast that had just found a prey, caused a madly grandiose idea to germinate in his bold mind, which began by seeming paradoxical and only worthy to serve for amusement, but which then ripened and became imposing, materializing day by day in order to conclude in the most audacious and strangest of projects.

Dr. Albin, he said to himself, can die without regrets; he has nothing more to expect from this world. He can disappear in full glory, surrounded by all homages and al sympathy. His party, which holds the best political positions, will not reproach him for having caused its ruin.

Thus, since there are two men in me, let the official man, the hesitant individual linked by friendships, entangled in the past, weakened by self-esteem and sentimentality, disappear; and let the other, the strong man, the just man, the free man, the true scientist, survive, destroy the false work, and proclaim the Truth!

In brief, I duplicate myself, I witness my own funeral, with all the respect that I owe to my first personality; then, once the doors of the tomb close, I inaugurate a second life, I become the scientific enemy of Dr. Albin, and I annihilate his false glory! I'm forty-six, it's true, but I'm educated and rich, I won't have to waste time acquiring a fortune and knowledge; in ten years, I'll reach the goal.

What do I have to lose? Nothing. The being that I loved the most is dead; the one for whom affection might reattach me to life doesn't understand me, and no longer even takes the trouble to hide her love for someone else. I'm weary of honors, I'd be ashamed to teach what I no longer know to be the truth. The intellectual and moral strength that remain within me can be utilized in a new incarnation. Nothing more remains for me to do, therefore, except die…in order to be resuscitated!

What do I have to fear? More ardent struggles, greater obstacles and sharper suffering! But it's doubtless because I haven't suffered and struggled enough that the truth has taken so long to appear to me. Dr. Albin was nothing, in reality, but the perfect expression of the *aurea mediocritas*[8] that leads to everything; I shall be able to say: I am the man of genius!

What mortal has ever had a destiny like mine: two existences of honors, combats and glory?

---

[8] The golden mean.

I shall make arrangements for posterity to learn, without being able to doubt it, the marvelous adventure. I shall be the man with two faces whose audacity and genius will astonish the world!

"Unless," he murmured, "death really does come to interrupt me... Bah! Everything leads me to suppose the contrary."

He stood in front of a mirror, as if to observe the still-powerful vigor of his vitality. He was a man of slightly above medium height, with a broad forehead, a dominating gaze, a jutting chin and a pale face framed by abundant black and slightly curly hair.

"And that's good for another ten or fifteen years," he said, thumping his chest. "And as Meng-Tze[9] said, 'It's never the strength that's lacking, but the will.'"

---

[9] The Confucian philosopher more usually known by the Latinized form of his name, Mencius. He was a great believer in the power of Destiny.

Chapter II

The scientist, having taken the definitive, unbreakable decision that day to accomplish his fantastic design, reflected at length. It was a matter of dying officially and in an incontestable fashion—which, for a man of his notoriety, was not a banal trick easy of execution.

First of all, what would be the evaluation of the act from the social viewpoint, and what might be its legal consequences? Was it a fraud in the legal sense of the word? No, since there would be no false declaration on his part, nor any usurpation of entitlement, since civil death would result from it and suicide was not punishable by law. One could, at the most, be considered as accomplice to an error committed by the registrar of births and deaths—which is to say, by Society.

The lie was, however, indisputable; but that was a deceit of which he would be the sole responsible judge; is not genius, like royalty, above human laws?

Now, in what fashion ought he to attain his goal? He searched for examples in history but found none. The comedy of the death feigned by Charles Quint had no similarity to his case.[10] The imagination of poets and dramaturges did not come to his aid either. The majority of romantic or fanciful inventions did not even have the appearance of reality. He wanted the veracity of his action to be undeniable.

Two projects appeared to approach his objective most closely.

One consisted of provoking apparent death by a lethargic drug, and then, having woken up a few hours before the funeral, substituting some other cadaver in his place. The expedient, it is true, would irremediably remove Dr. Albin from the offi-

---

[10] The Holy Roman Emperor Charles V (1500-1558) did not literally feign his death, but did abdicate all the parts of his empire piece by piece.

cial world, but he judged it dangerous and complicated, and above all, it required and intelligent and reliable accomplice. The absorption of such a philter might, moreover, damage his organism; it would at the very least be indispensable to put himself gradually into a cataleptic state, like the Hindu fanatics who died and were resuscitated at will.

The other means, of less complete result, had the enormous advantage of dispensing with any confidant. It consisted of departing for some unexplored region at the head of a more-or-less scientific expedition and seizing the first favorable opportunity to disappear. It would infallibly be supposed that he had been massacred by savages or devoured by wild beasts.

Circumstances decided him to prefer the latter. The Tonkin expedition was taking on the proportions of a major war.[11] Field hospitals were being organized in Paris; it would be the very devil if Dr. Albin, an influential member of the Red Cross, could not find a glorious death in that distant land that would crown his first life worthily!

That idea appealed to his pride, and gained more determinate consistency by the day. Indiscretions, notes and then interviews published in the newspapers of all parties did not take long to announce the news:

The author of Biological Chemistry, *the eminent surgeon Albin, with the patronage and support of the government, is organizing a model field hospital and preparing to join the expeditionary corps.*

Requests flowed from all directions from young and brilliant surgeons of the capital soliciting the honor of following

---

[11] The Tonkin campaign, led by Admiral Amédée Courbet, began in June 1883, suggesting that the story opens in that year—a hypothesis eventually confirmed by calculations based on other data; it is unclear, therefore, why the author refrains from specifying the last two numbers when he cites dates in the story.

the illustrious example, but the master, under various pretexts, rejected all those who were closely connected with him, and preferred colleagues he scarcely knew.

During that period of organization, Dr. Albin made arrangements for the future that seemed to him to be indispensable. The possessor of a large personal fortune, he was able to divert a part of it without attracting the slightest suspicion. Five hundred thousand francs appeared to him to be sufficient to ensure his future independence. The immediate purchase of securities risked creating problems later, so he realized that sum in banknotes and deposited them in a financial establishment under the name of Jacques Liban, an anagram of Albin, stipulating that it should be payable on the simple presentation of a justificatory document whose duplicate he left.

All the preparations having been made, the equipment sent to Marseilles and the surgeons ready to depart—in consequence of an agreement with the authorities, the orderlies would be recruited out there from among convalescent soldiers—Professor Albin wanted to give a farewell lecture before handing his chair over to Dr. Larmezan.

The vast amphitheater was overflowing with people. Students, scientific and political notables, and even socialites wanted to manifest their sympathies. The professor's entrance was saluted by an enthusiastic ovation. When the lecture was over, new acclamations burst for from all the benches. The professor signaled that he was about to add a final word.

"In lavishing me with such marks of esteem," he said, in an emotional voice, "you render the separation more painful for me; and if the idea that I am about to accomplish a duty to the fatherland did not sustain me, I would feel my courage weakening."

Frenetic bravos welcomed that declaration.

"Death," he continued, "does not strike all those who risk it, and I hope to have the good fortune to return among you, but if destiny decides otherwise, do not be surprised or afflicted. Let us envisage the end calmly and without too many regrets: to die is to live again, to reenter the mysterious crucible

23

of nature. Our remains are transformed and our spirit survives in our deeds and works. I did not want to leave you, my friends, without saying that to you. Let your deeds be noble and your works be beautiful, in order that that survival will be glorious for you and profitable to humankind."

Cries of admiration escaped all throats. For the first time, a remorse invaded the skillful scene-setter. Why was he playing with all those souls? What was the point of that invocation of the Fatherland? Was it not impudent of him to speak of duty, when he intended to desert it?

But was it not necessary to prepare that brilliant audience for the sensational news that it would not he long delayed in hearing, and was he not still Dr. Albin, the man of official pomposity and social hypocrisy?

Professor Albin's field hospital, as soon as it was disembarked at Hai-Phong, was placed at the disposition of Admiral Courbet and recruited its orderlies. The eminent doctor had divided it into two sections. One, established on the bank of the Red River in proximity to the troops then in the region of Son-Hai, was rapidly transported to the combat zone, where it picked up the wounded, gave them first aid, operated in urgent cases and evacuated them as soon as possible to the huts installed at Hanoi, in more hygienic and comfortable conditions.

Dr. Albin had put himself at the head of the first group, and, without losing sight of his audacious project, accomplished his mission with surprising courage, marching bravely toward rifle and cannon fire, enduring all fatigues and not recoiling before any danger. His colleagues had observed to him more than once that he had come to heal the wounded, and that it was therefore imprudent to take too many risks, but the illustrious scientist, without demanding the same devotion from them, paid no heed to their sage advice. He wanted his bravery to be proclaimed, so that his death, when it came, would be considered as the inevitable result of his temerity.

His desire did not take long to be satisfied, the courage of a celebrated man having few efforts to make in order to be noticed. Dr. Albin was mentioned in dispatches, and the Admiral himself implored him to be more careful of such a precious existence in future. Finding his reputation for boldness sufficiently established, he then judged that he could die with a brilliance worthy of his renown.

The general staff had warned him that a decisive action was in preparation and that it would be hot. He assembled his colleagues, assigned them posts that disseminated them along the battle line, and stayed with two aides and the orderlies and the hospital's main base.

The favorable opportunity was not long in presenting itself. That same day, heavy rifle fire broke out on the banks of the river in the direction of Son-Tay[12] and soldiers of the Foreign Legion, unexpectedly attacked by the Black Flags and overwhelmed by force of numbers, had fallen back in haste, abandoning their wounded to the field hospital. The most lightly injured had been able to flee, but the rest... And the officer who told him the story shook his head sadly.

"Let's go to their aid," the surgeon proposed.

"It would be running to death pointlessly, Doctor. Those bandits, as you know, always finish off wounded and take their heads as trophies. Tomorrow, when our troops have cleared the terrain, you can go to see whether they've neglected any, but be prudent—the village isn't secure."

He obtained the most precise indications, and spent long hours meditating. If he found a decapitated soldier of a similar height and age to himself, with a similar skin tone and distin-

---

[12] The Son Tay campaign, in which the French Expeditionary Corps eventually overwhelmed and smashed Liu Yongfu's Chinese Black Flag Army, took place in December 1883. Although there is no evidence that the Black Flags routinely took heads as trophies, Liu Yongfu did offer a bounty for the heads of French officers, and much publicity was generated in Paris when the body of naval officer Henri Rivière, who was also a notable writer of imaginative fiction and whom Gineste might well have met at *Le Chat Noir*—which Rivière helped to decorate in 1881—was found beheaded in May 1883.

guishing marks on his body, a substitution of identity would certainly be preferable to a pure and simple disappearance, which would always leave a certain lingering doubt...

The Foreign Legion is composed of soldiers of all ages and conditions. The majority of them conceal their identity under false names. No one worries about their lives. They disappear as suddenly as they emerged, not even leaving a slight foam on the surface of the human wave. As for him, the colleagues who had accompanied him scarcely knew him, and the orderlies even less. A decapitated cadaver would be found wearing his insignia. The pockets of his clothing would contain numerous evidences of identity. Who would take it into his head to have the slightest suspicion?

His body, it is true, would probably be transported to Paris and the coffin would be opened before his closest acquaintances, but in the three or four months that had gone by, decomposition would have done its work, and it would then be difficult for any doubt to arise. How could a half-putrefied and headless cadaver be recognized? The clothing and items found on him would be irrefutable witnesses. The particularity of decapitation was eminently favorable to the complete success of his plan. Apart from the facial features furnishing numerous indications, Dr. Larmezan had once taken anthropomorphic measurements of his skull in the anthropological laboratory, but that certain data would have been rendered useless by the saber of a pirate!

After mature reflection, and making all his preparations, he resolved to attempt the adventure.

The next day, at dawn, a cannonade burst forth from all the positions, soon followed by the long crepitations of rifle fire. He confided the care of the wounded to his two young colleagues, had his horse saddled, and set off upriver.

The fusillade, which gradually became more distant, proved that our troops were gaining ground. There was, in any case, no risk, as long as he stayed behind the French lines. The post attacked the day before was a few kilometers from his camp; it did not take him long to reach it. Smashed palisades and a burning house at the entrance to the village indicated the location of the battle.

He went into the rubble, and the most horrible spectacle met his eyes. Mutilated and decapitated cadavers lay here and there in pools of coagulated blood. Some were entirely naked, others half-stripped, as if some alert had interrupted the bandits.

He had seen floods of blood flow, and autopsies and the amphitheaters had shown him human remains a hundred times more deformed, and yet he was shaken by a quiver of fear. He thought about the true heroes, that elite intelligence, his friend, the unfortunate Commandant Rivière, who had suffered a similar fate.

That thought brought him swiftly back to his plan. He overcame his repugnance and chased away the vague terror that had enveloped him. One crime more to the account of those barbarians made no difference, and the reputation of Dr. Albin would benefit from it. He had edified the glory of his life on an error; the glory of his death might as well be a lie; the old man would thus be complete. Anyway, the deceit would not harm anyone; it only consisted of a substitution of individuality; had not the unfortunate legionnaire whose place he was taking really been massacred? Instead of being listed as dead, he would be considered as missing—which, in this merciless conflict, came to exactly the same thing.

He had made these last reflections while examining the cadavers minutely. One of them, especially, had attracted his attention. It was almost naked and had no apparent wound. Doubtless he had been taken prisoner and decapitated immediately. The section of the neck was so neat that the savant biologist, used to carrying out experiments on guillotined heads that were frequently badly cut, could not help remarking on it.

"Monsieur de Paris could take some lessons here," he murmured. "The head of that poor devil would have been an admirable subject of study for a transfusion of blood."

He continued his examination. The whiteness of the skin and the quality of the underwear indicated a certain origin. The summary measurements he made, the approximate age that he calculated, the color of the tegument and hair, all seemed to confirm the choice.

Hazard is favoring me, he thought. *I probably won't encounter a similar concordance again. Now it's a matter of finding some wounded, so that I can send my men away, and come back here.*

He immediately resumed his march. The village seemed deserted, but frightened faces glimpsed in several places proved that the inhabitants were hiding. As he progressed, the signs of a recent combat were multiplied; the cadavers of indigenes and Chinese regulars were strewn on the road. A few marine fusiliers, gathered in haste and arranged along a barrier, were awaiting the sepulcher. He had barely passed past the last habitations when he perceived, under the scintillation of bayonets, a somber mass that seemed to be guarding a position. To avoid any mistake, he waved his Red Cross flag. A navy surgeon hastened to come to meet him.

"You've arrived at a good time," he said. "Several of my men are more or less seriously wounded, and I'd be glad to evacuate them. We might receive orders to advance at any moment."

He immediately had the marines loaded on to cacolets, and resumed the route to the field hospital.

"I'll accompany my orderlies to the other side of the village," he said, as he was about to depart. "There's a house there that was recently built, and I want to check to see whether there are any wounded in the vicinity. Then I'll come back to put myself to your disposal."

"If we're still here," the navy surgeon replied.

"In any case, leave the rest of your wounded under a good guard; we'll be back in four or five hours."

As soon as he arrived at the site of the ambush he told his men that he was going to rejoin his colleague, instructing them to effect the transport as soon as possible and then come back.

When he had seen them disappear he swiftly dismounted, went into the tragic house, rapidly put on a check costume in the English style and his operating blouse, which he had brought in his saddlebag, cut the beard that he had allowed to grow, and then set about dressing the chosen cadaver.

As he was taking off the legionnaire's undershirt he perceived a small bag suspended from the stump of the neck. He detached it, put it in his pocket and immediately went back to work. The rigidity of the body rendered it singularly arduous; it required a great deal of effort to dress the limbs and the trunk in his own underclothing and his braided uniform, which he had previously stained with blood. He eventually succeeded, and dragged the decapitated man to the road. Taking off the soiled blouse, he replaced it with a dust-coat, put a green veil over his colonial cap, remounted his horse, and disappeared in the direction of Hanoi.

The orderlies were bringing back the ambulance when he passed close by, forcing the gallop. The two young colleagues and the personnel were heading for the wounded.

"Jacques Liban, correspondent of the American newspapers, Messieurs," he sniggered, although he was much too far away for anyone to hear him.

The victory of Son-Tay had enthused the European population of Hanoi. The correspondent of the American newspapers, who claimed to be arriving from Haiphong, collected all the details with an urgency that his profession was sufficient to justify. He learned thus that an irreparable loss had afflicted the victorious army. The celebrated Professor Albin, a victim of his heroic devotion, had been found dead on that glorious day.

Surprised by pirates, or perhaps indigenes, at the entrance to a village he had thought deserted, he had been decapitated by the savages and found a few hours afterwards by his orderlies. His death, as soon as it was known, had not gone unpunished for long. The village had been burned to the last hut, and everyone hiding there had been massacred pitilessly.

Of the obscure legionnaires who had given their lives for an adopted fatherland, not a word was breathed.

A few days later, the mysterious journalist read a telegram from the government ordering everyone to do everything possible to recover Dr. Albin's head and embark his remains on the next steamer bound for Marseilles.

"That's also the one I shall take," he murmured. "I shall have the honor of accompanying those famous relics."

But when, on the eve of the departure, the correspondent was informed that the head of the illustrious surgeon had finally been recovered, he had all the trouble in the world hiding his surprise.

"The word impossible isn't French!" he sniggered.[13]

The fashion in which the remark was greeted reminded him that it was neither the time nor the place for joking about such a grave subject, so he judged it prudent to shut up, and remained pensive.

---

[13] Dr. Albin is quoting Napoléon Bonaparte, in an 1813 letter to General Lemarois.

Chapter III

The *Indo-China*, which had disembarked Dr. Albin at Haiphong, was destined to take is glorious remains back to the motherland. When the gunboat transported the coffin to the steamer the troops and the crews rendered the military honors, the cannon thundered as a sign of mourning, and all the flags were lowered to half mast.

Among the passengers who followed the transshipping operation with a respectful curiosity from the height of the deck, Jacques Liban, agitated by the most various sentiments, his gaze lost over the low-lying coast of the Delta, was reflecting on the tragic and deceptive adventure.

"Dr. Albin is dead," he murmured, "but as long as he isn't buried, the life and personality of Jacques Liban will remain vague, indecisive and problematic. I hadn't reckoned on the head. The body alone won't furnish any conclusive data while that accursed head might compromise it. If Larmezan takes it into his head—and it can't fail to occur to him—to take its anthropometric measurements, he can boldly demonstrate that it's not his master's."

"The reply can be made to him, to be sure, that if there was an error with the head, the body found in the environs of Son-Tay is indubitably that of the famous surgeon, but the door opened to doubt might lead to the truth. Bah! So much irrefutable evidence will remain—the disappearance, the underwear, the clothing, the documents contained in the pockets—that the cadaver, with or without the head, can't fail to be officially recognized and buried as such. Anyone who dared to suppose the truth would be taken or a madman.

"No one, except for Jacques Liban, knows the reasons that Dr. Albin had for disappearing!"

Nevertheless, it would have been preferable if things had happened exactly as he had anticipated.

The steamer had raised anchor and moved off. The mariners, standing on the yard-arms of their ships, launched a last hurrah. The passengers and crew of the *Indo-China* responded by waving their hats and handkerchiefs. Jacques Liban, isolated in a corner, was still thinking about the cadaver saluted by such honors.

To what infamous and mysterious individual might it really belong?

He took out of his pocket a yellowed letter, the sole object found in the bag hung around the legionnaire's bloody neck, and reread it for the twentieth time.

You're right, Paul; one can escape human justice but that of heaven and death, as you've recognized, is the just and necessary denouement. But do not attempt to take your own life. A war is being fought far from here; the Foreign Legion does not require any identity papers; take another name, another nationality, another age, enlist and then fall on some battlefield, and merciful God, after you have given him repentance, will soon grant you death. Then...only then, will I have the strength to forgive you, for you will have proved your sincerity to me.

Your unhappy mother,
Gilberte

The surname had been neatly excised with a pen-knife.

What abominable crime had been able to wrench such a monstrous wish from a mother?

The steamer reached the open sea. Jacques Liban would soon find himself at table with the ship's officers who had known Dr. Albin; he locked himself in his cabin, shaved himself cleanly, darkened his complexion slightly, re-dyed his hair and side-whiskers, whose black had become blond, increased his height with high-heeled shoes and put on tinted spectacles. His check costume, red neckerchief and English accent completed the transformation.

32

A subtle observer would only have been able to observe the resemblance if he had had a capital interest in doing so, and the observation would not have led to any result. The American passenger, therefore, responded to the bell without the slightest anxiety. Hazard placed him next to the officer responsible for escorting the remains of the scientist who had died on the field of honor. The conversation revolved almost exclusively around the dramatic episode of the battle of Son-Tay. The officer's version contained amplifications and precise details unknown to the American.

"How was the head found?" he hazarded.

"That cost us a great deal of trouble and blood," the narrator replied. "The Minister's orders were formal; it was necessary to recover it at all costs. A strong column charged with going up the Red River explored both banks. Numerous villages suspected of being favorable to the pirates were destroyed, and notable recalcitrants imprisoned or shot. Our troops finally found a dozen heads planted on spikes in the vicinity of Hung-Hoa; they were brought back to Son-Tay, where the hospital staff recognized the head of their courageous chief; besides which, it fitted admirably to the stump of the neck."

The passenger had listened to the story with equivocal signs and frowns.

"The Black Flags are brigands," he declared. "They finish off the wounded, torture prisoners and decapitate them; I'd like them to be killed to the last man; but it's perhaps regrettable that unarmed indigenes were subjected to the punishment of a crime of which they might be innocent."

"The indigenes," the officer replied, "are almost all accomplices of the cruel pirates, the vile dregs of the yellow race."

"They doubtless believe that they're defending their independence, while you—I mean all the European nations—are only defending interests."

"We're defending civilization and progress," declared the Commandant, who was presiding over the table, sternly.

"Oh well, I'll admit that the indigenes merited being massacred—but that search must have cost the lives of several of your own."

"The column didn't sustain heavy losses," the officer relied. "Ten dead and thirty wounded, at the most."

"At the most! At the most!" the foreigner ventured, prey to the most vivid agitation. "Celebrated as the victim was, the head wasn't worth such a price, as Dr. Albin himself would agree. If it were necessary to shed so much French blood to avenge each of the obscure heroes who fall victim to their duty every day, wars would become odious butchery and there wouldn't be enough tears and mourning-dress for the mothers of France."

Angry and malevolent gazes welcomed these reflections; the guests whispered among themselves.

The officer shrugged his shoulders. "Go give lessons in humanity to those who slaughter Indians, lynch negroes and massacre Chinese workers to suppress competition," he responded, curtly.

"Monsieur," observed the Commandant, "there ought not to be irritant words at table; I beg you not to recommence."

From that moment on the imprudent stranger was held in suspicion. No one any longer addressed a word to him, and people affected to avoid him. Even the servants approached him in a disdainful fashion, and it was with a sigh of satisfaction, a month later, that he finally perceived the Byzantine tower of Notre-Dame de la Garde.

The ship entered the lazaret, and the Commandant, assembling the passengers, told them a few minutes later that they had been subjected to six days quarantine. A single exception had been made for the remains of Dr. Albin and the escorting officer.

Jacques Liban was profoundly affected by that measure; he was in haste to return to Paris, where not only did he desire to attend the funeral of the glorious surgeon, but could draw upon the considerable sum of money that he had left on deposit there. His resources had run out; he barely had enough to get back to the capital, and in order to do that he would have to sell the few objects of value that remained to him.

He spent that period of observation plunged in a mortal ennui, devouring all the newspapers he could procure. He successively learned, by that means, about the tributes rendered on the disembarkation of the coffin, the official reception at the Gare de Lyon, the unanimous vote in the Chambre, decreeing that the State would met the funeral expenses, and then the formal identification of the cadaver by his relatives and Dr. Larmezan.

The joy that the last news caused him was not exempt from a hint of bitterness. The illusions he had had regarding the moral value of is favorite pupil evaporated. Dr. Larmezan, it is true, had as much interest as he did in his master's disappearance being irrevocable!

The *Indo-China* obtained clearance on the very eve of the obsequies in which Jacques Liban wanted to take part at any price. Disembarked at eight a.m., he sold his watch for a derisory price, exchanged his colonial cap for something more appropriate, and had his hair and side-whiskers dyed again. Then, regretfully contemplating the total sum of 145 francs he had left, which obliged him to keep his frayed Yankee outfit, he ran to the railway station, took the express, arrived in Paris at eight o'clock the next day, did not wait to reclaim his trunk, and leapt into a cab.

The funeral was scheduled for ten o'clock. The coachman, stimulated by the promise of an exceptional tip, took him to Dr. Albin's town house at top speed.

Funeral hangings decorated the coaching entrance and the interior courtyard, which preceded his laboratory, transformed into a chapel of rest. The crowd had already been admitted to file past the coffin. He joined the queue, and penetrated, his heat gripped by an indescribable emotion, into the vast room where an entire happy life of labor had flowed by.

The setting was worthy of Professor Albin. The high shelves, encumbered with their alchemical apparatus, formed a strange décor well made to strike the imagination. In the middle, a raised catafalque, an ancient sarcophagus sustained by sphinxes, surrounded by silver lamps in which blue flames were burning, covered with palms, laurels, wreaths and flowers, bore the coffin of precious wood, and displayed the illustrious scientist's ermine-trimmed red robe and decorations. A tricolor flag, its shaft broken, lay dramatically at the foot of the stage. An insipid odor of wax and flowers weighted upon the ambient air, and students in frock-coats mingled with marine infantrymen, bayonets fitted, formed a guard of honor.

The visitors had received the order to leave in order to make way for the official delegations. He found himself back on the street in the middle of an incessantly growing crowd that the police had difficulty restricting to the sidewalks. Soon the butts of rifles clattered on the pavement, and the dull rumble of an artillery battery was heard. The representatives of the government and the school of medicine in formal dress, magistrates, academicians, superior officers of all the military services and even senior members of the clergy had come into the courtyard and were gathering in their respective places.

The coffin was placed on the pompous plumed hearse, where sprays and wreaths of flowers were heaped up, and the cortege moved off.

Hardened as Jacques Liban's heart was, and although he had followed the road that he was traveling today many times in thought, he could not remain indifferent to the grandeur of the spectacle and the respectful emotion of the crowd, whose tightly packed ranks formed thick hedges.

The professors in scarlet or purple robes, the groups of students from all the Universities, the dress uniforms whose braid scintillated in the sunlight, the glorious men holding the cordons of the pall, the giant wreaths carried on stretchers, the drums veiled with crepe, the military bands whose funeral marches seemed to summarize and translate a universal grief, and the multitude of unknown friends who were gravely following the cortege, plunged him into a kind of anxious intoxication.

For the second time, he was ashamed of what he had done.

Was that social suicide not stained with sacrilege? Had not the favors and honors with which he had been so lavishly heaped created special obligations toward the society that he was deceiving so brazenly? By what right had he made himself the unwitting accomplice of this macabre and solemn masquerade?

In the name of Truth, his conscience replied. *By the right that Dr. Albin had to die, and the right that I, henceforth his enemy and contradictor, have to live*, added his pride. Has Dr. Albin not died officially on the field of honor? Let someone tell the contrary to the surgeons who had recognized him and all the people following his convoy. One sole being was alive: Jacques Liban might, if the worst came to the worst, be the victim or the plaything of this adventure. There was, therefore, no knavery or lie that injured humankind.

And the villages burned and hundreds of innocents massacred, and the soldiers who died to avenge Dr. Albin's death? his conscience murmured.

Bah! That was the excess inherent in the abominable scourge of war. It was a collective crime in which his illustrious past had, in fact, played a large part, but for which he, Jacques Liban, was no longer responsible.

The cortege was engulfed by the porch of Notre-Dame. As a sign of mourning, the Hôtel-Dieu had veiled its doors with black. Pale invalids and convalescents in gray gowns appeared at the windows and raised their nightcaps respectfully. A regret more intense than the others gripped him. He would probably never again cross the threshold of the refuges of suffering where he had struggled so many times against death.

But was it not his pride as an admired clinician that was making him experience that chagrin? He would no longer hold forth by the beds of poor devils, surrounded by a circle of fervent admirers. What would prevent him from lavishing cares as efficacious and more discreet on other wretches?

In the immense nave of the cathedral hung in black, while the senior priest of Notre-Dame celebrated the sacrifice of the mass, the choir sang the *De profundis* and the *Requiem*; then the venerable Cardinal Archbishop of Paris, surrounded by his clergy, came to pronounce the absolution solemnly; the *Dies irae*'s cries of menace resounded in the depths of the vaults, and the convoy took the road to Père-Lachaise.

Less emotional now, Jacques Liban watched the people and events with more self-composure.

The groups already had a different appearance; the gravity and silence were by no means as marked as at the beginning; oddments of conversation were being exchanged now; distracted gazes were shifting to the right and left; friends were recognizing one another and meeting up in order to walk together. Even the crowd seemed less reserved and more curious; altercations rose up in its ranks, gestures pointed out famous people and acclamations greeted a group of radical députés as they passed by.

Soon the cortege picked up speed, and people deserted it at every crossroads. The official delegations and patriotic societies, to be sure, stuck to their duty until the end, some with bored and preoccupied expressions, while others consulted their watches; one divined that they were in haste to get back to business, or the hour for dinner was soliciting them.

Jacques Liban was not astonished by that change of attitude; had he not done likewise many a time?

In the Rue de la Roquette, the conversations became noisier and more free-flowing. Drawn by habit, he too experienced the need to interrogate his neighbor, an obese man who as continually mopping his brow.

"Did you know Dr. Albin?"

"No, Monsieur. Did you?"

"I knew him…slightly."

"Not at all, myself. I didn't even know he existed, but as yesterday's newspaper recounted the details of his horrible death in Tonkin, my wife said to me: *As you have nothing to do tomorrow you ought to go to the burial, because it will give you a little exercise and you'll see some famous people, hear the speeches and..."*

The unknown man had moved away toward other groups.

Some were talking finance, politics, commerce or theater. Others, local physicians, were calculating the fortune that the deceased must have accumulated.

"How much did they pay for his visits?" one asked.

"Four louis, and two for his consultations."

"And to think that for a hundred sous, or even three francs," a third added, bitterly, "we do more ingrate and more disagreeable work, and the clients still find excellent reasons for cheating us out of our honoraria."

"Renown, my dear, has welcomed you as a hospital physician, and you can flay your patients without making them cry out. The public demand guarantees; they suppose, most often with reason but sometimes wrongly, that a man clad in all the official titles is better able to cure them. Then, what economists call the law of supply and demand comes into play. Our colleagues in view, solicited by too many clients, are obliged to diminish their number by raising the price of their collaboration."

"But the medical profession isn't commerce!"

"An old song, my dear—it's an apostolate...when Society or the State gives us the means of existence."

He slipped into a group of military surgeons who looked at the intruder suspiciously.

"Jacques Liban, editor of the *American Chemist*," he said to his neighbor.

The professor at the Val-de-Grâce bowed graciously. "You see, Monsieur," he said to the foreigner, "that France knows how to honor knowledge and bravery."

"All those who die struck by an enemy bullet don't receive such honors," the American insinuated. "It's the personality of Dr. Albin, not his virtues, to which these homages are being rendered."

"The example that comes from above has more impact on the crowd."

"Because the ignorant crowd is unjust; otherwise, merit and devotion would only have more value when they're obscure."

The suspicious gaze of the old soldier made him understand that he was out of order. He let a few ranks pass and found himself among teachers, among whom he recognized Dr. Perraud, an unfortunate former rival of Dr. Albin, a conscientious scholar whose modesty had always relegated him to the background.

A name than he had just overheard excited his curiosity to the highest degree.

"It's said that you loved her madly," said the interlocutor to the old professor.

"It's true," Perraud replied.

"Why didn't you ask for her hand?"

"I didn't dare; I was poor, practically unknown; she was rich and the daughter of an influential professor. She would have thought that I was only motivated by interest."

A snigger of pity greeted that confession of that naïve delicacy.

"She's free now—enter the lists!"

"I'm too old, and it's too late, as you know full well; the other was able to find the way to her heart."

"It's said, in fact, that Larmezan..."

"It's not true—or, at least, only half true. Madame Albin, beneath her frivolous appearance, is naturally honest, but her husband neglected her too much. She's beautiful and good— I've never understood Albin's blindness. She loved him...."

"Do you think so?"

"She loved him, I tell you, in spite of the neglect, in spite of everything; a simple misunderstanding doubtless separated them."

"He loved her too, then?"

"As much as an ambitious scientist can love his wife—which is to say, less than his work, less than his honors and less than his glory."

"In a latent state, then—an amorous state that women scarcely understand and don't admit."

"They're right. A life together is made of reciprocal concessions; love has need of manifestations and tenderness. Marriage isn't only an alliance of interests; if the worship of science or arts has to come before anything else, let's do as priests do and refrain from marrying. It's the decision that we'd all make if we were wise. The children that we make—our works—serve humankind usefully, and the Fatherland will forgive us our celibacy."

"And nature?"

"Nature! We render her the homage she merits and the duties she imposes on us, of course."

"In a brothel, once a week? You're raving, Perraud."

"Then accept marriage with all its duties, all the charges and inconveniences it involves. Don't take a wife to serve as a stepping-stone and forget her afterwards."

"Dr. Albin wasn't as casual as that!"

"Very nearly, but it was written that he'd have every chance. In spite of the Benedictine life, made to exasperate a young woman who was elegant, pretty, avid for life, happy to shine, his wife, an elite intelligence, always respected the illustrious name she bore."

"And Larmezan?"

"It was natural, given the increasingly egoistical indifference of her husband, that she had a certain penchant for someone who never missed an opportunity to flatter her tastes and distract her. Larmezan was thus the servant cavalier, the preferred friend, and nothing more. If he'd been the lover, Albin might have been able to remain ignorant, but believe me, I would have known; I would have divined it."

The teacher continued, sadly: "Now, the situation is quite different. Death has destroyed the obstacles; Larmezan isn't a man embarrassed by overmuch delicacy. It's probable—I

41

could even say certain—that he'll marry his master's widow and be appointed professor. It's him, at any rate, who's leading the mourning."

Although, rationally, Jacques Liban, no longer had anything to debate with Dr. Albin's self-esteem, he was nevertheless not sorry to learn that the latter had only played Sganarelle.[14] The conversation that his appearance as an American scholar had permitted him to overhear was not absolutely true; the portrait of Madame Albin had been made by a painter visibly too much in love with his model; her husband had not forgotten his conjugal duties at any point. If his absorbing labors had rendered him egotistical and indifferent, she, for her part, had not made any effort or any sacrifice to conquer his affection. Apart from a few exaggerated or false details, however, the ensemble was accurate. Perhaps Dr. Albin would not have admitted it, but Jacques Liban, more disinterested, had been forced to recognize it. And suddenly, knowing that she was appreciated and loved by others, the widowed Madame Albin appeared to him in a new light.

Is Perraud's admiration contagious? he wondered.

The conversation, momentarily interrupted, had returned to the illustrious deceased.

"What a bizarre idea to go in search of death in Tonkin," one of them remarked.

"Albin's determination didn't surprise me overmuch," replied Dr. Perraud. "Although the chagrin caused by his daughter's death had, so to speak, put him off his stride, his combativeness and, let's say the word, his pride, couldn't remain inactive for long. Acquired notoriety and glory is insufficient for such minds. They're always aiming higher, but it's the immediate result that they seek; the slow and obscure work that posterity will acclaim can't content them; they want to enjoy their triumph and are always running after new conquests. They're unsatisfied; their ambition drives them to all

---

[14] As in Molière's *Sganarelle ou le cocu imaginaire* [Sganarelle; or, the Imaginary Cuckold] (1660)

kinds of metamorphoses. Art, science, politics and the battle-field attract them by turns. So their brilliant work almost always lacks foundation and is only temporary. They brush the surface of everything but don't plumb the depths of anything."

"What about the *Biological Chemistry*?"

The *Biological Chemistry* will suffer the fate of hundreds, thousands of scientific theories that have preceded it. Posterity will put it in its place. It will recognize that Dr. Albin added his stone to the communal edifice, but how many others, misunderstood today, will shine alongside him and perhaps eclipse his glory."

"You're an interested party," muttered the unknown, but added: *Well reasoned, all the same, Perraud; I'm not sorry to have heard those words. Jacques Liban will henceforth pursue one single goal: to destroy the false work of Dr. Albin and publish his principles of* Dynamic Chemistry.

"Were you present at the exhumation of the remains?" someone asked.

"No," the teacher replied. "I know, though, that the cadaver was in an advanced state of decomposition, and that Larmezan, having already taken anthropometric measurements of his master, repeated the experiment on the head accompanying Albin's body."

"And he concluded?"

"Evidently that it really was our regretted colleague's head, since he didn't raise any objection on that subject."

Jacques Liban was delivered from his final doubt.

Someone existed who could have objected, who was surely certain as to the inauthenticity of that head, and that man had said nothing! Dr. Albin was, therefore, really dead, irrevocably dead, and in a few minutes, when the slabs of the crypt were sealed over the coffin he was accompanying, Jacques Liban, still plunged into limbo unless then, would have acquired, definitively, the right to live and to act!

Further away, the official delegates, constrained to greater gravity, were only exchanging rare comments. There, doubtless, he was being judged by his peers in eulogies full of reticence and implication. What did all that matter now? Was he not soon to become, himself, the pitiless detractor of the illustrious dead man? Had he any need to observe once again the ingratitude of the obligated and the jealousy of rivals? Was he not awaiting, on the contrary, critics a hundred times more unjust, a hundred times more acerbic?

Fundamentally, all these people were indifferent to him. Had he not been like them? What were the veritable griefs he had experienced? Those caused to him by the deaths of his relatives, and no others. What reciprocity did Dr. Albin have the right to expect from all that official company?

Often, it is true, a temporary chagrin had darkened his soul at the disappearance of a friend or someone he admired, but that was one of those afflictions that is quickly chased away with a strong dose of the natural philosophy with which every combative man is provided. So-and-so is dead, what a pity! He was a great artist, a great poet, a great scientist. But we're all mortal, aren't we? Others come, others will—make way for the others...

What should all those people say, even the most sympathetic, except what he had said himself in similar circumstances, without hatred, without envy, driven by the egotistical and instinctive need that we have to conquer a large place in the sun?

Dr. Albin certainly had no cause for complaint; the dolor that was accompanying him to his last abode was as profound, as complete and as true as any official dolor can be,

The procession traversed the Place de la Roquette. All gazes turned toward the place sprinkled with human blood by the executioner's blade.

"The decapitated individual who is being borne triumphantly to the refuge of the dead," sniggered the mysterious stranger, "perhaps merited ending up there. Bandits, blind instruments of destiny, took responsibility for carrying out the task. Perhaps there was some element of genius in his crime that merited these honors."

The cortege bunched at the entrance to the vast necropolis.

To the sound of vibrant fanfares, the troops had filed martially past the cart. Then the delegations had gone to the family tomb, where the gaping crypt awaited its new guest, and, around the coffin ready to descend into the darkness, a compact circle had formed over which the respectful silence and restrained emotion of the first hour hung.

A dozen speeches were read or pronounced. Unknown friends and rivals lavished the same eulogies, formulated the same regrets. All of them celebrated the marvelous discoveries of Dr. Albin, praised the ardent patriotism that had led him to his death, affirmed that he would enter into glory and immortality, decreed that his example would engender heroes, and that his work, a torch for humankind, would cast its dazzling light until the end of time. All of them implored the young men to take him as a model, to follow in his tracks, to honor, as he had, French Science, and to be, like him, ready to die for the Fatherland!

If all that they're saying were sincere and true, thought Jacques Liban, *I'd never be able to destroy a reputation so well usurped; fortunately, hyperbole and the flowers of rhetoric grow vigorously in the garden of funeral orations.*

The soldiers fired the salvo of honor; a priest in a surplice sprinkled holy water on the coffin; it was taken down into the tomb. He heard the friction of ropes and the dull sound of the bier touching the floor. Then workmen swiftly sealed the slabs, while others heaped up the wreaths and flowers; a cemetery garden closed the entrance to the sepulcher, and the stranger found himself alone.

He wondered now whether he might be the victim of a dream. His fascinated eyes could not tear themselves away from doors forever closed, seemingly open wide to oblivion. A strange impression of emptiness had suddenly invaded him, and in the confused spider-web that blurred his vision, the past seemed to retreat and fade away into a prodigious distance.

He had wanted, before going away, to leave a souvenir to his venerated father, to his adored Jeanne, but now he thought he saw them loom up before him, irritated, to reproach him for the impure promiscuity of the unknown cadaver that he had just placed beside them.

A vague and dolorous far had taken possession of his entire being; he was in haste to escape that remorse of sorts, when, timidly and slowly, emaciated and poorly dressed, a young woman approached the grille and placed, in the midst of all the sumptuous wreaths, a humble bouquet of violets, and then knelt down to say a brief prayer.

Jacques Liban went to the pauperess, who stood up, her eyes devoid of tears but full of a soft sadness.

"Did you know Dr. Albin?" he asked, in a low voice.

"He cared for me last year in the hospital, Monsieur. He was good to the poor invalids."

"And you prayed for him?"

"I knelt down as a sign of gratitude."

"That's good, Mademoiselle. How are you now?"

"I live as I can. I'm so often weary!"

"I was a close friend of Dr. Albin. You action touched me. Take this in memory of him."

And Jacques Liban fled at a rapid pace, leaving his last louis in the hands of the bewildered and delighted young woman.

Chapter IV

Dead and buried! The man in the blue spectacles sniggered, gripped again by his pride, as he headed for the exit. *Free of the old man! But not of the public man, for Dr. Albin's glory survives, and as it's at his expense that I have to edify mine, it will be necessary to annihilate him.*

He stopped, and emitted a burst of strident laughter.

I would never have thought that social sanction had such great force. Have I not already arrived, like everyone else, at believing that Professor Albin is well and truly dead, and that I'm a completely different man, a being really and absolutely different from the other. It is, however, the same brain that is thinking and the same organs that are functioning. Is what has happened to me, from the biological point of view, a change of state analogous to a chemical transformation? Is the metal about to pass to the state of a salt, an acid, a base, or vice versa?

So much the better, after all, since Destiny is calling me to destroy my first work. Destiny? Vain word; it's Will that I ought to say.

He took a diagonal path to shorten his route and suddenly found himself confronted by thirty grave individuals groups around a stele. A man with an inspired expression had detached himself from the group and advanced toward the coffin.

"*Vita in Morte sepulta est,*" he proclaimed, in a loud voice. Life is buried in Death![15]

The passer-by was already far away, but the enigmatic text was still buzzing in his ears like a menacing knell.

---

[15] The quotation is from one of the epistles of the French theologian and poet Peter of Blois (c1130-c1210), whose name is rendered as Petrus Blesensis in Latin.

He emerged from the necropolis and found himself on the exterior boulevards. Facing him, the terraces of wine merchants and restaurateurs were invaded by a noisy and joyful crowd. Young women were mingled with bands of students, the tables were filled with food and wine. Calls to the waiters, bursts of laughter, emphatic speeches, toasts and the clink of glasses overlapped with the choruses of traditional songs. The *Pomponnette* succeeded the *Chanson de Bicêtre* and *C'est la reine d'Angleterre-terre-terre-terre* and the *Esprit-Saint descendez en nous*. Gascons, Auvergnats and Bretons confused their accents and rolled their *r*s in energetic interpellations, hoarse bellows or bacchic challenges. Girls grabbed by the waist fled the brutality of kisses with shrill cries. An "extra," alarmed by demands or liters intoned to the tune of *Lampions* and the reproaches of the proprietor, dropped a pile of plates, to the great hilarity of the customers, whose frenetic cheers saluted his clumsiness. An exuberant manifestation of life seemed to want to redeem the few hours consecrated to the cult of death.

The passers-by paused to smile at that juvenile gaiety, which an April sun caressed with its medial rays. Workers solicited as they went by hastened to come and clink glasses fraternally.

He felt comforted, then, cheered up, attained by a prodigious desire for movement and noise. He would have liked to mingle with the groups, to rediscover some of the distant impressions of youth, but time was pressing; the banks closed at three o'clock and he was at risk of being found wanting. Carried away by generosity, he had just given his last louis to the grateful pauperess and could not have much left. He opened his purse, searched all his pockets, and found two francs fifty.

"Just enough to take a cab," he murmured. *I'll go withdraw my money, and then I'll eat at the first place I come to—I'm dying of hunger. Then I'll take a room at the Grand and send the bellboy to fetch my trunk from the Gare de Lyon. Let's take care of the most urgent matter first.*

He hailed a coachman and had himself taken to the Crédit International in the Rue Saint-Lazare. It was the day of a share-issue; the hall of the vast financial establishment was overflowing with people and long queues had formed at the windows. In any other circumstances he would have postponed the operation until the following day, but hunger was clawing at him, and he no longer had a sou, or very nearly. He joined the line of people withdrawing their deposits in order to buy the new shares, and his turn finally arrived.

The employee who received his entitlement, seeing that he was faced with a special case, made a characteristic grimace and asked him to come back tomorrow. The depositor had to protest energetically. The sum was payable on demand; he had only deposited it after a preliminary agreement and on that condition. The bank was open and he needed his money immediately; he demanded that it be given to him.

The subaltern referred the matter to his superior, who deemed the demand well-founded, obtained a few signatures, carefully verified the entitlement and sent an order to the safe.

Jacques Liban, momentarily anxious, uttered a sigh of satisfaction. He sat down in a corner and rapidly counted his bills. The fifty wads of ten thousand francs formed a voluminous package, which he could not think of putting in the summary pockets of his coat. He asked a passing office-boy whether he could obtain an old newspaper.

"Permit me to offer you a copy of the *Times*," said a stranger with a strong English accent.

"Many thanks," replied Jacques Liban, bowing. "That's a great help."

The ranger had unfolded the immense sheet on a corner of the table. "There's enough there to wrap two million," he exclaimed, on seeing the awkwardness of its recipient—and with a rapid movement he made a perfect roll, which he hastened to hand to its possessor.

"That's how we do it in London," he said, bowing.

After thanking him again, Jacques Liban was heading for the stairway to the exit when the obliging person ran after him.

"A thousand pardons, Monsieur," he said, "Would you be kind enough to return half of the paper that I gave you. Here's my friend Sir William Reynolds, who has just withdraw six hundred and fifty thousand francs, and is in the same situation as you."

A respectable gentleman displayed his pockets, stuffed with blue wads.

It would have been difficult to refuse the reciprocity of the service that had just been rendered to him. The three of them retraced their steps and sat down at an empty table at the back of the hall, where Jacques Liban opened his roll, detached a double page of the great English newspaper and held it out to its former owner. The latter rapidly wrapped up the wads that his friend passed to him, and had quickly made up his parcel.

"No, not like that," he said, laughing jovially at the slowness with which Jacques Liban was reconstituting his own. "You haven't profited from my lesson."

He took the package from his hands again, finished it with a marvelous dexterity, returned it to him, then uttered a cordial "Good morning," and disappeared.

Jacques Liban, who had not eaten since the day before, was in haste to appease his hunger. Fortunately, he was in the vicinity of the Gare Saint-Lazare, where restaurants abound. He went out without losing a moment, but stopped at a kiosk to buy newspapers with the last sous remaining to him, and went into the Café Mansard, on whose windows he saw written: *Lunches, dinners and suppers, all day service.*

"Waiter," he said, on going in, "serve me something to eat quickly; I'm in a hurry."

The waiter looked at the clock. "It's after four," he said. "We don't have anything left at this hour but cold meat. Would you like a slice of roast beef while we prepare your order?"

"Anything you like, but be quick, and order a Chateaubriand with apples."

The manager, a thin man with harsh angular features and a narrow forehead surmounted by thick hair, with hooded and avid eyes, who was leaping from table to table with a napkin over his arm, had come to ask what the customer wanted.

He repeated the order and was assured that it would be immediately satisfied.

"We don't have any roast beef left," the waiter returned to announce. "Would you like ham instead?"

"Whatever you like," he relied, discontentedly. "How many times do I have to tell you?"

He took off his blue-tinted spectacles, which were annoying him, and devoured the ham, for which he did not have to wait very long.

The service was despairingly slow. He had finished his hors-d'oeuvres a long time ago, and did not see anything coming. He had questioned with his head and gaze, but the indolent waiter made him hand signals bidding him not to be impatient. He looked around. The vast room was full of noise and movement. At every moment, travelers were coming in, their meager luggage in their hand, obtaining a hasty snack, asking for the bill or scanning a newspaper, and leaving immediately.

The lady cashier, with a vague smile tamped on her lips, on the lookout for the slightest incident of service, awoke the attention of the waiters with the aid of a shrill hand-bell. The latter, accustomed to the haste of customers who were afraid of missing their train, seemed to take a malign pleasure in proceeding with the perfect tranquility of people prepared to carry out their tasks but having to intention of putting overmuch zeal into them.

It was nearly five o'clock and the famished diner as beginning to get seriously impatient. Perhaps the manager had forgotten the order or the waiter, with his mocking expression, was venting a little ill-will. He made the observation several times, and the cashier's irritated ringing and the manager's reminders ended up causing an altercation.

"I can't bring a dish that isn't cooked," cried the reprimanded waiter. "Complain to the boss."

The manager made his excuses. The morning dishes had run out, the evening ones were only just starting to cook. It was necessary to give the chef time to carry out an order transmitted to him—and then, to be truthful, it was rarely necessary to serve a dinner at such an hour.

"Why put *all day service* in your window then?" muttered the demanding diner.

"I don't refuse service, but it's necessary to give us the necessary time."

The fillet so much desired cut short the explanations. The diner, profiting from experience, had ordered two more dishes, and set about satisfying his hunger. The manager and the waiter observed him from a distance, whispering.

"It's always the bad customers who make the most fuss," muttered the waiter. "And this is another one who doesn't look like much to me: a bookmaker or a pickpocket. He looks like the old man a week ago who had your dinner and ours and took you for a mug. You didn't want to send for the police, and now he's sending you his friends, damn it!"

"Let's not make assumptions," replied the manager, aggravated by the unpleasant memory.

"Look at him, then," said the waiter, "with his English suit, his red kerchief and his dirty overcoat, not to mention the blue glasses that he had on when he came in."

"Oh! He had blue spectacles?"

"Of course, that's part of the get-up, the blue glasses. But you can see how he's guzzling—one would think he hadn't eaten for a week. I'll bet you a pernod he's a crook."

"Agreed," said the manager. "If I lose, of course, I promise you that I won't let this one off."

Jacques Liban had vaguely perceived, several times, that the manager and the waiter were looking at him in a singular fashion, but he had put that affectation down to his anterior protests, and had not attached any importance to it in any case. Having finished his meal he ordered a coffee, a small glass of Chartreuse and an excellent cigar, and then started reading the newspapers, which were singing the praises of Dr. Albin endlessly. Then, perceiving that it was almost six o'clock, he decided to go and book a room, deposit his cash in the safe at the Grand, and go to the theater.

He asked for the bill and, knowing that he had to more money, opened his parcel in order to take out a banknote.

A cold sweat immediately formed on his brow. The first note he detached was play-money. Seized by a feverish agitation, he examined the others rapidly; they were all the same. A cloud passed before his eyes and he nearly fell over. There was no doubt about it; the obliging stranger who had offered him the *Times* was an audacious pickpocket who had substituted this derisory parcel for his own.

How had he allowed himself to fall into that crude trap? Where was his intelligence? His first impulse as to run after the thieves; he stood up abruptly, but fell back on to the bench immediately. It was more than two hours since the thieves had pulled their trick.

The waiter had arrived with the bill on a plate, and presented it to him. He contemplated it, dazedly, and mumbled a few incoherent words. The manager, on the lookout, hastened to appear.

"Robbed—I've been robbed," murmured the customer, pale and distressed.

"I know that one," the employee replied, in a mocking tone. "Would you please settle your bill: it's seventeen francs."

"I've just been robbed," repeated the unfortunate, lamentably.

"That's nothing to do with me," replied the manager, harshly. "Don't play games: pay me."

The customers watched the scene incredulously. The exotic appearance of the insolvent did not inspire confidence. The man had stood up and was rummaging through his pockets with a tragic despair that made them laugh.

He fell back, as if stunned. "Nothing," he murmured. "Nothing." He revived. "Would you like my coat and hat?" he said, in a strangled voice.

"You're joking! Your dirty dust-coat and your hat! They're not worth three francs, and this isn't the Temple square."

He made a gesture of deliverance and took out his luggage-ticket. "This will redeem a trunk full of linen, and you'll be fully compensated."

"This is simpler. I'll have you accompanied by two waiters—you can pay for the cab, of course—you can get the trunk and settle the bill."

The man made a gesture of negation. "I can't pay for the cab and there's nothing in my trunk but linen."

"Once again, I'm not a second-hand clothes merchant, and you're going to explain yourself at the police station."

"The police station!" exclaimed the unfortunate, recovering a little energy. "You can't think so! The police, for such a trivial sum. I swear to you that you won't lose anything. I'll go and get my trunk, sell the contents myself, and come back to pay you."

"Tell it to someone else, old man. One last time, are you going to pay me or not? I don't have time to argue."

The fake American, devastated, stood there open-mouthed.

"Émile," said the manager. "Fetch the police, and go with the monsieur."

Chapter V

The police, always numerous in the neighborhood of the Gare Saint-Lazare, did not keep them waiting long. Jacques Liban, whom the terrible misadventure seemed to have plunged him into a stupor, followed them mechanically and found himself facing the Commissaire without having had time to make the slightest reflection.

The latter had just put on his overcoat and was preparing to leave. He sat down again, cursing, and listened to the explanations of the waiter from the café like a man weary of that kind of misdemeanor.

"You refuse to pay?" he demanded. "What do you have to say?"

The customer emerged from his torpor.

"The man is twisting the facts. I'm not refusing to pay, but I can't do it at present. I was robbed in a financial establishment about three hours ago, and I only perceived just now that I couldn't pay."

"What proof is there that you were robbed?" the waiter advanced. "I think you're using that excuse to avoid settling the bill."

"Wretch!" replied the accused, incapable of controlling himself.

"No insults, please," said the Commissaire. "You haven't been robbed of everything at a stroke, I assume?"

"I beg your pardon, Monsieur, but they took everything I possessed."

"And you possessed?"

"Five hundred thousand—or, more exactly, 499,500—francs in banknotes, rolled up in newspaper.

"Damn!" exclaimed the honorable magistrate, who could not help laughing. "You had a sum like that wrapped up in newspaper and you don't have a louis in your pocket!"

"Alas, no."

"Well, at least it's extraordinary. What proof do you have that you're telling the truth?"

"The Crédit International just paid out that sum to me. Send an agent."

"The banks aren't open at this hour. But you must have money at home, or objects that can present a sufficient guarantee."

"I only have a trunk at the Gare de Lyon. It contains linen and toiletries."

"The boss doesn't accept linen in payment," declared the waiter.

"Bizarre! Bizarre!" the magistrate repeated. "What's your name?" he asked, abruptly.

"Jacques Liban."

"Where do you live?"

"I've just arrived from Marseilles."

"Which hotel are you staying in?"

"None; I arrived his morning at eight o'clock.

"Where do you live in Marseilles?"

"I arrived from Tonkin on the steamer *Indo-China*."

"From Tonkin!" said the astonished magistrate. "What were you doing out there?"

"Correspondent for the American newspapers."

"Which ones?"

Caught out unexpectedly, the unknown had a fatal moment of hesitation, and then cited at random the titles of two or three newspapers of the New World.

"Where do you live in America?"

"New York."

"That's a long way away. Do you have papers establishing your identity? Do you know anyone who can answer for you? Have you a friend or acquaintance who can settle your debt?"

The pseudo-correspondent answered *no* to all those questions.

"What proof do I have, then," the magistrate went on, "assuming that you had a parcel containing five hundred thousand francs, firstly that the money belonged to you, secondly that it was stolen from you, and thirdly, that the pretended theft isn't simply a pretext to avoid paying for the copious meal that you had."

"My word as an honest man, Monsieur."

"Your word? You're joking, I think."

"Monsieur!" exclaimed Jacques Liban, revolted. "You don't have the right to doubt it."

"Say rather that I don't have the right to believe you. If I accepted words of honor, all the crooks and scoundrels I interrogate would be the most honest men in the world."

"But I'm not a crook!"

"Don't shout so loud, or pay what you owe."

The unfortunate made a desolate gesture

"Search this man," ordered the Commissaire.

Agents searched him from head to foot. His pockets contained, in total, some newspapers, two handkerchiefs, blue-tinted spectacles, a luggage-ticket and, in a leather bag, the letter found n the legionnaire.

The magistrate read the letter, and looked at the enigmatic individual, frowning.

"Oho!" he said. "Here's a document that doesn't lack interest."

"It's a letter I found in Tonkin," Jacques Liban hastened to declare. "It's addressed to some legionnaire. I don't know what it signifies."

"It will, however, be very interesting to the law to find out. I'm arresting you."

The unknown became suppliant.

"I swear to you, Monsieur, that I'm an honest man."

"That's up to others to decide," said the Commissaire. "If you are who you say you are, prove it to the court. No papers except for his luggage-ticket and this letter, which requires to be clarified. In addition, a fraud, wads of false bills, and not the slightest reference—and you expect to walk out of here tranquilly?"

He adopted a friendly manner and put on his most engaging smile. "Come on, play the game. You've been caught; your explanations don't hold up; admit the truth. Aren't you, by chance, one of those light-fingered gentleman who practice theft in the American fashion, with a magisterial impudence?"

Suddenly gripped by rage, the accused drew himself up to his full height. "What you're saying is imbecilic," he protested. "If I were a thief I wouldn't have got myself caught in such a stupid manner. I'd have papers, a domicile and answers for everything. You're accusing me of an infamy of which I've been the victim. It's shameful."

He advanced toward the magistrate menacingly, but the two burly fellows who had searched him, after a volley of punches, held him solidly by the arms.

"Insulting the authority," mocked the agents. "That's all that was lacking."

"Put him in handcuffs, since he's ill-disposed," said the magistrate. "Send him to the lock-up as soon as possible."

A terrible anguish gripped the heart of the accused.

"Appearances, I admit, seem to condemn me," he said, "but I swear to you again that I'm a honest man, and if I haven't satisfied your legitimate curiosity, it's because a mystery that I can't reveal envelopes me, because..."

"Good, good," interrupted the incredulous magistrate. "We're not at the Ambigu, and it's one reason more—the court loves mysteries! Take him away."

"Joker," he murmured, on seeing him disappear. "He claims that someone's stolen half a million francs from him, and doesn't even think of lodging a complaint!"

Taken to the police cells, Jacques Liban spent his first night back in Paris prey to the most bitter reflections. Was it really him, a former député, a former minister, who had just taken a beating like the most infamous of hooligans?

No, he had to admit, the powerful man of old no longer existed; the individual who had fallen victim to his lack of foresight, whom the law had legally arrested, was no longer anyone but Jacques Liban, the enigmatic unknown devoid of resources, devoid of a roof, devoid of a fatherland, devoid of any civil estate. Why hadn't he thought that a theft or some other hazard might deprive him of his fortune? What was he going to do? How could he defend himself?

Confess the truth? But that would be to sink into general reproof, to become legendary, the butt of the entire world's mockery, to play the role of an unintelligent knave. His action, if it were not redeemed subsequently by an indisputable glory, could only be considered as the criminal fantasy of an unhinged mind. It was even impossible for him to complain about the major theft of which he was suffering the unfortunate consequences.

To what would that complaint lead? Dangerous investigations that might lead to the discovery of his identity. It would be necessary to indicate the provenance of the large sum, justify its possession, etc., etc. On the other hand, the indications that he could furnish to the police were too vague; he would not even be able to recognize the man who had stolen it! It was, therefore, necessary to support as stoically as possible the catastrophe that had just overwhelmed him. What did he have to fear, after all? A few days or a few weeks in prison...

A fatal stupidity had backed him into such a dark and dangerous corner, when it would have been so easy for him at least to create a domicile and obtain papers! Was it his instinctive confidence in his lucky star that had prevented him from preoccupying himself with those trivial details?

The next day, after being given a preliminary shower, Jacques Liban submitted to the infamous formality of anthropomorphic measurement,[16] and Monsieur Bertillon, his former

---

[16] It was in 1883 that Alphonse Bertillon persuaded the Parisian police to establish the anthropometric service, which routinely measured the supposedly-unique facial features of everyone arrested. Photographic "mug shots" were not added until 1888. Bertillon could not have been a former pupil of Dr. Al-

pupil, scarcely suspected, in not sparing him any detail, that he was applying them to one of the most ardent investigators of that incontestably useful institution. The operation did not, any case, furnish any information regarding the mysterious accused. It was merely observed that he had dyed hair and an artificially tanned face, which he made no difficulty about admitting.

"And yet, I know that face," the anthropometrist affirmed. "It's surely not the first time I've seen it."

The legionnaire's letter found on the delinquent of the Café Mansard had attracted the attention of the examining magistrate, who brought an insistence and unaccustomed skill to interrogating him without being able to obtain the slightest clue as to his identity. It was only after many interrogations that the magistrate, despairing of removing the mask, had sent him to court for the minor offence.

There, between two gendarmes, on the bench soiled by so many ignoble contacts, the torture did not last long. The judge had swiftly consulted the file.

"You don't want to admit your identity, so far as I can see. You claim to be named Jacques Liban?"

"Yes, Monsieur le Président."

"You say that five hundred thousand francs was stolen from you, and it transpired as a result of enquires that that sum had indeed been withdrawn that day from the Crédit International by Jacques Liban. Where did that sum come from?"

"It belonged to me; I had earned it honestly."

"Yes, but when?.... You have nothing to say? You arrived from Tokin—that fact has been ascertained to be correct. What is the significance of his letter, addressed, you affirm, to an unknown legionnaire?"

"I don't know."

"Get away! You doubtless have the greatest interest in hiding it. The legionnaire is you!"

---

bin's, as he had had no real higher education and entered the Prefecture as a low-level clerk.

"No, Monsieur le Président."

"Then what were you doing in Tonkin?.... You remain mute, and for good reason! You say that you're a correspondent for the American newspapers. But no one, either at the legation or at the editorial offices of the newspapers you cited, knows your name. You lied, then?"

"I admit that."

"You had dyed your hair and darkened your skin artificially; in brief, you were disguised."

"That's correct."

"The examining magistrate has not been able to discover anything, in spite of the interest that we have in knowing who you are. Do you persist in concealing your true identity from us? By doing so, I warn you, you're exposing yourself to the severity of the law."

"Reasons of great importance oblige me to do so, but I'm an honest man."

"Or a deserter, a spy, a criminal—what do I know? Your obstinacy permits all suppositions. In any case, you refused to pay for the meal you had."

"I couldn't pay. You know why. As soon as I can. I'll settle the debt."

"Nothing obliges me or encourages me to believe you. You admit the fact of the accusation?"

"Alas, yes."

"If would be difficult to deny it."

The police commissaire, a fundamentally generous person, had dropped the charge of insulting the authority. After muttering a few lines from the penal code, the tribunal condemned the anonymous individual to three months in prison. He had already been detained for two months, and as ill luck would have it, the prisons of Paris were overflowing, so he was transferring to a suburban jail.

After the shame of the Mazas and the petty sessions, he endured the promiscuity of the exercise yard, subjected to the interrogations and the familiarities of the rabble. To complete the misfortune, the governor, shocked by the sight of his renascent hair, whose roots were black and the summit blond, had his head shaved on the pretext that it was dirty. Thus travestied and in the gray penitentiary uniform, he had the ignoble appearance of a veritable criminal.

The thirty days passed in a kind of despairing stupor empty of all thought. It was like an uninterrupted series of the kind of bad dream in which incoherent and inconsequential ideas tumble from one precipice to another without being able to cling on to the walls of the abyss.

He wanted to reflect, to analyze his situation, to think about the future, but it was impossible. During his sojourn in the Mazas he had been solicited by the need to defend himself, and his mind, absorbed by that concern, had found a meager aliment therein. Now his mind was floundering in a kind of nauseating marsh, darkened by thick fogs. He had been condemned to prison! He had a criminal record! He had allowed himself to be caught in the gears, and what was going to become of him?

He would have no more money and domicile when he got out than when he came in. He was employed sowing school notebooks, but would a single sou of that problematic pittance remain to him? How would he live? How would he escape further pursuits, further inquisitorial tortures? The police were not going to lose sight of him; they were interested in removing his incognito. What would become of him if they succeeded?

He muttered incoherent phrases and bit his fingernails, huddled for long hours on his iron bedstead.

Chapter VI

Those who are vowed to misfortune at birth; those whom vices or infirmities lunge into the mire of social life; even those whom bad luck pursues stubbornly: the poor in spirit, the pariahs and the undisciplined—all those, in sum, who live in the constant practice of misery—quickly acquire a kind of experience of which they make use to soften their fate.

They know all the shelters, all the refuges, all the soup kitchens, all the bureaux of assistance, all the charitable institutions. They know the times when the barracks, the big restaurants, the educational establishments and convents dispose of their surplus and the remains of their meals. They divine the door that opens, the heart that is moved, the hand that gives, the places where people are laughing, the places where people are weeping, the instant when people become compassionate. They do not disdain the temple where conversion is rewarded, the confessional where the penitent is helped. They sense the baker who gives good weight to the purchaser of a morsel of bread, the grocer who consent to sell a sou's worth of cheese, the butcher who is not miserly with his bones. They sniff out the debris of markets and the damaged goods of Parisian alimentation. They know the street-corners where genuine offers of work are posted on the walls.

They also know the thousands of petty métiers to which public circumstances and the dunghill of civilization spontaneously give birth. They are the merchants of festival insignia, the street-traders of every sort, the sandwich-board men, the newspaper hawkers, the openers of carriage-doors, the collectors of cigar-butts, the finders of lost dogs, the sellers of groundsel, wild flowers or wild birds; they are the improvised moving-men hired by the day, the auxiliary street-cleaners of Paris on snowy or muddy nights, the distributors of prospectuses, the weepers in funeral corteges, the clowns that surge forth in the vicinity of weddings, the poor who smile at newborns. They are on the lookout for suitcases to carry, vehicles to unload, shop windows to wash, chairs to bring out or take in, saleable places in bank queues on issue days, theaters whose plays in vogue, free spectacles or sensational trials. They are, in sum, the anonymous artisans of those innumerable tasks that municipal statisticians ignore and Bottin does not register.

All of those people contrive to live, sometimes with greater ease than veritable workers. No easy prey escapes their jackal flair. They seek, divine, enquire, assist one another, and almost end up grouping together. They have their respective districts, their specialties, their meeting-places, their customs, their conventions and their verbal laws. They know the way to the drinking dens of the Barrières and the suburban taverns; the pigeon-trap and the fricassee of the Seine are not myths, and they never really suffer from hunger.

But those whom an unexpected event precipitates suddenly from opulence into distress; those who, rich and powerful one day, wake up poor and disarmed the next; the inexperienced, the improvident, the ignorant, the debutants of poverty; those who are only educated in political discourse or humanitarian books; those who, for the first time, find themselves literally without a sou, will have to sustain a pitiless and murderous struggle in order not to die of starvation.

Now, not only is Jacques Liban one of the latter, but the cruelty, plenitude and lightning rapidity of the disaster that he had not had the sagacity to anticipate seem to have struck him a mortal blow on the head. The triumphal arch elevated by pride has collapsed; he is lying under the rubble, which is crushing him, hiding the light from his eyes, preventing him from crying out and only giving him just enough air for him to support a longer agony.

What is going to become of him? What is he going to do? The prejudices, the pride and the delicacies of old still enlace him and paralyze him; ignorance of the milieu into which Fate has thrown him leave him at the mercy of hazard, with his hands and feet bound. His head is empty, his will almost extinct; his intelligence, a formless larva, is crawling painfully in the dark; instinct alone might be able to save him.

Here he is, out of prison. Instead of fleeing immediately and disappearing, as all the others do, he stops, bewildered, for a few minutes outside the door, and seems to make a considerable effort to arrive at a decision.

The shopkeepers opposite observe him with suspicious and mocking expressions. A group of schoolboys stop and direct their curious eyes at the "thief."

A uniformed policeman accosts him. "Let's see, now! One would think you were missing the box? Well, at least one's always sure of bean soup, eh? Move along—it isn't here that you'll find work."

He shrugs his shoulders and flees, in the direction of Paris. What is he going to do? The twelve sous remaining from his pittance, which he was given on leaving, will suffice for today, but tomorrow? He'll sell his dust-coat and look for work.

He reaches open country; the June sun that warms and comforts him almost makes him forget his distress. He breathes in the morning air, gladly; he knows now the real and direct value of the word "liberty." A ray of hope gives him illusions.

"I'll find work," he murmurs, confidently, looking at the tall chimneys of a factory vomiting smoke. "I'll do no matter what; I'll accept the most menial tasks while waiting for something better, and that necessary, inevitable humiliation will be the very crucible from which my soul will emerge more noble and better tempered. A man of my worth can't remain in difficulties for long!"

Anguished, he mutters: "My worth! My worth! Can't it be said that that vanished with the identity of Dr. Albin?"

He strives to react against the enervating uncertainty that has paralyzed him for three months. His pride rears up. A banal misfortune, a monetary loss, a severity of the blind law, won't put an end to a man like him. The fabulous wellbeing of the past hasn't turned his head; he won't allow himself to be crushed by a vulgar catastrophe; and even if he has to pass through all the stages of poverty, even if he has to bruise his feet and hands, he'll march without flinching!

A placard pinned to the door of a worksite attracts his attention. *Good workers wanted.*

"Why not?" he mutters, with a bitter snigger. *Dr. Albin once supervised masons when he had his villa at Trouville built. Jacques Liban will serve them.*

He goes into the site, where buildings are beginning to emerge from the ground. The laborers are working at a fast, steady pace. A foreman approaches and asks him what he wants.

"To be hired as a manual laborer, if that's possible," he replies.

The man looks him up and down. "You don't look the part," he remarks. "Have you done it before? Do you have any experience?"

"No, but I assume that with intelligence and good will, it won't take long to learn."

"You might think so," mutters the other. "A good manual laborer is rarer than a good mason." He adds: "Do you have papers? Where have you come from?"

The beggar is nonplussed.

"You've come from the country house, I'll wager," says the foreman, raising his arm in the direction of the prison. "You'd do better to go offer yourself to a shoe-factory. At least you could say you've served your apprenticeship."

Two or three companions have drawn nearer to them.

"Monsieur is weary of working in the shadows for the government," affirms the Limousin, with a coarse laugh. "He wants to serve you."

Red with shame, the liberated man hastens to disappear, pursued by insulting gibes.

He resumes his route, invaded again by an anguished sorrow. Market-gardeners' vehicles, returning from the market, go past him continually. They know the time of release; they hate the malefactors that the State nourishes at their expense, and who, when summer comes, steal their fruits as they go by. Every morning, they make a brutal game of humiliating them.

"Another one from over there! Get, away, good-for-nothing!"

"Watch your pockets!"

"Dirty tramp!"

"Burglar!"

Etc.

He is in haste to get away from an environment whose vicinity seems to identify him to all scorn. A side-road appears to him to be more direct and less busy. He takes it and increases his pace.

Time goes by, the sun climbs, fatigue and hunger begin to make themselves keenly felt. He goes into an inn and asks for something to eat.

"An omelet, a steak, a cutlet?" asks the proprietor, in the middle of a game of Zanzibar with a group of carters.

Jacques Liban is not yet familiar with economical meals, and remains confused.

"Sort it out with the wife," says the innkeeper. A slattern emerges from the kitchen and asks in her turn what the customer desires.

"I only have twelve sous," he murmurs, ashamedly.

"A soup, half a liter and two sous'-worth of bread, replies the woman, accustomed to this sorts of bargaining. "Will that do? It's more trouble than profit."

He dare not refuse, and devours his meager fare with remorse. His infinitesimal resources have been exhausted at a stroke; he would have done better to buy a loaf of bread on the way.

"Am I far from Paris?" he enquires, as he leaves.

"Nearly four leagues," the woman replies.

"Which is the shortest route?"

By the indications that he is given, he observes with annoyance that he has gone astray. He continues walking, cursing the adventure, cursing the stupid self-regard that first made

67

his lose precious time and then prevented him from refusing the innkeeper's relatively costly proposal. He trudges his fifteen kilometers angrily and find himself at the Porte des Prés-Saint-Gervais at about three o'clock.

"Finally," he murmurs, collapsing on a bench on the exterior boulevard. "At least I'll go unnoticed!"

But what will become of him, without a sou to his name? Where will he eat this evening?

And his mind, once so fertile in resources, has no response, no suggestion to offer!

Thick darkness extends before him, not the slightest glimmer of light to show him his route. He feels his energy abandoning him at the very moment when he needs it most, and if he still has any hope for the future, the sentiment of his present impotence plunges it into torpor.

It is, however, necessary to tear himself out of this despairing daydream, doubtless occasioned by the fatigue of his long march. Above all, it's necessary that he finds some money right away!

Perhaps, by selling his still-presentable dust-coat and exchanging his almost-new hat for an old one, he can obtain the ten francs that he can use, first of all, to get back his trunk, three months on deposit, and then subsidize his initial needs. He goes into the wretched shops of three or four local second-hand dealers in succession and attempts to carry out his plan; but it is the first time in his life that he has gone into such hovels. Dr. Albin only ever knew the Mont-de-Piété by name. He has no knowledge of the ignoble bargains to which the starve-lings who fall into the dens of these birds of prey are subject and the prices offered seem so derisory to him that he emerges beside himself with wrath.

In the Rue de Belleville a more spacious and less sordid shop appears to offer a better prospect. He goes into the dark shop, a long tunnel cluttered with ragged religious and military uniforms and seamstress' rags hanging from the ceiling, where the walls are covered with frayed dresses and faded ilk shirts, lamentable collections of clothing sold after death or contagious diseases, the wardrobe of the morgue and the hospital, a lumber-room corrupted by odors of benzene, grease, musk, dirt and old leather.

An obese man whose flaccid cheeks are marbled by dark red capillaries emerges from the depths and comes to meet him.

"Monsieur," the passer-by proposes to him, indicating his traveling garment. "I desire to sell this. How much will you give me for it?"

"Nothing," grunts the broker.

"That's not much," declares the stranger, trying to take it in good part. "The garment, however, cost me dear and it's still in good condition."

"It could be brand new and I wouldn't give you two sous for it."

"Why not?"

"Because it's only well-off people who wear things like that, and they don't come to my shop to dress themselves."

"I'll make you another offer, then. Here's a hat that's almost new, which it will be easy for you to sell at a good price. I'll willingly exchange it for an old one if you'll give me a few sous in return.

"How much are you giving me with the hat?" replies the merchant, playing the fool.

"I'm not giving you anything, I'm asking you for money."

The merchant examines the bowler and sniggers.

"Let's put our cards on the table," he says. "No need for subterfuge. I can see that the hat embarrasses you, and the coat. You want to be rid of them—I understand. It happens all the time. Well, I'm a good fellow, you know, there's nothing to fear with me; I have what you need. I'll give you a good one in exchange—that's to get you to come back when you've got something better."

"He takes me for a thief," mutters the hungry man, quivering with rage, but he quickly suppresses his initial impulse. "You're mistaken; I'm not trying to get rid of the object for

the reason you suppose. I need money, that's all. If I had another hat I'd simply sell you this one, but as I can't go around
bare-headed, I'm offering to exchange this one for one of less
value with a small sum in return. Do you understand?"

The two men look at one another. The clothes-dealer
continues to snigger in an incredulous and arrogant fashion

"Say," he says, "can you give me the address of the Figa-
ro whose cut your hair so well?"

Jacques Liban, remembering the ignoble way in which
he has been recently sheared, experiences a pain in the heart,
but if the man has observed him so well and has had the cruelty to remind him that he has come out of prison, he will have
his revenge in his turn.

"I'd be wrong to give you the address you're asking for,"
he replies, in the curt and trenchant voice of old, "for if your
hair were cut short, you'd catch cold, and if you caught cold,
you'd be a dead man."

"What! What do you mean?"

"I mean, you poor devil, that you're afflicted by a very
dangerous disease, diabetes, and you're in a bad way."

The merchant opens his eyes wide in alarm. "How do
you know that?" he ends up asks, fearfully "Are you a physician or a sorcerer?"

"Both."

"A bone-setter, perhaps?"

"A bone-setter, indeed."

"It's true, what you said. I have diabetes—so my doctor
claims, at least. For months he's been drugging me, and I'm
no better for it. I'll wager you know a good remedy."

"Well, those I've cured affirm it."

"Then we can make a deal, if you like," the salesman
proposes, suddenly becoming honey and sugar. "I'll trade your
hat for one of mine, I'll take your dust-coat, and I'll give you
two francs for the lot—on condition, of course, that you tell
me your remedy. All right?"

"Two francs—what a joke! You put a low price of your health. There are people in your situation who'd pay a fortune to get it back."

"Go on, I'll go to three. That's my last word.

The bone-setter accepts the bargain, examines the patient, writes a long prescription, exchanges his new hat for an old one, abandons his traveling-coat and receives the agreed price in return.

An impulse of hatred and malevolence has just got him out of difficulty temporarily. He cannot help noticing that, and does not experience any regret; the merchant's impudence merited a lesson.

That sum of three francs, which he palpates fondly, gives him new strength. The immediate care removed leaves a little more clarity in his mind.

He goes down the Rue du Faubourg du Temple, arrives at the Place de la République and notices the handwritten posters stuck to the barracks of the Château d'Eau. All the offers aimed at specialist and well-determined métiers are no good to him. A few are asking for apprentices between the age of twelve and fifteen to train up, and others only propose tasks for immediate pay. It's too late, anyway, to attempt anything. But tomorrow...

Toward what goal will his search be directed? The teaching profession seems indicated. He will surely find some institutional head who will take him on as a professor or a junior.

Chapter VII

Since he has been poor his stomach digests rapidly, with an ironic punctuality. He perceived very quickly that the meager aliments devoured that morning would not permit him to wait until the following day. His sojourn in prison had taught him frugality; that was a fortunate training for the circumstance, but he had not yet served an apprenticeship in fasting. He found himself in proximity to a philanthropic restaurant of which he had often heard mention, and hastened to it in order to appease his hunger.

A long file of shabby individuals were forming a queue, as at the theater; the majority had small loaves and bottles under their arms.

"They don't supply bread, then?" he asked his neighbor.

"No bread or wine. You have to go buy those elsewhere. Hurry up because it's late and the queue's already long."

He profited from this advice and came back to join the queue. He found himself next to an old man with dirty clothes, a long yellow-white beard and a face illuminated by alcohol, a classic type-specimen of the beggars that run around the cafes under the pretext of selling pencils or letter-paper.

"Why do they make us wait at the door?" he asked.

"You're coming here for the first time! It's because you have to go past the cash-box before going in. They sell meat-tickets for four sous and vegetable-tickets for two. Get your money ready and do as I do."

They penetrated into the immense bare hall, exchanged their tickets and sat down at a table beside forks and cups retained by iron chains. The vast room, full of people, was almost silent. Nothing was audible but the click of cutlery and the sounds of mastication. Only a few words were exchanged in low voices.

"Is it forbidden to talk?" he asked.

"No, but the people here don't have the time or the desire; it's necessary to make room for others."

"A great many people come here?"

"Until the day's provisions are exhausted; then they shut—too bad for latecomers. It's doubtless curiosity that brings you here?" The old man stared at the check suit as he made this supposition.

"No, Monsieur, don't trust this slightly garish outfit, which isn't in accord with my situation. It's harsh necessity—and as everything is relative, I can even say that this evening I'm having a veritable feast."

The alcoholic became more amiable. He had brought a liter of cheap wine. "Permit me to offer you a glass," he said, taking out the bottle. "It's the sixteen, and I know it—it's good."

"With the hope of returning the favor one day," acquiesced Jacques Liban. They clinked their cups amicably and drank to their health.

"Excellent," remarked the guest, for the sake of condescension.

"Isn't it? All the same, I'll wager that you've drunk better in the past."

"That's quite possible," the stranger admitted, smiling, "but the good days will come back. I'm going to work. I..."

"Work!" sniggered the old pauper. "Work! You'll be lucky if you find any. If you have a manual skill, I don't say no, and then...but I deduce from your appearance, your reasoning and your white hands that it's not the case. But I was wrong to say that to you—what's the point in discouraging you?"

"Is it so difficult, then, to earn one's bread?"

"I hope that you don't have an experience like mine—but I, who am talking to you, who, like you, once occupied a very honorable position in a large provincial city," confided the man with the rubicund nose, caressing his long beard, "who was a ministerial officer, searched for work for years without being able to find any in a stable and remunerative fashion."

"Is it possible?"

"As I have the honor of telling you. I've been admitted as a model into the studios of student painters, because of the beard," he declared, proudly. "At other times I've written love letters for maids and whores, etc., etc., but all those occupations were precarious, and then..."

"Then?"

"I sold penholders and pencils—you know what that means, don't you? I begged, I'm a beggar," the old man confessed, in a low voice. "Oh, the early days were hard! Begging, you see, is a métier like any other; it's necessary to know it; one doesn't succeed overnight, especially when one isn't a child of the bullet and doesn't possess some repulsive infirmity to excite pity in passers-by. Look, dressed as you are, I defy you to extort five sous a day from the compassion of your contemporaries. You'd be taken for a thief, a fraudster, for anything you like, but for an unfortunate—never! You don't have the gaze, the voice, the gestures, or, above all, the look. There also, Monsieur, form plays its preponderant role, setting the stage is indispensable. Such as you are, you couldn't go into a café without the waiters throwing you out, and you wouldn't take a hundred steps in the street without the cops feeling your collar."

"But I don't have any intention of competing with you," Jacques Liban affirmed, with a forced laugh.

"Don't be disgusted, there's no dishonor in it. It's necessary to live, and at our age, when one hasn't a sou and no work, there are only two resources: to take or to receive. Well, it's more difficult to be a good beggar than a good thief, so there are far more thieves than true beggars. I'm not talking about occasional beggars, of course: those who, caught in want, implore the passers-by in order not to die of hunger. They aren't serious, and never receive anything anyway. No, I'm talking about true mendicants: professionals, artists, who know how to soften the heart of Harpagon and Monsieur Vautour—those, in a word, who have no need to beg to live.

"They, you see, are stronger people than one night think. I know some who could go to live on their income and play politics in some jolly provincial corner, if avarice or passion for the métier didn't prevent them from retiring. There are beggars' places under the porches of churches that are sometimes sold more dearly than a clerk or a bailiff's evidence.

"But the men of genius in the corporation are the specialists. If I weren't bound be professional secrecy," the tireless chatterbox declared, "I could tell you some good stories. There is, however, one item of information I can give you, because my friend Bouton is dead and his place is up for grabs. He knew all the famous men by name and mainly worked the vicinity of the Institut on session days. How does one refuse an obol to an erudite solicitor who admires your talent?

"Me," he added, modestly, "I don't have that ability, but all the same, I've a few tricks in my bag. On pay days and Mondays I move the drunkards to pity. As soon as a man starts perorating and gesticulating in front of a counter, I go in and ask humbly for a drink of water. The wine merchant, who's in on the trick, brings me a carafe, asks me questions; I reply that I don't have a sou, and the soft-hearted drunkard doesn't take long to offer me a glass. The proverb's right, you see: water-drinkers have no heart; there's no one more charitable than a lush, firstly because he doesn't like to drink alone, and secondly because the booze makes him forget poverty and chase away the egotistical concern for the morrow."

They had finished their meal. Jacques Liban, ashamed of the acquaintance, had bid his importunate companion farewell—but he changed his mind.

"Do you know a place where I can spend the night cheaply?"

"Of course. Firstly, one can sleep in cheap lodgings for two and four sous in the Rue Mouffetard and the Rue Galande; then there are limekilns in the environs of Paris where one can stay warm—but watch out, one can asphyxiate there, and the cops often mount raids there; when the suburban commissaires and gendarmes have nothing to do, they go there in search of work. Finally—and this is where it's necessary to go if you're not accustomed to low dives, there's a night-shelter in the Rue St-Jacques where you can have onion soup. There's no denying that it's a fine institution—perhaps the bath is vexing, one isn't always disposed to play the duck; but the soup and the bed aren't to be disdained. Unfortunately, it's necessary to present oneself before eleven, and when one wants to play a hand of manilla or cultivate the fair sex, that can be very hard."

"What's the exact address of the shelter?" he asked, dreading some new digression on the part of the enthusiastic talker.

"I've forgotten the number—ask a cop." The mendicant added: "You have no domicile, then? Your situation is grave, very grave, and I don't want you to have any difficulty with the police. Look—a piece of advice before we part; go without food, go without drink, but always have a domicile."

Jacques Liban was about to draw away, but the tenacious old man was not ready to quit.

"You won't go to bed without having accepted a little glass? I'll pay, and I'll take you to my regular place."

"Might as well," he murmured, sheepishly. "He won't let me go otherwise." Aloud, he said: "I'd like that, on condition that you let me pay."

"Oh, if your self-respect is at stake, I won't object," said the dirt-stained old man, who took him by the arm in a familiar fashion and drew him toward a den in the Rue Galande.

Shady individuals—whores and pimps of the lowest rank—were at the tables. The mendicant' arrival was acclaimed.

"Hey, Père La Glue, the redhead's been waiting for you for two hours—what a dance, old boy!"

An ignoble woman of an uncertain age had stood up in her corner, furious. "This is how you pay for dinner, you old sot!" she complained.

The former ministerial officer, winking, pointed to the stranger and made her a sign to keep quiet. "I haven't made

76

ten sous," he told her, in a low voice, by way of excuse. "And no music—I have business with Monsieur."

That pompous declaration seems to calm the pitiful whore.

"Come and have a glass," the beggar said. "It's Monsieur who's offering."

Sickened, Jacques Liban was in haste to get away, but he made a sign of acquiescence, paid for the three glasses that had just been served, shook the hand that the man held out to him, and uttered a sigh of satisfaction when he found himself back in the street.

Those, then, were the degraded beings with whom he was going to rub shoulders and to be constantly subjected. Not that it could last—that bird of ill-omen had lied. Vice and debauchery had surely caused the abortion of all the former ministerial officer's attempts, but a man of his knowledge and worth would easily find a place in the sun.

Before anything else, he had to shake off the kind of idiotic torpor that had weighed upon his intelligence since the catastrophe, and prevented him from fixing and immediate and practical goal.

He counted his wealth; he still had forty sous. He promised himself not to repeat the sumptuous meal he had just had; twelve sous a day would suffice. He therefore had three days ahead of him to look for work. At dawn tomorrow he would set out on campaign and visit the various institutions of the quarter.

He had wandered at random, and suddenly found himself, as if some mysterious will had led him there, facing his former dwelling.

The old house had a forbidding appearance that he had never noticed, and which surprised him dolorously. Nevertheless, everything there respired calm and comfort. Although the high windows and the laboratory doors were closed, the windows of the drawing room were joyously illuminated, and his old concierges, whom he could see, plump and shiny through the curtains, were still at table, digesting, and supping a small glass of liqueur. The man, an old soldier, was making energetic gestures to his wife and making chopping gestures with his hand. Doubtless he was explaining the tragic death of his master to her for the hundredth time.

Although his memory seemed to have been abruptly attenuated since the day of the funeral, and the past no longer agitated before him except in a confused fashion, as if through a veil, chagrined comparisons came in a host to assail him.

A man in a hurry, elegantly dressed in mourning, who brushed past him without apology and rang the bell at the coaching entrance interrupted his dolorous meditation. It was Dr. Larmezan, who slammed the heavy door behind him, as if he wanted to shut it in someone's nose.

He fled rapidly, with a kind of resentment and promised that he would henceforth avoid the placed that had been witness to such a fabulous prosperity.

At the street corner, an old pauper that Dr. Albin had had the habit of helping emerged from a corner and put out his hand. Instinctively, he dug into his pocket and gave him two sous.

He quickly regretted his unthinking generosity bitterly. Alms were a luxury that he no longer had the means to offer. Two sous! That was now life, independence, perhaps honor for an entire day. He had never suspected that such a minimal sum could acquire that relative value. He, who had once philosophized on so many subjects, given brilliant lectures on social deprivation, already glimpsed the almost insurmountable abyss that separated the benevolent, but rich and fortunate, theoretician from the poor devil really at grips with poverty and hunger.

It was about nine o'clock. He spotted two uniformed policeman whose heavy and regular tread made their boots ring on the sidewalk, and asked them for the exact address of the night shelter.

"At the top of the Rue St-Jacques," replied one of them. Addressing his colleague, he added: "Do you know the number?"

"No," grunted the other. "Let him ask."

"That's what I'm doing," the questioner pointed out.

"Go to the top of the Rue St-Jacques. The locals will tell you."

He set off in the direction indicated.

"Hey!" called the grumpy policeman. "Come here a minute, with your exact address. What's your name?"

"Jacques Liban."

"So you don't have a domicile, since you're asking for the exact address of the night shelter?" He emphasized the word *exact* as if he saw it as a reproach to his ignorance.

"Yes," the vagabond replied, striving to laugh, "but I've fallen out with my landlord over a slight delay..."

"That's all right, go on," the policeman eventually said, after looking him in the face carefully.

That incident proved to him that he ought to avoid the slightest contact with the authorities in future, and that, Jacques Liban having a criminal record, it would be prudent to assume another identity. Anagrams of Albin—since he was absolutely intent on retaining an anagram of his old name—being numerous, he was spoiled for choice. After a few seconds, he settled on Balin.

"The life of Jacques Liban was brief and unfortunate," he murmured. "Five hundred thousand francs lost and ninety days in prison in five and a half months! May Charles Balin have better luck!"

He reached the Boulevard Saint-Michel, exhausted by fatigue, and crushed by discouraging memories. It was there that he had once been saluted by the crowd, acclaimed by the students, and passed for someone triumphant; and now, a problematic unknown, he was dragging himself along the same street in search of a little rest in a night shelter!

The cafés were inundated by light, the terraces full of noisy customers; an unaccustomed turbulence reigned outside all the fashionable establishments. Groups of policemen posted at every street corner were ready to reestablish order.

At the height of the Café d'Harcourt and the Place de la Sorbonne the agitation was in full swing; rowdy students were going in and out incessantly; some were singing, others shouting at one another or proffering threats. Shrill female voices dominated the racket.

He had stopped momentarily to take account of that effervescence. He had not read a line of newsprint since the day of his arrest. What could be the reason for all this fuss? Probably some scandal at the School of Medicine or Law, perhaps a political demonstration.

A woman tugged on the sleeve of his jacket and drew him to one side.

"They'll fall on you," she murmured, in a horse voice. "Get away."

He thought it was some joke and looked at her, smiling.

"Why do you think those young people would fall on me, Mademoiselle? For that, there's have to be a reason."

"Oh, pardon me, Monsieur, I'm mistaken. I thought you were Fanny Tripette's lover—she's a mate from the Bullier. It's the check suit that caused the error. All the same, Monsieur," she added, "believe me, get away. The students have been up in arms for three days—they see pimps everywhere."

The passer-by thought that the advice was not to be disdained. *In fact*, he thought, humiliated, *this check suit, glabrous face, short-cropped hair, dirty hat and red neckerchief must give me a singularly shady appearance, if even a professional was able to mistake me for one!*

He took an oblique route to the Rue St-Jacques, crossed the hospitable threshold of the night shelter, registered under the name of Charles Balin, represented himself as an unemployed teacher just out of the hospital, made the compulsory ablutions, and slid into the narrow bunk, where a reparatory slumber came to extract him from his sufferings for a few hours.

Chapter VIII

Equipped with letters of recommendation that the director of the shelter had spontaneously offered him, Charles Balin set out ardently in quest of employment. The head of the first institution to which he addressed himself sent the response via the porter that the vacant position had just been filled. A second looked scornfully at the note of recommendation and grimaced.

"You've come from the night shelter! A poor reference, Monsieur. Anyway, my staff has been complete since yesterday."

The mere fact of emerging from a shelter is, in fact, enough to make these people suspicious, he thought. *I'll take due note of the observation.*

A third schoolmaster received him in his study; he made his request.

"What are your qualifications?"

"Doctor in medicine and sciences," he replied, modestly, announcing a few of his former official titles

The master started humming in an insolent fashion. "Well, Monsieur," he ended up declaring, "I have no place for you in my establishment. It's not a well of knowledge I need, it's a good master of studies, thirty francs a month, food and lodging."

"My God, Monsieur," the naïve petitioner relied, "the situation isn't, in fact, the height of my ambition, but necessity has no law and if you care to take me, I'll accept the place you're offering."

"Very good, Monsieur. Show me your certificates and diplomas."

The disconcerted solicitor stammered that he had no papers or parchments on him, but that he would come back.

"Ta ta ta," the pedant interrupted, brusquely. "No point in lying, you won't come back! You don't have the titles you claim. You want me to swallow that with all those diplomas you'd accept a place as a junior! But that's stupid, implausible—or you'd have had to have murdered your father and mother and be just out of prison, and no one wants to see you any more, in the flesh or in painting. Doctor of sciences! But if I were a doctor of sciences I'd have been a professor of the Faculty for ten years! Go away—I don't like frauds."

Charles Balin went out, discouraged. The man was right; why announce that he had titles he could no longer justify?

Those three attempts, the long walks and the hours of waiting had absorbed the whole of the first day. He went back to the night shelter, where he ruminated various projects during tedious hours of insomnia.

As soon as daylight appeared he recommenced his way of the cross. He had obtained several addresses from a Bottin, and presented himself there at hazard. Some were not yet up, others had a complete staff, and would not in any case have taken on a new employee on the eve of the vacation.

One of them was looking for a good professor of physics and chemistry; he thought that luck was finally smiling on him; the man, caught in need, having numerous pupils to represent for the examinations, received him with open arms.

"Monsieur," he admitted, frankly, "I have the most serious qualifications for the position I'm soliciting, but I can't show them to you, having lost them in a fire and not having had time to procure duplicates. If you'd like to take me to your laboratory, question me or take me on trial for a few days, you'll be astonished, I can confidently announce, by the extent of my knowledge."

"Do you imagine that I'm going to test all the teachers who present themselves?" observed the fabricant of baccalaureates, probably conscious of his own ignorance. "To do that, I'd have to have time to waste. If you have qualifications, go look for them, If your parchments are destroyed, bring me a simple certificate from the Sorbonne or the Faculty that received you. Simply show me attestations from honorable and well-known men, and I'll be content—I'm pressed for time—

but how can I take a teacher without a guarantee, a certificate or a reference? It's impossible. My institution is a reputable one, frequented by an elite. One doesn't come in without a recommendation, without proof of honorability and knowledge."

Toward the end of the day, the director of a suburban bedlam gave him a better welcome. He was an enormous fat man enveloped in an immense dressing-gown with a green foliage pattern on a red background, coiffed in a grenadine velvet bonnet. With the rubicund face of a heavy drinker and carrot-colored hair, he would have cut an excellent figure in a German tavern.

"You're looking for a place as a teacher?" he asked, before the solicitor had opened his mouth. "Sit down, please, my dear Monsieur."

"I'm a bachelor of letters," the postulant began, "but..."

The hundred kilos interrupted swiftly. "That doesn't matter. What good are all those university diplomas to me? None, my dear Monsieur—keep your parchments in your pocket, I've no need to see them. I need a study-master who can teach the kids to read, that's all. I won't insult you by supposing you incapable of doing the job. In consequence, in principle, I'll take you on—if you accept the conditions, of course.

"I'm not one of those headmasters insistent on discipline who make their institution a branch of Mettray.[17] No, I leave my pupils a certain liberty; I excuse the natural thoughtlessness and turbulence of youth. I close my eyes to a good deal of mischief. But in order that that paternal liberty doesn't degenerate into intolerable license, I need schoolmasters both firm and flexible, who can master the pupils without employing violence or brutalizing punishments. No caning, no detentions, no lines! It's not easy, you can imagine, to maintain good order without that arsenal dear to pedants, so I only take my professors on trial. I lodge them and nourish them for the first

---

[17] The Mettray Penal Colony for children and adolescents—a pioneering installation of that kind.

month, and if they possess the necessary qualities I give them fifty francs for the second. Fifty francs!" he repeated, in order to emphasize the enormity of the salary.

Food and lodging alone were a meager perspective, but it was the certainty of sleeping under a roof, of not dying of hunger, of being able to wash his only shirt. It was the hope of acquiring payments later that would help him to get out of the rut. Charles Balin accepted, and was introduced to "the ladies," Madame and Mademoiselle Béguinard, two thin, hypocritical individuals as stiff and yellow as quince paste. The ladies greeted the new schoolmaster with a scarcely-dissimulated grimace; there was a long conference in a corner in low voices. The imposing head of the institution seemed to make the most of his reasons of necessity, and they ended up acquiescing.

He was immediately informed of the usages, conducted to the study and solemnly enthroned in his functions as a junior master. One thing that struck him was that he was the unique teacher in the Béguinard school; Monsieur, Madame and Mademoiselle Béguinard directed the first three classes, and he found himself charged with general surveillance and teaching twenty brats to read.

From the very first day, the patience of the new martyr was subjected to the most ridiculous proofs: papier-mâché pellets, projectiles in the back, pins embedded in the chair, itching powder in the sheets, etc.—nothing was spared him. Once a day pupil in one of the great lycées of Paris, he had only known the backlash of the laxity of childhood by hearsay; he could now meditate upon that pitiful subject at his ease and in ample knowledge of it.

It was necessary to have one's back desperately to the wall in order to endure that imbecilic and odious suffering. Many a time, in that ridiculous pulpit of black fir-wood, where he served as the target for the malevolence and scorn of the little suburban grocers, he thought about the magisterial lessons of the eloquent Professor Albin, to which a crowd avid or instruction listened in silence and admiration. A week of that degrading ordeal did more to teach him to master his anger than twenty years of his past life.

At the end of the first fortnight, Monsieur Béguinard, who had never ceased for an instant to lavish smiles full of encouragement and beatitude upon him, asked to speak to him for a few minutes.

"My dear Monsieur Balin," he said, "you're not perfect, it's true, and you don't yet have experience in the métier, that's obvious, but I'm nevertheless satisfied, even delighted, with your services. Except that—don't take offence at the observation—the ladies find your check suit a little...how shall I put it?...extraordinary for a house of education. Without demanding a severe costume, a puritan aspect, our profession requires a certain bearing, a correction that you're far from having, it's necessary to admit. You look like an American tourist! They've also remarked that your linen isn't always irreproachably clean. You even, it seems, went a whole day shirtless. The children notice all that; your lack of authority stems from it; it's necessary not to give leverage to their mockeries. Quit this eccentric dress, then, suitable at the most for a Yankee steamboat, and change your underwear, damn it, change your underwear! At your age, one ought to look out for personal cares!"

"Monsieur," the junior master confessed, painfully, "I have no other clothes than these, and I was obliged to separate myself from my only shirt to wash it. If you would be kind enough to advance me the five or six francs necessary to reclaim a trunk left on deposit at the Gare de Lyon three months ago, I can satisfy you."

"Damn!" muttered the soup-merchant. "Damn! Not even underwear! If I'd known..."

"Once again, if you care to advance me..."

"I never make advances," Monsieur Béguinard interrupted, brusquely. "That's a principle."

That alarm bell warned the unfortunate junior master that he ought to expect dismissal, or the entrepreneur of cut-price education would not have would not have refused such a minimal advance. In any other circumstances, he would have hastened to take the initiative, but those two weeks of assured life had been so useful to him that he felt that in a few days more he would have got a grip on himself again, become once again the man of sure judgment, prompt determination and resourceful intelligence that he would not have ceased to be without the sledgehammer blow that destiny had brought down on his head. He had observed with so much joy the symptoms of the imminent awakening that he kept quiet, energetically determined to bury his pride, submit to all caprices, endure all villainies, support all shames and swallow all insults, provided that he was not thrown brutally on to the sidewalk, with his pockets a empty as the day of his arrival.

The next day, a Sunday, he was taking his children for a walk when an individual of Mephistophelean appearance, bony, toothless and grimacing, decked in a long threadbare frock-coat, accosted him on the main road.

"Are you the study-master at the Béguinard school?"

"Yes, Monsieur."

"Food and lodging for the first month—and what nourishment! Fifty francs salary the second, if the victim has the gift of pleasing?"

"I can see that you're well-informed."

"I should say so. I'm one of your predecessors. Well, Monsieur, I'll make it a duty to warn you that the second month never arrives; the unfortunate dupe always displeases at the end of the first. That's the crapulous hypocrite's game."

"I suspected as much."

"There's never any lack of excuses. Monsieur Béguinard is always delighted with your services, he's in despair at losing you, he'll regret it as long as he lives, but one displeases the ladies—two dirty sluts, in parentheses—a ridiculous feminine caprice to which one is obliged to submit for the sake of domestic harmony, etc. Conclusion: pack your bags and make way for the poor devil who'll be exploited in the same fashion. With that system, the wretch has solved the difficult problem of having study-masters—what am I saying…galley-slaves, pariahs, negroes—without taking a sou out of his pockets. If he weren't a former wrestler, things wouldn't have passed that way with me! Have you been with him for long?"

"About a fortnight."

"Well, in a week, he'll commence his confidences; he'll tell you about his debuts in the team of the illustrious Marseille; then he'll pass on to a little demonstration, lifting enormous weights, carrying heaving chairs at arm's length and challenging you to do the same."

"He really was a wrestler, then?"

"Big Béguinard, the rampart of St-Quentin! That's common knowledge. He became the director of the school by marrying the founder's daughter; the establishment is still in the father-in-law's name. He'll soon give you all the details himself. At first, one's astonished by the cynical display of a past so little commendable for a headmaster; it's only when the coarse reproaches replace his honeyed words and wheedling monkish smiles, and he throws you out brutally, that you understand the meaning and value of the whole comedy."

"What you're telling me is abominable!"

"It's the pure truth, Monsieur, I swear, and if, after that confidence, you persist in remaining in the house until the end of the month, you'll play the sad role of simpleton and métier-spoiler."

"Have you another situation, however precarious, to offer me?" asked Charles Balin.

The other junior master remained mute.

"Well then," his interlocutor continued, "while thanking you for your advice, permit me to handle the matter as I please."

The unknown man was continuing on his way when one of his pupils took it into his head to throw a stone at him. To turn round and administer one of those beatings that provide relief was the affair of an instant. The master of studies tried to extract his pupil from the angry avenger, but could not prevent him from receiving a magisterial correction.

On returning from the walk, Monsieur Béguinard, immediately informed and convinced that his altered dupe was about to leave him in the lurch, hastened to take the initiative. He could make light of all that a thief, an ignoramus defrocked for inadmissible reasons, had been able to tell him, but he could not tolerate that anyone would allow the dear children confided to his care to be assaulted!

"That's all right, Monsieur; I'll leave tomorrow," replied the sacked master, coldly.

"This very instant!" howled the rampart of St-Quentin, his fists on his hips.

"No, Monsieur," replied the victim, calmly. "I'll leave tomorrow, after you've given me a certificate of good conduct. If you refuse, I'll make a complaint to the Academic Council and take an article to the *Moniteur des Maîtres d'étude*. Know that it's not stupidity, but dire necessity, that caused me to tolerate the ridiculous role that I'm playing. Don't push me to extremes; your quality as a former wrestler doesn't impress me, and you might learn at your expense what an intelligent man is worth in such circumstances."

Suddenly softened, the headmaster judged it prudent not to demand an instant departure.

Chapter IX

"Not even an unemployed junior master," murmured the unfortunate Charles Balin, as he headed for Paris the following morning. "It's very difficult to eat bred by the sweat of one's brow, to the detriment of one's intelligence!"

He searched his pockets; he had had sixteen sous on entering the Béguinard school; he had spent four having his shirt laundered, so he still had twelve, enough not to die of hunger for two days.

However, that brief sojourn at the suburban pseudo-school had had several important advantages for him. He had rested from his physical fatigues and mental anguish; he had eaten regularly for a fortnight; and he possessed three documents of identity: a letter recommending a pupil to him, the certificate extracted by threat from Monsieur Béguinard, and a legalization of signature that he had procured under a pretext from the local Mairie. He had, therefore, the commencement of a legal existence. He was emerging from place that he could indicate, and he possessed papers—insignificant, to be sure, but papers nevertheless.

It was about one o'clock in the afternoon when he arrived at the Porte de X***. His stomach, lacking the dried peas and haricot beans of the institution, was gurgling consistently. He started nibbling pieces of bread thrown at him by the pupils and picked up covertly the day before. Then, embarrassed by the passers-by who were watching him eat with a scornful curiosity, he climbed the bank of the fortifications.

The July sun cast a little gaiety over the meager landscape of the suburb. The formless huts of the military zone, made of planks or plasterboard covered with bituminous paper, were hung with clothes in the process of drying. The ground, blackened by the dust and mud of Paris, constellated by the scintillations of shards of glass or porcelain, concealed its pestilence beneath vegetables and green bushes. Innumerable factory chimneys blurred by thick mist emerged therefrom, vague and somber, in the distance, vomiting floods of black smoke plumed with grey in vertical jets. On the horizon, the indecisive lines of hills melted into the sadness and uncertainty of the azure, soiled by so much impure breath.

Moving aside the greasy paper, the repugnant debris of improvised snacks, he sat down on the short, thick grass, which idleness, somnolence or the enlacement of wretched couples sprawling thereon for long hours seemed to have prevented from growing. Here and there, shady individuals lying on their backs, legs bent, hands behind their heads by way of a pillow, were sunbathing. A girl in a red smock was picking daisies and singing a sentimental sing; another kneeling next to a side-whiskered lout adjusted the locks of her hair and then, a female in heat beside a somnolent male, tickled him with blades of grass, laughing in bursts. An old groundsel-merchant, basket overflowing, drew away, curbed beneath the burden, while a dog-clipper armed with his scissors, and surrounded by brats, sheared a mongrel extended at full length.

The man with the check jacket, the dirty hat, the wan face and the forehead creased with anxiety for the morrow; the downfallen man whose hard crust cracked between his teeth, felt that he was in his element there, that he did not spoil the view, that he was, in fact, the individual characteristic of it and indispensable to it, the poor shameful fellow who did not yet dare to sate his hunger before the eyes of passers-by. Thus Dr. Albin, under the bushy shade of his luxurious villa, parading his meditation in a solitary park, listening to the distant rumbling of the sea, had once completed by his presence the décor made for a life of prosperity.

This, he sniggered, *is what one might call a nice day in the country: a green carpet, choice neighbors, a rural, and above all frugal, feast.* But why was it necessary for him to hide in order to eat? It was necessary for him to get used to wearing his poverty brazenly; there was nothing infamous about it!

A man had stopped in front of him, with a ferrety face almost entirely covered with unkempt hair, within which the anxious eyes of a jackal gleamed. He contemplated him with an open, drooling mouth, like a fog that can hear bones breaking.

"You wouldn't have, by any chance, an extra piece?" he implored, wiping the corner of his mouth.

He dipped into his pocket and brought out one last crust, which he threw to the vagabond. "That's all I have left, my poor fellow. It's a little stale—don't break your teeth."

The stranger had caught the piece of bread in mid-air, and devoured it with a kind of frenzy. "I'd like to have one like that every day," he mumbled, with his mouth full.

A frisson caused him to shudder. There were, therefore, creatures even more wretched than himself!

"It's a pity," groaned the starveling, "when one has arms, and can't make use of them to eat. In the provinces, there are rubbish-heaps, one can still unearth something by digging, but in this damnable Paris, one's worse off than the dogs. And to think that I've come so far to die of hunger! By dint of hearing it said that it was a land of Cockayne! In God's name, what a Cockayne! I'm no good-for-nothing, though; must be unlucky, can't find a blow to strike!" He paused, his interrogative and malevolent eyes igniting with sinister hatred. "You wouldn't be in need of a mate?" he went on, lowering his voice. "I'm a man who'd let himself be shortened rather than spill the beans—one can count on me."

He takes me for a gang-leader, thought the master of studies, invaded by disgust and sorrow. He stood up abruptly and drew away, to avoid the temptation to give him a sou.

He went back into Paris. The drinking-dens of the Barrière were full of workers celebrating holy Monday. The reek of soup and the scent of stew were already escaping from kitchens. Two coachmen with shiny faces were eating large steaks in the open air. A fat peasant-woman with a Norman bonnet, in front of an oven surmounted by a cast iron pipe, on which melted butter was sizzling with an appetizing odor, was turning over a large thin pancake, round and gilded, like a nimbus. A sudden greed, mingled with childhood memories, overwhelmed him. He bought the pancake and ate it hot, seasoned with regret for his prodigality, which made it seem even more delicious.

He walked on a short distance; a young woman whose face was shaded by the eccentric headgear of the Salvation Army approached him with the smile made of pity and scorn that believers accord to sinners, and offered him a pamphlet, which he took, and read the epigraph mechanically:

I have seen the doors of the tomb open and searched in vain for the remainder of my days. Ezekiel.

Seized by a sudden superstitious terror, he threw it away urgently. The citation launched by some clergyman at the moment when he was leaving the cemetery returned to his mind.

A child ran after him. "Monsieur, Monsieur, you dropped something." The child brought back the disdained pamphlet.

"Keep it. my lad." He replied. "I'll make you a gift of it."

A little further on, an older salvationist, whose ugliness was aggravated by colored spectacles, handed him another copy of the haunting pamphlet. He felt a surge of wrath that it was impossible for him to repress.

"Devil take these fanatics," he growled. "They always have some discouraging verse from a psalm to offer you; they'd do better the replace the celestial nourishment they dole out to passers-by with something more substantial."

"If you're deprived of resources and work," replied the propagandist, "go to..."

He drew away, grumbling, and did not hear the address she indicated. A brief moment of reflection sufficed to make him regret his outburst. He tried to retrace his steps to obtain the information that had been offered to him, but the Salvationists had disappeared.

He found himself outside a fashionable restaurant, where wedding vehicles were arriving in procession. Louts and ragged individuals hastened toward the landaus, opened the doors and received tips. He was watching them, almost envying their lot, when he saw the hairy man who had asked him for bread again.

The starveling tried to slip into the midst of the door-openers and share their windfalls, but the improvised lackeys would not stand for it; they would not allow an unknown prowler to benefit from a profit impatiently awaited for several hours. Surrounded in the blink of an eye, jostled and belabored with punches, and the luckless individual was forced to quit the place, piteously.

The spectacle revolted him. Was the struggle for existence so pitiless in its ferocity, then? But in that case, that pariah, chased away everywhere, was logically driven to theft, to crime. He went to him.

"Go to the night-shelter in the Rue St-Jacques, my poor fellow; you'll sleep in a bed and have some good soup."

By the inflexions of his head, the man let him know that the resource was not unknown to him.

"You're only let in there three nights in succession," he murmured. "Necessary to find myself something to eat, though, or I get myself put in prison; they'll be obliged to feed me there."

He quickly resumed his course, escaping the temptation to give him a sou for the second time.

Had the practice of poverty hardened his heart to that extent? Poor as he was, ought he not to aid someone poorer than him? Would he not have a small share of responsibility for the evil deed that the desperate man was bound to commit? But what sentimental folly it was to occupy himself with another when tomorrow, or the day after, he might perhaps find himself in the same situation, or one even worse? For after all, what was going to become of him? To what sad necessity would he be reduced?

Yesterday, he had been able to affirm that he had been, and would always be, an honest man; was he sure now of not committing a theft, if he were placed in that alternative and that of dying of hunger? Had his poverty not just been exploited unworthily? An idea of revenge might have germinated in his brain, weakened by suffering, revolted by bad faith! He had been born with good instincts, but not all the actions severely punished by law arise uniquely from our evil inclinations! Who knows whether our perverse instincts themselves might not be atavistically born of a long series of injustices and tortures?

He had believed once that he had torn away all the veils, explored all the charnel-houses; he had made great speeches, pronounced sonorous words; but, in reality, he had not had an accurate conception of matters that he had imagined he knew thoroughly. If all legislators had the rude apprenticeship that he was in the process of undergoing, their laws would be more indulgent to the weaknesses and impulses of the starving. He had never understood more fully Renan's remark that "No one has a right to anything but what is necessary; the excess belongs to those who have not."

He found himself in the Place de la République and wandered, mechanically around the flower-market. Women in bright summer dresses, nurses whose long ribbons hung down to the ground and who were proudly carrying heaps of linen and lace in which the white faces of babies were glimpsed through veils of tulle, idlers, soldiers and amorous couples cluttered the edges of the covered market.

Rows of flowers in pots were aligned on the asphalt. Climbing roses, honeysuckle and clematis clung to iron uprights, coiling their flexible stems around the slender supports. Gladioli with bright corollas, petunias as velvety as lovers' gazes, heraldic lilies and swooning or smiling roses promises perfumes and colors to the windows of mansards as well as the balconies of rich town houses. Ferns, fleshy plants, dwarf palms, dracaeanas, elegant umbels, disorderly tresses and bizarre nodulated stems declared their affinity with the Japanese bronzes of drawing-rooms. Gardeners in haste to sell their last merchandise were making seductive offers, commenting on the language of flowers, complimenting the ladies with banal circumstantial comparisons. And all those odorous effluvia, all those sparkling hues, emitted a kind of dizzying sadness that went to his head, as if the flowers had become animated in order to sympathize with him, seemingly astonished to see him so unhappy, and vague amorous memories emerged dully from the past.

The voice of a peasant woman attracted him from his reverie.

"Is there a ticket-porter here?" asked the flower-seller.

He turned round, a stout gentleman with a jovial and self-satisfied expression wanted to buy an orchid.

"No ticket-porter," repeated the florist.

Charles Balin presented himself. The purchaser looked him up and down. "Don't you have a plaque?" he asked.

"No, Monsieur, but you can trust me."

The bourgeois looked in all directions. A ticket-porter with a copper medallion in his buttonhole finally responded to the appeal.

"Here, my good man," the buyer instructed. "Take this plant to the address and the person indicated on this card, and then come back." He turned toward the solicitor he had dismissed; as if to compensate him for the refusal, he slipped two sous into his hand and said: "And you, my friend, have a drink."

His self-respect reveled against that casual offer. "I don't need a drink and I don't ask for alms," he said, proudly.

"All my apologies, Monsieur," laughed the parvenu, returning the coin to his pocket. "I thought it would please you." Addressing the flower-seller, he added: "It takes away the desire to be charitable; I won't take the risk of receiving the lesson again."

Humiliated by the incident, he drew away and at down on a bench facing the barracks. Soldiers in battle-dress were returning from maneuvers, harassed by fatigue, streaming with sweat, covered in dust, weighed down by their kit; they were swallowed up at the double by the arched entrance.

Once, the sight of a regiment had engendered patriotic hopes in his heart; now he thought before anything else of the abominable costs of war; he saw once again the bleak faces returning from a siege, the silent files of decimated and vanquished troops, horizons ablaze, fields of snow covered with the dead and the dying, the bloodied and muddy Tonkinese paddy-fields, and that house full of decapitated cadavers, the fatal cradle of his rebirth. The victims immolated to the false manes of Dr. Albin loomed up before him, and the collective crime appeared to him in all its hideousness.

Men, individually mild and benevolent, by the mere fact of being united into a band and dressed in a certain fashion, burned villages, pillaged houses, took pride in murdering their fellows, and the Fatherland circled their heads with laurels!

Was that not the antagonism between collective and individual morality displayed in all its nudity?

When would humankind reestablish equilibrium? When would the river of tears and blood that is war be dammed?

A sigh seemed to reply to him. A woman of distinguished appearance and a certain age, pale and thin, with a package on her knees, was sitting beside him. Her gaze, lowered to the ground, seemed to be fixed upon some terrifying sight; it was as if she were frozen in an attitude of dolor, nothing capable of deflecting her from her despair.

He fled immediately, as if he had scented the odor of death.

Why, he asked himself, are so many miseries once unperceived surging forth before me today? Is it my own misfortune that has removed the scales from my eyes, or do great dolors attract one another? I'd swear that that unknown woman is going to die, and I only have that intuition because I can't help her...

The sun was beginning to do down. He observed, cursing, that he had wasted an entire day wandering and that the futile vagabondage, complicated by hunger, had left him greatly fatigued. He went through Les Halles, gradually drawing nearer to the night-shelter. A sudden rumor erupted behind him: cries of "Thief!" and "Stop him!" multiplied.

He turned round; in the man who went past him, fleeing at top speed, he recognized once again the starveling of the fortifications. Two or three strong market porters and butcher boys were on his heels; workers who were coming in the opposite direction blocked his path; it was not long before a trip brought him down. The unfortunate lay on the ground, his forehead bloodied by the fall. Policemen approached and lifted him up.

"What is it? What has he done?" they asked.

A fat old woman ran up, out of breath. "He stole a sausage from me, Monsieur. On reflection, let him go, I'll give it to him. He must be rudely hungry to take it like that, with his fingers, from the hot stove!"

The audience started to laugh.

"You stole a sausage," said the policeman. "Where is it?"

"I don't know. When I saw them chasing me, I dropped it. I stole it for nothing!"

Further laughter greeted the unfortunate's heart-rending disappointment.

"Go on," said the policemen, amused themselves. "Don't do it again and be off, since it's been given to you."

"It's been given to me! cried the starveling, his eyes lighting up. "Where is it?"

"A dog ate it," replied a street-urchin.

"Oh, damn it! I burned my fingers for the cur!" groaned the grotesque delinquent. Astounded by the unaccustomed clemency of the police, he added: "It's a bit stiff, all the same. Caught red-handed and they didn't even arrest me!"

The hilarity became general, but no one thought of helping him.

"Too bad," murmured Charles Balin, who, being better informed, was almost moved to tears. "If heaven is just, it will take my action into account." He put two sous into his hat and made a collection for the poor devil.

Chapter X

"Obtain information everywhere," the director of the shelter advised him. "Read all the placards on the street-corners carefully. To begin with, go to the small ads section."

He followed the advice. A crowd of men, most of them young and vigorous, were cluttering up the exhibition hall and the environs of the newspaper officers. Some were taking note of the offers pinned up, others, standing around, were waiting disconsolately for an opportunity to present itself. Sometimes, a busy individual who looked like a caterer came in: a laborer was wanted, a manual worker, a delivery man, etc. A compact group of solicitors raced toward the Messiah; the man made his choice and the others, brows furrowed by care, immediately resumed their places.

He spent hours thus in vain waiting.

"No luck today," said a little, rosy-cheeked old man, timid and neat, who had come over to him two or three times with the evident intention of striking up a conversation. "We're wasting our time here."

"I'm very much afraid," he replied, "that we're too numerous. People are spoiled for choice; they'll always prefer the young ones to us."

"There are however, instances where people look for men of a certain age, serious men of respectable appearance."

"What are they?"

"When it's a matter of certain small tasks demanding a good deal of decorum: client of a page-four physician or an American dentist, for example; put on a frock-coat and a respectable appearance, and the occupation is within the range of all intelligence; it's sufficient to work the antechamber and sing the praises, with sufficient skill, of the illustrious healer. If I, who am speaking, had had a single one of all the cancers they've cured for me, I'd have been dead long since.

"Sometimes, manufacturers of specialties are in search of good launchers. You present yourself in recalcitrant establishments, ask for a glass of Quina Machin; the waiter, who hasn't got it, offers you a glass of Quina Chose; you spit fire and flame, declare that you have no wish to be poisoned, and leave. Or you run around all the small pharmacies of a neighborhood asking for a bottle of L***'s famous tonic wine; the pharmacist apologizes for not having any, asks you to come back in a few hours, sends out for some—and you don't go back, of course.

"But those roles, you understand, require to be played seriously; if the appearance or the manner arouses the slightest suspicion, the end isn't attained. Unfortunately for me, they necessitate a frequent change of personnel; that's the cause of my current lack of employment. Oh, if only the police hadn't stuck their noses into the affairs of the *** matrimonial agency, I wouldn't be here; that's where I collected some nice fees.

"What did you do there?"

"Noble fathers, rich uncles, bishops *in partibus*, opulent gout-sufferers in quest of a devoted companion, etc., etc."

"So those are the only employments that a man of a certain age can hope to find here?" he asked, in a melancholy tone.

"Well, those who don't have a métier, properly speaking, and don't want to take on dangerous and ingrate tasks like appearing as false witnesses, are very happy to accept them."

There was a long moment of silence. The little old man coughed; it was evident that he still had something to say.

"There are also," he eventually added, "photographers who come here in search of intelligent models, and who pay quite well, believe me."

"I thought it was entirely the opposite."

"I'm talking about photographs for export—those who specialize in pornographic pictures."

"Oh!"

"I can assure you that it's agreeable," the old choirboy confessed, his eyes gleaming with lust. "One sees funny things. One isn't always bound, of course, to take one's role seriously; the most robust of men couldn't do that. No, one makes a semblance—which already isn't a sinecure—but it's well paid, and there's nothing to dread, for if the woman is as naked as Truth, the man is usually disguised as all kinds of great individuals; lord, boyar, prince, sultan, financier, senator, magistrate, curé, monk, general, etc. etc. No danger that you'll be recognized!"

"It's evident that you're speaking from experience."

"Once, I posed as the King of the Belgians," replied the lubricious old man. "My doctor has forbidden me to do it anymore."

"You must have played the scenes with too much conviction!"

His forehead furrowed by disgust, Charles Balin, scenting some adroit tout, hastened to break off the conversation, but then, seeing that he was risking waiting even longer without finding the slightest opportunity that he could accept without falling from grace, took down twenty addresses and promised himself that as soon as he had eaten in haste in some corner of the square, to recommence active research.

Everything seemed to be in league against him, however; the rain that had been threatening since the morning began to fall in buckets. As his unique garment did not permit him to confront it without danger, and his thin and elegant shoes were not made for walking in mud, he quickly took refuge under a vault of the Louvre.

Oh, the despairing sadness that invaded him there, during long hours of waiting. The low gray sky put the royal courtyard in mourning; it seemed to him that the sun was extinct forever, that the desolation of things, so concordant with that of his soul, would never end, and that they were veritable teardrops that were falling in front of him. Could he ever have imagined, once, that such a banal accident could take on for some people the proportions of a veritable catastrophe?

Who, then, would take pity on his distress if nature herself came out against him?

Every moment lost brought him closer to absolute deprivation. Although he had gone to bed the previous evening without dinner, the two sous sacrificed to his greed and the two given as alms had reduced his derisory capital to forty centimes, only enough to keep hunger at bay for a few hours.

The rain did not stop until late. He immediately set forth once again, and fate seemed suddenly to favor him.

He was passing through one of the narrow back streets that still surround Les Halles when he saw a man in the process of sticking a notice on the panel of an old coaching entrance. *The written notice read: Immediately required, coachman and delivery man, good salary.*

He immediately raced after the employee, into the vast warehouse of a fruit wholesaler, and asked for the job.

"Already!" exclaimed the proprietor. "We won't lack candidates."

The man considered him at length. "Where have you come from?" he asked. "Have you done the job before?"

"It's the first time I've sought employment of this kind," the unknown admitted, frankly, "but you can put me on trial; you'll see that I can drive perfectly, and I know Paris thoroughly."

"Do you have papers? I want a man I can trust; my delivery man is often called upon to collect invoices."

"These are the only papers I have on me," replied Charles Balin, slightly abashed, holding out Monsieur Béguinard's certificate and the legalization of signature.

The wholesaler scanned them and scowled. "These papers only relate to one thing," he remarked. "That's that you've been a schoolmaster for a fortnight. I don't see any connection between that métier and that of coachman. What proof do I have that you can even drive?"

"I'll tell you the truth," the solicitor replied. "Not long ago, I was a rich man., very rich. I had horses and carriages. I took pleasure in driving them myself and I guided them with a veritable skill."

"That's possible," murmured the fruit merchant, indecisively, but ended up adding: "Come tomorrow at five. A trial won't cost me much. You'll have a hundred sous a day to start. If you suit me I'll hire you by the month, and feed you."

The petitioner dissolved in thanks, and went out radiant.

"A hundred sous a day," he repeated, "and a job that I'm sure I can do with honor; that's deliverance in a short while."

His joy, aided by the demands of his stomach, caused him to forget all precaution. He returned to the philanthropic restaurant, spent what remained to him and hastened to return to the shelter.

The next morning, at five o'clock precisely, he presented himself at the fruit warehouse. The wholesaler made a gesture of annoyance on perceiving him. A truck loaded with crates emerged from the courtyard.

"You're too late," he said. "The job's taken."

"I've arrived at the agreed time," stammered Charles Balin.

"I told you four o'clock and you've come at five."

"Don't lie!" growled the ousted petitioner.

"Oh, we're turning nasty," replied the other, in the same tone. "Bad move, friend. You want the truth, well, here it is: didn't you tell me that you've just lost a large fortune and that you learned to drive in order to conform with the fashion of the day?"

"Very nearly."

"Your reason seemed good to me at first, but on reflecting a little, it didn't take me long to perceive that it's worthless. It's admissible that in the capacity of a rich man you learned the métier of a coachman, but it's even more certain that you refrained from learning that of a groom. Now, my horses need to be well-combed as well as well-guided. The errand-boy ran after you to tell you not to bother, but you'd already disappeared. And as several solicitors presented themselves immediately after you, who had their papers in order and whose honorability was attested by certificates of good conduct and mores, I didn't have any difficulty making my choice."

"You've made me lose time," grumbled the unfortunate.

"Don't think so," replied the wholesaler, becoming coarse. "I've got you up a little earlier, that's all. It's time gained, my man. And there's enough of it, isn't there? If you think I've done you wrong, address yourself to the law.

Charles Balin mastered his anger with great difficulty, and left, distraught.

The streets were full of busy people running to their work. He envied their good fortune and felt near to tears.

"What!" he muttered. "So many mediocre or worthless individuals find employment, and I, a man of the elite, can't earn my bread?"

He wandered for a while at random. The shops and workshops were only just beginning to open. Then, shaking off the torpor that gradually infiltrated into his soul with every setback, he recommenced his painful endeavors with a new ardor, determined to continue for as long as he could.

Having remembered, during his insomnia, that he had heard of people making a start as proofreaders, he started with the printers and publishing houses.

"Proofreader?" they objected. "Where have you come from? Are you in the trade?"

"No," he replied, "but I've spent my life correcting proofs and my knowledge of dead and living languages puts me in a position to render the greatest services."

"No matter—you're wasting your time. First of all, the position of proofreader, like that of overseer, is a kind of marshal's baton that we award to old employees; then there are friends, protégés, those of our shareholders and our clients. Where would we be if we gave places as proofreaders to unknowns? You must have exercised some profession during your life; address yourself in that direction; you'll find sentiments of solidarity and benevolence there that you won't encounter elsewhere."

In fact, the man was right. He could not, it is true, make appeal to the sentiments that had just been mentioned, but he would have more assurance by looking in the direction indicated.

He went into a pharmacist's shop; the druggist was in search of a laboratory assistant.

"Did the agency send you?" asked the chemist. "Where have you come from? If you're from the provinces, there's no point in looking for a place; I need someone up to date with Parisian pharmacy."

"I can make the most delicate preparations and the most difficult analyses," he declared, confidently.

"Then you're making a mistake applying here. It's not an aide I want, it's a lab boy."

"Who can do the most can do the least. I'll accept those functions, and you can put me to the proof for the rest."

The apothecary looked him up and down disdainfully. "And you imagine that I'd let my preparations and my analyses be done by my lab boy? What do you take me for? Here, everyone stays in his place, you understand. In addition to domestic services, I only ask one thing of my assistants, and I can judge your work right away. Take that bottle, that paper and that wax, and we'll see whether you're capable of labeling a potion with a little chic."

The unfortunate petitioner had never labeled a bottle. After a few moments of trial, the certified grocer sent him packing without further ado.

"Chemical analyses!" he cried, indignantly. "You don't even know how to make a simple pleat!"

Now he knocked at random on all doors. "You have need, I hear, of a bookkeeper...a salesperson...a representative...on office boy...a clerk...an overseer...an aide...a manager...a tutor...etc., etc." Everywhere, he was found to be too old and too debilitated for the employment; everywhere, proof was demanded of his capability and morality; everywhere, he was sent away with more or less ironic pity.

He went into employment agencies and bureaux; they offered to sell him lists of vacant positions. A problematic banker asked him for three thousand francs of security; a dubious enquiry agent in need of a sleuth to follow a trail and provoke a divorce did not forgive him for a momentary hesitation that he could not help betraying.

A manufacturer who wanted laborers confronted him with a heavy crate and instructed him to load it on to a truck; he could scarcely shift it.

Dusk fell. He no longer had a sou, and it was the last night that the rules permitted him to stay at the shelter. At all costs, however, it would be necessary for him, like the wretch of two days before, to find food and shelter. Was he going to sleep on benches? Take refuge under bridges or go to earth in quarries? To what infamous promiscuity was he about to be subjected? The old mendicant had told the truth; one could no longer find work at his age. And the crapulous logic of the former ministerial officer returned obstinately to his mind; there were now only two alternatives: to take or to receive; beggar or thief.

A mortal chill traversed his heart; the two alternatives were as repugnant as one another—but nor did he want to die of starvation.

He dragged himself as best he could to the shelter whose doors would be closed to him the following day, exhausted by fatigue, and ended up falling into a sleep full of bad dreams, the slumber that is no longer repose.

He woke up near to collapse. The vegetarian regime to which he had been subjected since the day of his arrest was not made to support privations, but the vague nourishment, truly too summary, that he had taken in the last three days had not even served to stave off his hunger. It required all his energy to set forth again.

The first thing that struck his gaze was a placard attached to the facing wall:

Men wanted who know Paris well for easy and rewarding work, very urgent.

The notice had surely been put there intentionally. He armed himself with all his courage and went to the indicated address, in the vicinity of the Museum.

The grocer who received him insisted on offering him a glass of white wine; he had the habit of killing the worm when he got up, and business only went well after clinking glasses. Although certain of the harmful effect, he dared not offend the man who could get him out of trouble with a refusal. The merchant lisped in an irritating fashion and had the air of an utter simpleton. He began by tell him about his debuts and explaining all the inconveniences and frustrations of the grocery business in detail. After interminable digressions, he finally got to the point.

"This is it," he said. "I've decided to get into wholesaling, in a small way. I have, therefore, procured oils, wines, soaps and petroleum products at low cost; I can offer exceptional prices to clients; it's a matter of placing my products with solvent people in any fashion you please. My competitors take accredited brokers or travelers; me, I reason as follows: the more placers I have, the more merchandise I'll sell, that' s clear as day, so I put up notices in places frequented by people without work; I'll be delighted to come to their aid. Occupy yourself with selling my stock, then, and I'll give you a ten per cent commission, payable in cash as soon as the thirty-day invoices are settled.

"And in the meantime?" asked the disappointed work-seeker.

"In the meantime what?" said the astonished grocer.

"How do those in search of an immediate salary eat?" He was gripped by anger. "Are you stupid? You put up a notice like yours opposite a night-shelter; the people who come out, it can be assumed, don't have the time to wait a month for the price of their work."

He went out, irritated by the imbecility of the individual who had wasted his increasingly precious time, excited by the white wine, which had gone to his head. The heat was oppressive; noon was chiming on the clocks. He went through the

Jardin des Plantes, almost deserted at that hour. His head heavy and his eyes leaden, he sat down on a bench to rest briefly...

The burning rays of the sun brought him round. Had he gone to sleep? Had he lost consciousness? He hastened to apply compresses of cold water to his aching head, and started walking again. Hunger was beginning to torture him, thousands of black dots were dancing before his eyes; he felt himself vacillating; he made an energetic effort to collect himself.

"Come on," he sighed. "Who sleeps dines. I've dined."

A newspaper thrown from the top deck of an omnibus fell sat his feet. He picked it up feverishly and turned to page four. There were many requests for employment and few offers. The majority came from agencies; he was already informed on their account. Other were seeking boys between twelve and fifteen to undertake courses or apprenticeships for a rapidly-remunerated métier, or financial backers for exceptionally advantageous businesses.

A dentist was in search of an assistant.

It was in the Temple district. Hope restored his strength. He ran there.

Once, in guard-rooms, he had devoted himself furiously to the extraction of molars. If he did not know how to label a bottle with the dexterity and elegance demanded by a Parisian pharmacist, he could show the dentist that he was capable of extracting a tooth.

The operator examined him with a singular suspicion. He had ruminated his speech on the way, and, with the aid of the white wine, delivered it with an admirable fluency. The clamp no longer had any secrets for him and the forceps, in his hands, accomplished veritable miracles. There was not a caried tooth that could resist him, no ungraspable stump that he could not uproot.

The dentist whistled while he listened to him.

"I'll do without your services," he replied. "Apply elsewhere."

"But Monsieur, if you need someone, what I've told you is true; I'm not boasting. As for salary, I'm not demanding; give me what you wish. Look, just take me on trial for a few days—food and lodging; you'll see then what I'm worth and pay me what you please."

Negative shakes of the head greeted all these propositions.

The unhappy petitioner, with desperate persistence, swore again to the great gods that he was telling the truth.

"It's possible, even probable," the dentist ended up declaring, "and that's why I don't want you at any price, even if you were to offer me money. Do you imagine that I haven't guessed, at the first glance, what you're up to? But your attire, your appearance, your smooth talk, your disinterested proposals give you away sufficiently. You're some fairground dentist or provincial charlatan. You want to work with me to perfect your skills and then set yourself up in Paris. Well, it's not in my school that you'll learn the chic of the capital. Go away, decamp, my good man. Find another mug—I'm not going to make a rod for my own back."

Decidedly, fate was determined to doom him. He had a moment of terrible discouragement. Then, shaking off his stupor, he went back to the great boulevards like a wolf emerging from the woods, with the vague and foolish hope that someone might recognize him, guess who he was, come to his aid. Would a man like him be left any longer to die of hunger? A discreet hand would reach out, aid would fall from the sky.

The double current of the busy crowd occupied the entire width of the sidewalk; passers-by were arguing and gesticulating, friends were bumping into one another; foreigners and provincials were mingling the awkwardness of their gait; prostitutes in search of dinner or bourgeois coquettes, their meager purchases in hand, were variegating it with garish colors. He was marching automatically, like a specter, his feet no longer feeling the ground, his eyes staring, his complexion livid. At every step personalities from all walks of life passed him, and people who had once saluted him, bowing to the asphalt, did not even glance at him.

Had he changed to that extent, then? Or is it too difficult to recognize those one no longer expected to encounter?

Here comes Dr. R***, his former rival, his gestures broad, his head high, his gaze assured, the rosette in his buttonhole. The boulevard seems to belong to him; he is saluted by the crowd as he passes, they make way for him; heads turn, fingers point him out. Once, he had been treated thus, while now...

Instinctively, the wretch feels himself; he feels flat, effaced, ignored, annihilated. He no longer counts. He has the sensation, now quite clear and definite, that he is part of the crowd, part of the people. He is englobed, confounded, lost in a mass; he is the anonymous being one looks at without seeing, that one jostles without apologizing, the vague unit that moves in the midst of number; he is so alone, so astray, that he finds himself in the middle of the vastest desert.

He listened to the cries of newsvendors without hearing them, and without even trying, as he had on the previous days, to read the day's events in the headlines of newspaper he was unable to buy. What did political events matter to him? The events that would have impassioned him only a few months before left him plunged in the profoundest indifference. The intrigues of the Chambres, upheavals in the ministry, adventures in princely alcoves, financial scandals, frontier conflicts! What can all that mean to those who are in immediate need of something to eat? Oh, if he could see a band of starvelings passing by who were talking about breaking into a food store...! The disorders of the street would perhaps not appear to him as reprehensible as they once did.

Tragic visions passed before his eyes, of roads stained with blood, muted and horse rumors rising from the populace; the anemia sounding in his ears had the lugubrious chimes of a tocsin.

Weakly, he leaned against a column of posters. Facing him, the terrace of a political café was packed with customers.

Why were all those people looking at him without seeing him, seemingly without wanting to recognize him? The ugliness of the demonstrative gestures and the vulgarity of the grimacing faces recalled him to reality. Scales fell from his eyes; it was no longer the place of old made for cordial encounters and witty conversation; it was a vile gehenna where gazes shone with cupidity or hatred, where consciences were sold, where conspiracies were woven, where cabals were organized, where reticence, treason and cowardice mingled with ophidian undulations of smoke escaped from bloody or discolored lips.

Irritated by the appetizing odor of absinthe, he made an effort, crossed the boulevard and found himself facing Potel et Chabot. The monstrous salmon, the fillets Rossini, the sole pies, the pheasant galantines, the carps *à la Chambord*, the lobsters *à l'Américaine*, the scarlet bushes of crayfish, the giant shrimp from the African coast and the monstrous fruit from the Asiatic islands excited the curiosity and desire of passers-by. He could not help laughing bitterly. "Once," he muttered, "I drank absinthe; now I dine with Lucullus."

But all those dishes, once familiar, did not occasion any regret; he would have been content with the most vulgar dishes.

What would become of him? A vague glimmer of hope was born in his mind. What if he could find the alcoholic beggar and borrow two sous from him? He was the only being to whom he could address himself. He knew that he operated in the cafés of the left bank and he headed painfully in that direction.

As he passed over the Pont des Arts, during one of the numerous pauses that his weakness necessitated, he leaned on the balustrade.

The sun was setting in a luminous mist behind the Palais de l'Industrie. He gazed sat the Seine, whose waves, turned crimson by the last light were lapping the quais. How many times, on emerging from the Institut, he had admired that spectacle! Now, as he contemplated the water that seemed to fascinate him and promise eternal repose, he wondered if that bloody silk was not about to be the shroud that bore his cadaver, with the debris of the sewers, to the sea.

The sea! He would not even have the vast and poetic tomb of the desperate! A mariner's hook would bring his tumefied body back to the surface; he would go to the Morgue to serve as pasture for the unhealthy curiosity of idlers. Then the quicklime of the communal grave would devour his bones.

By an energetic effort of will, the man drew himself up to his full height. No, he would not seek Death. Let hunger continue its slow and sure work, and let it kill him. But he would struggle until the last minute, until the last breath. Had he voluntarily abandoned so much glory, so much wealth and so many honors, had he conquered a second life at the price of so many dangers for an obscure suicide to undo it a few months later?

That could not be; it would not be. He, who had once stimulated the enthusiasm and admiration of an elite crowd, was incapable of finding, today, a poor crust of bread? That was absurd, impossible. A thick veil covered his eyes, and the lid of a tomb weighed heavily upon his intelligence, but he would lift up the slab, tear through the darkness and tame Fate. Avoid the struggle by flight, like a coward, dive head first into Oblivion like the hero of some trivial news item? Get away! He would look the enemy in the face, and no matter how cruel his wounds might be, no matter how powerful the iron hand that had gripped his through and tried to strangle him, he would fight to the end. He had gambled with death, he had snatched from Destiny the few years that Dr. Albin still had to live, and he would confess himself vanquished already? Rather shame, rather theft, rather blood, rather...

The blasphemy caught in his throat.

On the arm of Dr. Larmezan and under the crepe that seemed to tear for him, so beautiful, so blooming, so languorously happy, such as he had never seen her and never suspected, a woman in full mourning, the widow of Professor Albin, passed slowly in front of him.

Chapter XI

As if to mock him for having made the energetic resolution to live, hunger—inexorable hunger—was devouring his entrails. How he regretted the two sous that a sentimental impulse had made him give away three days ago, how he regretted above all the obol that his pride had caused him to refuse. Now, there was no longer any stupid self-respect; as soon as night fell, he would beg. Yes, since he must, since he wanted to live, the man who had been Dr. Albin would beg.

His vanity would have adapted better to theft, but the most vulgar common sense, the immediate and future interest, the lack of know-how, all prevented him, so he had to fall back on that hideous necessity; he would beg. He had never refused alms to anyone, why should someone not render him a little of the charity that he had once lavished?

In the meantime, he sat down on a bench, facing a town house whose basement allowed irritating odors of cooking to escape. The darkness thickened, the mascarons grimacing menacingly above the arches. He got up and went to lurk in a corner near the coaching entrance, but the concierge came out, irritated.

"What are you doing there? You've come here to beg, or rather to spy on the house. Wait a minute—I'll fetch the police."

The unfortunate drew away, went down on to the quais, hid behind a tree and advanced toward a hurried passer-by, who made an abrupt sidestep and continued on his way, cursing the untimely apparition.

On the Pont des Saints-Pères he approaches two gentlemen in the midst of a heated argument under a gas-lamp.

"Charity, Messieurs, please!" But his dull voice his curt, his gaze anxious and piercing; the two men examine him suspiciously.

"Is that an order?" exclaims one of them. "Your money or your life! You think we're in a corner of the woods? Get away, quicker than that, or I'll bring out my revolver."

"Must be a communist," adds the other. "He asks for alms as if he were demanding his due."

The disconcerted beggar goes for some time without daring to renew the attempt. In the Avenue de l'Opéra, a woman of a certain age is trotting before him; he hastens his pace and approaches her; the respectable lady turns round indignantly.

"You're mistaken, Monsieur!" she cries, in an English accent. "I'm an honest woman, and if you persist in following me I'll call for help."

A young man in a black suit comes out of the Café de Paris; he hurries to meet him, sticks out his hand and stammers...

A "no money, my good man," immediately closes his mouth.

On the great boulevards, he immediately perceives that the too-compact crowd renders begging almost impossible. Passers-by solicited at too close a range recoil, muttering, the idlers huddle together. Monsieur Vautour is astonished that the police do their job so badly; Monsieur Rapace blames the ever-increasing audacity and cynicism of the false poor; Monsieur Prud'homme advises him to work and Monsieur Homais sends him to the bureaux of charity.

In the Place de l'Opéra, a street-vendor is offering all-comers transparent maps.

"Do I look like a provincial?" cries an obese stroller in a vexed tone.

"No, Boss," the lout replies, in his hoarse voice, "I can see that you haven't arrived from Quimper, but I've been fleeced at the course; give me two sous—it's to buy groundsel for my little canary!"

The simpleton laughs and complies with a good grace; the tempted vagabond extends his hand in his turn.

"Oh, no!" exclaims the gentleman. "Come back tomorrow, the till closes at three! Word of honor, they take me for their banker."

He wanders in the direction of the Madeleine, sketches a suppliant expression and implores an old beau about to cross the Rue Royale.

"Have pity on me, Monsieur, I haven't eaten!"

The man looks him up and down, mockingly. "It's bit too old, that one, old man; you've been telling me that for years!"

Twenty times he recommences his attempts, and the same fatality remains obstinate in making them fail. Perhaps he will have the opportunity to open a few coach doors when the theaters empty?

Midnight chimes. He retraces his steps hastily; a flood of spectators emerges from the Vaudeville; carriages and fiacres advance in a file; he wants to try to open them, but a swarm of street-urchins and prowlers, more alert and more skillful, take possession of them before him, jostling him brutally, warning him that this carriage is *theirs*, that they've sought it out, and shoving him backwards. He remembers the poor devil that he once saw showered with blows, and retires, discouraged.

Gradually, the crowd ebbs away, passers-by become increasingly rare, the terraces of the cafes empty, no one any longer remains on the boulevards but night-walkers, prostitutes and pimps.. The street-vendors and newsvendors, reckoning the day ended, gather in groups, counting their receipts, calling out to the whores, heading for the taverns that are still open. The animation is concentrated at the corner of the Rue du Faubourg-Montmartre. There he makes a few final attempts, as fruitless as the preceding ones. Policemen harass him, abuse him, order him to desist from begging and threaten to arrest him if they see him on the boulevard again.

Where can he go? His feet are bruised; he can scarcely walk. He takes a few steps in the direction of the Boulevard Bonne-Nouvelle and collapses on a bench almost directly opposite the Barbedienne foundry. His eyes mist over; he vague-

ly distinguishes shadows coming and going before him; a sei-
zure grips his throat; he needs all his will-power not to faint.

Suddenly, a brutal hand falls on his shoulder, and shakes
him awake.

"You're still here," complains the policeman. "Go to
bed, or I'll take you to the station."

The wretch opens his eyes wide.

"Go to bed, you old drunk," the policeman repeats, "and
quicker than that. Come on! Up! Move along!"

"I can't," he murmurs. "I haven't eaten. I'm hungry."

His voice is extinct, his face livid, his gaze tearful. The
policemen, slightly disconcerted, exchange a few words in
whispers.

"Leave him there," says one of them. "It's too late, they
can't give him anything at the station."

The two agents resume their round at a slow pace, and a
few passers-by, brought together by curiosity, disappear without saying a word. Then a whore sits down beside him.

"Is it true that you haven't eaten?" she asks him.

The unfortunate looks at her without replying; two large
tears trickle slowly down his cheeks.

"Wait for me," she said. "I'll buy you some buttered
bread over there." She disappears rapidly and comes back a
moment later.

"Here, eat."

The man falls avidly upon the pasture that hazard had
sent him, and devours it dazedly without saying a word. Two
or three other women have joined the first, and contemplate
him with pitying expressions.

"Are you still hungry?" asks a newcomer.

"Oh, yes," he murmurs, in a low voice. The prostitutes
club together, boldly soliciting contributions from passers-by,
and Mariette, whose benevolent impulse has just saved the life
of the starving man, soon comes back with victuals and wine.

"We can't leave him to eat all that on the bench," she
says. "The cops will come back again to move him on."

"Where do you live?" asks another whore.

"Nowhere," the man replies, still in a low voice.

"You're doubtless out of work. What do you do?"

"I'm a professor."

The women look at him curiously, and confer again.

"You don't have a lover—give him a bed," one of them proposes. "A professor's a toff!"

"Do you want to come with me?" says Mariette. "You can eat all that at the house."

"I'd be putting you out, Mademoiselle."

"Putting me out? Oh, at this hour I'm not risking anything by going to bed, for all that there is to do."

"That's true," approve the others, in chorus.

"Let's see—can you walk?"

"Yes, I feel a little better now."

"Come on, then, we'll sort it out. You can't spend the night on a bench."

With the docility of a small child, the unfortunate, vanquished by fate and disorientated, drawn by the odor of warm bread and meat, takes the arm that Mariette offers him and heads toward Montmartre with her.

The air is fresher; a pale light is already announcing that dawn is not far off. The little nourishment he has had has sufficed to render him courage and strength, the certainty that he will eat more on going inside causes him to forget the bruising of his feet.

They have scarcely exchanged a few words during the journey; here they are at the "Hôtel de la Dordogne et du Calvados," where Mariette lives.

The whore rings, lights candle-matches, and the poor devil, after having climbed two flights of stairs, finally lets himself fall, with manifest gladness, on to a threadbare sofa.

"Don't get impatient, my dear," his companion hastens to announce. "I'll light the candle and we'll eat."

The good woman has quickly set out her provisions on the table.

"No cutlery, plates or napkins here, you know; one's furnished—necessary not to be difficult."

The guest scarcely thinks about such details. The slices of ham and larded veal disappear rapidly into his mouth. Mariette, who is nibbling, watches him eat with a veritable contentment.

"Well, truly," she murmurs, "if someone tells me tomorrow that you're a fraud, I'll tell him he's lying. That's an appetite! How long is it since you've eaten?"

"About thirty hours."

"That's not too much!"

"Yes, but I'd eaten so little in the days before."

"Poor dear. You're a professor, then?"

"Yes."

"I thought professors were rich people."

"As you can see, not always."

"Why are you calling me *vous*? So I won't say *tu* to you, perhaps?"

"No, my dear Mariette," he exclaims, already feeling better and almost cheerful. "You're a good, a lovely girl, and I thank you cordially for the service you've just rendered me." This time he addresses her as *tu*.

"That's nice—we'll have to clink glasses on that—to the health of my poor old man!"

"To yours, Mariette, to the luck that will permit me to repay my debt to you worthily."

"You don't owe me anything—one can't let people die of starvation."

"Without your good heart, however, that's what would have happened to me."

He considered her with a keen gratitude. A slight blush colored the prostitute's cheeks.

"You must have suffered a good deal," he added, after a pause, "to have taken pity on a stranger like that."

Mariette's expression darkened. "Bah!" she murmured, by way of response. "A woman like me, a slut, can always find something to eat; if it's not one way, it's another. You've lost your place suddenly, then? After all, you don't seem like a poor man. You're well-dressed, you have nice shoes—without the hat, one could take you for an Englishman."

"I've lost everything, Mariette, from one day to the next. I found myself on the streets of Paris without work and without a sou in my pocket."

She continued to gaze at him attentively. "I don't know why," she ended up saying, "but it seems to me that we've known one another for a long time."

"That isn't possible."

"Well, there are faces like that, which come back to you, and people with whom you're old acquaintances right away. What's your name?"

"Charles Balin."

"Charles, Charlot! I like that. Will it annoy you if I call you by your first name?"

"It will give me the greatest pleasure," he affirmed, like a well brought-up man.

They had finished eating; there was a long pause. The rising dawn caused the candlelight to pale.

"Shall we go to bed?" Mariette interrogated, in a caressant voice.

"It would indeed by a good time to rest," her companion admitted. "Go to bed, then; I'll sleep on the sofa. Don't be afraid to undress—I won't look."

"Do I frighten you? Silly!"

"No, my dear; it's a matter of discretion."

The prostitute looked at him, surprised.

"Discretion?" she said. "Oh yes, I understand." She started to laugh while getting undressed. "It's the first time a man has said that to me," she added.

After a few moments, seeing that he was no longer moving, she went on: "What are you doing? Don't you understand? Get undressed, I tell you—there's room for two in the bed."

"But that would be indiscreet on my part," he stammered.

"Since I tell you no! One can sleep like that *en camaro*, as mates—unless I disgust you?"

"How can you think that, Mariette!"

Be quick, then; it's getting light and you need sleep."

She blew out the candle, and got into bed. He undressed in haste and slid in beside her.

"Good night," she said. "Or rather, good morning, and sleep well." She laughed softly, and pressed herself against him.

"Not going to give little Mariette a kiss before going to sleep?" she sighed, seductively.

He put his arms around her and held her for a long time in a chaste embrace. Then carnal desire invaded him, and he tried to hold her more tightly, but the young woman pushed him away gently.

"You're too tired, my dear; go to sleep—until tomorrow," she murmured, turning toward the wall.

When Charles Balin woke up, the sunlight was flooding through the curtains. A profound astonishment gripped him. Where was he? The events of the previous evening returned rapidly to his mind.

Beside him, Mariette was still fast asleep; he contemplated her, invaded by a instinctive sadness. She was a brunette, meager and slender, with drawn features, rings around her eyes, a straight nose and a delicately oval face. She might have been twenty-three or twenty-four, and was not ugly. Her uncovered forehead did not lack nobility, the nape of her neck was elegant, her long hands and fingers delicate, but the stigmata of debauchery, the precocious wrinkles, the residues of make-up brightening her cheeks, contrasting with the morbid pallor of her complexion, the black harshly accentuating her eyebrows, the thinness of her hair, the cracked and discolored lips, and the mouth vitiated by specific treatment, initially produced an impression of pity and disgust in him.

He turned his head and looked at the miserable room in the poor lodging-house in which he had just awoken. The dazzling light brought out its disorder and bareness.

The bed, an old wooden-framed bed in the Empire style, was garnished with dirty linen. Wallpaper with blue flowers, now torn, stained and discolored, had once covered the walls.

A dressing-table surmounted by a commonplace mirror was cluttered with utensils of intimate usage. A bucket and a pitcher of water were on the floor beneath it. The battered sofa that had seemed so soft the night before testified to the innumerable assaults to which it had been obliged to submit. Opposite, a glass-fronted cupboard in varnished walnut contrasted by virtue of its newness with the general obsolescence of the furniture. In the middle, a table covered with a faded cloth presented a heap of disparate objects: dirty glasses, a withered bouquet, a coverless novel soiled with stains, the debris of the evening meal, a spirit lamp, a small iron saucepan, candle-stubs, scattered cigarettes, lumps of sugar, etc.

On the mantelpiece there was an old clock with twisted columns that no longer had any hands, and small objects brought back from fairgrounds: chipped porcelain, roses in brightly-colored paper, toy trumpets, Japanese screens, spiced-bread rigs, cockades and fairground insignia. On the walls there were incomplete and discolored chromolithographs: a *Monk confessing a Spaniard*, a *Portrait of Monsieur Thiers* and a *Drunkard imbibing a glass of wine*.

He turned his gaze back to the sleeping Mariette. He saw her in profile now, and found her less repulsive. His adult life had passed in the continence of an ascetic scholar; there had been months on end when his desire had not awakened on contact with other flesh. An ardent blood ran in his veins, however; involuntarily, and wretched as he was, he was not indifferent to the woman. The feverish overexcitement of the last few days even seemed to have exasperated his senses. Slightly troubled by that unaccustomed itch, he sought to master himself by considering the abjection of the common prostitute, but sentiments of compassion and gratitude came to the rescue of his suddenly-unleashed appetite.

Had she not saved his life? Had he not eaten her bread and slept in her bed? Would he make her the supreme insult of disdain? Certainly, Dr. Albin had never lowered himself to such impure contacts, but Charles Balin did not have the right to the same scruples. Had he not already, perhaps..?

His memories became more precise; the simultaneously tender and delicate refusal before sleep returned to his mind, and moved him; he considered her with a more tender indulgence. Poor Mariette! She was faded, withered like that bouquet of red roses etiolating on the table, and yet, gratitude had just transfigured her in his eyes; he forgot the defilement, he wanted to ennoble her by means of sincere kisses.

Certainly, he knew that he was not going to love her with a veritable amour; he even thought that this idyll of the gutter, born of his pitiful misery, would be of brief—very brief—duration; but one day, might he be able to lift her out of the mire, redeem her, provide for her needs? What joy he would experience in rendering her, a thousand times over, the aid that she had given him, the hospitality that she had offered him!

Gradually, his sentiments and desires excited one another. He had been about to die; at the very moment when he had sworn that he wanted to live, a prostitute had snatched him from the jaws of death, and he dared to analyze her features coldly, debate her charms, and appreciate her morality with the prejudices and delicacies of old! He must be stupid and ingrate; she was good beautiful, desirable; she was worthy of being loved!

He leaned toward her and deposited a long and tender kiss on her pale lips. Mariette slowly opened her eyes, smiled at him silently, and put her arms around him...

She told him about the lamentable beginnings of her crapulous existence; her first stigmata, when she was scarcely out of childhood, her precocious amours with louts of her own age, then the flight from the paternal house, the long poverty of the braid-seamstress, her successive relationships, the ever-descending sequence of falls that had brought her to the sidewalk, her reiterated troubles with the moral police. Now, for six months she had been tranquil, she no longer had anything to dread: she had her number; she was registered.

Charles Balin suppressed a shudder of dolor, and made an effort to master his chagrin.

"You're a Parisienne?" he asked, by way of diversion.

"I was born in the Rue du Faubourg-du-Temple. What about you—where are you from?"

"I'm not from anywhere, Mariette. I understand that that astonishes you, but I can't explain."

"You're in hiding, perhaps?"

"Yes, but the reasons I have for hiding aren't dishonest."

"Oh, I'm not curious, me—nothing delights me more. I know that such extraordinary things happen. How old are you?"

"Forty-seven."

"Liar—that's not true, you're younger than that," she affirmed, laughing. In a low voice, as if speaking aside, she added: "I'd like you to be even older. I like gaiety, noise too much. I'm still very young, though—twenty-three. I could be your daughter! Many of those years, it's true, I could count double." She sighed, sadly. "And to think they call that having a good time! Oh, this is nice, it really is a good time."

"That's nicely said, Mariette—it fills me with joy. So, this life of hazard, of misery and debauchery disgusts you; you'd like to become and honest woman again?"

"An honest woman, my poor dear—how you say that! An honest woman! But you're crazy. A slut like me can't become an honest woman again—there's the number. That's not what I'd like. I'd like to live, but not today's slog. I'd need clothes and money to act as I pleased, to send the disgusting ones packing and choose the ones that please me, and have a lover at my convenience that I could maintain well and with whom I could go for walks in the country."

Charles Balin had a surge of nausea; repugnance, momentarily overcome, began to invade him again.

"Unless," she added, with a sigh, "someone was really able to love me..."

"And then?" he asked.

"Then, I'd do anything he wanted. I'd steal, I'd kill—it even seems to me that I'd have the strength to go back to work." She pronounced those words in a passionate tone that surprised him. "But all that's stupid," she added, after a moment's silence, as if to chase away an old dream. "Things like that only happen in feuilletons or plays. I've never had any luck, and when one's started badly..."

"One ought to finish well."

"That's stupid."

"I'm not joking. Look, I whom am speaking, started too well, and that's why I'm afraid of finishing badly."

"It's a fact that yesterday you weren't doing very well."

"And without you, my dear Mariette, I'd be in a sorry state," he acknowledged, affectionately recalled by that memory to less lofty sentiments. What did the vulgarity and decadence of this poor creature matter to him? Was he not bound to her henceforth by that moment of pity? Had he not just held her in his arms, kissed her lips, murmured amorous words to her?

The viler she was, the more she needed his help!

Prideful and insensate, he was already thinking about helping her, and tomorrow, perhaps this evening, he was going to be at grips with hunger again!

Both delivered to their reflections, there was a long interval of silence. But what was he doing there, wasting precious time? Ought he not to be thinking about finding work? He leapt out of bed abruptly.

"What's the matter?" asked Mariette, surprised.

"Time's passing, my dear. I need to look for work."

"And if you don't find any?"

"If I don't find any," he relied, disconcerted, "well..." He stopped dead, gripped by a sentiment of anguish.

"Well, you'll come back and find your little Mariette, silly!"

"That's right." He laughed, sardonically. "I'll come to live at her expense, I'll eat the money she earns by..."

"You ate it gladly yesterday!" she retorted, carried away by a surge of anger. "That's how you take it, is it? Well, as you like—do as you please."

"Mariette!" he exclaimed, humiliated. "Excuse that impulse of self-esteem; I'm wrong, a thousand times wrong! You speak to me, moved by your good heart, and I respond with sentiments to which I have no right: I ought to be blessing you, putting myself at your knees, and I dare to offend you!"

"Just kiss me, and let's not mention it again," replied the good woman. "I'm not proposing to keep you—for a start, I can't; the times are too hard. I'm saying that if you haven't found work, instead of going, tomorrow or the day after, to collapse on a bench or throw yourself in the river...I'm telling you that you'd do better to come and find me at two o'clock in the morning at the corner of the boulevard and the Rue du Faubourg-Montmartre; I'll have made the thousand-and-one paces, but I'll always have found the means to have something to eat. You know, what I'm saying, I don't say to everyone—but I like you; it seems to me that I've always known you, I respect you. Look, tell me the truth: you weren't a curé?"

In spite of his poignant preoccupations, Charles Balin could not help laughing.

"Well," he admitted, "You're not too far off; I must once have been something similar."

"Then it's understood," aid Mariette, getting up in her turn."

"That whether I find work or not, I'll come back; but what if..." He hesitated, feeling a blush rising to his cheeks.

"If what?"

"If you meet someone who wants to take you away?"

"That's my business. In any case, I never bring anyone here—but again, you don't have to worry about that; I'm offering sincerely, you'll pay me back when you can."

"Well, then Mariette, until tonight," he said, kissing her.

She called him back. "Hey, what are you going to do for grub all day?"

"Oh, I'm solid now, I won't get hungry," he affirmed, in spite of the pangs in his stomach. "I'll catch up tonight, if I don't have any luck."

"Come on, don't be proud—you'll pay me back, I tell you." And Mariette gave him a twenty-sou piece, which he did not have the courage to refuse.

Chapter XII

The tranquility of soul with which he devoured, a little while later, the bread and sew of a cheap eatery, did not fail to surprise him.

"Damn," he murmured. "Have I a ready-made disposition for the role that Mariette wants me to play?"

He left, and stopped in front of a shop window in order to contemplate his reflection for a few seconds. "Charles Balin, chemist and pimp," he sniggered, as if introducing himself to himself.

In fact, did he not have the costume of the employment? He remembered the mistake made, a few days before, outside the Café d'Harcourt and cursed the eccentric garment that the necessity of being completely different from his former self had caused him to choose. That jacket, as intolerable as the shirt of Nessus, was not unsuited to all these frustrations. Perhaps he owed the sympathy of a registered prostitute to it? And to think that, "from the height of his final heavenly abode," Dr. Albin was watching him wallowing in the mire. Oh, the fellow would be well content: his enemy was on the right road, already living on immoral earnings!

He quickly regretted his sardonic reflections. A wretched but good woman had had an impulse of pity, perhaps mingled with a little perversity. At any rate, whether it was caprice, sentimental whim or veritable delicacy, she had offered with a touching simplicity to come to his aid; why should he refuse? Because the help she was offering had an infamous origin? But had he had a choice? Did he now? Did not all considerations disappear before the necessity of living? Had he made any effort to create the dubious situation in which he found himself? Had it not been imposed upon him by pitiless hazard? Shame and dishonor were in the intention far more than the fact. What relationship was there between the abject individuals who deliberately exploited prostitution and him?

He had looked for work and had not found any; he had asked for alms and had not received any; at the moment when he was at the end of his tether, when he had felt will and life slipping away from him, help had unexpectedly appeared; ought he not to take it, since he wanted to live? Could he debate quibbles, indulge in the slightest objection? Was it not necessary, now, to accept the consequences, bonds and duties created by that primary fact? Was he not a new person, outside all the prejudices and all the sentimentalities of yore?

It was therefore better to receive as given, that which he was determined to repay in the most generous fashion; that was the surest means of liberating himself rapidly, since that acceptance would permit him to find employment.

What employment?

That interrogation, already made so many times, put his mind to the torture. He felt lost in the immense labyrinth of the Parisian hive. Buried alive in inextricable catacombs, he gazed indecisively at the thousand gaping holes open before him. By what route could he climb back to the light? He did not lack physical vigor or intellectual capacity; his lack of success came from the fact that, all the links attaching him to the past having been broken, all the social sanctions destroyed, he was solely reliant on his own strength, and, great as it was, he had learned by harsh experience that one cannot isolate oneself with impunity.

It was therefore necessary to reenter, one way or another, the bosom of society, even if he had to pick the lock of the door, wriggle through the hole of a drain. If not, death, from which a prostitute of the lowest class had snatched away its prey the previous evening, would fall upon him again with a new rage.

Had he not made his first searches with too many scruples? Had he not been wrong to scorn the dubious opportunities that had been the only ones offered to him?

It was necessary to choose between life and death, and once again, since it was necessary to live, he ought to have less delicacy.

He promised himself, putting more method into his new steps, first to visit all the establishments closely or remotely related to the legal fraternity.

The results of his first encounters were as discouraging as those of previous days; it was a bad time of year, the clients were in the country, there was no supplementary work, they had been obliged to sack all the clerks etc.

Nightfall found him careworn, it is true, but his discouragement was far from having the black intensity of the previous day. The interest that Mariette had shown in him, the support that he was almost certain to rediscover, was like a lifebelt to which a shipwreck victim clings desperately.

He had just entered the philanthropic restaurant and had scarcely begun to eat when a young man of about twenty, with long chestnut-colored hair, a nascent beard, blue eyes, an elongated face, refined features and prominent cheekbones, after having looked attentively in all directions, came to sit down facing him. In the ensemble of his physiognomy there was something dolorous and enigmatic. His forehead was broad and high; the curl of his lip, both ironic and bitter, contrasted with the softness and sadness of his gaze. Attracted by a sympathetic curiosity, he could not help looking at him and smiling.

Emboldened, the young man spoke to him. "Do you know someone who is looking for work, Monsieur? I've come here almost certain of finding companions of misfortune."

Charles Balin experienced a quiver of joy.

"Do I know someone?" he said. "But that someone is me."

I was sure of it, the young man's smile signified. "Well, Monsieur," he said, "the owner of a copy agency, Monsieur Lampe, 122 Rue des Petits-Carreaux, has asked me to find him a employee. I warn you that it's poorly—very poorly—remunerated."

"No matter."

128

"Then present yourself at this address tomorrow morning at seven, on the part of Monsieur Raphael. You can write legibly and rapidly, I assume?"

"As rapidly and as legibly as an educated man can."

"He'll employ you in copying addresses. He's a maniac—he'll put you through a kind of petty examination and ask you various more-or-less indiscreet questions. Don't contradict him in anything."

"I won't forget the recommendation."

"Once again, you'll be poorly paid; if you earn two francs a day, that will be all."

"I'm not in a position to be difficult."

"Good luck, then, Monsieur, and it will be a pleasure to see you again. I'm employed in the house that you're probably going to enter." The stranger bowed and disappeared.

Two francs a day! But that was the Pactolus!

The distracted man uttered a profound sigh of satisfaction. He perceived a glimmer of light. He would finally be able to live on his work; with his iron constitution and frugal habits, he would even be able to make savings. He went out with his soul inundated by joy; it seemed that his miseries has suddenly vanished. He had never felt so bold, to audacious, so ready for the struggle; a foot in the stirrup and the beast was soon straddled. Another service that Mariette had rendered him; without the twenty sous slipped into his hand, no such windfall would have been presented to him. He hesitated over going to meet her, but was it not to give her the good news? He would make it a duty to go.

He wandered at random for hours, delightedly clinging to the flowery branch of hope that a sympathetic stranger had just held out to him. For the first time since Dr. Albin's funeral, his tormented mind enjoyed a little clam. Wellbeing was a very relative thing, then? A meager hope had sufficed to dissipate the blackest despair.

As he was crossing the Pont Neuf a bare-headed man emerged slowly from the shadows and held out his hat with a trembling hand. He had suffered too much the day before to refuse his obol today. He threw the two sous he still had left into the hat; the beggar raised his head abruptly and started laughing...

He realized that, believing he was playing a farce, he had bitten a hook. He recognized the apologist for mendacity who, his face lit up with libations and the pleasure of having proved his know-how, was still guffawing.

"Two sous," remarked the former ministerial officer. "Wonderful—you must have had good luck since the other day?"

"No, but I have work for tomorrow and I've given you everything I had left."

The old man looked at him in surprise. "That's folly, prodigality—you'll die in the straw," he predicted, laughing.

"Those two sous might have been indispensable to the person asking for them," he replied, thinking about the terrible anxieties of the previous day.

"If I'd really needed them, I wouldn't have known how or been able to ask you for them in the same fashion, and you doubtless wouldn't have given them to me. I'll keep them all the same, but I'll pay for a glass."

Charles Balin excused himself: he was not thirsty; it was necessary to conserve is resources; he would accept another time.

"I see how it is," the fake hawker suggested. "You're afraid of embarrassing me. Don't worry—I've made eight francs today, and, as the claptrap says, it isn't over yet."

He persisted in his refusal.

"All right, all right," the individual growled, abruptly turning his back on him. "Play the proud man, and good luck to you!"

That's how I should have maneuvered yesterday, thought the previous day's starveling, watching him go away and solicit further alms. *That slow walk, so as not to surprise and frighten the passers-by, that lowered head, that humble attitude, suppliant and respectful, that hand trembling with weakness and alcoholism! The lesson is well worth the two sous it*

cost me; it ought to have been given to me two days earlier,
and I would have profited from it. Eight francs! He's extracted
eight francs' worth of it from the hard hearts of fortunate peo-
ple, and I, who was dying of hunger, couldn't get a single lib-
erating sou! That old thief was right, begging is a métier. A
man has to be flattered and duped to soften his heart; that's
an apprenticeship that the true poor haven't had time to make,
and because of that, the crooks and the experienced live at the
expense of the genuinely unfortunate.

Bah! He had nothing to regret. First of all, those two sous
repaid the glass of wine that he had accepted before; and then,
he had believed that he was saving a poor devil from hunger.
His action, in itself, was consequentially good and praisewor-
thy; it would be held to his credit in the mysterious book of
Providence.

A painful observation crossed his mind: since he had
changed his identity, all the good sentiments he had had before
had turned against him. The rare good luck that had come his
way had come from an impure source. It was a malevolent
impulse that had obtained three francs from the clothing dealer, and it was the produce of prostitution that had saved his
life.

Would he be compelled henceforth, armed by suspicion,
to envelop himself in lies, expel all pity from his heart, show
his teeth and claws, and use all possible means to live? It was
impossible that misfortune would change him completely; Dr.
Albin had never employed and of those shady and inhumane
methods to arrive at fortune and honors. It was true that that
anterior self, born in clover, profiting from collective injustices and hypocrisy, had had no great merit in retaining his personal dignity; the society in which he moved had taken charge
of accomplishing all the infamies necessary to his success,
while today, the orders of the factors was inverted. Left to his
own devices, outside that corrupt organization, deprived of its
support and assent, obliged by that fact to defend himself
against it, he could not see things from the same angle and
actions in the same moral context. Dr. Albin, individually vir-

131

tuous, had had his share of the collective criminality; but for the time being, he was only responsible for his individual actions. He was their sole judge, and if fatality had caused him to fall into the mud, and he could not get out of it without being splashed, he would be no more culpable or vile than fatality!

It was nearly midnight. He was thinking about his rendezvous, and idly drawing toward it when he suddenly saw Mariette coming down the Boulevard Sebastopol at a rapid pace. He was about to go toward her when the prostitute made him a signal of intelligence and changed course swiftly to avoid him. Surprised by the maneuver he turned round...

Shame turned his face crimson. Some provincial or foreigner, a colossus with a flowing beard wearing a broad-brimmed hat with a stout umbrella under his arm and a satchel slung over his shoulder, had just accosted the streetwalker.

They had stopped at the edge of the sidewalk. The trapper seemed to be haggling over the price; he even made as if to beat a retreat, but Mariette caught him by the sleeve and seemed to make up his mind with more seductive offers. Now, arm in arm, they headed hastily for a sleazy hotel in a small side-street.

He stayed there, bewildered, his feet stock to the asphalt, his eyes fixed on the wan lantern under which the licensed prostitute, accompanied by the giant, had just disappeared.

"It's me you're waiting for," said a streetwalker, approaching him. "Come in, I'll be very nice and not demanding, you'll see how naughty I can be. Come with me—I don't live far away—or to the hotel you're looking at..."

Thinking that her propositions were insufficiently explicit, she started whispering the filthiest promises.

He emerged from his stupor, and the calm that he had briefly recovered immediately fled from his soul, the appeasement vanishing before the infamous reality. So, he was about to be obliged to kiss those soiled lips, on which vile contacts had left their traces! Yesterday, he had seen nothing, he could, if necessary, maintain an illusion. But now that his eyes had witnessed, now that his will was no longer annihilated by hunger, could he accept the degrading situation? No, a thousand times no. He would not see Mariette again; he would write to her to apologize; he would repay her generously for the first occasion.

He hastened his steps, muttering and gesticulating. People grouped around a bench caused him to slow down. He drew nearer; policemen were shaking a vagabond, giving him an order to move on and threatening him with the lock-up. The man drew away, his eyes heavy with sleep, tottering.

That simple incident served to shake his resolution; the previous night's situation reappeared to him in all its horror. Where would he sleep if he scorned Mariette? Would he wander all night, at the risk of no longer being presentable when he went to solicit the job of copyist? Would he not be arrested for vagabondage? Did his distress permit him to have excessively delicate instincts?

It was yesterday, not today, that he would have been truly courageous in showing so much disdain. Why had he not had those scruples? Did he not know what the situation was? Had not the prostitute naively displayed her corruption to him from the outset? Did he not know he provenance of those twenty sous too easily accepted and spent without veritable remorse? Had his imagination not traced retraced for him the scene he had just witnesses and others even worse? The day before, he had been hungry, he was no longer in possession of himself, the beast dominated his spirit, his weakness was explicable—but this morning, when he had woken up in the hovel, why had he not fled? Why had he kissed those lips, hugged that body, murmured passionate words? It was then that it had been necessary to avoid the slightest corruption; now, it was too late.

Certainly, the situation could not last long; tomorrow, he would think again, but tonight, he would go to find Mariette, and since it was necessary for him to purchase a little repose and security by means of a new shame, he would drain the chalice to the dregs.

133

It was a holiday, the night was warm, the boulevard was full of animation, of joyous groups carrying armfuls of wild flowers descending from the Gare de l'Est, seemingly leaving behind them a wake of amour and pleasure. A leaven of perversity that he had never suspected was suddenly fermenting throughout his being, carnal desires rising to prickle his skin; an unhealthy appetite invaded him, and he was in haste to see the whore again, hungry for debauchery and avid with lust. He felt almost proud of being preferred by the woman who was, at that very moment, ignobly parodying amour and who would soon enlace him with a sincere embrace, cover him with disinterested caresses—him, the old man, the wretch, the accursed!

Then another frisson of disgust and fear shook him: was he about to wallow voluntarily in the mire, accept with a glad heart the exceedingly dubious role that fate as causing him to play? Into what monstrous avatar was his dignity about to sink?

He approached the rendezvous; he had one last impulse of retreat. Mariette who was looking out for him, ran radiantly to meet him, hung on his arm, and, without giving him time to say a single word, explained to him, as if it were the most natural thing in the world, while mingling vague excuses therein, the reasons she had had for avoiding him. It was necessary: a wonderful type, a man returning from America, a goldprospector, had followed her for half an hour; she had scented prey and could not miss such a good opportunity, windfalls were so rare, provincial clients so coarse and Parisians so demanding!

He hastened to change the painful subject.

"I've mainly come," he affirmed, "to tell you some good news; I've been promised work for tomorrow."

"How much will you earn?"

"Oh, almost nothing, perhaps two francs a day, but in my situation, I consider that sum welcome—besides which, I'm not spoiled for choice."

"Well, I've found you a marvelous place!"

"You, Mariette! Speak, quickly."

"The lover of one of my mates, Valentine, is a café waiter; they live in the room next to mine and I saw them after you left. Naturally, we talked about you, and we told Émile that you looked respectable and were still solid. 'We need an extra hand at my place,' he said. 'I'll see about it this evening, and if I get the go-ahead, I'll take charge of getting the job for him. I'll lend him a coat and linen to begin with. Just think: if you take that, you'll get four or five francs a day and you'll be well fed."

In spite to the prospect of earning such a considerable salary, the proposal scarcely made him smile. He did not, however, want to offend Mariette with an immediate refusal, although he promised himself that if he had the choice he would prefer the position with the copying agency.

"Now," Mariette continued, taking his silence for an acceptance, "let's go get a quick glass at the Avenir."

He protested that he was not thirsty, that it would be better to return tranquilly to the hotel, and that the cafes were about to close.

"The Avenir stays open until three," she affirmed, "and that's where Émile will come to meet us."

Chapter XIII

They walked a short way along the Rue du Faubourg-Montmartre, went through a large coaching entrance, traversed a narrow courtyard, at the back of which the brasserie was located, and sat down near the entrance. The vast room was overflowing with a noisy and variegated crowd. Soldiers on leave, workers on the spree, provincials and curiosity-seekers were rubbing shoulders with specimens whose eccentric jackets, gaudy cravats, flashy rings and attitudes that were simultaneously masculine, pretentious, arrogant and suspicious brazenly betrayed their means of existence. The businessman of the quarter had nicknamed the place "the brasserie of the backbones," the journalists opposite called it "the Aquarium" and the regulars, who found themselves very much at home there, called it "the workshop."

That evening, as every evening, the majority were playing billiards or interminable hands of manilla. A few others, the cream of the crop, off-course bookmakers or noted burglars, were proudly affecting to comprise a company apart, distinguished by ratting dogs or mastiffs, emptying glasses of champagne and causing the diamonds they wore on their fingers to scintillate. From time to time, women in garish costumes, leaving trails of violent perfumes as they entered, came to whisper a few words in their ears, took a hasty glass, and went out again. Here and there, other women, alone or in groups, awaited opportunities, simpering at consumers facing them, had successes, took out their cards, called out to people coming in or going out, changed tables, softening up the waiters for the saucer for which some recalcitrant pigeon had refused to pay. Sometimes, the commencements of disputes rose up in a corner, but the manilla-players, standing up, turned toward the disputants, the billiard-players, the Jupiters of the establishment, frowned, and order was restored. The caravan of flower-sellers, cockle-merchants, olive-vendors, profes-

136

sional deaf-mutes, dealers in fake jewelry, etc., did business there casually, is if in a familiar oasis.

Mariette had ordered two glasses of brandy.

"Are we going to stay here long?" asked her companion, who was ill at ease.

"Émile won't be long," she said. "Here's Valentine, Lucie Pognon and Nini—this is general headquarters."

The three newcomers sat down at their table, looked curiously at the man they had seen half-dead of hunger the previous evening, made maladroit allusions to the service that they had rendered him, and, as before one of the gang from whom nothing is hidden, started recounting the evening's encounters, their arguments over prices with bad-tempered provincials, their refusals to give in, without a supplementary fee, to some filthy caprice, the affectations they had put on and the malicious tricks they had played.

Nini Nichon, a plump flaxen blonde with a low forehead, thick lips, small eyes and overflowing enticements, a Flanders slattern or Norman milkmaid, had had no luck—not a single dirty swine had wanted her!

"What do they have in their eyes, then, all those tools?" she exclaimed, bouncing her breasts. "That's not socks or cotton, that. What about you, Mariette, did you get a bite?"

Mariette was momentarily embarrassed. "Oh me," she ended up replying. "I was lucky tonight, very lucky."

Lucie Pognon, a tall stiff brunette of about forty, and old warhorse who had been wearing away the Parisian pavement for twenty years, addressed herself directly to the previous evening's unfortunate, pointing at Mariette.

"I told her," she proclaimed, with the authority of a matron. "Get a lover; it'll bring you luck, you'll see; there's nothing like it to pep a girl up; it forces you to get moving. You don't waste your time any longer gossiping or playing bezique. When it's necessary to earn for two..."

Charles Balin, horribly humiliated and embarrassed, told himself privately that it would be best to face ill-fortune with a stout heart and take things ironically.

"For two?" he queried. "Better say three, Mademoiselle, for I alone have an appetite for two. I've already eaten twenty francs of Mariette."

"He's a liar, don't listen to him," said the latter, laughing. "Not everyone's as demanding as your Git-le-Coeur."

"Fortunately," added Valentine de Volaille, a stout redhead with milky skin, a turned-up nose and a bulbous forehead invaded by pretentious golden curls, "demanding men aren't essential. If Émile wanted to rake off my earnings, I'd soon give him a shove in the back." While saying that she looked at her neighbor with a menacing expression."

"So you don't give your Mimile gifts, then," insinuated Nini Nichon.

"Oh, gifts, I don't say no—one has to maintain amity. Then again, I don't like to go out with a man who's poorly dressed—but I want a man who works, or else: Out!" She was still looking at the unfortunate with an instance that made him lower his gaze.

"Finally, here's Émile," announced Mariette, annoyed by the almost aggressive attitude of her friend.

A short young man with a smiling face, a heart-shaped mouth, pomaded hair, a thin black moustache and hooded, almond-shaped eyes—a vulgar specimen of brunet good looks—had just come in. He shook hands with the manilla-players and seemed to want to join in their game.

"Over here, Mimile," shouted Lucie Pognon.

Émile, doubtless to give himself importance, or out of the old habitude of a playboy, did respond to the first appeal, but gestured with his hand to indicate that he had seen and was about to come. A few moments later, observing that he was no longer being summoned, he left the card-players and came to join them.

"What'll you have?" Mariette asked. "Come and sit here."

They made room for him on the bench, and the Don Juan of the brasserie ordered a small glass of Benedictine. Charles Balin found himself directly opposite, and the waiter finally deigned to look at him. He considered him for a few seconds, with a surprised expression, and then started laughing.

"This is the man Mariette told me about—the one who was dying of hunger on a bench?"

"Yes, what's the matter?" asked the astonished prostitutes. "Do you know him?"

"Oh, no, it's too good, let me laugh. Good God in Heaven! I'll have a good laugh tomorrow with the boss."

"Come on, Émile, what does that mean?" asked Valentine, looking at him hard. "You're laughing like a guttersnipe."

Bewildered, Charles Balin considered him anxiously.

"Necessary to put gloves on for an individual who took you for a mug not long ago, is it?" said the fop.

An exclamation emerged from all mouths.

"You know him?" Valentine repeated.

"Of course I know him. It's the Englishman I told you about, the pickpocket of the Café Mansard, who had a seventeen-franc blowout, and the boss sent to the police station."

"Are you sure?"

"It's me who served him—no tip and three fifteen-sou cigars into the blue. I don't care about the boss, but the cigars were on my account—I'm the one who danced, dirty old thief."

The man caught in the trap, at a loss, fearing a scandal, incapable of defending himself, bowed his head again. The women frowned, and the waiter continued to twist the knife.

"And you all chipped in yesterday evening, on the bridge—you paid for the stuffed galantine, and it's Mariette who, after having taken him in, proposes that I get him a job as an extra at the Mansard! Oh, no, it's superb! What a laugh we'll have tomorrow at the joint!"

Extremely pale, Mariette had risen to her feet.

"It's true, then, what he says," she said, hoarsely. "You're a swindler, a liar, a thief, and it's me who nourished you, me who gave you a bed, me who paid for your drink. Hypocrite! Swine! Here, this one won't do you any harm!"

And the furious prostitute, seizing the glass in which her lover of a day had scarcely moistened his lips, threw its contents in his face.

Rumors rose up; curious individuals arrived from all directions. The dazed man, wanting at all costs to avoid a more prolonged fuss, instinctively took flight, followed by the jeers and laughter of customers delighted with the incident.

Mariette, her fists clenched, her eyes haggard and her lips pursed, had collapsed on the banquette.

"Well done," said Valentine de Volaille. "You were warned, but you're incorrigible—you persist in picking up stray dogs. It was bound to happen to you sooner or later."

She emerged from her prostration. "What was bound to happen to me, then?" she demanded, with a surprised expression.

"That you'd pick up a thief, whom you paid to eat and swindled you out twenty francs from you into the bargain."

"What do you know about it?"

"He told us so himself!"

Mariette shrugged her shoulders. "Where has he gone?" she asked.

"He didn't leave his address and didn't settle his bill," said the waiter, laughing. "I'll bet he's still running."

Mariette looking askance at Émile and fell back into silence.

"Bah!" observed Nini Nichon. "One rabbit more or less, it's no big deal."

"It's humiliating, all the same, to be turned over by an old man," remarked old Lucie.

"An old man who can't be very appetizing," sniggered the harsh Valentine.

"Well, maybe that's why she had luck this evening," suggested the fat Nini.

"Say, if he gives you a kid I'll adopt him!" cried the café waiter. The three women burst into loud laughter.

All heads turned toward them. Again, Mariette went pale; tears came to her eyes. "Look," she ended up mumbling, dully, "you're annoying me, you'd do better to shut up."

"That's a bit much," Valentine recommenced. "She's crying! I'll wager she's missing him."

"What's it got to do with you, you dirty redhead. Do you want me to talk about the things you do, you who are so disgusted by old men?"

Émile hastened to intervene. "Shut up Valentine—that's enough. Come on, Mariette, don't get upset over that smooth talker."

Git-le-Coeur, holding his billiard-cue like an eighteenth-century cane, his head round, his hair russet, his eyes like lot-to-balls, his moustaches turned up, looking like a bulldog ready to bite, had come to find out what was going on, and grunted in a significant fashion. He claimed that Émile was a police informer, and never lost an opportunity to express his horror of the police.

"Well, what's all the racket? Why is Mariette peeling the onion?"

Lucie Pognon told him the story in brief,

"Well, what does that prove?" he declared, in his thick voice, not without menace. "That some poor old bugger pulled a fast one to get a meal. So what? So you think the chap, if he had cash, would be amusing himself taking a nap on benches and risking getting pinched up by the cops? You think it's funny, you lot, to have sod all to chew on? And what do you think he's done to Mariette? He didn't ask her for anything, promise her anything. If she let him sleep over, it's because she wanted to, because she has a kind heart."

"He's a pickpocket," hazarded Émile.

"Did he pinch anything from you?" Git-le-Coeur demanded of Mariette.

"Oh, as to that, no!"

"I tell you he's a thief," affirmed Valentine's lover, again

"And you're a nark, you little rat."

Émile, who knew the other, thought it prudent not to insist. Mariette sensing that she was supported, held her head up boldly. "Who are you to call other people swindlers and thieves?"

"She's mad," stammered the mongrel, held at bay by the bulldog.

"Yes, what are you?" she continued, "you who filch by short-changing customers, and brag about it."

"Oh, that's not the same thing," claimed the waiter, proudly. "The rich are exploiters; when one finds an opportunity to take revenge, it would be stupid to miss it!"

Git-le-Coeur had drawn away, shrugging his shoulders disdainfully. Mariette took out a fifty-franc bill and paid for the drinks. All the women eyed the hundred-sou coins that the waiter gave her in change.

"Those are some back wheels," observed old Lucie. "It's no joke, you're old colonist brought you luck. Say," she added, "Since you're in pocket, you could give me back the ten sous I gave you for the fraudster."

"Here, there's your ten sous. Who else chipped in?"

"Me," cried Nini Nichon, "but I'm not asking for anything, I don't begrudge them." Enticed by the well-garnished purse, she added: "Come on, my little Marion, you're a widow, I haven't made anything; we could go for a stroll, and then you could give your big cat a stroke, couldn't you? I don't like letting mates down, myself."

"Especially when it's a matter of drinking or whining," muttered the redhead.

"That way, we can stop quarreling," hazarded the handsome Émile. "Come on, Mariette what do you say?"

The irritated prostitute's only response was the word that saved Cambronne from oblivion.

After leaving the brasseries, Charles Balin had walked at a rapid pace, pursued by the jeers that were still ringing in his ears, trembling like a guilty man caught in the act by the police. Seeing that the Rue Richer was deserted, he turned into it furtively, slowed his pace and recovered a little of his composure.

After all, perhaps the humiliating scene of which he had just been the victim was a fortunate event; it had saved him from the real danger, had put a end to a situation that was more than dubious, in which he was in the process of allowing himself to be ensnared. The first money that he earned would serve him to pay Mariette back, and everything would be settled. He would have done better to follow the good impulse that had urged him to break off the crapulous liaison immediately. The scene that he had witnessed in the Boulevard Sebastopol gave him the right to do so, and the duty. Where would his procrastinations and laxities have ended? With the supreme insult that had just been hurled in his face, and which debased him a little more.

He had been afraid of a sleepless night? Was he not obliged to pass it? The sole appreciable result of the adventure was that he was rid forever of that strange prostitute whose sudden inexplicable tenderness had not left him indifferent. Was it the sentiment of gratitude, excited by burning kisses and sudden appetites? Was it the promises of debauchery he had made himself few hours earlier? His heart, belying his reason, experienced, now that it was all over, a vague regret for the unforeseen rupture.

With his only handkerchief, in tatters, he wiped away the drops of alcohol that were still trickling down his face, turned mechanically into the Rue d'Hauteville, reached the Boulevard Sebastopol and followed the market gardeners' carts that were descending heavily toward Les Halles. The animation of that quarter would help him pass the time, and, when the time came, he would not be far away from the copyist.

The peasants were already beginning to unload their carts full of flowers, vegetables or fruits. Porters were passing bales or baskets, forming a chain, and the last in line was staking them methodically in the indicated spot.

What if he were to follow the example of those men and earn a few sous? He asked for directions; an overseer showed him with a gesture the place where men were forming a queue. He joined the end of it; his turn arrived; he helped to unload a few carts, every time receiving the meager habitual salary.

Daylight had arrived rapidly; the vast market was swarming with people. Whores and *bon viveurs*, exhausted by partying and emboldened by drunkenness were mingling casually with the crowd of workers, who were not sparing with their gibes.

He was in the process of unloading a cartload of cabbages when two women who were the butt of the filthiest mockeries attracted his attention. A shiver ran through him; it was Mariette and Nini Nichon, hats askew, hair in disorder, their gait uncertain, their eyes lit up by drink, who were riposting with insults as vitriolic as they were colorful to the gibes of the market gardeners amused by the spectacle.

Suddenly, Mariette saw him, and stopped dead.

"What's the matter," hiccupped Nini Nichon. "Move! You can see that they're taking the piss out of us!"

"Charlot! My old man!" she murmured.

"Come on!" snapped her companion. "We're going to get pinched."

"Charlot!" Mariette tried to protest. "I want to talk to him, I want to apologize, I want him to come with me. Charlot!"

"Come on! What did I tell you—you're making the bumpkins laugh. Look at all those turnip-heads! One would think it were a game of Aunt Sally!"

"Charlot! Where's Charlot? She's asking for Charlot!" cried mocking voices from all directions.

"There he is," replied the drunken woman, pointing at the unfortunate. "I want him to come."

"Triple malediction!" murmured Charles Balin. He quit the chain and, beside himself, ran toward the tenacious drunkard.

"Go away, you wretched woman! Go away, you're preventing me from earning my crust."

"I want you to come!" proclaimed Mariette, between two hiccups.

"A domestic scene!" the voices clamored.

"Go!"

"Don't go!"

"Go!"

"Get going!"

"She needs someone in her bed!"

"She's had a drop too much!"

"She'll take you home."

People were beginning to form a circle. He took her by the arm brutally and dragged her behind a truck."

"Go away, save yourself."

"I want you to come," the drunken women persisted, cling on to him. He pushed her away so brutally that she collapsed several yards away.

The prostitute, partly sobered, got to her feet as best she could. Fortunately for her, the crowd was amusing itself around Nini Nichon, who, rendered furious, was pouring out her interminable repertoire.

Ashamed of his unconscious violence, he watched her come back, humble tearful, head bowed, like a beaten dog. She was weeping!

"I've said I'm sorry! Why can't you come?" she sobbed.

Before that persistence, a tremor of rage suddenly took hold of him.

"Wretch," he replied, in a dull voice. "Can't you see, can't you sense, that I've run out of resignation, and that after the insult you've offered me, if I went with you, I'd be capable of killing you! Go away!"

His gaze was so piercing and his voice so imperious that Mariette, returned to reason, hastened to flee.

Chapter XIV

The effort he had just made, the energy he had expended, seemed, like a flash of lightning, to tear through the darkness that enveloped him momentarily: he had an exact consciousness of the situation.

Is it possible, he thought, *as he paced back and forth outside the copyist's door, that a man of my worth and my intelligence, by the sole fact of being unexpectedly deprived of money and a domicile, can be reduced at a stroke to dying of hunger? Is it possible that a being, until then of exemplary morality, by virtue of a logical and fatal series of adventures, has consented to play the role that I have played?*

Is it possible, again, that after so much misery and emotion, I'm not ill or mad?

The half-hour chimed on the clock of Saint-Eustache. He climbed up four floors and stopped in front of a door on which he read, in impeccable longhand: *Aristide Lampe, copies in all genres. Enter without knocking.*

He opened the door and found himself in a large room where tables of blackened wood, with piles of Bottins and papers, porcelain inkwells and various accessories, were lined up methodically in two rows. A voice emerged from a large desk situated in a well-illuminated corner.

"Who's there?"

"The person sent by Monsieur Raphael."

"Ah! Good, come in." A little old man, thin and hyperbolically bearded, his head ornamented by a Greek bonnet and his sleeves covered in lustrine, considered him from head to toe in a cavalier fashion.

"What can you do?" he asked, in a bantering tone.

"Anything you wish to confide to me in the manner of handwriting."

"Anything I wish! That might be saying a lot."

"Would you care to try me, Monsieur?"

"I should think so. Many who pretend to know everything know nothing. You have some suspicion of what an address is? I don't demand perfection, but have you even the slightest idea, the slightest suspicion?"

"I think so,"

"You think so! We'll see. Most people who have sent letters to their parents or girls of their acquaintance imagine that they know how to write a subscription, the cretins! If you put them to the test they present you with something formless, devoid of order, clarity, elegance and style. Well, me, purely by the organization of an envelope I can appreciate and judge the true value of a man. I'm not a graphologist, mind—graphology is a fraud, since it's sufficient to have the vaguest notions to make a mockery all the experts, and I, Lampe, a mere entrepreneur of copies, guarantee that I can imitate any handwriting and cover all their assertions with ridicule."

He writhed in his armchair with shrill laughter, as if he had just carried out his threat and was enjoying his triumph.

"Certainly, I'm no graphologist," he suddenly went on, with a kind of anger, as if to reject an imaginary accusation, and added sententiously: "but show me how you write a address and I'll tell you who you are, what you've been worth, what you're worth now and what you'll be worth in future."

He changed his tone. "Take an envelope and prepare to write." The patient did as he was ordered. "Here you are: Monsieur Aristide Lampe, entrepreneur of copies in all genres, 122 Rue des Petits-Carreaux, Paris, Seine, France." The pretentious gnome added: "Everyone knows that Paris is in the département of the Seine and that the Seine is a département of France. If I'm dictating superfluous things, unnecessary in practice, it's because I need it in order to judge you on a complete address. You've finished?"

Charles Balin passed him the envelope.

"Has ha! Ha ha!" coughed the exclamatory minuscule individual. "Not bad: there's order, firmness, correction; no general conception, of course, no flight, no artistic sense; the good little writing of a modest man, with no energy, down to

147

earth, incapable of a brilliant or audacious action; the down-strokes of a heavy, materialistic mind, a sybarite; a hint of eccentricity but no imagination; apart from that, qualities, usage, above all, enormous usage. You've written a great deal in your lifetime. Wait, don't enlighten me, I'm not asking you anything—I want to have the merit of the discovery."

Père Lampe picked p the envelope again, looked several times at his future employee, absorbed himself in a profound meditation, and then suddenly slapped is forehead.

"Eureka!" he cried, like Archimedes. "You're either a former clerk in the customs service, or a former employee of the State. Ha!"

Charles Balin in a state of legitimate defense against human stupidity, simulated a comical astonishment. "How the devil did you divine that?" he murmured.

"I'm never mistaken," declared Monsieur Lampe, radiantly. "So you are?"

"A former customs clerk."

"So you have a retirement pension that permits you to live."

"Oh, very little, Monsieur."

"Yes, I understand that you need little supplementary resources, to found a few pleasures. You're a bachelor, are you not?" He winked and hummed a popular tune: *Que c'est gentil les p'tites femmes*.

"Don't contradict him in anything," the young man had advised. The petitioner sketched a smile of approval.

"So you want to work for me. Well, these are my conditions: you'll write addresses for prospectuses at a rate of seventy-five centimes a thousand for Paris, a franc for the provinces, one franc twenty-five for other countries. I pay on Saturday."

"I will, however, need a small advance at the end of the day, if only a few sous."

"We'll see about that. But come a little closer, and bend down."

The entrepreneur of copies raised himself up in his arm-chair, sniffed him like a dog and uttered an exclamation of disgust. "You reek of alcohol, you know. Take this as read: I don't tolerate drunkenness in the studio; at the first sign of intoxicated handwriting, I'll sack you."

"You can see, Monsieur, you who have just proven your astonishing perspicacity, that I don't have the appearance of a drunkard. In any case, look: no sign of an alcoholic tremor." He held out his two hands.

"Why are you doing that?" asked the old ape.

"Because if I had the habit of drinking, my hands would start to tremble."

"You think so? Let's see." He tried to do the same; his hands were agitated characteristically. He withdrew them rapidly. "All that's nonsense that physicians say," he growled. "Let's pass on to serious matters. If you accept my conditions, here's your place."

He sat down. Eight o'clock chimed. Three other employees, including the young man from the previous evening, came into the studio and came to occupy their desks after a silent salutation. Père Lampe distributed the work, gave a few instructions, and soon, nothing could any longer be heard but the scratching of pens and the rustle of paper.

No one said a word. Maître Lampe walked back and forth, looking over the shoulders of his scribes like a schoolmaster.

"Above all, Messieurs," he suddenly exclaimed, "I recommend you to silence." He went on, in a slow and monotonous voice, as if dictating an imposition: "A copyist, if one speaks to him aside, is likely to commit errors, to mistake one word for another, to neglect his work. It's time and paper that one wastes, it's a loss that he inflicts on his employer and himself."

The newcomer, momentarily distracted by the attention he ought to pay to those words, swiftly resumed work.

The door slowly opened, and a frightfully pale man, a lamentable apparition of an emaciated Christ, appeared on the threshold, timidly.

"Ah, there you are, Monsieur Benoit!" cried the employer. "Very sorry, my dear Monsieur; you haven't come for five days, and as you can see, your place is taken!"

The poor devil, with tears in his eyes, considered the occupied place sadly.

"I sent word that I was ill, Monsieur," he sighed.

"It's precisely for that reason that I've replaced you. Is it my fault if you're ill? Ought my work to suffer? You're ill, my friend, go take care of yourself. When you're completely cured, come back. I'll give you work...if I have any to give you."

The unfortunate bowed and disappeared, closing the door discreetly. Charles Balin felt his heart gripped. So he had taken the place of that poor fellow! The struggle for existence, pitilessly cruel, required that the bread he was going to eat should be snatched from some other mouth!

Behind that man who had just appeared to him there might perhaps be a wife and children who no longer had anything to eat.

Raphael, his neighbor facing, passed him a piece of paper with a few words written in haste: *If it hadn't been you*, he read, *it would have been someone else*. Charles Balin thanked him with a nod of the head.

"Above all, Messieurs, I recommend you to silence," Maître Lampe repeated.

A smile from the young man seemed to say to him: *Pay no attention; it's a mania.*

"Silence," the entrepreneur of copies continued, "is indispensable in a place where one is writing. The slightest distraction might have the most unfortunate consequences. One has seen wills broken, lawsuits engaged, fortunes lost for a misplaced comma."

He had stopped behind one of his pen-pushers, a middle-aged man who looked like an old soldier.

"Ah!" Explain to me, I beg you, why the devil you persist in underlining the word Paris in your addresses?"

"But yesterday, Monsieur, you instructed me to do it."

"Yesterday, yes, because the prospectuses you were doing were to be distributed by post and it was, in consequence, necessary to call the attention of that administration's employees to the proper name and the city. But today, haven't I told you that these addresses are to be distributed to domiciles by a porter?"

"Yes, Monsieur."

"And you have not divined that it is, in consequence, unnecessary to waste your time and my ink underlining the word Paris. Have you not understood that it would be much simpler and quicker to put the initials E.V., which signify *En Ville*? You therefore never show a little initiative? It's necessary to tell you everything, explain everything?"

The bewildered employee kept quiet.

"Above all, Messieurs, I recommend you to silence," the maniac added, by way of conclusion.

After several hours of work in which the accomplice of Guilleri[18] never ceased chattering, knocking over piles of books, thumping chairs and shifting tables in order to make sure that they were stable, a curt tap on the desk announced the lunch break.

"Have you the habit of frequenting a restaurant?" Raphael asked him, as they went downstairs. On his negative response, the young man proposed an advantageous creamery in the vicinity.

"I only have eight sous," he confessed."

"For that you can have a set meal. Anyway, don't worry about that—I'll be able to get you credit."

"That's all the more obliging as you scarcely know me."

"I know you well enough to know that I'm not risking anything by doing it."

---

[18] "Compère Guilleri" is a once popular song about a highway robber, which begins "There was a little man...."

He thanked him cordially.

"Do you think," he added, "that the little man will give me something on account this evening?"

"Yes, if you ask him for it in order to buy lustrine sleeves. I'll lend you a pair tomorrow."

"You're my good angel."

"Père Lampe," Raphael continued, "only allows himself to be softened by one pretext—lustrine sleeves—and only tolerates one weakness, "little women." When I say *little*, it's a manner of speaking, for the women he decorates with that dainty qualification are always veritable monuments."

"The law of contrasts."

"He only understands lust in a massive form; it's not rare to encounter him, around midnight, in the process of gravitating in the orbit of some Callipygian Venus. If you ever happen to arrive at the studio late, for whatever reason, allow him to believe that you were delayed in some alcove in a furnished house."

While they took their meager repast, the amiable your man brought him up to date with the eccentricities and caprices to which he would be obliged to submit.

"You passed the examination?" he asked, laughing. "You didn't deny the divination, at least?"

"Thanks to your recommendation, I carefully refrained."

"And you did well; he would have held it against you. Anyway, you must have pleased him—he hasn't covered you with the sarcasms that he hardly ever spares newcomers. Now, if you're armed with patience and you intend to stay with him for a few months while waiting for something better, don't forget what I'm about to tell you: he only admits that one earns two or three francs a day, so never do more than three thousand addresses. He always dismisses those that surpass that number on some pretext or other; his standard reason is that work too rapidly done is always poorly done. It's thanks to that observation that I've been able to keep the job."

"I note, and have already noted several times, that you have a veritable gift for observation."

"Since my earliest childhood, Monsieur, I've been obliged to earn my living—one quickly acquires experience in that game."

"You're an orphan?"

"Worse than that, alas—I'm a poor bastard."

"Many people who were the honor of their nation have been in the same situation. Anyway, we no longer have the same prejudices today as of old."

"Do you think there were as many prejudices as that, in olden days? Then, as now, poverty was much more culpable than vice; the bastards of great houses never had any cause for complaint."

"You're educated, I can see."

"Not as much as I'd like; I have so little time. By day I copy addresses; by night I perform minor roles at the Théâtre du Châtelet."

"You act at the Châtelet? How much do you get for that?"

"Two francs a night. Would you like to follow my example?"

"It's an anonymous situation I'd accept without reluctance."

"With a small lie it should be easy. You have one of those faces before which one remains indecisive as to whether it's the face of a physician, a priest or an actor. Be a former actor—you've come back from abroad, you're in difficulty; I'll answer for the rest."

"You're a veritable providence for me!"

"Something great and mysterious that envelops you draws me to you: you must be good, you must be indulgent."

"Raphael," proclaimed Charles Balin, greatly impressed by that divination, "you ought to have been born in an epoch and a land where seers were honored."

"That's true," murmured Raphael. "I sometimes have the fatal gift of reading the thoughts of others; I must be near death."

153

"I know that you're ill!" exclaimed Charles Balin, forcefully. "I was once a renowned healer; I shall care for you, and save you!"

"No, let me die. It's necessary that I die. Only death can wash away the stain."

He did not reflect then upon the infinite sadness with which his young companion pronounce those words, or perhaps put them down to his disreputable origin.

The very next day, thanks to his new friend, the apprentice copyist made his debut in a non-speaking part in *La Princesse au coeur de verre*, a spectacular fantasy play, which, defying the dog days, attracted the provinces to the Châtelet. He was thus, by turns, a guard, a genie, a statue, a big head, a eunuch in a seraglio, a melon in the realm of the vegetables, a great lord of the court, a village peasant, a scullion in a hostelry, a vase in the realm of porcelain, a ferocious beast in the depths of a wood, a dragon at the entrance of a cavern, an ophicleide in the Temple of Harmony, a demon in Hell and a marine monster in Neptune's court. The lie that Raphael had told also brought him an unexpected windfall; in his capacity as a former actor a few lines were confided to him, which he delivered marvelously.

He found himself singularly at ease in that new situation; he had the bizarre impression that it was really his place and that he had never done anything else throughout his life.

After a few days he had earned three francs and the theater and two francs fifty at the copyist's. Half of that sum allowed him to live, the other was religiously set aside. His first priority was to recover his trunk.

A month later, he found himself in possession of a fortune: ninety francs! He rapidly consecrated them to ridding himself of the odious check suit, buying a suit in black cheviot, a hat etc. He was just in time! The Châtelet, preparing its winter spectacle, had dismissed the supplementary personnel and Maître Lampe, perhaps confused by that transformation, which gave his subordinate an aristocratic allure, or vaguely aware of his superiority, had taken a dislike to him and was giving evidence of an angry humor. Raphael, familiar with the Lilliputian's habits, warned his friend to employ his hours of liberty seeking other employment.

As they were going past a music publisher's shop one evening, Charles Balin stopped to look at the new publications.

"Are you by chance a musician?" Raphael asked him.

"Well, I was once an appreciated pianist."

"What!" exclaimed the young man, delightedly. "And you didn't say anything? What were you thinking? You play the piano! But in your situation, that's a veritable lifebelt! Quickly, follow me."

The young man immediately took him to a Montmartre dive whose accompanist he knew. The musician, an obliging fellow, sat Monsieur Charles down at the keyboard, made him decipher and then accompany two or three songs, asked him whether he had any notions of harmony, and seemed delighted with the trial.

"My dear colleague," he affirmed, "with the talent that you have, you can present yourself without dread anywhere. Here's my card. Go to ***, the well-known lyrical agent; he'll have you fixed up in no time.

Charles Balin left, penetrated with gratitude for his young friend, whose fertile and resourceful mind had come so powerfully to his aid. He expressed his affectionate sentiments, but Raphael brushed his gratitude aside.

"You're not reasonable," he proclaimed, laughing. "You could occupy a position a hundred times preferable to the one that renders us slaves of that malevolent dwarf, and you hide your talent. Why haven't you thought of taking advantage of it?"

"To tell you the truth, my lack of initiative is a subject of perpetual surprise to myself. Perhaps I've been stunned by the unexpected event that plunged me into poverty. But now, thanks to you, it seems to me that the veil will soon be torn."

The two friends had finally found a relatively well-paid position in the administration of a daily newspaper in the process of foundation. They still had a week before them, in which they set about doing four or five thousand addresses per day. The dwarf, outraged by that sudden augmentation, could not master his wrath.

One could not do such a great number of addresses without carelessness; the handwriting was no longer legible; his porters had returned some of them, which they could not decipher; his clients had made him reproaches; quantity was only obtained at the expense of quality; who embraces too much grips poorly; everything comes to him who waits; the pitcher that goes oftenest to the well...the entire book of proverbs passed his lips. The two copyists, attained by an incurable deafness, continued to achieve a fabulous production.

On the last Saturday in September, while Maître Lampe, who had just paid them, grumbling, indulged himself in hand-rubbings and lip-pursings preliminary to some insolent formula of dismissal, Charles Balin interrupted him just as he was about to open his mouth.

"Permit me, Monsieur," he said, "to recognize the welcome that you have been kind enough to give us, but having, along with Raphael, found a much more advantageous situation, we are in the fortunate necessity of quitting this studio— of which, believe me, we shall retain a tenacious memory."

"Good, good," grunted the dwarf, full of rage. "Don't play the clown with your priestly humbug and get out." He had second thoughts. "Tell me, child," he insinuated, addressing Raphael, "is it in the land of the Hebrews that you've found a place?"

"The Jews are less hard than you are on the unfortunate," replied the young man, sharply.

"Especially those of Sodom," sniggered the entrepreneur of copies.

"Wretch!" exclaimed Charles Balin, beside himself at the enormity of the insult. He pounced on the copyist, took him by

156

the collar and shook him like a rag. The other employees, utterly enchanted by the adventure, intervened for form's sake.

"Go fetch the police!" howled the little old man.

Raphael dragged his defender away. "In the name of
Heaven, let's get out of here," he murmured. "The man's malevolent; he'll make a complaint and have us arrested."

They walked for some time without saying anything.
When they arrived on the quais they slowed down.

"Could I support such an insult to you and to me?" exclaimed Charles Balin. "The wretch! I regret not having
slapped him; his calumny is the greatest insult one can throw
in a man's face."

Raphael bowed his head. He was weeping.

A dolorous suspicion crossed his companion's mind.
Nothing, however, in the bearing, the gaze or the appearance
of the young man could authorize such a supposition. His
slightly effeminate mannerisms could legitimately be attributed to his delicate health. He was a good judge; his medical
functions and expertise had put him in the presence of vile
degenerates who parodied amour. However, allusions and
sniggers that he had overheard while they were appearing at
the Châtelet, vague insinuations made one day when they were
soliciting employment at one of the great Parisian hotels,
Raphael's profound sadness, and his inexplicable refusal to go
to certain places suddenly came back to his mind. He took the
young man by the arm and looked at him fixedly.

"Well, yes, it's true, or at least, it was true," the unfortunate confessed. "At ten years old, left to myself, forced by
poverty to suffer corrupt companionship and promiscuities, a
wretched procurer drew me into the vice. I went into a shady
establishment as an errand-boy, where I was skillfully delivered as pasture to ignoble lubricities. As soon as I was really
capable of judging and understanding, I wanted to get out, to
become an honest man, but in the ten years I've been strug-
gling to erase the stain, all my efforts have been vain. Just as I
think it's disappeared, some passer-by, a stranger, perhaps a
companion of hazard or debauchery darts a comment or a

glance at me that kills me. You understand, now, why life becomes more odious to me every day, and why I want so much to die!"

After a pause, he went on: "I sense, I know that it's necessary for us to part forever. Don't hold it against me too much for having hidden the odious, infamous truth from you; I had so much need for a little amity and esteem; I divined in you a mind so indulgent, so just, and so elevated that I put off the painful moment of confession for as long as I could—but if hazard and malevolence had not put you on the track, I swear to you that, considering it a duty, I would not have taken long to tell you my dire and lamentable story. You bear on your forehead the mark of some unusual adventure that separates you forever from other men; you're the only one from whom I would dare demand aid and pardon."

"Wretch! Wretch!" murmured Charles Balin. "Raphael" he exclaimed, suddenly, "would you really like to become a man?"

"Can you doubt it? Have I given you the slightest reason for suspicion in my conduct, my words or my actions?"

"Then this is what you must do. You've told me that you have some savings and that you speak a little English. Flee these places where the past weighs so heavily upon your existence, where the streets know your shame and the roofs have sheltered your infamy; change your name and face. If someone seeks to recognize you, boldly spit in his face and tell him that he's a liar. You're not solely responsible for your corruption; society owes you a reparation, and your intelligence will be able to attain it. Go to England, or America, or the end of the world, wherever you wish, but please don't stay here for another moment. You deserve to live. Give me your hand; I hold your efforts in esteem, and it's purely in your interests that I speak."

Raphael had wiped away his tears; his eyes where shining with resolution.

"Thank you for your kind words," he said. "It seems to me that they have suddenly cured the disease that was eating

158

me away. Thanks you too for the lessons and advice that you've given me, the cares you've lavished on me, the friendship with which you've honored me. Thank you above all for that pardon, which rehabilitates and redeems me. I owe you everything: life, honor, perhaps glory. Tomorrow, I swear to you, I shall no longer be in Paris."

He watched him flee in the direction of his dwelling.

Poor child! he thought. *Placed in normal conditions, with his intelligence, his natural distinction and his extreme sensibility, he might have aspired to anything.*

Then he glimpsed the dubious situation that that acquaintance had created for him. He had had a keen amity for the young man; they had lived side by side; that promiscuity might be interpreted in a malevolent fashion.

Were all the events of his new existence, even the simplest and most innocent, to serve to accentuate his fall? It was thanks to Mariette, and thanks to Raphael, that he had begun to emerge from oblivion; was it fated that all aid, all assistance, would come to him from an impure source? Could the man who had put himself outside society no longer be accepted, except by those whom society had cast out? Why was it necessary for his projects to be thwarted by the repugnances of old? Struck by the marvelous aptitudes of his young friend, penetrated with gratitude for the services he had never ceased to render him, he had resolved to educate him, to arm him for the struggle, to make a precious auxiliary of him who would have aided him in his task, and now an imperious necessity had separated them!

A storm that was building extended its heavy shroud of cloud over Paris. A long rumble of thunder resounded in the air. He lifted a menacing fist toward the sky; it seemed to him that Destiny was laughing at his vain efforts.

Chapter XV

Charles Balin had not forgotten Mariette, or the debt of honor contracted in her regard. If he had been slow in acquitting it, it was because he wanted to do it in a good and generous fashion; he estimated that an initial settlement of a hundred and fifty or two hundred francs, at least, was necessary. On the other hand, putting all sentimentality aside and sure of his intentions, he had told himself that before thinking about that largesse, he ought to be in a reasonable situation to make it.

His new position was infinitely preferable to the miserable employment he had recently occupied. He earned a hundred and fifty francs a month, the work was easy—he sent the paper to subscribers after having wrapped it—the conditions were agreeable and his relationship with his employer imprinted with urbanity. In addition, the lyrical agent to whom the Montmartre musician had recommended him had found him a few odd jobs and, finally, had sent him as an accompanist to a modest café concert in the Montparnasse quarter. That was another four francs a day to augment his budget.

After the martyrdom of the Béguinard school and the annoying eccentricities of the entrepreneur of copies, and above all after the apprehensions of his black distress, he experienced the joy of navigators who, having been tossed by interminable tempests, deprived of food and fresh water, end up landing on an enchanted island. A month of calm and repose, a more abundant and healthier nourishment, concerns of toilette whose privation had been very painful for him, soon rendered him a measure of composure. Numerous resources, of which that situation was the larva, of which the kind of torpor into which he had suddenly been suddenly plunged had prevented him from thinking, presented themselves to his mind. His bibliographical knowledge would permit him to earn a few sous dealing in books; he could undertake scientific or literary research for authors, orchestrate songs for the artistes he accompanied, etc., etc...

Did he not have the decent attire and the few advances indispensable to attempt approaches successfully? He hastened to rent a mansard in the Rue Vavin, buy a few items of furniture on easy terms, and on the eighth on November 18**, a little more than six months after Dr. Albin's funeral, Charles Balin lay down for the first time in a bed that was really his own.

It was a great and veritable joy, rapidly shadowed by bitter reflections. The fine success had arrived, after many privations, of sleeping in a narrow iron-framed bed for which he had not yet finished paying. How far away he was from his goal! He had scarcely had time to think about it vaguely; would he ever contrive to attain it?

He turned his attention backwards. A letter that had arrived a few days before from London had informed him that Raphael, employed by a major commercial company, was about to depart for India.

And Mariette? It was time to think about her. He could see her again with his head held high. But was he not going to find her still in the company of the accursed waiter? What did it matter? He had to fulfill the obligations that the pity of the prostitutes had created, and it was all the more urgent because his job as an accompanist in a low-level café concert might put him in the presence of one of them any day. He therefore put aside savings with that objective, and, soon finding himself in a position to do things honorably, set out in search of the poor registered prostitute.

At the Hôtel de la Dordogne et du Calvados he was told that Mariette had left the house four months before.

"She must still be in the country," the clerk told him in a mocking tone. He was not sufficiently acquainted with argot to understand the precise significance of the words.

Apart from the furnished lodging-house there were two places where he might find her: the Brasserie de l'Avenir or the corner of the Rue du Faubourg-Montmartre. He went back down toward the grand boulevards. It was Saturday; his Sunday morning was free, he could be up late without being inconvenienced.

He wandered the sidewalks that had witnessed his rude ordeal with the sensation of wellbeing that a convalescent experiences who has just escaped death. The street was more animated than usual; the cafes, wine merchants, patisseries and charcuteries were overflowing with clients. Bands of partygoers were coming back noisily from Montmartre, while artistes and journalists, their tasks accomplished, were returning to the heights at a rapid pace. Newsvendors were deafening the passers-by, trying to get rid of their last few copies, while the street-vendors, having become hoarse, had run out of patter.

A hubbub suddenly rose up. Idlers and curious passers-by ran toward a brawl, where two women thrown out of an establishment were tearing at one another's hair, to the great joy of the coachmen stationed outside the doors. Other whores were coming and going, running after belated pedestrians and grabbing the arms of night-prowlers. He recognized one of them and went over to her.

Lucie Pognon, enticed by the sight of the well-dressed man with the distinguished air and gray beard, who was coming toward her of his own accord, whispered the most seductive promises.

"You don't recognize me, then?" said the unknown man.

"Wait a minute—yes, I think so! You've been with me before! Oh, the old rogue, it's you who..."

He interrupted her swiftly. ""That's not it. I'm the man to whom you were obliging enough to lend assistance over there on the bench, about three and a half months ago."

"Impossible!" cried the stupefied prostitute. "In fact, I recognize you now. There's a surprise! How well-dressed you are, and how good you look! You've made a fortune, then?"

"Not yet, but I'm in a less precarious situation, and if you'll permit me, Mademoiselle, to offer you a little present in

162

memory of the service you rendered me, I'd be very obliged to you." He slipped a louis into her hand.

"Twenty francs," observed the whore, overjoyed. "Twenty bullets for the ten sours I put in the kitty—one can say that that was money well-invested. That's marvelous. Well, Mariette was right, you're a worthy, honest man.

"You weren't alone that evening in coming to my aid."

"No, there was also Nini Nichon."

"Is she here?"

"Hey Nini! Where's Nichon?"

Without exactly being a sylphide, the enormous blonde had rapidity.

"Here I am. What is it? Does Monsieur want two women all to himself? Judge and you'll know—with me there's no robbery. No tricks, you can see that, I bought them at Bon-Marché. 'We have them for all tastes, in metal wire, in rubber.'"

"You're drunk again," Lucie interrupted, dryly. "You obviously don't recognize Monsieur."

"Yes, I recognize him," said the stout Nichon, without even looking. "He's the Monsieur from the other night who..."

The tall Lucie put her hand over her mouth. "No blather, you stupid lummox, and look hard—he's a mate. I'll bet you a glass you don't recognize him. Ah, you see, you're flummoxed." She whispered a few words in her ear.

"My God, it's true!" exclaimed Nini Nichon. "Who'd have thought it? But he's up and running now, damn it!"

Charles Balin, in a hurry to cut the conversation short, slipped another louis into the hand of the buxom chatterbox with the same politeness. She squealed in delighted surprise, hid in the corner of a coaching entrance, lifted up her skirt and hastily stuffed the gold coin into her stocking.

"Now," he said, "I'd like to see Mariette."

"Mariette!" interjected the two women. "You don't know, then?"

He had a sentiment of anxiety whose violence surprised him.

163

"I don't know anything," he murmured. "Has something happened to her?"

"She's in Saint-Lazare."

"Ill?"

"In prison."

"Because of you," added Nini Nichon.

"Because of me?"

"A little, my lad. She bashed Émile, the waiter, the red-head's lover."

"She killed him?"

"No, but she smashed a tankard in his face. We were all witnesses, big Lucie, Valentine and me."

Charles Balin uttered a sigh of satisfaction. It was evidently just a matter of a tavern brawl, but he was interested to know all the details. His name might have been pronounced in court; he had to know what the situation was.

He offered to buy the two women a drink, provided that it was not at the Avenir.

Lucie Pognon refused; Git-le-Coeur was intractable on Saturday; it was pay day and, as in the administration of the cab company, he demanded higher fees at certain times and in certain circumstances, and she wanted to buy a dress with the twenty francs that had fallen from heaven, it was necessary for her to work.

Nini Nichon, to whom the offer of a drink was never indifferent, hastened to accept. She took him to the Clair de Lune, a dive that she called a night restaurant, but where it was nevertheless necessary to have the password to be admitted.

The hovel was worse than the Avenir, but it was too late to retreat and his companion, on familiar ground, hastened to order two well-garnished sauerkrauts.

"I'm not eating," he objected, timidly. "Only order one."

"Bah! I'll eat them both," affirmed his guest, with a coarse laugh.

He was in haste to be brought up to date.

164

"You remember," she told him, addressing him as *tu* like a comrade, "the morning when you were unloading cabbages at Les Halles—so Mariette said, because I didn't see anything. Well, the evening of that day, she came back to the Avenir and she wasn't in a good mood, I can tell you, because she hadn't made anything all evening and someone had taken, or she'd lost, all her money.

"Valentine—you know, Émile's redhead, who'd vexed her the night before—started teasing her again because of you. She said—and how she said it!—that you were an old good-for-nothing, that you were out of prison, that you wanted to have yourself kept by the girls, that she'd been stupid to pay you a louis, etc. etc. She gave her a clout, and what a clout!

"We separated them, and nothing would have come of it if Émile hadn't arrived. When Valentine, who's a coward, had her lover beside her, she started coming out with horrors again on your account, and Émile pitched in even harder. Well, if you'd seen Mariette! She was whiter than that napkin! Me, who knows her and heard her grinding her teeth, I thought to myself: something bad's going to happen here. 'Hey,' she finished up saying to Émile, 'leave me in peace—you're a liar, a dirty nark, and the thief is you!' The other tried to raise his hand, but he hadn't made the move when he got the beer-glass in his face and was bleeding like an ox.

"You can imagine that that caused a stink! The police came, they took them to the station. Perhaps nothing would still have come of it, but Mariette started calling Émile a nark again—for her, who isn't stupid, that wasn't very clever. In a police station, calling someone an informer burns the ears.

"The brigadier, offended, said she was insulting the police. She replied to that, because she doesn't like the agents, because her father was put in front of a firing squad during the Commune. Then they arrested her; she was brought up in the police court: assault and battery, insults to the authority, the whole shebang; and she was sent down for four months."

"Poor Mariette! It's me who caused her that misfortune," sighed Charles Balin.

"You can believe it! I don't know why, perhaps you have hidden talents, but she really thought a lot of you. Look, the evening when she threw the glass of brandy in your face, you'd scarcely gone out when she regretted it and started to cry. Then we went to get a bite in Les Halles—well, it was because of you. You'll understand that I couldn't let her drink alone!" Laughing loudly, she added: "Me, I never miss an opportunity. Waiter! Another half."

"You were a witness in the affair you said. Was my name mentioned in court?"

"Had to be! Émile said you were a crook, Mariette replied that it wasn't true, that's all."

"Was my name pronounced?"

"I don't remember. All I know is that Mariette hasn't spilled the beans—you can be sure of that."

"What! You still believe the waiter's accusations?"

"Me? What does it have to do with me? I don't care. It seems to me, though, that if you really were a thief, you wouldn't have given me twenty francs, unless..." She lowered her voice and winked. "Unless you'd pulled off a big coup."

Charles Balin shuddered with shame.

"Oh, you know, with me, nothing to fear. Look, *motus*," she said, clicking her teeth with her thumbnail.

He tried to protest his innocence.

"Motus, motus," repeated the stout whore. "After all," she added, cynically, "perhaps you're an honest man, but for me, you see, the most honest man is the one who pays me the most."

A surge of disgust nauseated him—and yet that vile prostitute had given her obol to save his life!

He remained plunged in humiliating reflections, and quickly reverted to the less filthy memory or Mariette. Why had he not made enquiries earlier? He would have been able to soften the rigors of prison, return to her then, in a more opportune fashion, the service that he owed her. Why had he thought of himself first? Why had he waited to accumulate a relatively large sum? Egotism and vanity, no doubt.

The few sous brought at an opportune moment are worth a hundred times more than futile largesse! But perhaps he still had time to come to her aid.

"She was arrested the day when you came to Les Halles?"

"That same evening."

"That was the end of July; it's now the end of November," he calculated. "So it's exactly four months that Mariette has been in prison. Perhaps she's even been released?"

"Certainly not. She'd have come to the Avenir."

"Then she'll be released before long?"

"Probably."

"No one has gone to her aid during that long sojourn?"

Nini Nichon put on a tearful expression, raised her eyes to the heavens, made a gesture of desolation and swallowed the rest of her half-liter in a single draught in order to forget her chagrin.

"Not that I know," she sighed. "Poor Mariette! We haven't thought about her once, but the times are so hard! Lucie has her fat leech, Git-le-Coeur, and I can't make ends meet."

"Well, Mademoiselle, as soon as you see Mariette, tell her, please, that I'm presently a pianist at the café concert whose address I'll give you, and that she mustn't fail to come to find me there.

"In the meantime, be kind enough to get these twenty francs to her, so that when she comes out of prison she can eat, get a room, and come to the establishment where I'm employed. Tell her, though, not to come to join me in the orchestra, but to wait by the door until it's time for me to leave."

"I won't fail," promised Nini Nichon, putting the address in her corsage. "But the twenty francs..."

"Well?"

"I'd rather not take charge of them. I'm afraid of eating them—or, rather, drinking them."

Charles Balin could not help smiling.

"You're slandering yourself, Mademoiselle. You'll remember that you might find yourself in a situation similar to

167

your comrade's; you'll remember, since you were taught when you were little, that it's necessary not to do unto others what you wouldn't want anyone to do to you, and you'll give Mariette the deposit I'm confiding to you."

"You're right," said the prostitute, who had instinctively stopped addressing him as *tu*. "I'll do as you say."

He paid, got up and left, without having been excessively solicited by the truculent individual, who nevertheless did not fail to expend herself in further compliments on the exceptional abundance of her charms, the comfortable breadth of her bed, the prefect tranquility of her furnished hotel, the near-virginity that a long widowhood had remade for her, the benevolent dispositions to which an abundant and well-watered nourishment had given birth, the obliging attention that she would have for a friend, etc. He replied, smiling, that he did not want to be unfaithful to Mariette.

It was three o'clock in the morning. He was in haste to get back to his domicile. The sight of the place where the drama of his misery had almost reached its denouement in such a banal fashion, the conversation he had had with the prostitutes and the news that he had just learned had revived the memory of Mariette in a disturbing fashion. After the four months in prison that she had received for coming to his defense, would he have the courage to see her again coldly? Would his determination not weaken?

What's the point? he replied to himself, immediately. Wasn't it necessary to bring the adventure to a prompt and definitive end? Why retie bonds that he would break the day after? It would be absurd, and perhaps cruel. He no longer had the right to treat that unfortunate woman as flesh for pleasure that one takes or leaves at will, especially if, a floret of amour grown on the worst of dung-heaps, she experienced the slightest feeling of tenderness for him.

It was pretentious, at his age, to imagine such a thing, but had not her comrade in debauchery just made that claim? Had he not believed it momentarily? Great misfortunes, especially when they are enveloped in mystery, have the attraction of the gulf, and fascinate the rebellious.

Certainly, Mariette could not have the nobility of soul that gives rise to blind devotions, but the instinctive curiosity that had pushed her toward him might perhaps have engendered a rudimentary sentiment of that sort.

On the other hand, he could not think of hampering his life with such a liaison. It would have been necessary for that for him to have money for her to live on and time to devote to her.

It was infinitely probably, anyway, that even in that event, the vagabond, irremediably degraded by a long past of vices, would not accept the calm and worthy life that he would want to impose on her.

He decided, therefore, and it was the wisest course, that Mariette would remain his friend, and that he would only see her again in that light.

He had almost arrived at the Rue Vavin while philosophizing thus, along the railings of the Luxembourg, when, just as he was telling himself that he had committed an honest action and that no harm would come to him, a man surged abruptly from the shadows and seized him bodily, another gagged him with two hands, while a third robbed him. In the blink of an eye his pockets were cleaned out, and the thieves had vanished.

Surprised by the rapidity of the operation, he had not had time to utter a cry or to put up a fight. He quickly wiped his soiled lips, bruised by the brutal hands of the aggressor, and then perceived, sadly, the loss of his wallet. Fortunately, he still had a little money at home. Mariette would not be utterly disappointed when she came to the rendezvous.

Gradually, thinking that he had received neither blows nor wounds, and that the skillful professionals had been content, like conjurors, to rob him with a magisterial dexterity, he accepted his fate stoically. Who, then, could have carried out the coup? Had he been seen giving money to the two prostitutes? Had they talked too loudly about his generosity? Had they confided it to eager ears? Or had the prowlers attacked him at random?

The last supposition might have been true, but a voice sniggered in his ear that his subjection to pillage was the logical consequence of his scrupulous restitution. "Clean him out properly," Nini Nichon must have said to the skillful pickpockets of the Clair de Lune, "but don't do him too much harm; he might be a high-class criminal, and in any case, he's Mariette's friend."

Bah! He wouldn't die of it. Half a million francs had been stolen from him and he hadn't been able to say anything.

Two uniformed policemen came down the street, making their regular footfalls ring on the pavement. They were arriving too late, like carabiniers in an operetta. He thought about confiding his misadventure to them, but did not take long to change his mind.

"With my luck," he murmured, "I'm capable of getting myself arrested. As the poet says, let's imitate the prudent silence of Conrart."[19]

---

[19] A sarcastic comment made by Nicholas Boileau, referring to the fact that Valentin Conrart (1603-1675), one of the founders of the Académie, who assembled some fifty volumes of letters, notes and other documents during his lifetime, which became an important historical resource after his death, never published anything while he was alive.

Chapter XVI

The Café Concert de l'Étoile, a former interior courtyard transformed into a glass-roofed hall, where "Monsieur Charles" exercised his talents as an accompanist, did not shine either in the renown of its artistes or in the luxury of its decoration. It was one of those improvised establishments in which the singing serves as an excuse for the poor quality of the fare and its slightly elevated prices. The habitual troupe consisted of three chanteuses, a baritone and two comedians, to whom occasional amateur performances sometimes lent their collaboration. The pianist, reinforced on important occasional by a cornet, a clarinet and a trombone, represented the entire orchestra. As for the public, except for Saturdays, Sundays and Mondays, when workers' families took possession of the hall, it was composed almost entirely of regular clients: local employees and shopkeepers, art-students in search of the Gioconda, Pygmalions in quest of statues, impecunious students and litterateurs as yet devoid of glory, whom the proximity of schools and the low rents attracted to the quarter in large numbers and whose hearts came to search for pasture.

It was, in fact, notorious in a certain milieu that the habituées of the Étoile, vaguely married women, sentimental local seamstresses and kept mistresses with time on their hands, did not come there in search of fortune, but were content with a little gaiety and amour. A few of them even made a specialty of allowing themselves to be subjugated by the pseudo-actors who hung out there

The men being almost their equals, they considered before anything else the matter of their employment. It was thus that the baritone and the pianists enjoyed an incontestable primacy; whether they were young or old, elegant or dilapidated, handsome or ugly, whether their hair was blond, brown, red or white, they immediately became the prey of some amiable habituée.

171

Monsieur Charles, initially surprised and even flattered by the languorous stares of which he was the object, had quickly suspected the truth. Seeing the same women devouring indistinctly all the ephemeral singers of the establishment, he mistrusted the advances they made to him and, without affecting puritanical manners or a prudish virtue discordant with the rather unrestrained milieu in which the need to live had placed him, he maintained a polite reserve, not avoiding provocative conversations but opposing the most profound deafness to insinuations of a certain kind. His situation was too precarious, and he had too much pride, to chase after such adventures.

A pretty blonde, a somewhat rough-hewn former chambermaid from the Franche-Comté, who had nurtured for years an insatiable caprice for all the virtuosos who succeeded one another in Père Antoine's establishment, had inevitably set her cap at the new arrival. Although he was not in the prime of youth, he had a distinguished air and polite manners made to flatter self-esteem. With the flair of a perverted soubrette, the lovely Annette divined in the pianist, whom her neurosis still lacked, a man of the world plunged into poverty by an unexpected catastrophe, and that supposition stimulated her monomania.

She had regular features, an advantageous and lithe figure, large gray eyes, a luxuriant bosom, ash-blonde hair, a suggestive neck and appetizing lips. She wore elegant clothes, expensive jewelry, paid ostentatiously for drinks and proclaimed, when she wanted to be heard, that she was a good and disinterested girl for whomever had the gift of pleasing her. The painters were mad about her, the sculptors licked her feet, and the poets brought out her beauty in the most impeccable sonnets, but—excluding commercial transactions, of course—a man only had the gift of pleasing her on condition of making his agile fingers fly over ivory keys. The most convulsive comedians, the most eccentric clowns, the most muscular gymnasts, the most charming baritones, the most disconcerting tightrope-walkers and the most dexterous jugglers had sought the way to her heart in vain; and yet, on simply hearing a pianist, that unassailable heart, not content with opening all its doors, resonated like a statue of Memnon.

The species of indifference with which Monsieur Charles had received her first advances plunged the beautiful Annette into the deepest amazement. Although she had judged him, instinctively, superior in education and delicacy to the bashers of chords she had known thus far, she had not expected to find the slightest resistance in a man who, in view of his age and situation, was scarcely spoiled by fortune. Perhaps she had approached the matter too abruptly.

Changing tactics, therefore, instead of the frontal assaults she was accustomed to making, and which ordinary settled the matter with an immediate victory, she stood down her batteries and laid siege methodically to the heart rebellious to her initial summons.

A long week passed in insignificant skirmishes; the enemy avoided combat and remained holed up. Never had the conquest of a performer demanded so much effort. She began to get impatient; doubtless he was married or had a mistress—but, having always considered inconstancy as second nature, and infidelity as the most sacred of duties, that reason could not have any value in her eyes. Did she not have a lover who maintained her? That did not prevent her from deceiving him—on the contrary!

Perhaps the artiste, who, in spite of his gray hair, seemed to her to be as timid and desirable as a novice, dared not take advantage of the windfall? Perhaps his reserve, as a well-brought-up man, prevented him from declaring himself too rapidly? She took the baritone Fernand into her confidence, and charged him with adroitly discovering the trouble in his heart.

The baritone, a Pandarus of the Barrière, was coarsely eager to transmit the gallant message.

"You've had a real stroke of luck, Monsieur Charles. The most beautiful girl in the quarter, a true bourgeois morsel, is smitten with you!"

"Who's that?" the accompanist had asked, feigning astonishment.

"You don't suspect, then? The great Annette, of course! A fine sprig of a girl, that one, not a hooker, not a painter's purée nor a gigolette at the Bullier: the kept woman of a rich wood-merchant, nice tits, neat, well-dressed, who has real jewels, fine furniture and doesn't run after a loaf of bread!"

The baritone, a former village blacksmith, who, after having dreamed of making a hundred thousand francs a year at the Opéra, had great difficulty getting hundred-sou gigs, and subsidized his needs by breeding racing greyhounds, was licking his lips as he enumerated all the advantages that such an acquaintance involved.

"Don't play the joker, Monsieur Fernand, I beg you," the pianist replied. "I'm only too well aware that at my age, one is no longer made for conquests; it's fine for you with your superb lungs and your curly moustache, which drive them all mad."

"The fact is," admitted the baritone, "that one doesn't do badly. But what do you expect—I don't like to make the darlings suffer, me, and when they're pretty, in truth, if they want a little bit of Fernand, I don't raise any obstacles!"

He made a self-satisfied gesture, tweaked his moustache, winked and hummed the scale, all the way down to the lowest register of his voice.

"But to get back to you, Monsieur Charles," the victorious baritone went on, "I assure you that Annette, without having one of those terrible crushes that women have for me, wouldn't be averse to receiving a few little piano lessons at home. Move quickly, or I'll steal her away!"

In a fit of mad enthusiasm, the irresistible singer was about to tap him on the belly; he stepped back rapidly.

"You'll die in the skin of a joker, Monsieur Fernand—stop it now, it's your turn."

Annette was watching them chat, curiously. The baritone came on stage and she addressed an interrogative gesture to him. Fernand replied with a doubtful grimace.

Excited by the difficulty, the tenacious blonde, increasingly seduced by the imposing air, the distinction, and the youthful and singularly keen gaze of the pianist, decided to make more precise advances. Fernand had doubtless acquitted the commission poorly. Perhaps—hadn't he courted her himself?—a sentiment of jealousy had even pushed him to put a spoke in the wheel. She could not admit for a moment that a man might disdain her, and in this milieu, where all the habituées were on the lookout, she sensed that she was becoming an object of humorous remarks for the host of rejected adorers. It was necessary for her to reckon with the recalcitrant accompanist.

That same evening, therefore, offering the pretext of being afraid to go home alone, she begged Monsieur Charles to escort her to her door—which the musician consented to do with the most amiable courtesy. When they arrived, she invited him insistently to come in for a small glass of liqueur, but the pianist did his best to escape.

"Are you afraid then, that I'm imperiling your virtue?" she exclaimed, laughing.

"My virtue, Mademoiselle, would be only too glad to succumb if you were to do it the honor of provoking it, but alas, I'm too old to hope for such favors," the cavalier replied, gallantly. "It's absolutely necessary that I go home immediately to do some very urgent work; don't see any other reason for my refusal."

He's afraid of being late, she thought. *His legitimate must be expecting him!*

The next day, driven to extremes, she employed the ultimate means, the one that never failed.

She knew how to play the piano, a little, and had, she had been assured, great dispositions for singing; she wanted to perfect them in his school, and begged him to come and give her a few lessons at home. She would pay him the fees that he habitually demanded of his pupils.

Monsieur Charles assumed his most desolate expression. "Impossible, Mademoiselle; I work all day, I don't have a single moment of liberty. As you can suppose, I can't live on the four francs I earn here!"

"All the more reason why you mustn't be alone," added the lovely Annette, a trifle vexed.

"What do you mean?"

"You have a wife, a mistress?"

The musician assumed a melancholy expression. "Yes," he ended up sighing, as if a painful confession were being extracted from him.

Annette he knew, as an old habitué of the concert, spending money without counting it, always trailing friends and suitors after her, had considerable influence with Père Antoine. Some even claimed that the cut-price impresario had not always been indifferent to the charms of "my child," as he always called her. At any rate, the old entrepreneur, an intelligent and rapacious man, who had become a wine-merchant after being a coal-merchant, the proprietor of a dance-hall after being a wine-merchant, and then the proprietor of a drinking-den that he had transformed into a flourishing café concert, placed a high value on such a generous client. He was already looking with a jaundiced eye upon his employee's obstinate refusal of the drinks he was offered.

"You could at least take a glass of milk or syrup from time to time," he complained. "It's refreshing."

"It's injurious to my health."

"Have a rum, then—that's fortifying. You're losing me three francs a night; with the four I give you that makes seven; for that price, I could have a Paganini." Any celebrated performer was a Paganini for Père Antoine.

The musician sought to calm the interested businessman's irritation with all kinds of soothing words, but he sensed that he had not been forgiven for his refusals of drinks, and that a few words from the lovely Annette would suffice to get him fired.

Monsieur Charles thus had a capital interest in not offending the title-holder of the pianist, and if it was necessary to end up passing under her Caudine Forks—which, after all, might be a very agreeable punishment, given the tales told left right and center about previous adventures—the near-certainty that once her caprice was satisfied, the beautiful woman's only priority would be getting rid of him, caused him to postpone as long as he could a denouement for which so many others, who did not possess a golden key, sighed in vain.

From that unexpected refusal, the blonde Annette had concluded that Monsieur Charles must be afflicted by some bad-tempered leech, and that that was the sole reason that prevented him from accepting her reiterated advances.

Bah! It would not be said that a single one of the Étoile's virtuosos had escaped her. She would end up triumphing over those conjugal dreads! Hysterically perverse and obstinate, she invested her self-esteem in it, donned dresses that were very elegant but more discreet, assumed the modest and amiable airs of a perfect lady, and every evening, from her habitual place behind the piano, uttered sighs, indulged in long conversations with Monsieur Charles, and acted in such a fashion that she soon passed in all eyes for the accompanist's accredited mistress.

The handsome Fernand had groused, her little comrades had gossiped. The hairy bohemians, furious at not being appreciated at their true value, were laughing at her disappointment; it was necessary at all costs to save appearances. Once the thing was well-established, if he continued stupidly to insist on ignoring her caprice, she would take it upon herself to get him fired. Sober for the practical drinks-merchant, virtuous for her! That really was too many good qualities for a dive of that sort.

Monsieur Charles divined the machinations of the persistent blonde, and redoubled his diplomacy. In any other circumstances, he would have made her an agreeable plaything; she was worth the trouble, and if the case was not very interesting in itself, the obstinacy that she put into pursuing the goal ended up flattering his vanity. He searched through all the chatter for the cause of that musical erotomania.

Annette's "pianistomania" had distant and profound roots. Since childhood, in the village, the piano, the privilege of the demoiselle of the château, had appeared to her to be the supreme mark of distinction and wealth. As a chambermaid, "playing the piano like Madame" was the culminating point of her dreams of the future.

Having progressed from lewd bourgeois to lyceans, from valets and coachmen and the Salle Wagram of the boulevards, the clients who possessed a piano had enjoyed all her consideration. Later, when luck, in the form of a wood-merchant from the Nord had ended up smiling on her, her first luxury as a kept woman had been to buy an Érard piano, and her first perversity as a faithless mistress had been to sleep with the professor charged with unveiling the secrets of the sonorous keyboard to her, and the blind tuner who maintained it in good condition.

As usually happens, her enthusiasm for the instrument had been of short duration; she had changed pianists and offered herself in holocaust to all the masters of the keyboard, but her numerous sacrifices had not developed dispositions in which she was completely lacking. When, after eight months of intense labor, she perceived that *Mon rocher de St-Malo* still remained inaccessible and that the *Sultan Polka* continued to be an undecipherable rebus, she had relegated her dreams of performing to the background, had no longer considered the instrument as anything but an item of furniture of indispensable ostentation, which her blind tuner, whom she continued to madden amorously, came to visit from time to time, and had transferred all her admiring affection to the privileged beings for whom arpeggios and demisemiquavers were mere child's play.

She judged the beauty of music by the quantity of ink that blackened the paper. The blacker a piece was, the more value it took on in her eyes. The cascades of notes and the racket of base-lines caused delicate shivers to run down her back Variations on the *Carnaval de Venise* and *Au clair de la lune* were an inexhaustible source of emotional astonishments.

The notes repeated in tremolo of the *Crépuscule* caused her to swoon. The amour she felt for the player was in direct proportion to his velocity.

Unfortunately, if the beautiful Annette adored the pianist in general, she very rapidly lost her appetite for the pianist in particular; she corrected the vivacity of her imperious caprices by an incurable inconstancy. As soon as she had realized her desire, as soon as she had observed, once again, that the lover could open all the treasures of his heart to her without giving her the slightest particle of his talent, the insatiable seeker of the rapid fingerer sighed after the unknown that he agency would not take long to procure for Père Antoine—and the latter, considering an accompanist as a kind of machine with which all the agencies were abundantly provided and Annette as an opulent client difficult to replace, played with regard to "my child" the role of a veritable accomplice. At the moment when the unfortunate pianist, infatuated with his personal advantages, was curling his moustache victoriously or caressing his beard with the utmost satisfaction, he was abruptly dismissed under some pretext or other; usually, Père Antoine reproached him for not playing quickly enough.

The adventure lasted for varying lengths of time, but the termination was fatal and regular. One of them, doubtless to retain the flighty Annette in his net for longer, had had the ironic and ingenious idea of persuading her that, although her dispositions for the piano were disputable—that was doubtless because she had started too late—she had a voice of incontestable beauty and it was necessary to reveal that treasure swiftly to the public. That new hobby-horse, mounted with enthusiasm and a deplorable credulity, had caused her to fall into another mania: that of the concert.

The prestige of the pianist had increased even further. In each new accompanist she saw the man who might bring out the scale that nature was hiding jealously in the depths of her pretty throat, the liberator of the nightingale imprisoned in her opulent thoracic cage. If the blonde Annette had heard the innumerable jokes to which her bland voice, limited in its

179

range, gave rise on a daily basis, she would have had a few doubts regarding her vocation as a future Star, but she had beautiful eyes in order not to see, and adorable ears in order not to hear.

That new mania was rendered all the more powerful because Père Antoine found it to his advantage. From time to time she attempted debuts that brought in serious benefits. It required so much money to make a good audience, and the claque was always composed of thirsty individuals. The pretty maniac confronted the footlights, the weekday audience applauded as a joke, but Sunday's whistled pitilessly. Père Antoine made "my child" understand that she still needed work, the professor who had been unable to make anything of his pupil's brilliant dispositions was sacked, and the story recommenced.

Monsieur Charles had learned or divined all that. He knew that, one way or another, his place would not take long to get away from him. His role as Joseph was becoming increasingly difficult to sustain, and Père Antoine was even reproaching Annette for no longer cultivating her voice.

Would it not be better to resign himself to being devoured by the pretty monster? He did not, after all, experience any repugnance for the neurotic. She was soulless, devoid of perfume, like an orchid born in ingrate terrain, but he found her worthy to excite his passing curiosity. Furthermore, the exploration he had just made at the corner of the Rue du Faubourg-Montmartre, and the memory of Mariette, had stirred up lubricities that his long continence as a scholar had only ever put to sleep He wondered whether he might not find in the elegant Annette a powerful distraction that would made him forget that of the ordure, that of the sidewalk.

He rapidly became ashamed of those sentiments of ingratitude. The unfortunate woman was worth at least as much, if not more, than the fortunate one. He was quite wrong to lose his memory so rapidly; had he not been a man of the street himself, a vagabond, a beggar, a starveling! Was he going to scorn the woman who had helped him?

No, he would not have the soul of a turncoat.

He regretted, nevertheless, not having chosen another place of rendezvous for Mariette, Her appearance of a brazen streetwalker, the poverty of her attire, and the vulgarity of her language, might attract the mockery of the regulars and the malevolent disdain of Annette.

Bah! She would wait for him at the back of the hall, he would collect her at the exit and steal her away rapidly from the curiosity of the artistes and the mockers.

Chapter XVII

For several days he had been watching the comings and goings in the hall anxiously, and that evening again—it was Thursday—nothing had revealed the presence of Mariette. She had, however, come in while he was playing deafening variations in the guise of an intermezzo, and, as she was wretchedly dressed, she had retreated into the darkest corner. Her friends had warned her about the change that had taken place in the attire and the bearing of the man she had helped; she had no difficulty in recognizing him.

The pianist had just played his final chords. Annette, authorized for some time by an affability, almost tenderness, that augured well, pressed Monsieur Charles closely, and the latter, making a three-quarter turn on his stool, responded with smiles to the provocations of his beautiful neighbor. Mariette had a frightful contraction of the heart.

A local prostitute had just at down beside her. "Do you know the blonde who's talking to the pianist?" she asked.

"Yes, that's the great Annette, a well-to-do kept woman—a real show-off! She has an air of looking down at you, because she's covered in silk and thinks that makes her better than the rest of us. Well, what can I tell you—some bitches have all the luck. Oh, if I had a lover who gave me the necessary, it'd be me who'd amuse myself deceiving him."

"She pulls strokes?"

"That's obvious—you can see by the moves she's putting on the pianist."

Mariette felt faint.

"Then the pianist…?" she said, effortfully.

"Is her lover of the heart, of course. It's not with the three or four francs he earns here that he can keep her and pay for the diamonds she has in her ears."

"Are you sure of what you're saying?" Mariette asked, clinging on to a last hope.

"Well, I haven't held the candle, but everyone here's joking about it. It's a young one who's wearing the horns and old one who's getting fed—the world upside down, eh!"

The poor girl lapsed into a mutism that the chatter of her neighbor could no longer interrupt.

For a moment, she had a desire to flee, but why should she go? He wasn't her lover; she had no rights over him. He had told her to come and wait; she had come. Doubtless, he wanted to give her some money, perhaps the other's money. She'd be stupid to refuse it. She wouldn't amuse herself playing the prude; she'd take her money and go, and never see him again.

Tears rose too her eyes. She had had such a pleasant dream in coming to this rendezvous!

Why had he brought her here, rather than somewhere else? To make her witness his scene, to brag, to avenge himself for the way she'd treated him in the Avenir? Oh, if she were sure of that, he's make him repent of it! She wasn't a girl to let herself be mocked. But in what way was he mocking her? Hadn't she insulted him, hadn't she chased him away?

He had taken another mistress; that was quite natural. He wanted to see her again to recognize the service she had rendered him, that was certain, the money he'd given to the others proved it. How many men in his place wouldn't even have thought of it? The only guilty one was her!

She gazed at her rival, radiant with pleasure; she compared the other's costume with the poor garments in which she was clad, and again, envy and jealousy fermented in her heart. With her beautiful dress and her jewels, she wasn't as pretty as all that, the slut. She hadn't done four months in prison for him. Ha! All it needed was for her to amuse herself looking down on her, damn it!

Then Mariette contemplated her lover of one night avidly, and observed with a stupor mingled with admiration the transformation that had been announced to her. Instead of the enigmatic individual clad in an eccentric check suit with the dirty hat and the distraught and morbid face, she saw an elegant man, with a dazzlingly white shirt, a neatly-trimmed beard, carefully-combed hair and a becoming smile. She considered fearfully the abysm that separated them now: her, the registered prostitute just out of prison; him, the distinguished man that a rich and beautiful woman seemed happy to possess.

All the projects that she had formed since Nini Nichon had told her the good news collapsed. All the hopes to which her naivety, mingled with perversity and tenderness, had given birth, fled. Why was he no longer the starveling, the old lost dog, the defrocked priest, the wretch, the thief, that his fall had brought down to her level and would have permitted her to associate her life with his?

Such was the true significance of the confused reflections that were passing through her soul.

Now, utterly resigned, having lost all illusion, she waited patiently for the spectacle to end. She did not have a sou. Nini Nichon, under some pretext, had not yet given her the twenty francs she had for her; she had scarcely been able to advance her twenty sous to get into the café concert. She too had not yet eaten that day.

The concert was over, the pianist played the retreat, the audience flowed toward the exit door. She waited in her corner. Soon, the last habitués would have emptied the hall.

The artistes, Annette, and two or three other women headed for the door in their turn.

Monsieur Charles suddenly found himself face to face with Mariette. Before the poverty of her appearance he had a moment of irritation and repulsion that made him hesitate. Would he have the cowardice not to recognize her?

A rapid vision of the past surged before his eyes, and he ran to her.

"My dear Mariette!" he cried, affectionately. "Here you are at last!"

He took her hands, drew her toward him and kissed her.

Sniggers and jokes burst out behind him. He turned round menacingly.

"This poor girl is worth more than all the women here," he declared, in an irritated voice. "I won't tolerate anyone mocking her."

The spell of sorts with which the great Annette had succeeded in enveloping him was broken; he was ready to scourge her mania.

"What do this heap of cowards and whores have against me!" howled Mariette. "Come here, then, bitch, and say it to my face, if you dare!"

She was about to hurl herself at her rival, but he grabbed her violently by the arm and drew her outside. He had suddenly calmed down; Mariette was still grumbling. She suddenly burst into sobs.

"Sorry, sorry," she stammered. "I heard someone call me a filthy whore and I couldn't hold back. Perhaps I've done you harm."

He was quick to console her. "Let's not talk about it anymore, my dear. When were you released?"

"This morning."

"Have you seen Nini Nochon? Has she given you the money?"

"Someone stole it all while she was asleep. She could only give me twenty sous to get into the concert."

"You haven't eaten, then?"

"Oh, I'm not very hungry yet."

"Poor Mariette! Come quickly, we'll go to a brasserie; it's not midnight yet, we still have time."

They sat down at table. Mariette continually interrupted her eating in order to talk.

"Eat first," he told her. "We'll chat later."

He thought, while he watched her devour the food with such a good appetite, of that long day without bread, on which the charity of the prostitutes had rescued him. He was ashamed of the vile hesitation he had just experienced and cursed the stupid vanity that had caused it. She had not been concerned about whether he was a pianist before coming to his aid.

185

He set about contemplating her. The four months of forced rest she had just taken had changed her visibly. Although her face had the characteristic pallor produced by the privation of air and light her cheeks were full, her wrinkles effaced, her complexion uniform, her large eyes less ringed, and her coiffure more modest. Her attire was almost sordid, it was true, but in her dirty black woolen dress she looked more like a poor seamstress just out of the hospital than a whore ready to resume her vile work. She resembled the pauperess he had seen kneel down before Dr. Albin's tomb. He was astonished by a change so advantageous for her, and expressed his satisfaction with it.

"Do you know that you're pretty like this, and have a respectable air about you?"

"Really?" she exclaimed, a gleam of joy in her eyes. "People won't take me for what I am, then," she added, quickly, and sadly.

"Embarrassed, he did not know what to say.

"Why don't you try to work?" he ventured, finally.

"Work?" she said, sardonically. "Go back to the sweatshop, wear myself out to die of hunger? Oh la la! If I weren't a slut, perhaps I could try to try again to get out that way, but what's the point now? I could never become an honest woman again, could I? So why put myself through the hard grind of honest women? What would give me the courage to do it? I'd need someone I loved to tell me that I had to do that and nothing else, or it'd be over."

He sank into dolorous reflections. The terrible logic of acquired vice, accepted corruption, caused him painful impressions. So, tomorrow, perhaps tonight, the unfortunate was about to descend into the gutter again. In a few days, that physiognomy, which had become almost chaste, would have resumed the bold allure, the brutal cynicism that would doubtless stigmatize it forever. Oh, if he could extend a hand efficaciously, take advantage of the calm that had broken her depraved habits, make her understand the debasement of her condition, give her the desire to get out of it...

He opened his mouth...

But what right had he to speak thus, to trouble her crapulous quietude, insert remorse and regret into her soul? Was she not unhappy enough already? It was actions, not words, that was required. Was he ready to become her lover? Did he even have the means to support her? He knew that he did not. Besides which, another task, much greater and more noble, solicited him. Charles Balin kept silent.

"What are you thinking?" she asked, seemingly having divined his disquiet.

"About you," he admitted. "But why are you no longer addressing me as *tu*?"

"I don't know. I don't dare."

"Have you forgotten, then, that we are and always will be old friends?" He added: "Nothing else alas, since destiny obliges us each to live in our own way."

"Ah," said the prostitute, with a gaze imprinted with resignation and reproach.

"Well, you see, Mariette, one day, perhaps soon, I shall be rich. Then, no matter where you are, I'll come to find you and I'll say: here's money, become free again, act as you wish; have a lover if you want, but no longer be at the mercy of passers-by."

"May the good God hear you," she replied, simply. Then the enigmatic young woman had an instant of ironic and bitter revolt. "And in the meantime," she observed, "it'll be necessary to go back to the game."

There was a long moment of silence. What could he say?

"So, my poor Mariette," he resumed. "You hadn't eaten yet today?"

"Bah! It's not the first time that's happened to me, and it surely won't be the last."

"It's always in moments of distress," he remarked, with thoughtless indelicacy, "that luck abandons you, for you might have been able to encounter a friend to come to your aid."

Mariette blushed to her ear-lobes. "I met a fellow coming to the concert," she murmured, "but I didn't want to. I wasn't thinking about that."

He gazed at her, astonished by her sudden blush and her sadness.

Had she by chance, been thinking about seeing him again as soon as she emerged from prison, of renewing the relationship that ought to have been irrevocably broken, of keeping the first fruits for him? He resolved to take away all hope.

"Where will you go now?" he asked.

"I don't know. I'll walk straight ahead, and arrive somewhere eventually," she replied, with a forced smile.

"Do you think I'd let you leave without money?" he hastened to add. "Why would I have asked you to come, then?"

"How do I know?"

"Certainly not, my dear. We're going to go to the Rue Vavin. I no longer dare carry money on me; I was robbed the other day going home. I'll go up and look for what I've put in reserve, and give it to you."

He paid the bill and left.

Mariette had taken the arm that he had offered and wanted to tell him about her quarrel with the waiter. He begged her not to rake up bad memories. Then she told him about her sojourn in prison, the books she had been lent to read. She had earned a few sous working, but she had been indebted when she was put away and had had to give them to her mates.

They had arrived at the door.

"Is this where you live?" she asked. "In a furnished room? You're all alone?"

"Yes. Why ask that?"

"Well, what would be extraordinary about you having a mistress?"

"Nothing, but I assure you that I'm alone. To have a mistress, it's necessary to be able to maintain her."

"Is that true, what you're saying?"

"I swear to you, Mariette."

She looked at him with a suppliant expression. "Well, since I'm alone," she implored, slowly, "take me. I won't be inconvenient."

He made a moment of irritation, which the prostitute saw.

"You must have a sofa, a chair," she said, in a low voice. "I'm not difficult, I'll sleep on that."

He remembered the night when Mariette had taken him in. A violent combat began in his heart. But the situation was not the same. Wasn't he going to give her money, permit her to sleep in a good bed?

"No, my dear Mariette, I'm sorry. I can't explain why, but it's necessary that we don't see one another in that fashion again."

"Tomorrow," she replied, dully, "It'll be finished. I'll go away, we won't see one anther again. I have no pretention to be your wife. You'll always hold it against me what I did to you in the Avenir, but you can see that I regretted it, because I fought for you."

"Mariette, I swear to you again that all these reasons you're imagining don't exist, but I can't, I mustn't have any other liaison."

"Since I'll go away tomorrow, as I told you, why are you afraid of my staying?"

His impatience increased. "Wait here; I'll come back," he replied, in a tone that was almost curt and harsh.

She straightened up, bold once again. "Well, go—but now I know what I was told at the café concert is true."

"And what were you told?"

"That you have a mistress. She's waiting for you up there, for sure."

"For the third time I swear to you that I haven't."

"Why won't you take me with you, then? I didn't disgust you the night I took you to my room!"

Visibly disconcerted, he maintained an awkward silence.

The strange young woman's expression suddenly softened. "I'm wrong to reproach you," she added, discouraged.

"You're right not to want me anymore, I'm nothing much. Go get me the money and I'll go."

He ran up the stairs, took the sum he had put aside and came down again in haste.

Mariette was no longer there. He saw a shadow fleeing in the distance.

"Oh my God!" he murmured. "Where is she going?"

He ran as fast as he could and caught up with her along the railings of the Luxembourg.

"Mariette! You're crazy! You know full well that I have to give you, pay you back, the money!"

The young woman turned on him like a wild beast. "Money! That's not what I came for!" she howled. "Keep your money, or I'll throw it in your face! Money! I have what I need to make it too!" She accompanied those words with a lewd gesture. "Go back to your jewel-box, your great blowsy blonde. Get away!"

Was he weak, perverse, afraid of letting her believe that another woman was keeping him, or was he vanquished by the young woman's disinterest? What the suppliant and meek Mariette had not been able to obtain, the unleashed whore, beautiful in anger and transfigured by that inconceivable amour, had no difficulty in getting. Was it not just that he should also render her the alms of pleasure that she had given him, since she put more value on that than all the rest?

"Come on, then," he murmured.

It was his turn to beg. One might have thought that she was trying to read the reason for his change of mind in his gaze.

"Swear to me that you're speaking with an honest heart?" she ended up by demanding.

He held out his arms; she threw herself into them recklessly, sobbing, avid for tenderness, famished for a little veritable love.

They went back to the mansard without saying a word, almost running, gripped by a previously-unknown intoxication.

The next day, Charles Balin went back to his office, emerging as if dazzled by a dream, wondering in what fashion he was about to pay the legitimate reparation that he owed Mariette. He was very late, the administration of the newspaper was capable of sacking him—but nothing came of it.

That evening, however, the concierge handed him a note.

Monsieur Charles, wrote the amiable person who was serving Père Antoine as a scribe for the circumstance, *after last night's scandal, and informed of the bad company that you keep, I am obliged to dismiss you.*

My action must be partly just and honest, he thought, *since destiny is inflicting such a light punishment on me.*

Chapter XVIII

Now, without veritably loving Mariette, he sensed that the bond that had been formed would be difficult to undo, entangling him with her.

The indefinable something that attracted him to her, the mixture of naïve perversity and delicate sentiments that caused him new surprises every day, had ignited his covetousness, and unchained his lustful instincts. The carnal sensuality that he had scorned for so long, belated by imperious, claimed its due, and the person who poured out the troubling liqueur, expert in enchantments, made him drink it to the dregs. He had found Calypso's island.

Already, many a time, he had tried to take back his liberty, but the revolt, soon repressed, had only served to make him aware of his weakness, to tighten the chain, to convince him of his cowardice. Mariette had only to look at him, and he fell submissively into her arms. The young woman who had wanted to leave the mansard the day after that night of amour no longer left it, and he was the one who had retained her.

Thus is was that his noble project, for the accomplishment of which he had given up everything, was relegated to the background, just at the moment when he had decided to set to work, and he was no longer thinking about anything but redeeming Mariette from her ignoble slavery.

To lift her out of it completely? It was necessary not to think of that; he did not have the resources and could not consecrate his entire life to her. But there are degrees of vice, castes in prostitution, a kind of hierarchy in corruption. It was that ladder that it was first necessary for his friend to climb. The further away she was from poverty, the better able she would be to follow the good instincts dormant in the depths of her heart.

It was necessary, before anything else, to find a little money. Since he had to live with Mariette for some time, he did not want her, at all costs, to have the slightest acquaintance with the degrading milieu from which he hoped to remove her. Once she was launched into another mode of existence, they would be able to part as good friends, he to resume his task, she and she to live more happily and even to raise herself up if she was truly worthy of it. But until they were able to recover their respective liberty, he demanded a common life exempt from any compromise; it was therefore necessary for him to provide for all her needs.

He racked his brains for a long time; a project of indisputable rectitude came to mind.

Dr. Albin, he thought, *has left his widow nearly a million, which he acquired legitimately by his knowledge. Could I not recover a tiny part of that sum? It no longer belongs to me, it's true, since Dr. Albin is dead, of my own will, and has given her all his wealth, but have I not some right to it all the same? Oh, I don't want to be demanding, all the more so as there would surely be danger in that. Two thousand francs ought to suffice.*

He took an ordinary piece of paper and drafted the following note:

I, the undersigned, recognize that I owe Monsieur Charles Balin, for a painting by Van Ostade, L'Opérateur de village, *which he has sold me, the sum of two thousand francs.*
Paris, 16 June 18**

Dr. L. Albin.

He had, in fact, bought the said painting at the time indicated and had placed it in his consulting room.

He put the note in an envelope and, modifying his handwriting, he added to it the following letter:

Madame,
The late Professor Albin, your husband, gave me more than a year and a half ago this recognition of a debt of two

thousand francs, a sum of which I now have the most urgent need.

I was far away from France at the time of his death and unable to bring my entitlement to your attention earlier. I know, Madame, that you are one of those elite individuals for whom moral obligations have as much value as written proofs, so I have not hesitated for a moment in sending you the justification of the debt. Dr. Albin, having no money on him at the time he bought the painting from me, gave me the acknowledgement you will find enclosed.

I have the honor, Madame, of being your humble and very respectful servant.

Charles Balin,
42 Rue Vavin.

Certainly, he was playing a dangerous game. Madame Albin, left to herself, he was sure, would pay immediately, but she had advisors. Dr. Larmezan must have taken charge of her affairs; there might be an investigation; he might be accused of having imitated the illustrious scientist's handwriting; his former employment as a copyist even rendered him susceptible of that suspicion. Fortunately, his concierge only knew him in his capacity as a pianist, obliged as he was to draw the bolt for him at late hours.

He awaited the result of his attempt impatiently. After ten days, a letter from Maître ***, a notary, invited him to call at his study. The cashier apologized for the delay; he had been obliged to have the note verified by experts and to seek information. That quest had not been absolutely satisfactory, but Dr. Albin's handwriting had been recognized indisputably, the sum he had demanded was therefore paid.

The facility with which that sort of fraud had succeeded occasioned him regrets. Why had he not thought of that means earlier? It is true that he had not had any presentable domicile then, and that a room in a sleazy hotel would have given rise to the most violent suspicions.

He silenced the scruples that murmured in his conscience. Was he not coming to Mariette's aid, and had he not once earned that money?

A thousand francs served to complete his furnishings and to provide his mistress with clothing and underwear. Mariette had never seen such a windfall. Her modest but elegant attire transfigured her; she never ceased looking at herself in the mirror, admiring herself ingenuously.

She tried with all her might to go out with him that evening. He had no difficulty proving to her that it was necessary not to show herself thus to her former friends, that bravado of that kind might excite their jealousy and covetousness needlessly, and that she would also expose herself to temptations that would separate them forever. That threat was sufficient to make her abandon the project, but she then demanded that he take her to the Café Concert de l'Étoile. She promised him that she would not say anything to the insolent Annette, who had looked down on her, but she wanted her to see her well-dressed.

That was a petty satisfaction of self-esteem of which he did not want to deprive her; in any case, he would not be sorry himself to destroy the poor impression that the people at the concert hall must have formed.

They went out, arm in arm, like two young lovers, to Père Antoine' establishment. Mariette, in her new outfit, had comical alternatives of silent gravity and exuberant gaiety, which amused him greatly. In the spontaneous reflections that joy inspired in him, he perceived, marveling, that she thought soundly and had wit.

They went into the hall. The great Annette was in her usual place and the pianist, a very young man, incessantly turned toward her, without paying overmuch heed to the singers. The entrance of Monsieur Charles and Mariette disquieted the pretty maniac and caused her a violent surge of resentment. She was, so to speak, caught in the act; the only pianist who had not fallen victim to her affectations had been able to see with his own eyes the scant regard she had for the individual and her infatuation with the employment. The thing was all the more sensible because the skillful resistance of the graying musician had disconcerted her flighty heart; his fine manners and fluency has fascinated her, and she had found herself on the brink of falling for him.

The baritone Fernand, perceiving his former accompanist in his turn, made signs of intelligence to him, and, few moments later, went to confer with Père Antoine, whom he notified of his presence.

The impresario drink-merchant immediately approached the lovely Annette.

"When you've finished distracting my employees, my girl," he exclaimed, in a fashion to make himself heard, "you'll tell me, won't you?"

The tall young woman, humiliated, rose to her feet furiously

"Oh, it's like that is it?" she declared. "That's all right, I'm going, and I'll never set foot in this dirty dive again."

"And you'll give me pleasure," Père Antoine approved. "You're really too demanding, and you turn the establishment upside-down."

"Come on then," she shouted to the young man. "Can't you see that you're about to be sacked. It's been fixed—the replacement's already here."

The young virtuoso, only subjugated the day before and hypnotized by the beautiful blonde, thought himself obliged to follow her. The director, who seemed to have been counting on that, hastened to approach Monsieur Charles. He was fed up with gigolos, he wanted a serious man like him; the artistes were right, one couldn't change accompanists every month without disrupting the service. He therefore begged him to take his place again; if Annette took it into her head to come back, he would throw her out.

Delighted with the proposition, the musician sat down at the piano and the triumphant Mariette took possession of Annette's chair.

Monsieur Charles was intrigued by the change of attitude on the part of the rapacious proprietor of the Étoile. The reasons he had given, although plausible, could not be the only ones. There had surely been a quarrel between them; the appellation "my girl," which had replaced "my child" was characteristic; it was almost a term of scorn, which Père Antoine only applied to lower class clients. At the exit, the baritone Fernand gave him the key to the enigma.

Annette's financial supporter, the wood merchant, had suddenly rendered his generous soul to God; the lovely woman, thus finding herself reduced to seeking her fortune anew, had had the unfortunate idea of wanting to exploit the gold mine lurking in her lungs, and not only had she not offered any money to prepare the room but had actually had the audacity to ask for a fee.

Confronted by that enormity, Père Antoine had almost fallen over; his nose, formed like an eagle's beak, had turned up in a menacing fashion; his indignation had taken on epic proportions, and he had not yet calmed down. "My child," denuded of all prestige, was no longer anything but an insupportable whore who debauched all his pianists and whom he would throw out at the first opportunity. The personnel had agreed, and the arrival of the former accompanist had precipitated events.

As for the irresistible baritone, he had not thought for an instant of avenging himself for the lack of success of his own advances; he could not care less about Annette; he could not satisfy all the women infatuated with him—but he was, all the same, not sorry to have rubbed it in.

While they walked back to the Rue Vavin, Mariette sang the songs she had just heard.

"You know," her friend remarked, "you're hitting the right notes—you have a musical memory; one might even think that you have a voice."

"Yes, I have a voice," Mariette affirmed. "I think told you I that have a voice. When I was young and better off, if

197

you'd heard me sing in the studio, you'd have been amazed. Here, listen to whether I have a voice!"

She intoned a popular song.

The joyful Charles Balin had found the solution to the problem, for which he had been searching since the commencement of the liaison. He would make his friend a singer at the café concert! It was the best and only relatively honorable fashion that was in his power to pull her out of the gutter and give her a means of existence, in order to be able to leave her to her own devices when he had the courage to abandon her.

The troubling dream in which he was living could not, in fact, last long. Remorse was beginning to assail him with increasing frequency; outside of his work, Mariette absorbed all his hours, all his thoughts, and deflected him from his goal.

The night of amour that crowned the fortunate day quickly stifled the first protests of his conscience.

The following day, he made his mistress party to the project he had conceived. At the mere idea that she might one day enter the café concert, she began to jump for joy.

He bought an old upright piano that was not completely worn out, books of elementary instruction and scores, and commenced the education of the near-illiterate slum girl.

The newspaper that employed him had just failed; he had a thousand francs in hand. His job as an accompanist and a few piano and singing lessons permitted him to live without taking up all his time; he was able to devote himself seriously to the ingrate task he had imposed to himself.

The success was surprising; after a mere five months the little Parisienne, willing, courageous, intelligent and extraordinarily malleable in his hands, had attained unexpected results. She expressed herself almost correctly, no longer remembered, except in rare moments of anger, the dirty argot of old, and had relearned everything she had known on leaving elementary school. In music, her progress had been even more rapid; she had almost mastered the scale, she had learned to read music a little, and endowed with a good memory, possessed a veritable repertoire. Her natural qualities, her desire to achieve something, and the verve she put into the slightest actions, had facilitated the task singularly.

He had, in addition, taken advantage of certain affinities, her ardent and enthusiastic character and her accentuated traits to steer her in the most favorable direction. It was thus that she had learned the majority of the popular songs of Italy and Spain, and, whether by assimilation or atavism, Mariette launched an *Olé* like a veritable Castilian.

He judged that she would soon be ready to make her debut, and envisaged, not without sadness, the moment of separation. The months they had spent together would have been even happier if he had been able to free himself from his remorse.

He earned between eight a ten francs a day; Mariette cooked a simple meal; they set to work, and then went to the concert, before swiftly returning home.

The humble lodgings in which they lived were situated under the eaves of an old building. Two windows, drawn back from the roof, which formed a terrace above them inundated them with light and pure air. Without equaling the splendor of the Hanging Gardens of Babylon, the convolvulus, clematis, roses and wallflowers that Mariette grew in boxes already framed the windows and promised imminent flowers. Day by day, they followed the progress of their cherished plants, and Mariette, who measured their height, announced the growth with a charming pride. In the distance, the verdure of the Luxembourg ornamented the horizon of their regal landscape.

Their furniture bordered on indigence: a big iron-framed bed, two tables, a few chairs, the old upright piano, a bulbous eighteenth-century chest of drawers unearthed in a local second-hand dealer's shop, a kitchen table, household utensils, a cast-iron stove, and a few pleasant prints on the wall formed the whole of it; but everything was neat and orderly, because Mariette applied herself to proving that she was no stranger to domestic chores.

It was there that a little happiness had come to console their poverty. Their communal life, it is true, had not always been exempt from storms. Mariette sometimes had disquieting reversions to a savage state.

Not that she had ever sought to deceive him; the advances that had inevitably been made to her by the habitués of the café concert had always been greeted with a singular coldness; but she sometimes suffered from sudden hungers for liberty, sudden revolts that troubled their union.

The slightest intemperance unleashed her impetuous character, when she vomited insults at the smallest irritation, regretted the time when no one could demand anything of her, cursed her slavery, declared that she had had enough of it, hastily packed her clothes and went out, slamming the door. She had had two or three fits of that sort, which had been very hard for him to bear.

But as she had quickly returned, ashamed, to the fold; as she had humbly begged his pardon and had returned, more courageously and submissively, to her study; as the pity he felt for her was infinite; and as he was determined to leave her some day, he had contented himself with making sensible reproaches, demonstrating to her the facility with which she could fall back into the mire if she allowed herself to be carried away by her indomitable nature—and it had all ended in tears and kisses.

Chapter XIX

It was in the month of June 18** that Mariette made her debut at the Café Concert de l'Étoile. Monsieur Charles, knowing the suspicion and avarice of the former coal merchant, had carefully refrained from making him the slightest proposition. Père Antoine gladly accepted amateurs in quest of a debut, but he obstinately refused, even if they had the voice of Faure or Patti, to grant them the slightest fee. His resolution in that regard was as unshakable as the granite of his natal region. For him, there were no veritable artistes except for those the agencies procured for him; all the others were Goguette singers.[20] Pay them—get away! It was, on the contrary, him who had the might to demand money; apprenticeships were served in all métiers. The great Annette knew what the obstinate attempts she had once made every few months had cost her! As if he were going to amuse himself paying debutants! All his artistes and waiters would bring him their good friends! He wanted veritable chanteuses, the professional chanteuses that the agency sent him.

The pianist, informed, went directly to the agency, introduced Mariette, had her audition, and left with a formal assurance that at the first request, she would be sent to Père Antoine at a salary of five francs a night, the maximum fee that the parsimonious montagnard granted to ladies.

"Your protégée has a voice and talent," he was told by the lyrical agent, an active young man on the lookout for artistes of the future, "her physiognomy has character, she has a good figure and her voice will carry in big halls; if her debut is favorable, which I don't doubt, and she becomes habituated rapidly to the boards—that's the main thing—we shan't leave

---

[20] Goguettes were groups of amateur singers who met up in cafés, organized as formal societies, approximately equivalent (as the name implies) to American "glee clubs."

her dragging her heels in a low-class café concert." Addressing the radiant and confused Mariette, he added: "And you won't forget later, Mademoiselle, that the agency helped you to find a brilliant situation. In brief, when you're offered serious engagements, come to find me: I'll obtain you more advantageous conditions, and get a commission."

A short time afterwards, Mariette received the summons so ardently desired. The day before, Père Antoine, alerted by a special letter from his supplier, which only happened in exceptional circumstances, announced to all his personnel an artiste of the first rank, from the top drawer, an Italian named Rose Gontran.

"What makes you think she's Italian?" asked the surprised accompanist.

"Look, read it for yourself!"

Monsieur Charles could not help smiling. The agent advertised a chanteuse *del primo cartetto*, Mademoiselle Rose Gontran.

"Well, Monsieur Antoine," he declared, "Mademoiselle Rose isn't Italian."

"Oh," said the disappointed director.

"She's Spanish," aid the pianist, to console the impresario. "A Spaniard from Paris," he added, laughing, "which is to say, Parisian, born of Spanish parents."

"You know her, then?"

"I've accompanied her often."

"Does she have the talent the agency says?"

"You're a man of taste, you have experience and flair, you'll judge her for yourself."

"Certainly," Père Antoine had replied, swelling up with pride, "but even so, what's your opinion?"

"I don't want to spoil your surprise. I'll bring her to you myself, tomorrow."

"You know her intimately, then? Admit it—your legitimate isn't here."

"Perhaps."

The next day, the former coal merchant, at the sight of Mariette, who presented herself with the letter of convocation, started comically in surprise.

"Rose Gontran, the Spaniard, is you?"

"Yes, Monsieur Antoine."

"Impossible! You name is Mariette."

"Rose is my stage name."

"You're a professional singer, then?"

"Your agency wouldn't have sent me otherwise."

"You've been here every evening."

"I was resting, on doctor's orders."

"Where have you sung, then?"

Mariette brazenly listen ten Parisian café concerts and twenty in the provinces. Père Antoine, too wily not to understand that his hand was being forced, scratched his head indecisively, but he left it there. There was hardly anyone in the place, and besides, she was an artiste that the agency had sent him, the sole consideration that could reckon with his mistrust.

Mariette, therefore, made her debut that same evening. The thing had been kept secret; her friend knew full well that if Annette had caught wind of it she would not have failed to organize a cabal; only the sympathetic clan of painters and rhymers had been alerted.

The result was all that could be hoped. The chanteuse had a few moments of weakness—no matter how small a stage is, one does not tread the boards for the first time without a dangerous emotion—but the help that the accompanist gave her, forgotten words whispered, tightness in the voice masked by energetic chords, and the powerful encouragement of friendly smiles, came to her aid at the critical moments. The debutante, recalled several times like a star, obtained a dazzling success. Even Père Antoine shelled out the hundred-sou coin without complaint. Rose Gontran had conquered all votes.

Charles Balin had demanded that is mistress change her name. The registered prostitute who had emerged from prison had to erase all traces of her past, to the extent that it was possible.

At first, Mariette wanted a sonorous name with a Spanish termination, but he had persuaded her of the futility of pretentious pseudonyms of that sort. Nevertheless, as her real name was Marie-Rose Gantron and his weakness for anagrams was able to satisfy the debutante, she received the name with the Castilian termination of Rose Gontran.

The success of the chanteuse was accentuated in the following days; bands of students came to acclaim her. For the first time, Père Antoine had an artiste who brought in receipts. Then he learned that Annette had hired whistlers. He talked about calling the police. Monsieur Charles begged him not to do that, and presented himself unexpectedly at the home of his former admirer.

"Let's put our cards on the table," he said to her. "I know what you're planning. If you have the audacity to carry it through, I'll send a signed circular letter to all the agencies asking them to communicate it to the pianists; I'll denounce your infatuation, of which some of them are already aware, and you'll become the laughing-stock or the prey of all the key-tappers in the capital. Believe me, don't waste your money satisfying imaginary grievances, the adventure will turn against you. Instead, make a friend of Rose, whose talent will open doors, and who might be useful to you later. Come this evening; I'll introduce you to her."

The beautiful Annette returned to the Concert de l'Étoile, and was the first to applaud her rival.

Two months later, aided by a fortunate hazard and the interested protection of the agency, Rose Gontran went to the Ambassadors at four hundred francs a month. There, her debut became something far more serious. Although she had acquired the necessary aplomb and the habitude of the audience, it was necessary to cope with the jealousy of rivals and the appreciation of the petty press. Aided by her friend's advice, modest, becoming and affable, she was able to maintain herself in a situation that was initially effaced, but became more brilliant by the day. When the dormant rivalries awoke, it was too late. Rose, applauded by the public, judged favorably by the theatrical press, was able to defy the envy of her comrades, the gossip of the wings and the gibes that her poverty attracted to her.

The intoxication of the stage had taken possession of her ardent nature. She put so much passion and consciousness into singing fashionable platitudes that the most banal lucubrations were entirely transfigured. Soon, authors were bringing her their songs. On that occasion again her friend made observations and suggested retouches, and only allowed her to accept works in conformity with her qualities. Success did not fail to confirm the choices.

An ambition that he had never imagined devoured her; she felt that it was necessary to take advantage of the favor that the public and the press seemed eager to lavish upon the previous day's unknown. She wanted to reach the first rank.

Unfortunately, their resources were blatantly insufficient, and poverty risked being an insurmountable obstacle.

In that milieu, of such a dubious artistic value, talent, although welcome, is often only an accessory; the beauty of the singers, the luxury of their costumes, and sometimes, the eccentricity of their genre, occupies the place of honor. How many stars of the first magnitude, without their charms and outfits, would become mere embers!

Charles Balin knew all that; he took account of the sufferings that poor Rose must be enduring. The ordeal must be hard, the offenses to self-esteem incessant and cruel; her rivals had sumptuous dresses and expensive jewels, of which they made the most. She, with the same two or three costumes that they had been only able to procure at the price of the greatest sacrifices, cut a rather paltry figure! Although she dared not complain too loudly, fits of rage followed by long period of sadness, bitter comparisons, eyes reddened by tears, sullen silences, became increasingly frequent and significant.

The situation would therefore, not take long to unravel of its own accord. He would suffer, perhaps more than he thought, but his task with regard to Mariette seemed to him to be complete. He awaited the painful moment with resignation. He wanted the separation to come from her, or that she would furnish him with a genuinely serious reason. Rose Gontran was still too close to Mariette for the event to be long delayed!

One day, without the slightest warning, Rose did not come back in the evening.

In spite of being prepared for it, the method affected him painfully. Why was she doing it is such a brutal fashion? A simple word would have sufficed.

He did not see her until three days later. Disdaining recourse to lies, she threw herself into his arms, weeping.

She needed clothes, she was weary of being humiliated by her comrades, the directors were looking askance at her penury. Yesterday, they had made the implication; tomorrow, they might give her the sack. So she had taken advantage of an opportunity, but an opportunity so exceptional that he wouldn't hold it against her. Who was she? A wretch that he'd taken out of the gutter. A few stains more or less were no big deal, especially if they were made in an intelligent and discreet fashion. Her new estate had terrible demands; he shouldn't object, then, to the rare blots that she might make in their communal life. He was the only one that she would always love, and it was to him alone that she'd retain an eternal gratitude.

He stopped her.

"I don't hold it against you, Mariette, and I've been expecting this dolorous moment, almost with impatience. Fatality has obliged me to leave you; it was necessary, as you know, that it would happen sooner or later, and as soon as possible. You've taken the initiative—so much the better! You've spared me the great chagrin that the fear of seeing you weep would have given me.

"You helped me on a day of terrible misery, and in spite of the primordial interest I had in living alone, I thought that I ought to devote a few months of my life to help you to escape from shame. It would be necessary, to redeem you completely, to give you all my soul and all my heart; I can't do that; that would be to abandon my plans; it would be to commit a cowardice, to transform a meritorious action of my past life into a futile sacrilege.

"It's necessary that I return to the mysterious task that is imposed on me, and I render your liberty to you. Let's separate, Mariette, without bitterness and without regrets, and let's remain friends, in spite of everything."

"The division that you'd like me to accept, I would have been able to forgive you when you were still wretched and you needed my indulgence and my pity; today, when you're capable of earning a living, I could no longer submit to it without dishonor and without scorn for myself. Now, I have need of all my strength and all my esteem to accomplish the miracle that I have to realize.

"I don't know what the future reserves for us, and how we might meet again one day; doubtless it will be in another milieu and under another name; don't recognize me then unless I recognize you, and don't seek to retie bonds that so many reasons oblige us to break. But if any danger threatens you, if any despair takes possession of your heart, don't forget that you'll always have a sure and disinterested friend in me, who will always make every effort to get you out of difficulty.

"Let's embrace one last time, Rose, and not for long, for you'll make me suffer needlessly."

She threw herself into his arms again. He pushed her gently toward the door.

Leaning on the banister he watched her go down the stairs sadly. A frightful pain gripped his heart; he wanted to call her back, but the cry would not emerge from his throat.

Oh, if Rose Gontran had only looked up and seen the anguish that had taken his breath away!

He left the door ajar.

Mariette might perhaps have come back. Rose Gontran did not.

Soon, other sentiments came to agitate him. The memory of the work that it was necessary to complete comforted him.

Since that absorbing liaison, born of the obligation created by misery and also, he was obliged to recognize, by an impulse of his heart, could only ever be temporary; it was a hundred times better that it end completely. Certainly, he was heartbroken to have lost Mariette, but he ought to deem himself fortunate to have recovered his liberty so easily.

The clock chimed midday; he resolved to go eat lunch at a restaurant. As he went past the church of Saint-Germain-des-Prés, his curiosity was solicited by a crowd of idlers who were forming a hedge to either side of the porch.

A wedding, no doubt, he thought. A long file of carriages, their coachmen and horses decorated with flowers, were waiting at the exit. He drew nearer. The head of the cortege came down the steps of the perron.

On the arm of Dr. Larmezan, majestically clad in a robe of blue silk, a woman, the bride, looked directly at him.

He hastened to flee like a guilty man, ashamed, humiliated, his heart bleeding, gripped again by an inexplicable regret at finding himself alone forever.

Chapter XX

Convinced that Rose, after having acquired the dresses and jewels indispensable to her success, would not take long to come back to beg his forgiveness; certain that he would be weak enough to allow himself to be recaptured, he resolved, in order to avoid the danger, to leave the sunlit mansard in the Rue Vavin.

In any case, the narrow abode, which she had filled with her presence, now seemed singularly sad and empty. Before the old piano, still open, on the stand of which the last song that he had had that her still remained, he had even felt tears rising to his eyes. It was necessary, therefore, since it was still haunted by troubling memories, to abandon that place, where dreams bore him, involuntarily, toward the absentee.

The Café Concert de l'Étoile had changed management and personnel; Rose would lose track of him and find a lover more in conformity with the demands of her new situation. The aid and advice of the old friend had incontestably been indispensable to Mariette; his presence and his love could only be injurious to the future of Rose Gontran.

He therefore rented the specious loft of a of town house in the Rue de Ile-Saint-Louis, installed his books and his furniture there, and then, thinking, full of remorse, that since the death of Dr. Albin, the search for quotidian bread and the education of Mariette had prevented him from taking a single step toward the sacred goal, he wanted to redeem his long inaction by means of intense labor, and finally begin the brilliant synthesis of chemistry that had reduced the totality of his past work to nothing.

The task was much more arduous than he had supposed. He could not repeat, for lack of money, certain fundamental experiments; the official laboratories were closed to him and the miserly libraries only opened their doors to the privileged. In spite of that, he worked day and night for more than two months, sustained by a feverish excitement, scarcely according a few moments to his meals, stealing hours from his sleep, forbidding himself the slightest rest. Carried away by a kind of frenzy, he succeeded thus in laying down the first foundations of the envisioned work—but at the price of what sacrifices!

The intermittent work he found: music lessons, translations of foreign works, sessions as a pianist, etc., was no longer sufficient to enable him to live in an adequate fashion; the few savings he had had the prudence to put by had been absorbed by Rose's dresses; his furniture, sold piece by piece, had been reduced to the strictly necessary. It would have been necessary to run hither and yon, interrupting his favored labor, and rather than waste time, which fled so quickly, he preferred to nourish himself wretchedly with meager portions purchased in a vague local creamery and shiver with cold in his large fireless room. Robust as he was, his health could not support so much effort and so many privations with impunity.

One day in November, on returning from the Bibliothèque Nationale, he went along the glacial Rue de l'Ile-Saint-Louis, exposed to all the winds, inundated with sweat, and felt ill when he got home. He immediately went to bed; violent shivers agitated him all night, and then the symptoms of pneumonia became manifest. He had his old concierge cover him with vesicants and cared for himself as best he could. Scarcely was he convalescent from that first attack, however, than a grave complication set in. A diffuse anthrax of the neck developed rapidly, in disquieting fashion.[21]

This time, the malady necessitated the intervention of another; it was necessary to quit the loft where no one had come to sit at his bedside. He covered himself up as best he could, informed the concierge, and, hanging on to the walls, his head hammered by the fever, dragged himself to the somber edifice that might perhaps shelter his death-throes.

---

[21] The reference is not to the contagious disease to which the name "anthrax" remains attached today but to what would nowadays be recognized as a staphyloccocal infection.

"The central hospitals are full up," he was told. "We have no more rom. Go to Lariboisière or Beaujon."

He demonstrated the impossibility of his taking a single step further, insisted on speaking to the intern on duty, explained his situation to him, protested against the humanity of a refusal whose result would be a certain aggravation of a condition already very grave, and ended up being admitted urgently.

By an ironic and mysterious will, number twenty of the St-Jean ward entered as a patient in the service that Dr. Albin had directed so magisterially for such a long time. He took refuge, devoured by disease, in the supreme asylum where, full of strength and health, he had so often leaned over the suffering of others. He sheltered, conscious of his own peril, behind the white curtains where he had seen so many poor devils die, with the vague and general pity that results from professional indifference. In the fashion in which an orderly helped him to undress, he already judged their value, the care of mercenaries for whom he no longer had the eye of the mater.

He spent a night of torment and hauntings. Policemen tracked him from bench to bench and his legs gave way beneath him; abject beings dragged him into an endless whirlwind and his heavy head was suddenly tipped back more forcibly by the gyratory movement. An immense jeering crowd chased him. He was buried alive in a tomb.

The next day, he was beginning to sleep, taking advantage of the brief morning calm, when the sound of footsteps and voices woke him up with a start. The chief of service, his successor, had just arrived and was making his daily round. A compact group of students was following him, stopping at all the beds, listening religiously to the lessons *in anima vili* that the master was lavishing upon them, trying to recognize maladies, examining wounds, fractures and tumors by turns.

"An entrant yesterday evening," announced the intern, indicating number twenty.

"What have you observed?" asked the eminent surgeon. "Reply in a low voice in order that these Messieurs don't hear; we're each going to judge the case. The intern obeyed. The chief of service advanced toward the patient, ordered him to sit up, hanging on to the rope that hung down before him, and examined him carefully.

"Look," he said. "He's been covered in vesicants."

"So, my worthy friend," said the chief surgeon, "you've been ill before coming here?"

"I've just had pneumonia," the patient replied.

"And who was the donkey who put those vesicants on you."

"It was me."

"My compliments—your remedy has put you in the state you're in now." He turned toward his audience. "That treatment for pneumonia is a little behind the times, but it still has ferocious partisans, it must he said. My illustrious predecessor Dr. Albin was one of them." He perceived one of his pupils.

"Diagnose this illness!"

The apprentice succeeded the master and palpated the tissues for some time.

"It's an anthrax," he finally replied.

"Very good; and you, Monsieur Boulon, do you observe the fluctuation?"

The inexperienced hands of the provincial of that name fell heavily upon Charles Balin's dolorous neck and attempted to resolve the question by repeated palpations. A third student advanced in his turn to observe the fact. The patient had allowed himself to fall back on his bed, moaning.

"I can't take any more," he murmured. "I'm cold; leave me, I beg you; you can examine me tomorrow."

"Let's leave him," the chief of service approved. "The poor devil's tired, and with reason. The case is typical and serious, Messieurs; we're in the presence of a diffuse anthrax." He gave a long and brilliant discourse to the audience, who took notes, without thinking that the patient could understand the meaning of the medical terms he employed.

"I can't yet pronounce on the outcome," he added. "How old is the patient? He looked at the placard. "Forty-seven.[22] If he's not an alcoholic, the prognosis might be good, Hey, my man, do you have the habit of taking a few little glasses with friends?"

The patient shook his head.

"They always say no," he observed. "This one doesn't look like a drunkard. "What métier do you follow?"

"Writing. You can open up broadly. I've never had syphilis and don't have diabetes," the patient added, as if to get ahead of the questions he was bound to be asked.

"Lucky you!" muttered the chief of service. He took his lancet and made broad cuts. The skin split under the steel. The poor devil, clinging to the bed-frame, horribly pale, supported the pain without flinching, but cold sweat beaded his livid face.

"Come on, my friend, don't worry; it's nothing," he concluded, after having informed his pupils of the contrary.

"You haven't noticed," he said to the intern, as he went on to the next bed, "that if that pen-pusher wore his hair long and shaved off his beard, he'd bear a strong resemblance to Dr. Albin?"

"Indeed," replied the student. "I wondered yesterday why I thought I recognized him.

Ill as he was, Charles Balin, subject of study, typical case, raw material for observation, no longer had the same way of seeing as Dr. Albin. While still admitting that the hospital ward ought to be a school for aspirants to the doctorate, he judged nevertheless that the situation of the indigent patient demanded a reserve, a delicacy and a respect that he now regretted not always having had.

---

[22] The annotation is mistaken; given the time measurably elapsed since Dr. Albin declared himself to be forty-six at the time of making his fatal decision, "Charles Balin" must be forty-eight, perhaps even forty-nine.

The patient spent several days between life and death; perhaps he did not take all the potions that his former colleague ordered for him, and did not always follow his prescriptions, but in spite of that, he found himself out of danger after a week.

Liberated from the instinctive and egotistical concern that had only made him think at first about his own existence, he examined what was happening around him. He watched, with his patient's eye, the long agonies that he had only glimpsed with his physician's eye. The gasps and coughing fits of the dying filled his nights with anxious pity. The hallucinated ramblings of the delirious evoked phantoms that had never appeared to him; the racking coughs and stifled plaints began to augment his own suffering; the insipid and penetrating odor of death gave him nausea.

He saw a cadaver carried away, enveloped in its shroud, still warm, without any pious hand closing its eyes. *Whose turn is it next?* the orderlies seemed to be asking as they looked to the right and left.

There were so many things that he would have sworn he knew thoroughly, of which he had had scarcely glimpsed the appearances. His dolor and misery had taught him to feel pity, and his compassion led to understanding.

The idea that I was working for the profit of humankind, he confessed, *too often made me forget humanity. There's something other than an anatomical specimen in a cadaver, and something other than a subject of study in sickness!*

His convalescence lasted a fortnight. Soon, he knew, he would be given his ticket of leave. What if he could stay for a while in the hospital, in the capacity of an orderly? That would permit him not to fall back without resources into the street. He needed once again to sell a few poor items of furniture, but it would be better to keep them. He imparted his desire to the chief of service, presenting himself as a former medical student whom reverses of fortune had deflected, and asked for his support.

A few days later, a place having been found in another surgical ward, the recommended convalescent was dressed in his smock and circled by the regulation apron.

The head of service, one of his old rivals, to whom the new subordinate was introduced, inspected him with a rapid glance.

"Why, it's Père Albin!!" he exclaimed, observing the resemblance. He started laughing; his pupils joined in chorus, and the soubriquet remained to him among his colleagues.

Soon, the new orderly gave evidence of singularly astonishing surgical aptitudes. He begged the interns and pupils to let him undertake a few dressings, a favor that the idle hastened to accord to him. He put a passion, a contentment and a skill into it that surprised everyone.

"Where did you learn all that?" asked the chief of service, brought up to date. He repeated his story of interrupted studies

"Aren't you, rather, some provincial bone-setter? There are, it's said, some who are very skillful."

The orderly tried to protest.

"Don't defend yourself," added the chief of service. "Some pork-butchers, not to mention amphitheater assistants, carry out disarticulations I wouldn't disavow."

The skill that the newcomer showed earned him some consideration at first; the pupils established laudatory comparisons between his dressings and those of the interns, and the latter, often in haste to leave, confided their work to him on more than one occasion. But the services that the orderly strove to render did not take long to become a source of trouble. One thing earned him a disgrace from which he ought to have taken a lesson. Several times without be instructed, he remade dressings that he thought badly executed. There was in that action a usurpation of function complicated by a kind of criticism that could not be tolerated. The offended interns forbade him to touch their dressings thereafter, and never missed an opportunity to treat him as a servant.

Charles Balin tried for some time to hold himself in check, but involuntarily, surges of impatience, authoritarian observations and occasional rude comments escaped him in confrontation with a lack of skill or a hesitation. It was not admissible than an orderly should dare to correct or criticize those to whom he owed submission and respect; everyone ganged up against him, and even his colleagues, initially full of admiration for is incontestable superiority, but rapidly becoming jealous, treated him as a black sheep.

He requested a transfer; the director, after having reprimanded him and warned him that in case of recidivism he would be obliged to dismiss him, consented to it.

The orderly kept quiet for another month, telling himself that he was, after all, in the wrong, that Dr. Albin himself would not have suffered such anarchy in his staff, and that, socially speaking, the intrinsic value of an individual ought not to be above the position he occupied.

Soon, however, an event that caused a certain noise in the hospital world was imputed to the surprising orderly: several errors of diagnosis had been corrected on the placards!

Taken to task, he strenuously denied any responsibility for that bold action, which damaged the reputation of a renowned surgeon. The latter, unable to admit that an orderly was capable of giving him lessons, insisted that he be sacked, but there was no proof and he was spared again.

A final incident, however, completed the measure.

A worker employed in roughcasting fell from the scaffolding, sustaining grievous wounds in the thigh, and was immediately taken to the hospital. A considerable hemorrhage endangered his life; a few more minutes and the man would be dead.

It was about two o'clock; no surgeon was there. The intern on duty, as was required, attempted a ligature of the femoral artery, but he had lost his composure groping and could not find the artery. Yielding to an irresistible surge of impatience, the audacious orderly, who was serving as his aide, suddenly took the scalpel from his hand, shoved him away without saying a word, discovered the artery in the blink of an eye and tied it off.

At a stroke, the situation was no longer tolerable; the astounded young surgeon had not breathed a word, but rumor of the incident spread rapidly. The following day, the director summoned him again.

"Monsieur," he said to him, with an involuntary respect, "you did something yesterday that in itself in perhaps worthy of praise, but which nevertheless obliges me to criticize you and dismiss you. You took on a very heavy responsibility that you were not entitled to bear. You did, in truth, succeed in that delicate enterprise, but admit that if the injured man had died in your hands, what might have followed. Can you imagine the scandal? All the newspapers in Paris would report that the Hospital allows patients to be butchered by orderlies in the face of the most distinguished surgeons! You can see the raising of shields from here. If someone dies in the hands of a physician, no one can raise any protest; his scientific qualifications are a guarantee for society, but in the hands of a ward attendant! I would, with every right, throw him out immediately. Go then, if you please; exercise your talents elsewhere. Yesterday, chance favored you; tomorrow, your vanity, give an appetite, might cause you to commit the worst blunders. Here's the account I've prepared; present it to the cahier."

Charles Balin, having argued the urgency of the case and *force majeure*, made the observation that a human life was at stake and that he was sure of himself, since he had succeeded.

The honorable director was intractable. A surgeon, denying all evidence, putting concern for human life below his whim, could obstinately refuse to apply antiseptic in his service; he found that quite natural, or, at least, not his concern. But an orderly, even if he saved a man's life, had to be severely punished for daring to take on the role of a qualified individual. The exceptional success did not justify the monstrosity of the action. The reasons that the subaltern tried to put forward could only have value among people with no social organization, in a land where rules were made to be broken and diplomas were issued without conferring any prerogative.

Chapter XXI

Desolate, but obliged to recognize himself the social log-ic of the outcome. Charles Balin quit the smock and apron that he had worn with joy and honor for more than three months. He had not spent a sou of his meager wages, had received meager New Year's gifts, and relatives of patients grateful for his attentions had sometimes slipped the modest offerings of poor folk into his hand; he could therefore take his time and search for an employment. He would continue his scientific work as soon as fortune had smiled on him a little. It was nec-essary before anything else to be sure of being able to live and not fall back into the tenebrous *in pace* in which he had almost left his intelligence and his skin.

He went back to his domicile on the Ile St-Louis, passed his cherished manuscripts in review, tidied himself up some-what, and headed with no precise goal toward the grand boulevards. The first thing that struck his eyes was a large poster with a portrait of a woman:

FOLIES NOUVELLES every evening ROSE GONTRAN.

Damn! he thought, *Mariette's making rapid progress; already a star of the first magnitude.*

A real pleasure inundated his soul. He had read in the newspapers, from time to time, laudatory appreciations of his pupil, but he had not imagined such a rapid and brilliant vogue. The registered prostitute who had been walking the streets scarcely a year ago was today bringing all Paris to her feet! She was, therefore, out of all poverty, in a position to live luxuriously, to follow her tastes and satisfy her caprices—and all that was his work; he was the good genie of that unex-pected metamorphosis!

Put in a good mood, he treated himself to a succulent dinner washed down by a generous wine. Then, enlivened by that small intemperance, he headed for the Folies Nouvelles. He wanted to hear Rose, observe her progress for himself.

Lost in the crowd of spectators, she would not see him or would not recognize him. Perhaps she was no longer even thinking about him?

He bought a ticket and hid himself in the discreet penumbra of the gallery.

Young women in opulent but garish dresses—export items—old much-decorated gentlemen, party-goers in suits with flowers in their buttonholes, Englishmen in check jackets that reminded him of the accursed rags of old and provincials in violation of conjugal fidelity were heaped up in groups or walking around at a slow pace.

The spectacle was encumbered with acrobatic exercises and clownish pantomimes, which bored him. A kind of almost-silent expectation and the accumulation of auditors in the most favorable spots announced to him the appearance of the Star. Soon, in fact, the orchestra launched into a seguidilla, thunderous applause brought the house down, and Rose Gontran came on stage.

With her mantilla, her short skirt, latticed with black silk on a yellow background heightened with jonquil ribbons, her half-naked breasts florid with blood-colored carnations, her features accentuated, her large eyes circled with bistre, her almost masculine forehead, her elegant slender legs, and beneath the floods of oxyacetylene light that enveloped her, causing the silk to gleam and her diamonds to sparkle, bringing out the pallor of her uniformly mat complexion, she was still not pretty in the dainty sense of the word, but beautiful, with a beauty full of enticement.

His heart beat forcefully, and a frisson ran through him to the marrow of his bones.

She sang, to the Spanish tunes that he had once taught her, filthy words emphasized by feline movements of the hips and vulgar but graceful gestures.

The success immediately took on triumphant proportions: acclamations, enthusiastic encores, and a rain of flowers; nothing was lacking. By the end, the delirium was at its height. Radiant with joy, she apologized for having run out of strength and made her exit, blowing mischievous kisses.

Charles Balin found himself leaning against an open box in which the two cavaliers serving a golden-haired demi-mondaine were making themselves noticeable by the warmth of their bravos.

"Wonderful, superb, stunning, amazing!" cried one of the young men, who never ran out of eulogies.

"What enthusiasm!" his neighbor ended up saying, with a hint of jealousy. "Are you infatuated with that Montmartrean Spaniard?"

"Why not? She's worth the trouble, I think."

"In that case, my lad, you can dig deep, if you have pockets," the golden-haired beauty assured him. "Rose Gontran doesn't want a lover. She doesn't like men."

"Really?"

"Try—you'll see."

"What does she love, then?" asked the other, feigning naivety.

"You're indiscreet, Alfred. Go ask her."

"All the same, these good little comrades, insinuations don't cost them anything."

"Damn! Listen, it isn't me, it's her who says it. Look, yesterday evening we were eating at the next table at Peters, and just between us, drinking champagne and eavesdropping. She was with Baron de Ramel, who was pressing her hard."

"The handsome, irresistible de Ramel?"

"The same. Doubtless he'd just made her some firm proposition, for Rose started laughing in his face. 'No, no, my lad!' she cried. 'Comrade, as much as you like, anything else, never! Men! I don't need them anymore; I've known too many in my life and they disgust me too much. I've only ever loved one; he was old, not handsome and poor; me, I was young and beginning to have talent, money, success, and he didn't want me anymore!'"

"Pooh! It's an affectation, like any other, to excite desire and raise the price. Look, if you want my opinion, it's fashionable in a certain milieu, to go to Lesbos, but fundamentally, it's a pose."

"A pose! A pose!" repeated the beautiful young woman, writhing. "What reason would she have, then, for always having that filthy old seal trailing after her?"

"A seal?"

"You can see, in the front row of the stalls, that fat common whore, decked out like an inmate of the Darcy."

Charles Balin looked in the direction indicated. Still fat, ignoble, but richly rigged out in a garish fashion, Nini Nichon was lounging in one of the orchestra stalls.

So it was for that that he'd wasted ten months of his new life, so short and so precious! Sickened, he was about to leave, the obligatory final ballet having no interest for him, when he thought he recognized the tall Annette marching toward him.

He was not mistaken; the svelte blonde, still beautiful and desirable, was nonchalalantly following the stream of strollers. What was she doing in this place, denuded of pianists?

He overtook her, turned round and looked at her, smiling.

"Monsieur Charles!" she exclaimed, recognizing him in her turn. "That's funny! I was just thinking about you a moment ago!"

"Good or bad?"

"Both. But perhaps you're waiting for Rose Gontran and..."

"I haven't been waiting for Rose for a long time."

"Yes, yes, I know," she said, with a knowing air. "It appears that she's conjugating the verb amour in the feminine."

He cut her off swiftly. "I left Rose of my own accord."

"Then I can ask you without indiscretion to offer me a glass of beer."

"With pleasure, Mademoiselle." They went into the winter garden and sat to one side.

"Ah!" sighed the great Annette, "that Rose Gontran truly has all the luck. She's a star, the newspapers talk about her,

her picture plasters the walls, the directors cover her with gold—and all that's your work, because without you, without your lessons, what would she be? Nothing, less than nothing. It's you who launched her; she still be walking the streets if she hadn't been your mistress."

"There is, in fact, some truth in what you say."

The beautiful Annette uttered a profound sigh. "And to think that if you'd wanted, it could have been the same for me!"

"Perhaps, but not in the same fashion, though."

"What do you mean?" said Annette leaning very close to him.

"Are you willing to hear the truth, the whole truth? You might perhaps be able to take advantage of it."

"Explain yourself—you're making me impatient."

"Well, until now you've been following a false path. Once again, excuse my frankness but you've always interested me."

"Speak with an open heart."

"It's not sufficient to love music and singing to become a musician and singer; it also needs natural gifts, which determination can develop but can't give us. Now those indispensable qualities, without wishing to offend you, you don't possess in a high enough degree."

"Oh!" said the pretty woman, disappointed.

"But," he said, "you're tall, well made, and, according to rumor, a good girl, although a trifle inconstant; you have a whim that pushes you toward the stage. Set your sights on dancing. I'm a good prophet and a good judge—Rose Gontran is the proof of that. You'll succeed."

"What an idea!" exclaimed the great Annette delighted. "I sense that what you're saying is true—it's like a revelation. And I never thought of it! I fact, I adore dancing."

"How old are you?"

"Twenty-five."

"It's not too late; a few months of serious study and you can debut as chorus girl at the Folies. Your fine figure, your beauty and your grace will do the rest." Laughing, he added: "You'll never get to the Opéra, it's true, but you'll acquire the notoriety for which you have such a great desire."

In her enthusiasm, Annette would willingly have thrown her arms around him; she could see herself already, acclaimed, recalled by a delirious audience. She looked at him tenderly; he felt a quivering of the flesh run through him. A languor full of softness invaded him; the lust that the sight of the other had just stirred up rose rapidly to the surface. Nevertheless, he dared not make an advance, fearing a refusal that, after all, would only be a legitimate revenge.

Annette, for her part, had had too many previous disappointments to issue a categorical invitation.

He had just paid for the drinks.

"Are you free this evening?" he sighed.

"Yes!" she hastened to respond. "Why?"

"Because if, by chance, you're afraid to walk home alone," he replied, smiling, "I'd be glad to accompany you."

"As far as the door?"

"And even further."

"You're not afraid that Rose Gontran might see us?" she said, mockingly, as she took his arm.

"I no longer love her," he murmured, gripped by a dull ager. "I never loved her. Come on."

This time, the great Annette could affirm, without fear of contradiction, that not one of Père Antoine's pianists had resisted her enchantments. Already, in the fiacre that carried them toward the Boulevard Montparnasse, the pretty vampire was devouring her prey with kisses.

Monsieur Charles had lost nothing by waiting.

Chapter XXII

That amorous adventure, born of resentment as much as hazard, had the ephemeral duration of the longest of Annette's caprices. He had imagined that the beautiful woman would make him forget the other, but he perceived, as soon as the next day, that nothing could tear Mariette out of his heart.

The malevolent insinuations he had heard at the Folies Nouvelles represented to him Rose Gontran in the grip once again of her vicious past, returned to the crapulous milieu from which he thought he had liberated her; ought he, however, to trust the gossip of some rival? Alas, the presence of Nini Nichon, whose appearance denounced that she was sponging on Mariette corroborated the accusation.

After all, what was astonishing about it? Had he not left her in a situation that was, it is true, less repulsive, but just as degrading as that of old? The price of the act did not wash away the stain. There would not have been a great difference between the high-cost Rose Gontran and Mariette whoring at a discount on the sidewalk. From the moral viewpoint, in fact, the state of the rich prostitute was perhaps even more despicable, since it did not have imminent destitution as an excuse.

Had not Rose Gontran instinctively felt that?

Reclaimed by the shameful past, she was escaping the repulsive merchandising of prostitution by means of a perverse caprice that he knew full well to be only a temporary phase in her disordered existence. He had been too hasty in quitting Mariette; he should only have abandoned her at the moment when, provided with the accoutrements and engagements necessary to earn a lavish living, she was able to become the disinterested mistress of some devoted friend; she would then have been on the road that led to moral redemption. Instead of that, he had seized the first opportunity to leave her; he had taken Mariette off the street merely to return her to the alcove.

He had feared finding himself in a dubious situation—a paltry excuse born of egotistical self-regard. He was outside of all social conventions, free in his actions, the sole judge of their intrinsic value; it had been necessary to stay with her, to channel her excesses, so to speak. He would have continued to earn his living honestly, no compromise being able to draw in into enjoying a life of dishonorably sourced luxury. Rose Gontran, thanks to his aid, would have continued to deny Mariette's crapulous camaraderie, and Nini Nichon, attracted by the fortune, would doubtless never have exploited debasing memories.

He had, in truth, a great and veritable excuse: that he was obliged to pursue a goal a thousand times more elevated, and could not attach himself any longer to Mariette's fate; but he ought not to be astonished, given that, if he found her in a moral situation almost as despicable as that of old.

Did he not have a partial responsibility for that almost immediate return to her vomit? If she really had loved him, had she not demanded of intoxication, a poor counselor, the forgetfulness of his abandonment? Of all the vices of the past, drunkenness had remained the most tenacious; he had only been able to master it to a degree by dint of patience, supplications and cunning. The deadly habit had surely profited from his departure to recover all of its empire.

An item published a few days later in a morning newspaper confirmed him in that opinion:

One of our most talented café concert stars, Mademoiselle Rose Gontran, to be precise, came on stage last night in a state of unstable equilibrium, which the audience almost failed to find to its taste, but with a presence of mind as rare as it is precious in such a situation, the witty artiste immediately began singing to the tune from La Périchole;[23] *'"I'm a*

---

[23] *La Périchole* (1829) is an *opéra bouffe* by Jacques Offenbach, the story of which features two Peruvian street-singers

*little drunk, a little drunk, but shh! You mustn't tell. Shh!,
etc." Needless to say, the incident was concluded by laughter
and applause.*

Now he was sure of it; Rose Gontran was as much to be
pitied as criticized. But what could he do about it? Had he not
already devoted too much time and vital energy to her, stolen
from the sole enterprise that was worthy of him? Had he not
returned, in the measure of the possible, the fortuitous aid that
she had once brought him? If he had not been able to redeem
her, she was sheltered henceforth from hunger and official
stigma, and if ever disgust for vice took hold in her, poverty
would no longer rivet her to infamy.

It was thus, with the sophisms of his intellect, that he
tried to dissimulate the anxieties of his heart, which, independently of his will, sought a thousand reasons to exculpate,
or at least to excuse, Mariette. Certainly, he had never loved
her, any more than he loved her today, in the true sense of the
word; otherwise, he would not have hesitated for a single instant to sacrifice his dream to her, to consecrate all his life to
her; and yet, a sheaf of sentiments, in which gratitude, perversity, pity and even curiosity flourished, still attracted him to
her by a thousand memories.

He sensed, more vaguely, that another motive had played
an important role in that kind of fascination, but that cause he
could neither define nor divine.

It was in that situation of mind and heart that he approached Nini Nichon, encountered one day in the environs of
the Trinité. The whore, initially surprised and annoyed, obstinately refused to recognize him, calling him a peasant and
threatening to call the police.

Rose must still love me, he thought, since the wicked angel was afraid of me; she doubtless imagined that I wanted to
take her back.

---

too poor to afford a marriage licence; it includes the "tipsy
aria" of which Rose Gontran here makes opportune use

227

Not wanting either to see her or write to her, he found an indirect means of reminding her of him. Remembering that he had once written verses—what had he not done?—he sent her the words and music of a love song, "*Chanson pour aimer*," the last quatrain of which was:

> *Since it is necessary that everything ends*
> *Let us separate loving one another;*
> *Our love will be the dream*
> *That endures eternally.*

involuntarily betraying the secrets of his heart.

That scarcely resembled the singer's vulgar genre, but she sang it with all her heart and veritable tears and, as the influence of her friend had always been beneficial, the success it obtained proved to Rose Gontran that she had no need of coarse words and provocative gestures to conquer the applause of the public.

In the following days, the theatrical press carried numerous advertisements saying that Mademoiselle Rose Gontran keenly desired to reach an agreement with the author of *Chanson pour aimer*, Monsieur Charles Balin, for new creations of the same kind.

He knew what that meant, and did not respond.

A few weeks later he learned that the Star, departed on tour, was reaping profits and laurels on the great stages of Austria and Russia. He was simultaneously pained and satisfied; the slightest encounter might have reunited them, and the mere presence of Rose in Paris was sufficient to trouble his repose.

Several months went by; on emerging from the hospital he had found a modest employment with a large manufacturer of chemical and pharmaceutical products with which anterior purchases had created a connection for him.

That position presented considerable advantages. Not only did he earn a living, but he had a well-equipped laboratory at his disposal, and although his employer did not always see

228

without displeasure one of his minor employees devoting himself to scientific research, the reliability of his analyses, the simplification of procedures and a few other exceptional services that he rendered caused it to be overlooked.

He repeated the conclusive experiments that overturned Dr. Albin's theory and found new ones to support then, bringing a definitive precision to the mysterious formulae.

Intoxicated by those results—which, after months of discouragement and forced inactivity had affirmed his convictions—he thought, unfortunately, that he was ready to commence the struggle. A preliminary article published by the *Revue des Sciences*, in which the fashionable theory was seriously criticized, burst like a bomb.

The article was signed Charles Balin. An investigation of sorts was mounted. The druggist, told by numerous official acquaintances that he was suspected of having encouraged the attack, hastened to dismiss the audacious employee. He had nothing for which to reproach him, but by keeping him he would have risked losing the greater part of his clientele.

Similar companies not want to inherit such a dangerous auxiliary at any price, he found himself out on the street again, and fell back into tenebrous despair. Although he no longer had, as before, the immediate anxiety of lacking a loaf of bread, the rudeness and rapidity of the riposte, and the ostracism with which he felt himself immediately subjected, taught him brutally that he was not yet strong enough or sufficiently well-armed to go into the arena.

He set out once again in quest of employment. A veterinarian, the director of an animal boarding establishment, was in search of an aide accustomed to the manipulation of pharmaceutical products. On the advice of his former employer he applied for the post and was accepted.

There, things seemed at first to present themselves in a favorable light. His employer, a great gambler against fate, exceedingly fond of racecourses and beautiful women, spending his days in the weighing-room and his nights in fashionable cabarets, gladly delegated professional cares to his auxiliaries. As long as the employee was subordinate and only had to prepare drugs, all went well; unfortunately, he could not help displaying his surgical and veterinary aptitudes, and the veterinarian, all the more delighted because he wanted to go to the races in Nice, immediately confided the administration of the hospital to him. That was the part of the establishment where sick inmates were placed, where poor tomcats were neutered, the ears of ratting dogs were cropped and bulldogs were deprived of their tails.

In spite of the irony of the situation and his repugnance for such work, the Chief of Service mastered his pride and set to work conscientiously. It was, after all, an excellent opportunity to experiment with the potency of certain antiseptics that he had recently discovered.

The most recalcitrant quinsies, coughs, galls and swine-fevers, and the most tenacious tapeworms could not rest his treatments. After a fortnight, the dogs had returned to their kennels, the cats, returned to old ladies' laps, were purring by the fireside, and parrots reinstalled on their perches were once again delighting children great and small.

On his return, the veterinarian, amazed by that unexpected evacuation, could not master his ill humor.

"I had sixty boarders when I left!" he cried, with comical chagrin, "and now I have no more than ten. You've either sent them away without being cured or you haven't followed my prescriptions."

"I have, in fact, applied treatments that I thought better."

"That, I can't support in my establishment! By what right did you take that initiative? What qualifications guarantee you? You haven't come from Alfort,[24] I assume! In any case, I expect you to respect my instructions, and I'm dismissing you." He muttered, inaudibly: "Go get hanged elsewhere. The health of an animal isn't as precious as that of a man; we have

---

[24] The École Nationale Vétérinaire d'Alfort, established in 1765, was, and still is, France's principal college of veterinary medicine.

the right to exploit the manias of people, almost all rich, who often threat their animals with more regard than their fellows. I'm a partisan of cures, since they ought to serve the good reputation of my establishment, but there's no need to obtain them with such urgency!"

"Monsieur," Charles Balin said to him, divining his thoughts, "I hold animals in no higher esteem than one ought to, but apart from the fact that any weak and suffering creature has a right to our pity, the most rudimentary honesty commanded me to act in that fashion. Your clients, via your intermediary, paid me to reestablish the health of their pets; I cured them as rapidly as I could, that's all."

"And you did well," replied the businessman, coldly, "but your reasoning runs into the brutal logic of a fact: so long as I had animals to care for, I needed someone to carry out that task. No longer having any, I no longer need the special employee. That's all, and goodnight."

The director, freed from paying wages, went out laughing quietly.

Had he not avenged himself in his fashion for the repugnant role of clipper of canine ears and castrator of cats that necessity had forced upon him?

In the meantime, Rose Gontran, returned from Russia, had resumed performing at the Folies Nouvelles, and her success was increasing by the day when the newspapers announced a sudden indisposition on the singer's part.

Observing that her name was still absent from the posters, he did not take long to become anxious, and ran to the Folies, where he was informed of the imminent return of the chanteuse. Nevertheless, he went to her domicile in the Rue de la Pépinière, where the Cerberus obstinately refused to unclench his teeth, and prevented him from going up. He had strict instructions not to give out and information and not to let anyone in.

Two or three days later, he learned from a theatrical newspaper that Rose Gontran, afflicted by a serious smallpox, would not be returned to the stage for a time as yet undetermined.

Smallpox! That was ugliness, despair, ruin for her, but he might perhaps be able to prevent her being disfigured. Determined to force all doors, he ran to the Rue de la Pépinière, where the concierge no longer tried to stop him and indicated the floor. He went up the stairs like a madman. The key was in the door; he went in without even thinking about knocking.

Everything seemed deserted; the cupboard doors were open, the drawers agape; clothing and lingerie was trailing everywhere; one might have thought that the apartment had been burgled.

He called out. A thin old woman appeared on the threshold of a doorway and, without letting go of the bottle of warm wine she was holding in her hand, half drunk, told him that the poor lady was very ill; the doctor had said that she would not recover.

He entered the bedroom that the megaera indicated to him with a finger, distraught. He had arrived too late! Rose Gontran, covered with horrible pustules, her face torn, her body lacerated, was writhing on the bearskin that served as a bedside rug. He picked her up and quickly replaced her in the bed.

Poor Rose, prey to delirium, had not recognized him.

"Is this how you look after the invalids confided to your care!" he shouted, seized by a violent anger.

The mercenary started stammering excuses; she had only left for a minute; the lady must have fallen while she was preparing the warm wine that she had been advised to take to preserve her from the infection; for sure she would not have taken long to perceive the accident and put her back in bed.

Mad with dolor, he sat down momentarily on the bed and took Rose's pulse; the unfortunate woman continued to ramble. He prescribed a potion and, not trusting the unsteady drunkard, ran to fetch it himself, returning a few minutes later.

"Why are you here on your own?" he demanded of the nurse.

"Well, Monsieur," the old woman replied, "there are maladies that scare people, not everyone wants to care for them. Me, although they say you can't catch it twice, I only agreed to do it to please the concierge, a friend of my poor late husband, and because he promised me a good fee. With that, I'm afraid of being robbed. Who'll pay me if she dies?"

"Shut up, you old fool—she can hear you. Has Mademoiselle Rose no servants, or friends, then?"

"Oh, friends—they're fine ones, her friends. In the early days, there was a fat blonde and a maid, sluts who didn't dare go into the room once and gave orders to the concierge not to let anyone in. The good-for-nothings spent their time plying bezique, as if nothing were happening, while the sick woman was moaning to break your heart! Yesterday evening the doctor said that she might well not recover, and might not even last the night; then they quickly parceled up linen and all kinds of things that were theirs—so they told me—because they lived together; they left in a cab, telling me they'd come back this morning, and I can see that they've done a flit. They're a dirty lot, all the same."

Charles Balin spent the night with the invalid and strove, as much as he could, to attenuate the ravages of the disease.

In the morning, Rose had a long sleep, after which she seemed to be emerging from a bad dream. Her eyelids were swollen; her closed eyes could not see anything.

"Nini," she murmured.

"Rose…Mariette," he replied, in a sift voice.

She shuddered and uttered a cry. "Charles! Charles! I recognize you, I know it's you! I no longer want to die! Save me!"

He could not help shedding tears, and took the hands that was groping, searching for him—but she snatched it away swiftly.

"Don't touch me," she said. "You'll catch my disease. It's catching—the doctor said so…"

From that moment on, the poor young woman gradually improved. She asked where Nini and the maid were; the old nurse told her about their departure.

"It's all over for me," she repeated, with resignation.

Two days later she was out of danger, but Charles Balin wondered fearfully whether she would survive her despair, when she saw the hideous traces that the disease had left on her face.

As if she divined his concern, she sighed: "I'm going to be very ugly now, aren't I?"

He tried to attenuate the truth and console her,

"Oh, I know, I sense that I'll be disfigured. The doctor who cared for me took precautions, but one night, I woke up with a start; I was afraid; I called out but no one came. I tried to get up, but I fell on the floor, and I can't remember anything more." Sadly, she added: "Why didn't you come sooner?"

He bowed his head and said nothing.

"Oh, I don't hold it against you. If I only had the hope of seeing you in future," she implored, "perhaps I'd still be happy. I'd resent this illness less, which has brought you to close to me again. I could even console myself for being hideous; you taught me resignation. I wasn't pretty before, now I'll be frightful!"

He promised to do everything for her that he could.

The convalescence made good progress. Soon, Rose was able to get up. The first time she looked in a mirror she uttered a scream of horror and nearly fainted.

He had, however prepared her with all kinds of circumspection for that despairing contemplation; it was necessary, besides, that she should not trust that first impression; the wounds, still poorly scarred, made her a thousand times uglier than she would be; the skin would resume its natural color in time; the inequalities would disappear.

"It's over, completely over," she replied, sobbing. "Adieu, beautiful dreams; I'll never set foot on a stage again."

That day, which he had put off as long as he could be keeping Rose in bed under countless pretexts, was for her a source of profound dolor. Rendered suspicious by the inhuman abandonment of Nini and her maid, she wanted to insect her cupboards. Her money, her jewels, all the objects of any value and a part of her clothing and lingerie had disappeared.

"The wretch!" she murmured, desolate. "The punishment is greater than I expected. Ugly and ruined—it's too much, all at once."

Again she dissolved in tears.

He tried to make her accept her disappointments philosophically.

"You didn't want me when I was pretty," she observed, "and now I'm a scarecrow, now I no longer have anything, and perhaps can't even earn a living any longer, how can you expect me not to weep, thinking that it will soon be necessary for us to separate again."

"I left you," he replied, gravely, "because you were rich and pretty and I thought you were able to do without my help. Now that you're appealing to me for help; now, above all, that your misfortune, more than anything else, might enable you to become an honest woman by obliging you to work, although I can't engage my entire future, if you swear to me never to get in the way of my projects, whatever they may be, if you promise to do as I ask blindly, I'm ready to extend my hand to you again. We'll earn our living as best we can."

An immense joy transfigured her. "I swear to you," she cried, throwing herself into his arms.

"You know," she added, in a curt, dull and resolute voice that that penetrated his heart like a sharp spike, "if you hadn't said that to me, I would have thrown myself in the river tonight."

A few hours later, Rose Gontran, completely reestablished, asked for the annulment of her engagement. The director of the Folies Nouvelles refrained from raising the slightest obstacle. Fortunately for her, he owed her a considerable sum, which permitted her to pay her rent and acquit all her debts.

The first thing to do was to abandon the costly apartment, sell the expensive furniture, now unnecessary and collect the debris that the thieves had left. She assembled thus about four thousand francs.

What were they going to do?

Mariette—for she demanded that from now on, he would no longer call her Rose Gontran—wanted to buy a small stationer's shop.

He saw nothing inconvenient in that. She would tend the shop, he would go to work or would do such work as he found at home; they would thus resume the communal life of old, the obscure life of calm and wellbeing that she had always regretted. Why hadn't he proposed that before? What could have prevented him? Could he not act as he wished, pursuing all his projects without her raising the slightest obstacle, without her even seeking to penetrate the mystery with which he enveloped himself?

They toured various quarters in quest of premises. A good opportunity having come up in the Rue de Belleville, they concluded the bargain. The foundation was already laid, and he completed it in an intelligent fashion by adding the sale of newspapers, and put a notice in the window:

Scientific and literary works, chemical analyses, translations of foreign works, redactions of pamphlets and prospectuses. Apply within.

After a few weeks, the encyclopedic stationer had enough work no longer to have to seek any outside. A former pork-butcher, his neighbor, aiming for academic palms, having had him write a pamphlet on *The Role of Tinned Goods in Military Alimentation*, the success of which had surpassed all expectations, immediately ordered a host of opuscules. It was thus that he published successively, under the name of the ambitious sausage-merchant: *A Rational Manner of Salting and Smoking Meat, Hygiene in the Breeding of Pigs, Let's Make Lard French, Italian Swine and Gallic Butchery* and *Long Live Bayonne and Down With York.*

Two or three maniacs of that sort, and the future was assured.

Mariette became cheerful again and set to work courageously; her friend had demonstrated to her from the start that veritable commercial skill consisted of never cheating the clients, having merchandise of all qualities and always selling items at their true value. She had taken advantage of this advice, and customers did not take long to flock into the small shop.

The perpetual comings and goings, the conversations she willingly exchanged with the regulars, the respect that her past reputation earned her—for she had ended up being recognized—and the sympathies that her affable manners attracted to her lent powerful assistance to the vanquishing of her chagrin; one would have sworn that she had been in commerce all her life.

Her friend, shut away in a first floor room, drafted his commissions or ripened his projects.

Soon, there was enough money to buy chemical products and a few accessories necessary to his experiments. Mariette never asked him the reason for those relatively expensive purchases or worried about what he was doing.

In reality, she did not hinder him at all; he had, therefore, taken the best course.

Chapter XXIII

Since Charles Balin had been able to analyze coldly the unforeseen situation created by the loss of his fortune, he had traced a program whose broad lines would first assure his material existence, which never losing sight of his scientific projects, and then to earn the sum of money necessary to the completion and the publication of his work. In order for him to be able to do that in advantageous conditions, however, it was indispensable that he should be in possession of official qualifications. The miserable failure and unfortunate consequences of his first attempt would have demonstrated that necessity, if he had not already been convinced of the fact.

His plan, prior to the theft at the Crédit International, had been to purchase an American, Belgian or Italian doctoral diploma, and, furnished with that parchment, to obtain the favor, easily done, of taking the examinations for the French doctorate. Thus placed, he would have sufficient qualifications to act fruitfully.

Events having disrupted those plans, instead of the few months that he would have needed, he might well have to spend years becoming an official doctor again. His situation, nevertheless, was beginning to improve. Mariette's commerce, increasingly prosperous, brought in a good income; his personal endeavors had already permitted him to make savings; another few thousand francs, and the University of Liège or Pisa would sing the *dignus est intrare* in his honor.

Hazard gave him the chance to earn them more rapidly. Passing one day in front of the shop of the foul-mouthed second hand clothes dealer from which he had once bought his hat, the curiosity of an old practitioner pushed him to discover whether the diabetic was still alive. He went into the wretched shop.

The obese man was still there; his condition even seemed to have improved.

"What do you desire?" he asked, on seeing him enter.

"To enquire after your health, Monsieur."

"Bah!" grunted the shopkeeper, still as peevish. "But I'm not ill."

"You have been, at least, and gravely, if I remember correctly."

"Perhaps," muttered the amiable broker. "What does it have to do with you?"

"I can see that you don't recognize me."

"Wait a minute," said the merchant.

"Have you forgotten the man in the check suit who gave you a consultation two and a half years ago?"

"The bone-setter!" cried the second-hand dealer, seized with a veritable joy. "I recognize you. Sit down, I beg you, and let me express my gratitude. I owe you a big debt—you put me back on my feet." He rummaged in the drawer of a dresser and pulled out a dirty piece of paper. "Look—do you recognize it? It's your prescription—I've been careful not to lose it. As soon as I feel ill I run to the pharmacist, and a few days later, I'm better."

"I'm glad to have been of service to you."

"It won't be said that you've come to see me without our clinking glasses."

The broker was so persistent that the visitor could not refuse the invitation. They went into a small neighborhood café. As they went past his shop, the stationer pointed it out.

"That's where I live now, Monsieur; we're practically neighbors. When you need newspapers or stationery, you know where to come."

"What! It's you that bought the stationer's!" exclaimed the second-hand dealer, increasingly delighted. "I can ask you for a consultation, then, if necessary?"

"I'll be happy to give you one."

"Do you know that, without suspecting it, you sank the doctor who was treating me. The imprudent fellow had told overly curious cousins that I only had two or three months to live. The others no longer left the house, they thought they'd already inherited. Perhaps you'd have thrown them out? I'm not so stupid. I let them give me a heap of presents and lavish me with care. After a while, when they saw that, instead of taking the train for the turnip field, I was continuing, thanks to your regime, to devour the oysters they bought me, they departed, furious. You should have heard them slandering the doctor—and the friend I told the story to made fun of him. As for me, I couldn't met him in the street without laughing in his face; he started making long detours in order not to go past the shop, and he ended up leaving the quarter."

The scrap merchant introduced his savior to the regulars of the little café, recommended the stationer's shop loudly, and whispered a few words in their ears.

After a few days, everyone in the neighborhood knew that the bone-setter who had cured Père Ravin was a stationer in the Rue de Belleville. Consultations began to arrive.

Mariette, knowing her friend's value, found it quite natural, and strove with all her might to persuade him to accept retribution. Why should his services not be recognized? The local doctors got paid for their cures, in spite of their blunders!

After all, Charles Balin said to himself, *am I not fundamentally an illustrious healer, and can I not accept two or three francs for advice for which Dr. Albin was paid twenty times as much?*

To the question "How much do I owe you?" he therefore replied: "Whatever you want to give me; you don't have any obligation; the law doesn't give me the right to receive a fee." A few consultants profited from the liberty, but the majority did not depart without leaving their obol.

Soon, his reputation grew and was propagated.

A former orderly at the hospital recognized him, told the story of the operation, and claimed that he had made a mockery of all the celebrated surgeons of the hospitals. The stationer, having become a famous bone-setter by public rumor, received visits from all the corners of the quarter, and even the heart of Paris.

In the beginning, the pharmacists filled his prescriptions, to which they found no grounds for objection, but, on receiving threats from physicians, they were soon obliged to refuse them. The bone-setter then had to advise his patients to go to establishments where he had not been blacklisted—which is to say, those that were outside the quarter. The physicians and pharmacists immediately fell upon him; he was denounced and threatened. It was necessary to surround himself with mystery and, with the aid of the persecution, his renown took on colossal proportions. The qualified doctors, afflicted in their interests, searched everywhere for evidence and witnesses, but the healer, with a remarkable flair, sent suspect patients away or treated them gratuitously, as was his right.

Unfortunately, a public event arrived, which gave redoubtable weapons to his adversaries.

A private carriage had tipped over in the Rue de Belleville. The passenger, violently projected on to the sidewalk, was gravely wounded; his left tibia, broken in two, had torn through the skin and was sticking out of the wound. Transported to a pharmacist's shop, prey to the most intense pain, he called loudly for help that did not come. No local physician was at home! The proposal was made to fetch the bone-setter.

"Whoever you like," he begged, "as long as I'm not left in this state any longer and can be taken home."

The stationer hastened to come, staunched the blood-flow, reduced the fracture, washed the wound and had the injured man placed in the least painful position.

Then he waited for one of the physicians who had been summoned to arrive.

Seeing that no one was coming, and judging that he had to apply a special dressing urgently, he said: "Would you like me to apply a dressing that will allow you to be taken home without danger, Monsieur? Once at home, you can call your usual doctor, and he will do what is necessary."

The injured man, already sensibly relieved, urged him to do so. He obtained bandages, wadding, cardboard and plaster and rapidly constructed a plastered apparatus, with the opening indispensable to the future care that the wound required. When the apparatus was complete he dressed the wound meticulously.

He had scarcely fastened the last pin when one of the physicians who had been summoned arrived.

"Who reduced the fracture and put on this apparatus?"

"It was me, Monsieur."

"Ah! The bone-setter. That's a surgical operation: what gave you the audacity and the right to do it?"

"The urgency there was to do it immediately, and the doubtless involuntary delay in your arrival."

"All right," growled the physician. "We'll see about that later." He prepared to take off the dressing."

"You mustn't touch that," declared the bone-setter.

"Who'll stop me?"

"The injured man, whose precious time you'll waste performing unnecessary maneuvers."

"You're afraid that I'll see your stupidities."

"The treating surgeon, Dr. P***, whose value you know, I think, will establish them."

The impatient victim paid the physician for the unnecessary disturbance, thanked the man who had just alleviated his suffering and asked him to accompany him to his domicile to supervise the care of the transportation.

Professor P***, alerted in advance by telegram, was waiting for him there. The invalid as put to bed with the greatest precaution, and then Charles Balin briefly put the illustrious surgeon in the picture. The case was very serious; he had thought it necessary to make a plastered apparatus that would permit the injured man to return home without suffering too much. Dr. P*** approved, removed the bandages that were covering the wound and examined it carefully.

"That's perfect," he declared. "You made this dressing yourself, you tell me?"

"Yes, Monsieur."

"All my compliments, my dear colleague; I couldn't have done better if I'd done it myself. In what quarter do you practice?"

The bone-setter did not know what to say. "I'm not a physician in the official sense," he ended up confessing.

"That's impossible. Where did you lean to do that?"

"I've been a medical student, and then a hospital orderly."

"Are you by any chance the famous orderly of whom I've heard talk—the one who did the ligature?"

"The same."

"Well, my friend, I'll tell you frankly that it's regrettable that you don't have a diploma in your pocket. Once again, I couldn't have done better myself, and my intervention is presently unnecessary" He addressed his rich client: "Monsieur will remake the dressing; I'll come back tomorrow."

"Doctor," asked the injured man, "do you see any inconvenience in me asking him to be my nurse?"

"Not only don't I see any," replied the eminent operator, "but I urge you enthusiastically to do it."

The bone-setter accepted the offer, and cared for the gentleman for more than a month.

The man, who bore one of the most illustrious names in the French nobility, endowed with a high intelligence, an extensive instruction and a perfect education, had a somewhat timorous nature. Delighted, to begin with, to have as a nurse a companion who could understand and reply to him, he quickly became intrigued, and then alarmed, by the surprising erudition of the Bellevillois stationer.

"Doctor," he confided to Professor P*** , one day when his guardian was not present, "I don't like mystery, and the man who is caring for me is truly too surrounded by it. He's no more a stationer or an orderly than you or I are chestnut-sellers or street-sweepers."

"Why do you think that?" interrogated Dr. P***.

"Because Monsieur Balin, or, rather, the so-called Monsieur Balin, possesses knowledge and an education such as

243

I've rarely encountered, and you know the kind and the worth of my acquaintances."

"Is that possible?"

"He knows Descartes, Kant and Hegel in depth. No question of science, art or literature is foreign to him; he plays chess better than I do and is polite to the point of letting me win. He knows three or four living languages. He plays Bach and Beethoven like a professional. Finally, you've told me yourself that he makes a dressing as well as you do, which is not saying a little! Until now, you've been able to respond to me that he was once a medical student, that he has perhaps received a very careful education, and that an incredible series of misfortunes has reduced him to the humble situation he now occupies, but wait—that isn't all. You know that, having long been a secretary to the ambassador, I know all the chancelleries inside out. Well, a few words escaped here and there have proved to me that that unknown man is aware of certain very serious diplomatic secrets. He knows things that a minister only confides to his night-cap."

"Damn!" aid the illustrious professor. "Who can he be?"

"That's the catch! At any rate, be certain that he's only a sham stationer. He's a man in hiding, a noted nihilist or a disgraced foreign diplomat, unless he's some defrocked papal nuncio. Anyway, I'm at a loss, and I confess to you that the mysterious fellow frightens me. In spite of the service he's rendered me, I'll be glad to see the back of him."

"That's simple enough. You're out of danger, well on your way to being fully healed—thanks to him, in fact. Give him a generous recompense and send him on his way."

"I'll give him a thousand-franc bill and…"

"Make it two thousand," put in the prince of surgery. "He hasn't stolen them, and wealth has its obligations. With the other two thousand that I'll demand for my visits, you'll be getting away lightly."

"That's all right; would you be kind enough to carry out the commission?"

"With pleasure. He took the two banknotes that the convalescent held out to him. As the stationer had just returned, he said: "Say goodbye to Monsieur de S***, and come downstairs with me; I need to talk to you."

Charles Balin and his patient made their reciprocal adieux, and he immediately rejoined Dr. P***, who was waiting for him in the antechamber.

"Here's two thousand francs that I've been instructed to give you," the latter said.

"Two thousand francs!" stammered the delighted stationer. "Oh, dear and illustrious master, you can't imagine the importance of the service you've just rendered me, and I thank you with all my heart—for that sum, I divine, it was you who requested, and perhaps demanded."

"Now, permit me to ask you a question," said the famous operator. "Who are you? Where have I seen you before? I know you, I'm absolutely sure of it, but I can only put the name of a dead man to the physiognomy of which you remind me."

"Master, you're never mistaken in making a diagnosis?"

"Sometimes I am," the practitioner assured him, laughing. "All the same, joking aside, who are you?"

"A simple Belleville stationer, and something of a bonesetter."

"That's not true," interjected Dr. P***, a trifle dryly. "You're in hiding, and it's showing little gratitude for the service that I have, indeed, rendered you to manifest such a great suspicion in my regard. Come on, confess!"

"If I were in hiding," the unknown replied, in a grave tone, "and I could tell someone my name, you would be the only person to whom I would wish to confide it."

"I understand what you mean to say," replied his illustrious interlocutor, softening. "Excuse my indiscretion; it's born of a sentiment of sympathy, and it's the same sympathy that leads me to give you some good advice before we separate. Since you have some reason for dissimulating your identity, and have chosen the profession of stationer for that, don't any longer display an instruction and an education out of all proportion to the mask you've put on. You've awakened Monsieur de S***'s suspicions—let that serve as a lesson for the future. Give me your hand—and I'm certain that it's not that of an unknown that I'm shaking."

They separated.

"That's *post mortem* sympathy," murmured Charles Balin. "That damned Dr. P*** has true flair—the scientist, a rare thing, is also an artist."

While the bone-setter had been serving as a nurse, his enemies had created a stir. The Faculty had taken the matter in hand; it was known that the healer had been an orderly; it was absolutely necessary that an example be made of him, else all the orderlies would set up as bone-setters. An urgent complaint had therefore been lodged and the Prefecture of Police had begun an investigation.

When the joyful stationer, brandishing his two thousand-franc bills, burst into the modest shop, he found Mariette in tears.

"Oh, my God! What's happened? What's the matter?" he demanded, fearfully. Mariette told him that an agent of the secret police, charged with carrying out an investigation, had come in search of information.

"Bah!" he declared. "I'm not saying that I don't care—I'd be lying—but that news is less disagreeable to me, since I have the money that will permit me to take a giant step forward in the realization of my projects."

"Yes but I haven't told you everything," Mariette replied, her tears not drying up.

"Explain—you're torturing me."

"The agent of the Sûreté charged with the investigation is Émile, the waiter from the café. He recognized me."

"That wretch again," he growled, carried away by a surge of anger. "Let him go to the devil!" He reflected for a few moments. "After all, the misfortune isn't as great as you imagine. They're going to know that Charles Balin and Jacques Liban are one and the same. Well, so what? What can they do to me? Give me a heavier sentence as a recidivist, that's all. The vagabond Liban has, however, paid society by three months in prison for the crime of having been robbed. It's true, though, that they're going to ask me once again who I am and try to hurt me by raking over the mud of your past..."

"My past?" said Mariette, surprised. "My past has nothing to do with the illegal practice of medicine."

"Ha! The court and the prosecution, to establish what they call moral proofs, won't see it like that. Whatever can cast a slur on an accused won't be passed over in silence."

"That's infamous! They'd better watch out. I'm not a woman to take things lying down."

"Don't worry; I'll try to ward off the blow, from which, as regards myself, I don't have very much to dread. There's no law to punish anonymity. If the law is intent on discovering my identity, let them try. I defy them to do it."

"What if we were to leave, quit the quarter, Paris, France?" Mariette proposed.

He hesitated momentarily.

"If I were alone, my dear," he ended up replying, "that would indeed by the surest and most logical means of avoiding further trouble. I could change my name, take another mask, and that would be the end of it. The bone-setter Balin, convicted in his absence, would escape their indiscreet curiosity. But we'd be obliged to sell the shop, which is your entire fortune, for a derisory price, and I don't have the right to put you in difficulties. The few savings I possess are absolutely necessary to the imminent realization of my projects. Besides which, that police agent won't lose sight of us again. I could easily give him the slip, but it wouldn't be the same for you."

He stopped, and set about reflecting profoundly.

So, whether he liked it or not, Mariette was, and perhaps always would be, an embarrassment, and obstacle!

The poor young woman sensed it. "What if you left on your own?" she said effortfully.

He reflected again. "No, Mariette, that would be to leave you the objective of that blackguard's persecutions; he'd set some trap for you and you'd be caught in it. You still need my help, and I won't abandon you for the moment. Later—I see, in fact, that I'll be forced to change my name and identity again—I'll probably ask you, as an indispensable sacrifice, to accept a temporary separation; but first I want to make certain of your material fate. Let's await events."

They spent a lamentable evening full of evil presentiments.

Chapter XXIV

Mariette, disfigured by the smallpox, perpetually absorbed by work, revived by the affection and advice of her friend, seemed to have forgotten the intoxicating triumphs of the stage, but Rose Gontran was not dead within her. Although she avoided going to spectacles, and had forcefully refused the piano that Charles Balin had offered to buy for her, she was still anxious about former rivals and friends, devoured all the theatrical papers and often fell into long periods of sadness that brought tears to her eyes.

"Rose, Rose," said her friend—at such times he affected to call her by her pseudonym—"poor Rose! You're missing the ovations of the public again, weeping for your vanished dream." She quickly wiped her eyes and tried to laugh.

"With a chestnut stove like this," she said, pointing at her face, "no café concert director would consent to give me three francs a night! Père Antoine wouldn't even want me for nothing."

"To be sure," he replied, "you could no longer, it seems to me, succeed as well in the genre that won you stunning success. It's necessary, to make the most of the filth that you sang, to have a great self-assurance, a certain charm, grace, beauty, and a crapulous boldness—in brief, an ensemble that it would be difficult for you to have today.

"If the concert bug has bitten you again, you'd risk vegetating in local cabarets or going to make the delight of subprefectures in barns hastily transformed into concert-halls. As for tackling the serious singing stages, that requires long and difficult studies, and there too, the physical plays an important role with regard to the directors and the audience. Perhaps, though, you could go into the real theater and play comedy or drama."

"You think so?" she said, falling into the trap.

"Ah—I see you're a liar," he observed immediately. "You can't get over your regrets; our humble existence weighs upon you."

With the most solemn oaths, Mariette swore that she would never set foot on the boards again—but not a day passed when he did not catch her in the process of asking her mirror whether it was necessary to renounce all hope.

Another blemish came to afflict her friend and cause him more real chagrin. Although Mariette's attitude from the viewpoint of fidelity had become irreproachable again, she adored and respected the only man to whom she owed a modicum of honor and joy, had even succeeded in restraining her indomitable love of liberty, and stuck to her daily task without proffering the slightest complaint, she still allowed herself to be drawn to drink, sometimes more than was reasonable. She gladly offered a little glass to the neighbor who came to gossip in her shop, and always had a bottle of rum or cognac hidden behind her bundles of old newspapers.

Charles Balin perceived the artificial excitement that delivered Mariette to unaccustomed fits of gaiety, anger or loquacity, but, knowing full well that habits of that kind are difficult to uproot, full of indulgence, rightly supposing that she was seeking to forget her disillusionments in drunkenness, he limited himself to amicable remonstrations to which his mistress could not take exception. In any case, ashamed and deploying an uncommon energy, she was genuinely trying to efface that last vestige of her debauchery.

Every time she had made a reference to the shameful past, he had told her to be quiet; now the reappearance of the baneful waiter, transformed into an agent of the Sûreté, had returned the conversation to the miry epoch in which they had met. That fop, scarred by Mariette, had suffered cruelly in his vanity; he would surely try to avenge himself. Already, when she was at the concert, he had planned a conspiracy that had turned against him; the whistlers had been abused by the audience.

What would he contrive now that he was in a position to do them harm and a favorable opportunity had unexpectedly presented itself to him? That question always left them sad and perplexed.

He knew approximately what he was facing: the story of the Café Mansard would be brought up again in court, his unconsciousness on a bench on the boulevard might be related; the matter of simulation would be held against him; but was not she, who had nothing to do with the case, also about to be covered in mud, the whole dung-heap raked over?

The methods of the law, he repeated to himself, to habituate himself to those execrable maneuvers of chicanery, were not always imprinted with great delicacy. The public prosecutor and the advocate of the physicians' syndicate would not let the slightest detail escape that might sully him and present him to the judges as an individual denuded of all moral sensibility. Mariette was snarling in a disquieting fashion.

To put an end to the affair of the Café Mansard, which his enemies would not fail to exploit, he went to that establishment, perceived the manager on the threshold and told him that he had come to settle a bill. The man, unused to events of that sort—he very rarely gave credit—considered him in surprise, without recognizing him.

He took a louis out of his pocket. "Take the seventeen francs that I consumed in your establishment on the fifth of May 18**, and for which you had me arrested."

Increasingly amazed, the manager stammered obsequious apologies. "Come in, Monsieur, please. I'm not the owner and I don't have the liberty to act as I please; otherwise, believe me, I wouldn't have had recourse to that extremity. Seventeen and three equals twenty; here, Monsieur, are the three francs, and come again."

"You're forgetting the receipt."

"That's true. Here you are."

He hastened to transmit the document to his advocate.

The investigation was singularly protracted; the examining magistrate summoned him numerous times. His entire past since the fifth of May 18** had been gradually reconstituted; they had even found the traces of his passage through the copyist's studio, and the latter had not failed to give his liaison with his former employee Raphael a less than honorable significance. He was frightened in spite of himself by the obstinacy with which they were trying to tear the veil that envelope him. Undoubtedly they thought they were on some important trail.

As he had the first time, he remained stubbornly mute; he could only be convicted of one misdemeanor: the legal practice of medicine. On that subject, he would have been able to invoke the testimony of Dr. P***, and have himself defended by the invalids he had cured, but he did not want, for reasons of scrupulousness, to have recourse to those means. He had dictated the arguments of his defense to his advocate himself.

Medicine is not only a science, but also, and perhaps primarily, an art. Now, artistry is a gift that diplomas do not deliver. If there are, therefore, outside official science, individuals endowed with the prescience that constitutes a healer, the society that benefits from their services has no right to condemn them, especially when their intervention is signaled by their success.

That the law, rightly excusing the errors of qualified physicians, should be pitiless toward those who, without any other title, render themselves guilty of negligence or awkwardness, all well and good! But for that law to punish a man who has nothing to his account but indisputable cures—his delicate situation having obliged him to refuse categorically to treat incurable maladies—is inhumane and tyrannical; it is to give an exorbitant and unjust value to a piece of parchment, which, all too often, alas, does not confer knowledge on its possessor. Furthermore, the accused could not be convicted of having demanded real fees; he had always left his clients free in their actions. His prescriptions, even in the opinion of the pharmacists, had been drawn up in a therapeutically impeccable fashion.

As for the bone-setter's incognito, he would make use of a perfectly rational hypothesis. Assume, the defender would say to the jurors, that a man has been assumed to be dead, that his wife has remarried, that his children have shared his patrimony; suppose that that voluntary exile, devoured by spleen and gnawed by homesickness, returns to the city of his birth, but does not want to sow trouble and annoyance among his relatives by an official return based on an admission of his identity. Assume that the unknown man had been a skillful qualified physician with multiple diplomas, and ask yourselves whether the accused, whose skill, cures and operations had surprised everyone, might not be that man.

Such were the broad lines of his defense.

Fearful that Mariette might be dragged into the case, he judged it appropriate to write to the public prosecutor and his adversaries' advocate.

The agent of the Sûreté changed with the investigation, he told them, had a personal grudge against them. Mariette Gantron, it is true, had an unfortunate past, but she had tried to rise above it by all possible means; she was none other than the charming Rose Gontran adored by the public and distanced from the theater by a cruel malady; she now lived with him maritally in the most correct fashion; she had nothing to do with the misdemeanor for which the bone-setter was reproached; it would be profoundly inhumane to recall corruption for which society bore a large part of the responsibility; he appealed to their indulgence, to the broadness of their ideas. Let them be pitiless toward him, if they judged it appropriate, but at least let them have pity on her.

The day of judgment, so long awaited, finally arrived. Mistrusting the irascible nervousness of his mistress, he ordered her categorically to stay at home, certain that at the slightest offensive word she was capable of resorting to insults.

In spite of the eloquence of his defender, and the relatively anodyne speech of the public prosecutor, the tribunal, based on a prior conviction , the proven fact of illegal practice and on the incognito that the accused obstinately maintained, sentenced the bone-setter Balin to three months in prison and a hundred franc fine,

That denouement was relatively satisfactory to him; there had been mention of a registered prostitute whose help had saved his life, but Mariette's name had not been pronounced. The duration of the reclusion was, it is true, longer than he had expected, but the steps taken by his advocate, combined with the protection that Dr. P*** did not refuse him, obtained him permission to devote himself to his cherished studies.

He had been put under immediate arrest; one of the Gardes de Paris who escorted him scratched his head with embarrassment had seemed to want to ask him something; he smiled at him to put him at his ease.

"I don't know what's wrong with me," the representative of the public force ended up admitting to him, overcoming his timidity and showing him his ribs. "For a long time I've had a pain that sometimes stops me sleeping; the horse remedies that the major gives me are no more use than a plaster on a wooden leg."

He could not help laughing. "So you want to submit me to a further conviction, wretch?"

The worthy soldier was nonplussed.

"Come on," he said, "let's go into a corner. What do you feel?"

He gave him a consultation, and took out a pocket note-book to write him a prescription.

Chapter XXV

Those three months at Saint-Pélagie, consecrated to the most regular and most assiduous work, passed with a rapidity that surprised him. Isolated and temporarily delivered from all care, receiving Mariette's visit every week, he scarcely thought about cursing his judges. Fundamentally, the law was playing its role, safeguarding the legal exercise of a difficult, delicate and sacred profession; it guaranteed the worthy public against the brazen and dangerous charlatanism of unscrupulous adventurers. Was it not sufficiently exploited by official charlatans? It had just struck him harshly, but what was he? An exception of which blind justice could not take account because his identity was hidden under a cloak of mystery. To what did he owe his worth and his success as a bone-setter? To real medical studies once sanctioned by the demanded qualifications. The law is only a means, it can only be just in the generality and *en bloc*. Why had he put himself outside the law, outside society? No more than the orderly, the bone-setter could not remain unpunished.

Now he was about to be able to re-enter into legality; he would go to Liège or Pisa, acquire a diploma there, return to Paris and pas his examinations. For that, a civil estate, documents—*papers*, as the gendarmes put it—would be absolutely necessary; he would find them in London. He had assured himself once that shady agencies in that city delivered veritable civil estates in return for a few. He would have recourse to that expedient, in general dishonorable, but legitimate and indispensable in this particular case.

It was necessary at all costs that Jacques Liban and Charles Balin disappear. Such individuals, possessors of a criminal record, watched by the police, stained by a wretched past, would have a very slender authority to combat the doctrines of the famous Dr. Albin. It was, moreover, probable that if the bone-setter Balin dared to present himself to the Faculty in order to take his examination there, he would not be welcomed with the greatest indulgence. It would be very dangerous to procure identity papers in the name of Charles Balin; he might be charged with forgery of official documents, and then it would be forced labor. He therefore required a new name for a new identity. Once in London and advised to the demands of the agency, he would make a decision.

So, under another mask, which he would strive to render as dissimilar as possible to the preceding ones, he would return to Paris and would not be recognized.

A mortal chagrin and a profound distress invaded him. It would be necessary, for that, to leave Mariette! Would she consent to it? Could she? It was, however, certain that if he stayed with Mariette, it would not be long before he was recognized, suspected, and paralyzed in all his enterprises. The agent dogging their heels would not lose sight of her again.

Mariette was, therefore, a dangerous obstacle, and he had to choose between two alternatives: either to stay with her and try to realize his projects in deplorable conditions; or to leave her temporarily, reappear after a further metamorphosis and put to work all the advantages that absolute liberty, a stainless identity and official titles would procure him.

Did he have any right to hesitate? Was Mariette not incidental to his existence? Ought he to forget his noble goal any longer?

Evidently, no, yes, and no.

He would therefore demonstrate to his mistress the absolute necessity of that temporary separation; but before leaving her, before even informing her of that cruel resolution, he would devote a few more months to her existence.

She was still, he felt sure, fundamentally haunted by regret for her past successes. He had surprised her reading the scripts of fashionable plays and attempting to declaim; it was in giving her that new position in conformity with her secret desires that he would console her and enable her to accept an inevitable departure.

The ideas that he had already resifted many times received a definitive sanction during his sojourn in prison.

The first person he saw on emerging from Saint-Pélagie was Mariette, who was waiting for him in a fiacre, impatient and overexcited. She fell into his arms and kissed him with a violence and an agitation that surprised him.

"How you're trembling!" he observed.

"It's nothing—a little anger, that's all."

"Caused by what—or whom?"

"That agent of the Sûreté, whom I perceived again as I came here. During your absence he's never ceased to prowl around the shop and spy on my every move. I wonder what he's trying to do?"

"Doubtless push you to extremes, to exasperate you, to profit from some insult to cause trouble for you."

"It's possible, unless he wants to assure himself personally that I'm no longer on the game."

"It's scarcely probable. He wouldn't dare to indulge in such maneuvers. I'm no longer a vagabond and you're not the Bohemian of old. We're legitimate, Mariette, and you have no idea of the social value of that word. Legitimacy is a file on which the reptilian individual would be advised not to damage his teeth."

"He's capable of anything," said Mariette, whose eyes filled with tears. "Hasn't he spread it around the quarter that I've had a registration number?"

"The cowardly wretch."

"He'd better not show himself again now that you're back," she snarled, menacingly.

"What would you do? You're being silly—that would be to fall into his trap." He seized the opportunity. "Look, we ought to sell the stationer's, if we can get a reasonable price, and shake him off our track."

"Perhaps you're right, but what will I do then?"

"We'll think about it; there's no urgency."

They hastened back to the shop. Several invalids notified of his release were waiting to consult him, which annoyed him; he did not want to start again. He would care for them later, since he would have the right."

"Let's close the shop for today," he said, toward evening. "I need some air; we'll go for a walk and celebrate."

"With pleasure," said Mariette. "That's the first time I've ever heard you say those words."

He had not said them without intention.

They confided the sale of newspapers to an obliging neighbor and went down the Faubourg du Temple. It was time for the return from work; like a rising tide, floods of human heads were emerging in the distance with vague undulations. Workers curbed under the burden of tool-boxes, their hands and faces blackened by manual labor of factory smoke, and women laden with needlework that they were delivering or taking away, were climbing the slope with sad smiles on their faces: the smiles of tasks accomplished; the resigned smiles of wage-earners cowed by poverty. Modest clerks and sprightly shop-girls marched at a faster pace. Housewives, purses in hand, in the summary clothing of women going to market, were besieging handcarts loaded with no-longer-fresh victuals or allowing themselves to be convinced by the seductive offers of rubicund apprentice butchers who hailed them as they passed. A reek of vitriolated absinthe emerged from all the drinking dens. At the street-corners, and the entrances to passages, compact groups surrounded ambulant artistes and young seamstresses, their songs in their hands, awkwardly trying to follow the singer's voice.

Mariette stopped in front of a rotisserie and was admiring the chaplet of gilded birds rotating over the blazing wood fire. He looked from side to side at wrinkled brows, shining gazes, lips retaining saliva. The anguish and hunger of old return to mind. He had an imperceptible surge of ill-humor.

"Better to eat them than look at them," he said. "You're wasting precious time; let's go to a restaurant so we can come out early, if the desire takes us to go somewhere."

The delivered themselves to the glorious sin of gluttony, drank select wines and branded liqueurs, and then, without a precise goal, followed the crowd that was taking advantage of the last five days.

It was the first time, for a long time, that they had walked along the grand boulevards together in the evening. Mariette's attire was simple but in perfect taste; nothing about her evoked the brazen streetwalker or the excessively elegant Rose Gontran of the Folies Nouvelles, whose city costumes were a little too similar to those of the stage. The astonishing facility she had for adapting to the environment in which circumstances placed her had made her a petty bourgeois Parisienne in the process of celebrating some family anniversary. She was able to go past the corner of the Rue du Faubourg-Montmartre with impunity, with no fear of being recognized.

Old Lucie, always solid at her post, was already on duty. Mariette shuddered on seeing her, and a tear escaped her eye.

"Poor woman," she sighed. "Poor woman! That's how I was, not three years ago. Let's go, quickly, I beg you."

They increased their pace and remained silent for a few moments. The nervous movements that Mariette's arms were making indicated a salutary terror of the past. She was painting, seemingly fleeing some imaginary danger.

"Why are you running like that?" he asked. "There's no hurry."

"This sidewalk would burn my feet," she replied, in a muffled and resolute voice that he was not hearing for the first time, "if it ever tried to take me back!"

He hastened to interrupt her. "Are you crazy to think of such impossibilities? Isn't there already a profound abyss between the present and the past? Haven't you redeemed your shame, first by talent and then by work?"

"Talent," murmured Mariette, sadly. "A paltry talent, which couldn't resist a few marks on the face. As for work," she added, in a low voice "who knows what the future has in store for us?"

"What do you mean?"

"Will I have the strength to work, if you're no longer there?"

"I've got an idea!" he exclaimed, to change the subject. "Today's a feast day: Holy Deliverance. It's necessary to talk like prisoners, because I'm out of prison. What if we were to go to the theater?"

The impressionable Mariette immediately cheered up.

"I'd never have dared to ask you," she confessed, "but that would give me the greatest pleasure." She added almost immediately: "Unless it would give me the greatest chagrin. Never mind—let's go. Perhaps it will stop me getting gloomy."

They deliberated for a moment in order to consult their taste. *La Périchole* was advertised on the poster for the Variétés. She knew the score, had read the eulogistic appreciations of the singer who was playing the title role; it was there that she wanted to go.

They went in. Poor Rose Gontran, happy at first and then gripped by an extraordinary excitement, murmured in her lover's ear that, without boasting, she guaranteed that she could sing as well and better than that, and soon fell into a profound melancholy.

The hubbub of the entr'acte led to a diversion. They had gone to the lobby; a theater gossip columnist recognized the ex-star of the Folies Nouvelles and approached her.

"Mademoiselle Rose Gontran! What a pleasant surprise!"

"What?" she replied, radiantly. "I'm still recognizable?"

"I wouldn't have recognized you otherwise," the journalist replied, laughing. "Come on, when's the comeback?"

"Alas, Monsieur, just look at me." She lifted her veil with a swift gesture. "How do you think I'd dare to set foot on stage with this pock-marked face?"

"You're exaggerating, Mademoiselle. I don't think you've changed as much as all that. Besides which, beauty is only indispensable to mediocre artistes; with the talent you have, you could get by, if necessary."

"Thank you for you gallant words," Rose stammered, blushing with pleasure, "but I take them at their worth—which is to say, for the delicate politeness of a charming man."

They returned to their seats. The pensive Mariette was only listening to the play with a distracted ear.

"Fundamentally, you were wrong to bring me here," she sighed as they left. "It's revived my dolors and caused my regrets to be reborn. When one's intoxicated by this milieu, when you've seen all gazes devouring you and all hands applauding you, it's hard to think that it's finished, all over."

"Who knows, Mariette?"

"What do you mean? Am I not disfigured? Do you think I took the flattering words of that well-brought up man for sincerity?"

"The journalist isn't so far from the truth as you think."

Surprised, she stopped and stared at him. "Are you speaking seriously or trying to drive me mad? Shut up. I'm ugly—fearfully ugly."

"Much less than I feared," he replied, without appearing to perceive her emotion. "Time has already greatly attenuated the ravages of the accursed malady; your mirror is there to tell you that; the lines of your face have regained almost all their purity. With the distance of the stage, intelligently made up, you could produce an excellent effect, and if, as I've explained before, you can no longer operate in the same genre, nevertheless..."

She closed his mouth with her hands, and then started kissing him madly, as if to belie what his lips were saying.

"Naughty," she said. "Don't blow on a fire that ought to go out, don't release hopes that I've locked away irrevocably in the depths of my heart."

The weather was good; they went home on foot. At the corner of the Rue de la Lune she had a hunger for a galette that she hastened to satisfy. She started devouring it first with her beautiful teeth, with a child-like joy; then she suddenly became somber and stopped eating, as if she hated the past, even in her most innocent memories.

"Poor girl!" she sighed, taking his arm again.

"Who are talking about?"

"The unfortunate who once, in this same place, soothed her hunger with two or three sous' worth of galette."

"Why always evoke the past, Mariette? Let's expel it from our minds, let's think about the future."

But the past, that evening, was obstinate in surging forth. Near the Château d'Eau, a monumental woman whose stride had the imposing gait of a Dutch cutter with the wind in its sails, went past them going in the opposite direction. A victim of the law of contrasts, the minuscule Père Lampe was navigating in Nini Nichon's wake.

He had once frequented too many intern's wards to resist the desire to commit a mischief.

"Above all, Messieurs," he shouted, "I recommend silence."

The dwarf, furious at being recognized, veered away and disappeared into the shadows, while the fat whore, sensing that she was no longer being followed, slowed her pace and then stopped, to scrutinize the boulevard in all directions.

"The stolen money has scarcely profited her," remarked Mariette, with an indifference that augured well.

They resumed walking, both plunged in their reflections. The encounter with Père Lampe had reminded him of Raphael. What had become of him?

"What are you thinking about?" Mariette ended up asking, troubled by the long silence.

"Things already distant and heart-rending, miseries and corruptions that have explained to me why, on a given day, the paving stones rise up of their own accord into barricades, and why energetic unknowns struggle ferociously until the last breath, solely for the pleasure of killing."

Chapter XXVI

The seed that he had sown in such favorable ground did not take long to germinate and grow. Mariette, hooked by the hope of a new debut, immediately wanted to return to study.

They sold the stationer's shop in Belleville and rented a small apartment in the Rue Lepic. They had about twelve thousand francs in hand, and it was agreed that that sum would remain intact. If circumstances obliged them to separate temporarily, they would each take half.

"Why are you talking about circumstances that might separate us?" Mariette had interrogated him, anxiously.

"Because I have a mission to fulfill," he replied, "and it will be necessary for me to reclaim my liberty when the time comes."

Mariette, nonplussed, became somber and taciturn.

"Oh, our separation won't be definitive," he hastened to affirm, "We'll surely find one another later, and we can then, if you still love me—for you'll still be young and I'm marching rapidly toward decrepitude—resume our communal life without cares and without remorse. But let's not talk about that, since the time hasn't come."

On the contrary, Mariette, as if to deflect him from his mysterious and incomprehensible projects, caused the dream of a happy existence to shine: she would make her debut in the theater, earn tidy sums. She knew, of course, that she would not have the same successes as before, but she would be living the life of which she dreamed, and he would devote himself to his favorite research; nothing would any longer come to trouble their happiness. She looked up at him then. He contented himself with shaking his head.

"Let's begin by working relentlessly. You'll make your debut, and then we'll see." He thus prepared her, little by little, to accept without too much surprise and chagrin the separation that he judged to be necessarily imminent.

At that moment he was carrying out research on the fermentation of wine on behalf of a notable merchant. Mariette was taking a course in declamation and spent the rest of the day learning roles. In the evenings, he made her rehearse, lavishing her with advice and accompanying her on the piano. He would have preferred that his mistress set her sights on an entirely serious genre; he found powerful dramatic qualities in her; in his opinion, she would have succeeded in passionate roles. But Mariette, wanting to utilize her voice, had a weakness for operetta; perhaps she would rediscover her formed success there? She had not graduated from the Conservatoire, had not passed through any of the usual channels, how could she make the most of her dramatic qualities? What theater would consent to put her forward? It was necessary to begin by accepting minor parts, and then...whereas the past successes of Rose Gontran might serve as a trampoline for a neighboring genre.

If he had had the design of associating his entire life with Mariette's, he would have imposed his will on her, but since he had to leave her, he did not think that he had the right to oppose her desire.

His chemical work was reasonably well-paid; he was putting some money aside and was relatively happy, when an accident, banal for anyone else, took on a menacing gravity for him.

The scientific and technical journals were making a great fuss about the new explosives that the European powers, armed to the teeth, were putting to trial. That gave him the idea of studying certain combinations of nitric acid with organic compounds, and he was able to fabricate a powder whose power surpassed that of all the detonating mixtures.

The wine merchant, already glimpsing the gleam of millions, became enthused with the idea and furnished him with the means to develop it.

The laboratory experiments having been satisfactory, it only remained to carry out a conclusive trial. They close a large garden in the suburb where the merchant had his warehouse, and only employed a small quantity of the substance. Even so, the explosion was so conclusive that all the windows in the neighborhood were shattered. There was talk of a bomb, successive attacks in London having awakened the suspicion of the police.

The prefecture made a minute investigation, which established the real cause of the accident. The delinquent manufacturer got away with a large fine and the payment of serious damages. His notoriety as a merchant put him above all suspicion—but his employee had all the difficulty in the world is extracting himself from the claws of the law, and the businessman, hearing about his two prior convictions, did not want to have any more to do with him.

That event having caused him to lose his job and put the former waiter on their tracks, they thought about changing domicile again. Mariette had made great progress; her dialogue was vivacious, compelling and astonishingly natural, and she knew a dozen fashionable scores; she could now grasp the first favorable moment to make her debut. The recent threats of arrest pushed him to encourage his mistress' impatience. Rose Gontran—she had resumed the name known to and loved by the public—made a tour of all the generic theaters.

In the most outwardly amiable fashion, the directors sent her away one after another; although the pretexts were polite and enlivened by the warmest eulogies, the refusals were nevertheless categorical.

Poor Rose came back in the evening desperate and dejected, putting her disappointments down to her ugliness. He did his best to console her. Was it not necessary to expect such hitches? When she had proved her talent, all the obstacles would disappear; it would no longer be her who was petitioning, it was the directors who would come to put themselves at her feet.

"How am I going to prove to them that I have talent?" exclaimed the poor young woman. "They don't even want to give me an audition!"

For his part, luck was not showing itself any more clement; all his attempts failed miserably. Hidden machinations and detestable allegations, whose source it was easy to divine, had him rejected everywhere. He had to dip into the money put in reserve.

In the meantime, a new and violent blow struck him in a sensitive place. The *Revue des Sciences* published a translation of an article signed by a young German scientist, Ludwig Keller, which also attacked Dr. Albin's theories and announced in veiled terms that he would soon be able to publish decisive experiments.

Thus, while he was wasting time preparing operetta debuts, someone else—a foreigner—was about to rob him of his future glory, and he had in hand the money that would permit him to act...

He spent several days in a state of overexcitement that skirted madness.

"My God!" said the frightened Rose, repeatedly. "What's wrong with you?"

"I need to leave," he murmured. "A great misfortune, the greatest one that could befall me, is threatening me, and it's my fault because..."

"Because it's mine, perhaps," she replied, weeping.

He consoled her rapidly, but in a fashion nevertheless to make her comprehend that she was, indeed, a real obstacle.

"No, Rose, darling, but it's absolutely necessary that you make your debut, that you can earn your living, that you can do without my help, and that I'm free."

"Debut!" cried the actress, in despair. "You know full well that it's my most ardent desire, but no one wants me. What can I do? Great God, what can I do?"

A few days later, Rose Gontran, overexcited in her turn, seemed completely changed. An influential journalist that she had met in the offices of a theater had taken an interest in her and had formally promised to arrange a debut for her in the imminent future. She never ceased chattering, building castles in Spain. He was a serious young man, a talented playwright, he was going to introduce her to several directors; if necessary, he would impose himself upon them. Her slightest desires would be taken into account. Her new friend had heard her, judged her and had seemed enthusiastic.

He feared that he understood, and frowned, but she did not notice, or did not want to notice anything.

Seen she was absent for long periods, came back well after nightfall on various pretexts, excited by drink and troubled by remorse. He no longer had any doubt that Rose Gontran, in order to arrive more rapidly at her goal, was deceiving him.

After all, it was an excellent opportunity, an opportune denouement. He resolved to bring the situation to a head. He did not go to bed that night and waited up fir her until three o'clock in the morning.

Anticipating the storm and following her habit when she wanted to avoid any explanation, she threw himself into his arms when she came in. She finally had an opportunity to make her debut!

"Where?" he asked, coldly.

"At the Théâtre de la Gaîté-Belleville." He pulled a face. "Oh, I know that it isn't famous," she hastened to add, "but what do you expect? My protector hasn't been able to find anything else for the moment. It's a means to have me judged. Didn't I make my debut at Père Antoine's when you got me into the concerts?"

"The circumstances aren't the same. In that epoch, you hadn't yet been on stage; you didn't have a reputation to sustain; you made your debut before my eyes; I was sure of the audience; I accompanied you, and your success was absolutely dependent on you. Here you're going to be hindered by ridiculous nonentities, comrades devoid of talent, an insufficient setting, an improvised orchestra, an audience prejudiced by your previous successes or ill-disposed to your attempt, and many other things."

"My God! What can I do? I've accepted, I've given my word."

"Debut, then, but instruct your new lover to make sure that you can show yourself in favorable conditions."

There was a long and painful moment of silence.

"My lover," she finally stammered, in a low voice, bowing her head. "My only, my true lover, is you."

"I have been, Rose, and always will be, but the time for our temporary separation has come. I'll leave France tomorrow."

She looked at him with an imploring expression, as if, knowing that she had been divined, she were humbly begging his pardon. He read her thoughts.

"I have nothing to forgive you for, my dear. On the contrary; it's me who's demanding your indulgence. The implacable logic of things has once again created the incidents that have happened to us. If I had not been resolved for a long time to leave you, for pitiless reasons, I wouldn't have pushed you into the path you're taking. I'm therefore the only one responsible for your actions; I know the reasons for which you've committed them, and I have no right to reproach you for them."

She threw herself into his arms, weeping.

He told her that his resolution was irrevocable, that he had already put off his duty for too long, that he did not feel any resentment toward her, that they would meet again in time, and that then, without reticence, they could swear an eternal fidelity to one another. Their liaison was a mutual obstacle that it was necessary to break through; he was even glad to know that, when he was gone, she would not be without support. He had learned from hearsay that her protector was a man of intelligence and heart; without egotism, he hoped that their liaison would be serious.

He spent the night giving her advice, begging her not to have the slightest acquaintance, under any pretext, with her old milieu. He implored her not to allow herself to be discouraged by the difficulty of her first forays, to work courageously, always to aim at higher goals.

He recommended her, above all, to avoid the slightest intemperance.

Rose never ceased to weep, trailing at his knees, swearing to him that she still lived him, that she was ready to give up everything to go with him. He was inexorable.

"Since I have to leave," he declared, "since it's necessary that I leave and that an action, although already pardoned, gives me the strength to do it, it's today that I shall leave."

He took six thousand francs, as agreed, gave her the other six thousand, promised her one last time that he would see her again, tore himself from her arms and fled in haste.

This time, it was Rose who leaned all her anguish on the banister. It was him who did not look up. It was him who did not come back.

Rose Gontran remained plunged in her dolorous stupor for a long time.

"Gone! Gone!" she murmured, her heart torn. "He doesn't want to understand, then. He doesn't want to know that since the moment that I met him, if my body has failed—what does a little more or less soiling signify to Mariette?—my soul and my heart have never ceased for a single instant to belong to him."

Then she clutched stubbornly at one last hope. He wanted to teach her a lesson; he knew that she had deceived him, he wanted to punish her—but he was good; he would come back; he was going to come back.

She waited for several days without going out, shivering at every sound of footsteps, waking up with a start in the middle of the night. The absentee still did not come back.

Gradually, her despair changed face; anger invaded her, muted at first and then explosive. She was very stupid, after all, to take the thing so much to heart! He had wanted to leave her; any pretext would do. A motive that she hated profoundly without knowing what it was, tore him away from her; she was not loved as she loved. Why, then, abandon herself to her chagrin?

She went out, returned to her new lover, ran around all the brasseries and cabarets in Montmartre, got abominably drunk and did not go home for several days.

Then regrets came to assail her again, she returned in haste to the communal abode, as if she were going to find him there.

"No letters, no visitors," the concierge told her. "Has Monsieur gone traveling, then?

"Yes," she replied, confused. "He might not be back for some time."

The apartment was in the name of Charles Balin. She paid a quarter's rent in advance, took her money and effects, ordered a fiacre and confided the keys to the concierge.

"Give them to Monsieur Balin when he comes back," she instructed.

"You're going too, Madame? But you'll come back."

"It's only the dead who don't come back," she murmured.

She gave the coachman the address of her protector and fled, swallowing her tears.

A few weeks later, on the eve of her debut as an operetta performer, Rose Gontran had returned to work ardently.

The intelligent and handsome young man, attracted to her by a keen sympathy, and whom she had abandoned, partly on impulse but mostly by calculation, made her a thousand protestations of love. She looked at him, astonished, smiling and sad. She surrendered herself mechanically to the slightest of his desires, strove to please him, even tried to love him, but it was the other, always the other, the mysterious individual she had helped, the first man that had not treated her as a whore, who still took up all the room in her heart.

The theatrical papers had already announced that Rose Gontran, the much-applauded star of the Folies Nouvelles, was about to return to the generic stage. Perhaps her friend had not put enough discretion into the publicity that his situation as a critic and author permitted him to make. Perhaps the newspapers made a little too much of the exceptional talent that the actress was about to demonstrate and the admiring astonishment that the public was about to experience. At any rate, Rose Gontran's debut was considered as a Parisian event, and the public, blasé about great premières, although grumbling, deigned to climb the hill.

In memory of the evening when her lover had taken her to the Variétés, the actress had chosen the role of La Périchole.

That evening, the Théatre de la Gaité-Belleville presented an unexpected aspect. Men in suits, former admirers of Rose Gontran of the Folies Nouvelles, journalists, critics, gossip columnists, socialites on the lookout for novelties, theater directors come to judge the debutant, and former comrades of the concert hall who did not consider that ascension toward a genre in vogue without jealousy, had taken possession of all the best sets and chased the small local theater's regulars from the boxes and the stalls. The hall was literally packed with spectators; the worthy public, relegated to the highest galleries, betrayed their ill humor by demanding with deafening cries and obstinate foot-stamping the raising of the curtain, which was late.

In the wings, Rose Gontran, emotional and immeasurably nervous, was running around madly, jostling belated employees and the bit-part players that it was necessary to drag away from the seductions of the bar, criticizing at the last moment the poverty of the costumes and the dilapidation of the set. Furthermore, in order to hide the traces of the smallpox, she was outrageously made up. Her first appearance on the stage cast a chill that augured badly. The gentlemen in suits, disappointed, interrogated one another with their eyes, with characteristic grimaces, the little comrades of old stifled laughter and whispered among themselves. The bulk of the audience remained indifference.

The first couplets were sung with vigor; she received a little timid applause; the entire first act passed without any notable incident.

She had vaguely perceived that several individuals among the spectators had cards suspended from their button-holes or affecting to keep them in view in their hands, but she had not attached any importance to the observation.

"I hope you placed the advertisement," the actor playing the Viceroy said to her during the entr'acte.

"What advertisement are you talking about?" she asked, astonished.

"Well, the cards that are being distributed gratuitously at the door; all the spectators have a card," he added, with a coarse laugh. She snatched the piece of cardboard that he held out to her from his hand. It was, in form and color, exactly similar to her old prostitute's registration card. On one side she read in large letters: *Mariette Gantron*, and in parentheses, *Rose Gontran*; on the other was the program of the play.

The blow struck home! A mortal anguish gripped her throat; a stifled cry escaped her, and she fainted. People gathered around her. She gradually recovered consciousness, collected her ideas, and wanted to leave. The director, who put the indisposition to the account of emotion, begged her not to do anything, assuring her that everything would go well. Inertly, she allowed herself to be persuaded, but only consented that the manager would announce to the audience that she had fainted and ask for its indulgence.

When her lover wanted to comfort her in his turn, suddenly gripped by an inexplicable surge of anger, thinking that he might perhaps have anticipated the blow or warded it off, she ordered him dryly to leave her alone.

The gallery, impatient with the length of the delay, recommenced its infernal racket. The curtain finally went up, and she made a superhuman effort. She knew now where the odious conspiracy originated. Émile, the former waiter, surrounded by shady accomplices, applauded madly without rhyme or reason.

"Shh! Down with the claque!" shouted the regulars, furiously.

The performance was interrupted in that fashion continually, and the disconcerted actors were obliged to await the reestablishment of silence before resuming the dialogue.

Soon, laughter and cries of every sort accentuated the disorder; poor Périchole, at her wit's end, lost her head and her memory, stopped dead. The prompter raised his voice clumsily; the curious heads of carpenters and scene-shifters emerged from the wings. The actors on stage could scarcely dissimulate their laughter, and the cabal profited from the opportunity to go full tilt.

Then the actress, her eyes haggard and her lips trembling, showed her fist to her implacable enemy, shouted: "Coward!" with all the force of her anger and her voice. The public, thinking that it had been insulted, demanded apologies.

"She's drunk!" cried some.

"It's her habit!" replied others.

"To the carnival!"

"Apologies!"

"We want our money back!"

The fashionable people smiled; the journalists and directors watched the debacle, almost indifferently; the little friends gave free rein to their laughter. Rose Gontran, half mad, leaned against an upright on the stage, breathlessly.

Suddenly, she summoned up all her strength, came resolutely to the front of the stage and made a sign that she wanted to speak. A silence full of curiosity immediately fell in the hall.

"My insult," she roared, "was not addressed to the public, whom I have always respected, and whom I respect more than ever, but to the agent of the secret police who has mounted an infamous conspiracy against me." She indicated Émile with a gesture.

All gazes turned in that direction; the agent, of course, was indistinguishable from everyone else, and no one could tell whom she intended to indicate. Cries of "Down with the cop!" and "Throw the nark out!" burst out on all sides.

If Rose had had a modicum of self-composure; if the slightest authorized advice had come to support her; if anyone, in fact, had even been able to identify the author of the disorder, the game might have turned around and the fall changed into a triumph; but Rose Gontran was alone; her lover, discouraged by the first rebuff and ashamed of the defeat, was hiding in the depths of the dressing-rooms or had perhaps already left; the dreamer who loved her had been unable to understand her and had removed himself from the action.

She left the stage and refused to go back on.

"I'll be obliged to return the money," begged the director again, who had followed her to her dressing-room. "You've caused me considerable damage; at least go on to the end; I've gone to considerable expense."

"How much have you spent?" she demanded, curtly.

"About two thousand."

"Here it is," she said, extracting two bills from her hand-bag. "Return the money; I'm going."

She undressed in haste, put on her ordinary clothes and left without saying another word. In the hall, the racket was at its height; people mistaken for policemen had been challenged and jostled; there was fighting.

It had begun to rain. She went down the Rue du Faubourg du Temple on foot, almost running, without knowing exactly where she was going. A fiacre, coming up behind her at the gallop, nearly crushed her; she threw herself instinctively to one side, and the movement dislodged her poorly-pinned hat. She did not even think of picking it up.

In the Place du Château-d'Eau she sat down, in spite of the bad weather, on the terrace of a café, and demanded several glasses of brandy, which she drank one after another. She paid the bill and resumed her course.

The air was damp, the sky heavy and low; drizzle was falling gently, the noise of fiacres and the din of the last omnibuses was muffled by the soft ground. Under the street-lights, surrounded by luminous haloes, the passers-by appeared as if behind a yellow net-curtain. Mariette, her hair almost undone, her make-up soaking, her shirts splashed with mud, looking like a drunken refugee from a brothel, marched straight ahead, her eyes haggard.

A burly lout who, coming out of a pimps' café in quest of good fortune, had seen her stop and drink the brandy, barred her passage with his arm, as if in jest, then offered her his arm and made gallant propositions.

She looked at him, bewildered, her arms dangling, her mouth open.

Fearing that he had not been understood, the man reiterated his suggestion, entering into precise details, alerted her to his habits and demands, and concluded by offering her money.

"Ah! Yes, yes, I know what you mean," she murmured. "It's all the same to me. As you wish; it's necessary."

"Come on then," said the man. "We'll get a hotel room."

She followed him momentarily; then, suddenly changing her mind, as if she were emerging from a frightful dream, she uttered a cry of anguish and fled at top speed.

The stupefied lecher watched her disappear.

Now, she knew where she was.

She took the Rue Turbigo, followed the Boulevard Sebastopol, traversed the Place du Châtelet, found herself on the bridge, climbed the parapet with a rapid movement, and threw herself into the Seine.

Chapter XXVII

Resolved to head straight for the goal, Charles Balin, as soon as he arrived in London, set out in search of the shady establishment that had already been identified to him.

The Monks Agency is not easy to find; no directory mentions it and some of the best-informed people have never heard of it.

"I don't know the Monks Agency," the aged cab-driver told him, "but I know a bookseller of that name who does business." He took the cab anyway, and it stopped in front of a shabby shop on Holborn Hill.

"Excuse me, sir," he said to the individual who emerged from behind a barricade of old books. "I'm looking for a Monks Agency, and the similarity of the name caused me to suppose that you might be able to inform me."

"Perhaps," replied the sales clerk. "I can tell by your accent that you're French; what sort of agency are you talking about?"

"One of those specializing in litigations and question of interest, which carry out research and procure certain documents."

"The boss does indeed do all that," the employee interjected, "and we sometimes receive people who come in search of the Monks *Agency*." He stressed the final word in a significant fashion.

"In that case, I'd like to speak to Mr. Monks."

"He's not here, Monsieur."

"When can I see him?"

"I don't know. If, however, you care to confide the subject of your visit, I can inform him of it tonight or tomorrow and ask him for an appointment."

Damn! thought the foreigner. *That's a lot of precautions; Monks the bookseller is evidently the man I want.* Even so, he hesitated.

"You can confide in me in complete security, Monsieur. I'll admit that if you want to see Mr. Monks, that's the only way that you can enter into communication with him."

"The Mr. Monks for whom I'm searching might, I'm told, be able to procure me certain papers I need."

"Who gave you that information?"

"A solicitor passing through Paris: Mr. Clifford, if I remember rightly."

"Speak frankly: what do you want?"

"Identity papers."

"That's clear; come this way."

He was introduced into a back room, where Mr. Monks, a sort of leather bag surmounted by a small neckless head and furnished with arachnid limbs gestured to him to sit down.

"You desire identity papers, I understand. What nationality? Real or false?"

"French nationality and real; otherwise my papers won't have any value."

"I can get you serious ones for five hundred pounds."

"Five hundred pounds!" murmured the client, with a grimace of disappointment. "My means don't permit me, then, to carry my project forward."

"The least French, English and German papers," said the fake bookseller, "sell for that price; if they include aristocratic titles or scientific diplomas I charge extra, but I have cheaper ones. The Swedish, Norwegian, Dutch and Danish are four hundred pounds, Russian, Austrian, Swiss and Belgian three hundred. For a hundred I can furnish Italian, Spanish, Portuguese, as many as you wish. All the rest—American, Asiatic, African, Oceanian—vary between thirty and fifty pounds. I'm talking, of course, about authentic documents; if you wish to equip yourself with false papers, they're cheaper—much cheaper—and between the two of us, Monsieur, the false ones are often better than the real ones. It depends on the usage you want to make of them."

"I'm very sorry to have disturbed you needlessly," the visor stammered. "I hadn't expected such high prices."

"Well, Monsieur, people who want to change their identity always have serious reasons for doing so; they're usually notaries or bankers on the run, former keepers of public houses, relatives of people condemned to death, executioners…in brief, people who want to escape dishonor and who, for some reason, have broken with the past. Those people don't care about the price, especially when they're certain of not being cheated. Now, the Monks Agency never leads its clients into error." With a little pointed laugh, he added: "It devotes itself to its dishonest operations with scrupulous honesty."

"The reasons I have…"

"Don't concern me," the businessman interrupted. "The identity papers I sell cost me dear. Even though I've taken my precautions—I'm not a merchant of old papers for nothing—I risk, in making that traffic, having disagreeable encounters with the law, so it's reasonable that I obtain some profit."

Charles Balin apologized again and left. The six or seven thousand francs he possessed, which had not only to serve him to obtain documents but also to support him and take his examinations, were scarcely in rapport with the demands of the Monks Agency.

He dismissed the cab and was going back to his hotel on foot when the bookseller's clerk caught up with him in the street.

"I know that you didn't make a deal with the boss," the individual said. "Would you find some good advice worth two or three pounds?"

"If the advice you have to give me is worth the fee, I'm good judge and an honest man; I'll recognize your service."

"I'll trust in your honesty. My idea is practical, excellent and realizable in a short time. You want authentic identity papers: go to New York and have yourself naturalized as a Yankee. With the directions I give you, and a few papers I'll provide, which will cost you another two or three pounds— let's say five in all—it can be very easily done."

Time was pressing; he was afraid of being anticipated by another; above all, he could not see how he was going to get

278

the 12,500 francs Mr. Monks was demanding. What did nationality matter, after all? Science and Art have no fatherland. He accepted the plan. Instead of going to Liège or Pisa, he would obtain his diploma from a university in the New World.

A fortnight later, Pierre Iblan, a chemist of Cuban origin, arrived in New York, went on to Philadelphia, registered at the university and requested naturalization. Antedated letters from Dr. Albin recommending him warmly to former correspondents immediately won him the eager support of several professors.

A few months later, the Cuban chemist, having become a Yankee citizen and received a doctorate, took the steamer, disembarked at Le Havre and returned to Paris.

The new individual who, under that further anagram of Albin, was about to go in pursuit of glory, no longer had more than a distant resemblance to his previous incarnations. The slightly darkened complexion, the narrow beard running beneath the chin, the long near-white hair, the simultaneously grave and bold manner and the exotic air he had about him allowed Dr. Iblan to go anywhere without running any risk of being unmasked.

A sufficient knowledge of the English and Spanish languages completed the illusion. He astonished himself with a transformation so complete, and began to wonder whether his aptitudes as an actor might have been one of the principal results of his past success.

A method for the fabrication of artificial ivory sold in the United States had brought him a few thousand francs. He rented a small apartment in the Rue du Faubourg Saint-Honoré, decorated the main room artistically with furniture and ornaments bought at the Hôtel Drouot,[25] and rapidly entered into communication with the American Legation. Then he solicited and obtained the favor of sitting the examinations for a French

---

[25] Then, and still, the leading auctioneers of high quality artefacts in Paris.

doctorate. He had no more to do than present himself before the Faculty.

Until then, the constant preoccupations, daily obligations and overwork, without causing him to forget Rose Gontran, had prevented him from making any serious search for her. He had heard vaguely about the failure of her attempted come-back, knew that her former domicile as uninhabited, and that was all. Now that he was completely reinstalled her and had no more to do than wait for the moment to subject himself to his proofs he was in haste to relocate his lover, determined to watch over her covertly and come to her aid if necessary.

People in the theatrical profession and the press were unable to give him any information about the present situation of the actress; even the man who had been her lover was completely ignorant as to what had become of her—but they told him all the details of the fatal evening and the abominable machination of which the unfortunate artiste had been the victim.

Then he had funereal presentiments; involuntarily, the statement that Rose had pronounce so resolutely on the day when he had promise not to abandon her—"If you hadn't said that, I'd have thrown myself in the river"—returned incessantly to his mind. He knew her violent character, her nervousness, so easy to excite, and her energetic will. He trembled to acquire some sad certainty. Failure combined with abandonment might have driven her to any extreme.

If, however, one way or another, Rose Gontran were dead, the fact would be surely known—but the Seine does not surrender all of its cadavers, and how many people who had had their moment of celebrity die abandoned and forgotten in obscure mansards? Enquiry agencies could not furnish him with any information.

He went to the Gaité-Belleville.

"Since the night when Rose Gontran left us flat," the director replied, "I haven't heard any mention of her. She must surely have regretted that impulsive action. A vile cabal had, it's true, been mounted against her, but the performance might have ended turning to her honor. She lacked composure authorized advice. I did what I could; unfortunately, I could speak any louder than my rights as director, and she closed my mouth by compensating me generously for the expenses I'd made."

"She had no one to look out for her? A husband, a lover?"

"There was the young playwright, but the fellow was the first to lose his head. In any case, he appeared to have no influence over her, and Mademoiselle Gontran, so far as I could judge, wasn't easy to manage."

He had already been assured that Rose had left their former domicile shortly after his departure. Supposing, nevertheless, that she might have left some indication there, and have reason in any case to recover the furniture and books he had abandoned in the Rue Lepic, he furnished himself with an authorization from his relative Charles Balin, and presented himself to the concierge. She, embarrassed by the apartment and glad to be paid, did not raise the slightest objection.

He took the keys, ran up the stairs and opened the door. Nothing had changed, but on the table, very visible, a letter addressed to Monsieur Charles Balin immediately struck his gaze. He tore open the envelope, trembling with emotion, and read the words, effaced her and there by tears:

Wicked man who makes me weep so much, I'll wait for you forever; don't forget your promise. Poor Mariette.

Poor Mariette, indeed! What could have become of her?

He wiped his eyes, because he was weeping too, and went back downstairs.

"So you've never heard any further mention of Madame Balin?" he asked the concierge again.

"Neither Monsieur nor Madame." She had second thoughts. "Yes, a man came several times to ask whether they still lived here and where they'd gone. Without being a witch, I'm sure that he was a cop."

He gave her a coin, told her that he would send removal men the next day, and left.

The concierge called him back.

"Oh, Monsieur, there's one thing I forgot to tell you. When the lady left, I asked her whether she was coming back. She said: 'It's only the dead who don't come back.'"

A sudden chill traversed his heart.

Bah! It was a manner of speaking; he could not draw any conclusion from a popular saying.

Perhaps Mariette had obtained some engagement elsewhere? It was not admissible that she had been reclaimed by her past.

He went so far as to wander in the vicinity of the Faubourg Montmartre and was accosted by old Lucie, whose offers he declined, but to whom he gave some money, under the pretext that he had known her a long time ago and had already encountered hr on his first voyage to Paris with someone named...wait a moment...

The American made a semblance of searching his memory.

"Nini Nichon, a big aggressive blonde, I'll wager."

"No."

"Valentine, then...a pullet from Le Mans? Jeanne Gambier? Fanny Béquille?"

"No," the foreigner replied, to each name on the list. "It's true that it was four or five years ago," he added, to put her on the track. "You probably don't remember."

"Four or five years...Mariette, perhaps?"

"Mariette—that was her name, Mariette! I'd like to see her again."

"Well, old chap, if you're waiting for Mariette to lose your innocence, you'll wait a long time. You'd do better to come with me."

"She's dead, then?"

"No one knows! She was in the theater; no one has seen her since the night when she had a fiasco. A chap named Émile said later that she must have gone to the provinces or abroad with her old mec."

"Oh...she had, what did you say?"

282

"An old mec, a mysterious old fellow, a lost dog, a former curé, a fellow who had ups and downs, a thief, perhaps a murderer—so Émile says, for I have nothing to reproach him for myself; he even gave me twenty bullets one day for nothing."

He did not want to know any more, and, ashamed of the investigation, which he had thought necessary, he resolved not to take his research any further.

Poor Mariette! He was almost certain now that, yielding to some crazy excitation, she had found repose and oblivion in death.

A long and dolorous sadness invaded him. An instinctive hallucination nailed him to the sidewalk, haggard. He saw Rose, maddened, coming out of the theater at a run, going down the streets and boulevards without drawing breath; he saw her nervous clenched hands hanging on to the hard stone parapet; he heard the muffled splash of the body that the Seine, the consoler of the desperate, had hastened to swallow.

He shook himself to chase away the nightmare; he had the painful impression that he had suddenly grown several years older.

Had he loved her, then? Did he love her still, to experience such cruel suffering?

It was impossible for him to reply.

He walked straight ahead, and found himself in the Place de l'Opéra.

It was the night of a première; municipal guardsmen enveloped in their dark mantles, their helmets dazzling in the glare of the electric lights, astride their large horses, were stationed hieratically on the edges of the large square. The spectacle had just finished; the steps of the monumental peristyle were packed with people, gentlemen in suits covered fur-lined overcoats; officers in dress uniform; warmly wrapped ladies their shoulders wrapped in marten or ermine, their faces hidden beneath silk capelines or lace mantillas.

Carriages were arriving slowly in single file, turning away and disappearing rapidly in all directions. Once, he too had been among that elite; his love of music had caused him to follow these artistic events passionately.

He was at the corner of the boulevard, outside the Café de la Paix; suddenly, he recognized his old coachman, traveling rapidly and extracting his vehicle from the curious crowd. In the coupé, which had almost brushed him, an involuntary glance showed him the woman who had long been his neglected wife, with whom he had spent an almost indifferent life, amorously enlaced by Dr. Larmezan's left arm.

A stupid and incomprehensible surge of indignation gripped him; the familiar attitude of Dr. Larmezan seemed to him to be grossly revolting. Tremulously, he watched the vehicle race away at the gallop. One might have thought that he had suffered an outrage.

The impression, it is true, was as brief as the apparition. "Am I going mad?" he murmured, almost immediately. "Only a moment ago, the memory of Mariette, the near-certainty of having lost her gave me a profoundly cruel pain, and now, the rapid vision of the woman who was legally and honestly my wife, with whom I lived for such a long time almost without waiting to love her, almost without wanting to know her, disturbs me and seems to engender a ridiculous sentiment of jealousy. It's absurd! I must be losing my mind. Why has that wall of glass reflected, so to speak, the regret of the other?"

The cold made him shiver, and he resumed walking. Now he was thinking, as he went through the same places, of that calvary of begging when his hunger, as heavy as a cross, had weighed so heavily upon his shoulders. He told himself that alongside him, perhaps, there were human beings whom his relative prosperity was already preventing him from recognizing, submissive to the same anguish. He examined the passers-by with eyes in which pity was mingled with fear. The providential memory of Mariette came back to haunt him, and now he saw her, hooked on to some laundry-boat jetty, icy, decomposed, her orbits empty: a human rag doing a *danse macabre* in the eddies of the rapid current.

He retraced his steps, shivering, and, in order to warm himself up, went into the first establishment he encountered on his route.

It was the Café Américain. Women enticed by his exotic allure immediately came to prowl around him, addressing suggestive twitches of the lips and languorous blinks to him. He gazed at them without seeing them, blinking his own eyes at the display of garish colors, sniffing with an unconscious sensuality the heady odors emanating from skirts and corsages, and drank a hot toddy, which did him good.

He gradually returned to a sentiment of reality. What the devil as he doing in this milieu, so out of tune with his sinister and grave thoughts. He now saw the maneuvers of which he as the object, and was in haste to get away from them—but as he summoned the waiter, a gross Rubenesque blonde draped in mauve velvet, who saw prey ready to escape, came brazenly to ask him whether he was not going to buy her a drink. He shivered involuntarily on recognizing Nini Nichon.

He grasped one last hope. Perhaps he might learn something.

"With pleasure, Mademoiselle," he said, adopting his circumstantial accent. "And entirely in your honor, I assure you."

"I can always drink another glass," sat the fat woman, whose sumptuous costume did not lend her the slightest distinction. "A grog, waiter. It's so cold tonight that I'd need twenty to warm me up," she added, laughing heavily. She sat down facing him and waited to be served. He seemed to be studying her intently.

"It seems to me that I know you," he ended up saying. "Where the devil have I seen you before?"

"Who doesn't know Nini Nichon? Not four in all Paris," she proclaimed, tapping her enormous bosom, which began quivering gelatinously. "There aren't two like me."

"Oh, I have it," he said. "I saw you once at the Folies Nouvelles."

"It's possible; I once went there every evening. Oh, those were the good times."

"Weren't you the friend of a singer—Rose Gontran?"

"The intimate friend," replied the mass of greasy flesh. "Poor Rose!" she added, drinking her toddy slowly. "She's dead." He stared at her; she seemed to be holding back a tear. "She died of smallpox. I closed her eyes myself."

Chapter XXVIII

In front of the modest table covered with a simple cloth, behind which three examiners were seated without ostentation, the foreign chemist prepared himself to submit to the terrible proofs of the French doctorate.

His companions in the line, timid and trembling, replied with discretion to the questions addressed to them; he had the clear voice and assured tone of a man of worth. A venerable professor interrogated him about the theories of Dr. Albin; carried away by the subject, the American emitted grave doubts about the merit of their point of departure. The examiner stopped him.

"You certainly don't lack knowledge, Monsieur," he remarked, severely, "but you're bringing us theories now for which we haven't asked, and which are only hypotheses devoid of authority, since no one has demonstrated them. Your affirmations might, perhaps, be affirmed by the scientists of the New World, or find grace among German professors, but they prove to us that you have not understood the beautiful discoveries of our illustrious and regretted master; you will therefore be kind enough to go and study them more deeply, your artistry in throwing dust in the eyes is insufficient for us; we shall hear you again on another occasion."

He was deferred!

If he had had time to waste the adventure would have amused him: he did not understand what he had invented!

After all, it was his own fault. Why forget that he was presenting himself as a pupil, why perorate like a master? He had not been asked to refute Dr. Albin's doctrines; he had been asked to explain then, and that is what he should have done.

The lesson was excellent. He easily passed all his other examinations, refraining from emitting the slightest personal notion, repeating all the theories dear to the professors who questioned him, submitted a thesis that was a collection of bibliographical researches and was received with the warmest eulogies.

On the twelfth of March 18**, Doctor Pierre Iblan of the University of Philadelphia donned the French doctoral toga and received the diploma that permitted him henceforth to speak on his own behalf, care for the sick and obtain glory, honor and profit therefrom.

He had thought it would take him five or six months to attain that objective; it had taken him nearly five years! Five years of poverty, persecution and groping, five years of thick darkness that only a single ray of light had traversed.

Fortunately, all of that was about to end…and the devoted friend of those dismal hours was no longer there! That thought alone mitigated the delirious joy that he felt as he emerged from the thesis hall. In the courtyard of the École de Médecine, a gleam of pride illuminated his eyes.

"It's the two of us, now, Professor Albin!" he exclaimed, raising a menacing fist against the Sacred Arch, while, pensive in his bronze envelope, Bichat seemed to be smiling at him and encouraging him.[26]

Dr. Iblan, doctor of the University of Philadelphia, doctor and laureate of the Faculté de Paris, comfortably installed in his apartment in the Rue du Faubourg-Honoré, waits for patients, but the patients do not arrive. A few consultants sent by the American Legation who come from time to time to ask his advice, relying on their quality as compatriots, let him know that they are not rich, and end up obtaining treatment for free.

However, the doctor has considerable expenses: a costly rent, a small household. The money he had melts away like snow; the local suppliers, not reassured by the information

---

[26] The statue of the pioneering anatomist and histologist Xavier Bichat (1771-1802) by David d'Angers was erected in the courtyard of the École de Médecine in 1857.

they do not fail to seek, began to refuse him credit. The rich American and Spanish colonies do not bring the contribution he expected; their patriotism vanishes before the slightest distress, and they prefers to address themselves to the leading lights of French Science. Who has heard of Dr. Iblan, anyway? Where does he come from? Where are his proofs?

I obviously lack connections, he says to himself. *It's necessary to launch myself into society.* He therefore sets out in search of invitations, runs around soirées easy of access, perorates in a brilliant fashion in cosmopolitans salons, makes music, attacks all subjects with authority—and achieves unexpected results. All the qualities that once aided in him his upward progress now work against him.

"He's too good a musician to be a good physician," snigger some.

"Too much of a physician to be an artiste," claim the others.

"These people who dabble in everything don't get to the bottom of anything," observe the specialists.

"These foreigners can try as they might," whisper the Parisiennes, "young or old, they never succeed in escaping the flashy category."

"Haven't you noticed," the foreigners confide to one another, "that Dr. Iblan has no character or mark of nationality?"

"He belongs to the neuter gender."

"A character out of Sardou, then."

"All dentists, these Americans," insinuate colleagues aggravated by his brilliant conversation.

"I have a horror of old doctors," confess the neurotics, ingenuously, "only young and cheerful faces inspire me with confidence."

These ephemeral connections, he soon thinks, in his consulting room, *too often barren, can't be of any great utility to me; I spend my time in too many places where I only pas through; people don't have time to appreciate me, or even to get to know me. I need to frequent a salon of repute, and in a sustained fashion. The circle will be more restricted, but I'll be better able to have myself judged and to create real sympathies.*

Here the difficulty becomes greater; one does not penetrate overnight into the intimacy of a house; the more amiable his smiles become and the more engaging his manners, the more the reserve is accentuated.

He finally succeeds in capturing the good graces of the Baronne d'A***, an Austrian lady of note—so it is said—who invites him to her intimate Thursday gatherings.

The Baronne's Thursdays are not as intimate as he had imagined. At the very first soirée he has the disagreeable impression of wandering through a carnival masquerade even more grotesque than those through which he has already passed. The drawing rooms are overly luxurious, the furniture excessively gilded; there are too many master paintings, heraldic jewels, family relics and regal snuff-boxes. Old gentlemen whose faces are worryingly pale or excessively acned, like vicious ostlers or debauched sacristans, wear too many sashes, decorations and necklaces of all sorts of orders. Dethroned princes play cards with too much luck. The ladies display too many diamonds and too much bosom, but seem nevertheless too reserved. Demoiselles who are too young and dowagers who are too old have smiles that are too enigmatic and gazes that are too bold. The buffet is too notorious in its insufficiency, and the servants contemplate the appetite of the guests with too much mockery. There are too many foreign generals, plenipotentiary ministers of unknown principalities, ambassadors of distant nations, Italian tenors, Germen harpists, Polish pianists, celebrated cantatrices, famous tragediennes and writers of genius. All those people have too much renown in their own lands for it not to be astonishing that one has never heard of them. The few Parisians astray in that milieu are considering it with too much curiosity. Finally, the Baronne d'A***, a buxom blonde of about forty, whose husband is often away, darts too many significant glances at Dr. Iblan. He is too fearful of the tariff list, and quickly escapes from the excessive intimacy of the place.

It was there, perhaps, that he might have circulated with the greatest ease and perhaps profit, but his scruples are still too keen and his delicacy too sensitive.

A few other attempts at intimate relationships succeed no better. Sometimes it is a milieu of extraordinarily dubious financiers who move millions in words and go home on foot on the pretext of getting a little air. Sometimes it is a cut-throat's den where the naïve are stripped gaming, sometimes the boudoir of a procuress where the heavy draperies seem to be designed to stifle screams; a mysterious lair where the reek of laxity, treason and crime seem to corrupt the air and creep in the corners. The doors of honest houses remain obstinately closed. It seems that people sense, divine or know that he has no name, no fatherland, no family and no personality.

He then resumes his peregrinations, banal but more honorable, around the fêtes where one merely passes through and receptions remain open, where the people who shake your hand one evening no longer recognize you the next.

Meanwhile, time is flying; his social connections, he observes fearfully, only lead to the subjugation of a few old hysterics that his self-respect sends away, and who then became redoubtable enemies.

His frequentations oblige him to futile expenses, the devil continues to lodge in his purse, and the goal is retreating instead of getting closer.

A victim of his mask, he then surpasses the measure, unconsciously taking on charlatanesque appearances, has recourse to newspaper advertisements affirming with aplomb and arrogance that he has as much and more merit than no matter which of his fashionable colleagues.

Serious people smile, a few desperate individuals rejected by other physicians and reputedly incurable finally come to him and permit him to live in a meager fashion, but the incurables die on his hands and the naïve, enticed by excessive promises, end up proclaiming his impotence; nothing remains of Dr. Iblan but a reputation for employing means of undeniable correctness.

He knows that by raising the tenor of his publicity and employing more money in his advertisement, he would better exploit the credulity of his contemporaries, but the sentiment of his real value inhibits him; the horror of lying, the professional honesty of old, still ties his hands. He only does things that succeeded partially, or not at all.

The need to put himself in evidence then leads to mistakes that awaken all suspicions.

One evening, he finds himself in a salon with well-known politicians, some of whom are former colleagues of député Albin. The majority profess so-called advanced ideas but are only, in reality, narrow minds nourished on bombastic words and imbued with prudhommesque doctrines, shamelessly ambitious, democrats or socialists by order, egotists whose convictions are expended in promises.

They have been taking about the occult sciences, and some are fulminating against mystical tendencies with all the more insistence because a talented young physician, brought into the limelight by recent occultist publications, is affecting to exempt himself from the conversation.

"So-called telepaths, theosophists, mages, diviners, magnetizers and *tutti quanti*," declares a rival of Maître Homais, pompously, "are merely skillful charlatans; coincidences and fortune hazards alone establish their reputation; the supernatural doesn't exist."

"That's precisely what the most authorized occultists assert," declares the young physician, finally picking up the gauntlet. "There is no supernatural; nothing exists outside nature and contrary to it; but it's nevertheless true that an infinity of redoubtable or beneficial natural forces of which so-called exact science is profoundly ignorant are revealed to initiates. There are properties as strange as magnetism, for example, in many other minerals; the physicists of the Institute have no doubt of it, and Asiatic herdsmen make use of them.

"Without going so far, for thousands of years, the fishermen of our Mediterranean coasts have known, profoundly mysterious as it still is, that a few drops of oil are sufficient to calm an irritated sea; science has scarcely begun to learn that; and how many uneducated peasants of our French provinces know secrets of herbs, enchantments and dreams, while the therapists of the Académie have forgotten that Hippocrates and Galen used them every day. The majority of our remedies—belladonna, digitalis, opium, etc.—come to us from sorcerers who maintained the tradition. What do we not owe to the Medieval alchemists, who were neither madmen nor ignorant?

"Believe me, don't judge too lightly doctrines that we haven't studied sufficiently, and let us look at important facts without prejudice! The day isn't far off when official medicine will perceive once again that, alongside the single force that we recognize today, vitality, there's another equally important, vitalism. That's a fact about which there's nothing supernatural, a fact known throughout the ages, as occultist physicians have proclaimed."

"There are occultist physicians then?"

"Why not. I know one who has just accomplished a miraculous cure in a desperate case of typhoid fever."

"The recipe! The recipe!" cry ironic voices.

"It's quite simple. He transmitted vital fluid to his patient, expelled all thought of death and rendered her the will to live."

"That physician is a criminal, since, having those powers, he still lets people die every day from that disease."

"Would you be ready to give your blood every time a patient could be saved by a transfusion? Can't you understand that, as the transmission of vital fluid is made at the expense of the operator, such a means can only be employed exceptionally."

"He ought at least to teach it to his colleagues."

"Some don't want to, other are unable to receive the words of truth; that's why there have always been, and always will be, phenomena known to some and unknown to the majority—which is to say, occult sciences."

"The only sciences that I admit," announces a humanitarian philosopher, "are those that are displayed in broad daylight, and profit humankind with their discoveries."

"Humankind," ripostes the occultist, with a bitter laugh, "a few centuries ago, hastened to burn, without rhyme or reason, anyone who lifted a corner of the veil. We cannot, we who are judges and parties, appreciate the conduct that the humankind of today adopts in their regard; posterity will inform our descendants when it judges our actions and our works, but it is logical to think that if people hide their discoveries, it is because they believe them to be baneful to their contemporaries or harmful, perhaps mortal, for themselves.

"Do you imagine that the age of persecutions has passed forever? Alas, the hydra that devours the pioneers of ideas has only changed its face and form; an immense myriapod, it enlaces the contemporary world in its viscous rings; there is nothing astonishing in the fact that the initiates are fearful.

"On the other hand, are you certain that all discoveries are profitable to humanity in the way that you mean? So long as alcohol, employed in the form of a cordial, was the secret of a few Alchemists, it was not belied by the name of *eau-de-vie* invented by Arnaud de Villeneuve.[27] Does it not merit the name of *eau-de-mort* now that science has put it within the range of everyone? And, as a great statesman has said, is it not more harmful to the human race that the three greatest plagues—war, disease and famine—put together?

"Certain discoveries can only be usefully unveiled to beings worthy to receive them. Not all races are equipped to the same degree to digest what you call progress. Entire peoples have died, and are dying, of the civilization that conquest

---

[27] Arnaud de Villeneuve (1238-c1311) was a physician and alchemist, one of the first founders of modern chemistry, in which capacity he is reputed to have discovered the distillation process that produces brandy from wine, and called the product eau-de-vie. The Church failed to suppress his activities, and condemned his writings in vain; the secret got out.

brings them, for under the fallacious name of civilization you almost always conceal vile commercial interests."

"That's the theory of the candle-snuffer," proclaims a radical député. "By what right do you hide from some what you teach to others?"

"Because not everyone merits knowing everything. Because superiority, intelligence and moral value are only acquired by successive efforts, which the law does not decree."

"If the law doesn't decree them, it prepares them."

"It ought to prepare them, but religious hypocrisy and materialistic egotism put a stop to it, and it's because the occult sciences proclaim the superiority of the spirit and its liberation, that they are persecuted or, which is worse, turned to ridicule."

"That wouldn't happen if people didn't make a métier out of astonishing their fellows and chasing after money with pretended secrets: exploiters on one side, imbeciles on the other. The love of the marvelous that simple minds have is fundamentally nothing but an aspiration toward the better, toward the best; it's inadmissible that they're cheated."

"Is it any more admissible that they're exploited, deceived and harmed by scientific hypotheses, yesterday's verities, tomorrow's errors? Your science is impotent and wretched, the means of which it disposes are so limited, its views so narrow and its pretentions so great, that its intervention is more often harmful than helpful. Wasn't it in the name of science, only to cite one example, that for centuries, physicians extorted and killed their patient by bleeding them left, right and center? Diaforus isn't dead yet. So combat cupidity and charlatanism wherever it seeks to insinuate itself, but don't declare *a priori* that all the honest people, all the scholars are on one side and all the rogues and ignoramuses on the other."

"You're not going to go so far as to admit the deceptions of spiritism, mythological fables and popular superstition?"

"Words—all that's just words. I'm not saying that; I'm simply affirming that alongside known phenomena, there are

295

occult phenomena that a few privileged individuals know and the revelation of which would astonish you prodigiously."

"I'd certainly like to be astonished," voices proclaim from various directions.

The young defender of occultism falls silent—but Dr. Iblan cannot resist the need to intervene

"That's very easy," he affirms. "I don't approve of all my young friend's theories and I'm not a mage or a diviner, but if it's merely a matter of astonishing you, I'll take responsibility for that."

The challenge is accepted.

He leans close to the ear of one and reveals a family secret; he reminds another of a parliamentary intrigue to which only a few individuals had the key; a third is amazed to find that confidential steps taken in a distant epoch are known to the American doctor; a député is astonished to learn the cause that had motivated his vote in a important circumstance; a former minister hears a state secret recalled.

Everyone looks sat one another, astounded. A glacial silence succeeds the animated conversations. The pseudo-sorcerer is almost made to understand that his presence is a cause of embarrassment and annoyance.

He leaves a few minutes later, under some pretext, perceiving too late that he has just committed an absurd blunder. Anxious people interrogate him with their gaze; no one can understand. He is a spy, a secret policeman, a dangerous individual, perhaps a master blackmailer.

No one dares say so aloud but everyone is thinking it.

Chapter XXIX

The American doctor owes several months rent, his suppliers refuse him any credit; stamped papers are beginning to rain down. The rare patients that arrive scarcely serve to prevent him from dying of hunger.

I've taken a false path, he thinks, *by attempting to gather an aristocratic clientele at a stroke. I'll go to a quarter more in rapport with my...I don't say Bohemian situation, but at any rate exceptional. It's in the real Paris, the Paris of artistes and men of letters that I ought to demand the means of existence; they'll understand me, they don't have stupid prejudices; they won't ask where I come from or who I am; they'll be content to judge me on my work.*

Seduced by that idea, which he thinks excellent, he hastens to rent an apartment in the Rue des Martyrs, and set out in search of connections. But there, although approaches are easy and camaraderies of the brasserie are established overnight, although his originality and his universal knowledge win him the admiration of painters and the consideration of singers, although the gentleman cabaretier of the *Chat Noir* takes him under his wing, competitors are innumerable and the clients have long since adopted the detestable habit of paying their doctor with the dedications of books or gifts of sketches. Between artists, one only exchanges favors, and Dr. Iblan is the artistic physician *par excellence*; the philistines do not want to hear mention of him under any pretext.

Within a month he perceives that he has taken another false route and is just about to go pitch his tent elsewhere, when a news item delays his determination. A *fin-de-siècle* dancer has just been shot with a revolver at the exit from the Moulin Rouge.

Dr. Iblan, a regular at a nearby café, hastens to the scene and finds himself in the presence of the great Annette. The bullet has penetrated her arm. He extracts it without further ado and has the injured woman, who has not recognized him, taken to her domicile.

Amicable relations are quickly established between the American surgeon and the grateful convalescent.

Annette is living in a richly furnished apartment; much-decorated old gentlemen, spirited reporters and even renowned artistes come every day to obtain news of her. She is in the full bloom of her beauty and, seeing her every day, white and pink in floods of lace in which languid charms flourish, Dr. Iblan senses appetites reborn that are all the more imperious for being exasperated by memory. But the beautiful Annette, who, without knowing it, is avenging the disdain of the former pianist, encloses herself in an indifference denuded of all artifice.

Certainly, she does not refuse to accord him a few hasty favors; that is how, she admits cynically, she always pays her physicians, but it is professionally and not otherwise. It is in vain that the foreigner attempts to reanimate the heart that was once so warm. In vain that his agile fingers run across the keyboard, to revive the enthusiastic gallops, the pointed polkas, the deafening variations and suggestive tremolos of yore, in vain that he exclaims many times, always hoping to put her on the right track: "It's extraordinary how much you resemble someone I once loved!"

The reciprocal question, the response he awaits, never arrives.

He provokes confidences, excites her to tell her story in order to recognize the trace that Monsieur Charles might have left in her heart, but the facts bear so little resemblance to those he knows, there are so many forgotten items and lacunae, that he cannot help smiling. It is a biography reviewed and corrected for the usage of serious clients. Neither his name nor those of others are pronounced; the attempted café concert debuts have become enthusiastic triumphs, Père Antoine's establishment an elegant confectionery frequented by the high life of the entire world and the rapacious coal merchant a generous impresario who covered her with gold.

"Why not continue such a brilliant career?" he asks, a trifle sarcastically.

"Singing fatigued me too much; it's not written in stone, though, that I won't return to it."

"Didn't a fashionable singer make her debut at the concert whose name you cited" he asked.

"You're doubtless talking about Rose Gontran."

"That's the one. Did you know her?"

"Very well; we had the same teacher of piano and singing—an old eccentric, in parentheses."

"What was his name?"

"Monsieur Charles."

"Monsieur Charles who? Monsieur Charles what?"

"Oh, you're asking too much; I never bothered to enquire as to whether he had another name. He gave me lessons; I gave him his fee, and then bonjour, bonsoir."

"And what became of Rose Gontran?"

"Probably what becomes of artistes after having lost their beauty or their voice—a singer in some provincial hole, star of a garrison, prima donna in some South American republic, unless she's a seamstress, concierge, domestic or street-sweeper, how do I know?"

"Or dead," murmurs the foreign doctor, sadly. After a long pause he adds: "And how did you get the idea of becoming a dancer."

"I had that in my blood," the forgetful individual affirms.

Decidedly the beautiful Annette does not want to see or hear. In the midst of the confusion of lies that she tells him every day, he succeeds, aided by local café gossip, in reconstituting her veritably history.

As he had suggested to her during the short liaison that followed their encounter at the Folies Nouvelles, she had resolved to charm her contemporaries with the elegance and flexibility of her figure. Instead of addressing herself to some high priest of Terpsichore, she had transposed her neurosis into the dangerous world of dubious dancers. Freed from her mania for pianists, but continuing nevertheless to consider amour as the supreme and sole initiator of all the arts, she had run around the fashionable dance-halls and swooned before the celebrities of the splits. There, however, things had progressed differently than at the concert.

Instead of deceptive virtuosos devoid of great energy, who toyed with her and were amused by her, she found uncommonly demanding individuals of bad character. The majority of master gigolos put a tariff on their rude and savage embraces, not being content with a brief infatuation, and put an excessive self-respect into not being dismissed.

The great Annette, direly put to contribution by her first essay, robbed of several jewels during the second, had the misfortune to want to attempt a third. She stole the "Gomme Elastique" of Madeleine de Commercy, an acrobat with gilded hair, like the delicacies whose name she bore.

As the capricious Annette put that price on it, the Vestris[28] of the Barrière agreed to accord her his favors and unveil the secrets of his unparalleled elasticity to her, but when, after a few days, carried away by her old habits of inconstancy, she took it into her head to cast envious eyes at the quadrille in which "Moulin à Vent" caused his flippers to spin, Gomme Elastique declared categorically showing her the extremity of his vulgar arms, that he would take charge of ensuring her fidelity in true affection. She could have as many clients as she wished, but so far as dancers were concerned, he alone would give her lessons henceforth. For the first offence, he would content himself with a little beating when she returned. It was not him who had come in search of her, was it? She had only to let him alone and he would not have left Madeleine, a woman of such good earning-power.

Tamed, the tall blonde finally devoted herself to study.

---

[28] Auguste Vestris (1760-1842) was a famous French dancer at the Opéra whose name became legendary, although its application to the "elastic rubber man" is surely an insult to his memory.

She had once tried to learn music and singing by means of intimate acrobatics; she learned the art of fluttering in public by means of punches and kicks.

"Look," her lover said to her, during the first lesson in dislocating arms and legs, "that's how it's done; it's no more difficult than that; it's necessary to lift yourself, that's the main thing."

The tried to imitated the master's acrobatics, and could not succeed.

"It's necessary to lift yourself, I tell you!" cried the lout full of rage. "Here, look at me, it's not a footbath to swallow. I'm lifting myself." The tall devil opened his legs horizontal, fell to the floor and rebounded briskly. Poor Annette tried to do likewise, but her legs obstinately formed and angle; she could not get up again, and the professor invariably came to her aid with a few kicks, delivered in accordance with the rules of the art.

"That's how I was taught the métier," affirmed the former acrobat, to console her.

After a few days, the lout, not sensing any serious vocation for instruction, threw his patience to the winds.

"All this is wasted time," he declared. To learn to dance, it's necessary to dance in front of people. That being the case, you're going to dance with me at the Moulin tonight."

The great Annette, put on the spot, made her debut immediately, and—who would have believed it?—in the midst of epileptic quadrilles and gross leg-movements, the elegant gaucherie and gracious inexperience of the pretty woman, attributed to a perverse refinement, won her an unexpected success. The lubricious old men and the "passionate" younger ones formed a circle around her; artistes seduced by hr beauty proclaimed that Annette's dancing was "the latest thing," and that renown, in search of which she had so often offered herself in sacrifice, suddenly arrived at the moment when, disenchanted by her guide's boots, she had promised herself to give up.

Her name, like Rose Gontran's at one time, was displayed in large letters on colored posters. The newspapers praised her grace, and she was imitated in end-of-the-year revues. The great Annette, alias "Crépuscule des Dieux," was the delight of the Elysée Montmartre, the glory of the Moulin Rouge and the ornament of the Jardin de Paris; noble foreigners outbid one another for her in the night restaurants.

Unfortunately, Gomme Elastique, believing himself to be the unique artisan of that vogue, made increasingly exacting demands; she was obliged to address herself to the Prefecture of Police in order to break the chain, and that was why the furious pimp had attempted to murder her.

"And now," says Annette, who has given him the final details herself, "not only is the dirty swine in prison, and I'm rid of him for a long time, but the revolver shot has given me wonderful publicity. I've been offered an engagement at the Folies Hippique; a Serbian or Rumanian prince—I don't know which, exactly—has offered me a left-handed marriage with a town house, a carriage, livery and all that...and if you were very kind," she continued, simpering, "you'd come to see me a little less often. I'm cured now, and your assiduity might compromise the success of the affair—unless you'd like to maintain me on the same footing?"

Offended by that appeal for discretion, Dr. Iblan bows ceremoniously, and shakes the dust from his shoes.

Chapter XXX

By what aberration of his sense and his mind has he wasted his time and his money in a crush worthy at the most of a schoolboy? A reversion to childhood? That senile caprice has devoured his last resources. He sells his overly luxurious furniture, settles a few accounts with his creditors and goes to establish himself in the Faubourg-du-Temple. It is in that populous quarter, in the midst of humble working people, that he ought to have come to begin with; those who are suffering know better how to ease the misfortune of others. He has, moreover, succeeded admirably in Bellevue as a bone-setter; his former clients would soon come to see him now that he could care for them overtly—but for that it would at least be necessary that the American doctor take off his mask, and it is impossible for him to do that.

So, there, no more than in the other, more fortunate quarters, luck does not consent to smile on him. The sick, it is true, are far more numerous, but the work is far harder; the stairs to go up and down all day leave him out of breath and exhausted by fatigue. The spirited thoroughbred of yore can scarcely resign himself to that toil of a coach-horse. If he could even obtain a just profit from it! But the majority of the clients to whom he presents his bill look at him peevishly and declare that they would rather pay the baker than the doctor. Others seize the slightest pretexts, claiming that they have been poorly treated, and heap him with insults; a few regretfully bring out a little money set aside and separate themselves from it with a heavy heart. No one understands that a doctor might have an immediate need to receive his honoraria; the same ones who claim to be exploited by the upper class and struggle righteously in the defense of their interests, do not admit that a physician has a right to eat.

Every day reserved a cruel disappointment for him, a further discouragement. One of his former admirers declares to him, furiously, that a Belleville bone-setter once cared for him in a much better fashion—that one, at least, didn't try to drag out sicknesses, as physicians do, to empty the pockets of their patients.

There, however, better than in the Faubourg Saint-Honoré, the physician succeeds in paying his most urgent debts and making a living—but at the price of what incessant efforts, what a murderous struggle!

Dr. Albin can rest in peace; the pitiless need to live has taken possession of his enemy more than ever, absorbing his days, troubling his nights, devouring his physical vigor, stifling his cerebral faculties and rendering him almost impotent.

He knows sleepless nights spent at the bedside of pauperesses with puerperal fevers in fireless rooms where the rags exhale the stink of misery. He has leapt up to answer the imperious ringing of the bell that summons him from his first sleep. He had climbed the calvary of flights of stairs, has stopped, out of breath, at doors standing ajar, where surly faces tell him that he has arrived too late and they have gone to find someone else. The pharmacists have deemed that his prescriptions do not bring in enough and the relatives of the sick that they cost too dear. He has been sent away for having said that he judged a case desperate—what is the point of keeping a doctor who declares himself impotent?—and others have reproached him for having dissimulate the gravity of the illness and allowing the client to die intestate. He knows mute reproaches before the dead and the hateful gazes of potential heirs before a cure.

In brief, he has learned to his expense the heavy responsibility of the poor local physician—a crushing burden, of which Dr. Albin, and even the bone-setter Charles Balin, givers of consultations at home, never felt the weight.

He thinks then, fearfully, that if Charles Balin, caught in the gears, had not taken long to be crushed by the social machine, Dr. Iblan, armed with the guarantees demanded by law, has nevertheless been thrown as fodder to the prejudices of a crowd in which collective injustice is accentuated by individual stupidity and ignorance.

That observation fills him with bitterness; an invincible disgust invades him gradually; he wonders whether it is really useful to suffer for the truth and if everything is not for the best in the worst of all possible worlds.

He no longer has the ardor that sustains, the faith that saves, the youth accessible to humanitarian dreams. The need to live squeezes in its claws the indulgence and natural generosity of his heart; poverty stifles his generous sentiments; he is snatching bread from mouths hungrier than his own, and that harsh necessity, which tortures and humiliates him, drives him to tears.

Again, if Mariette were there, he would find, on coming home in the evening, exhausted by fatigue, a smiling face and a few consolatory words, but he is alone, terribly alone. No hand reaches out toward him, no sympathy envelops him, no joy welcomes him.

At the moment when he thought that the coveted goal would be easily attained, an evil wind dissolves the deceptive mirage; the official titles that he judged indispensable and on the aid of which he counted so much, seem to be a weapon that destiny has turned against him. He regrets no longer being a bone-setter!

Perhaps, he thinks, *it's my status as a foreigner that is the cause of all these disappointments?* But a hundred others around him only succeed thanks to that status; it is, therefore, within himself, and only within himself, that he must seek the cause of his incredible bad luck.

Then an insurmountable discouragement invades him. It is true, then, that one cannot recommence one's life with impunity.

He knows now that to arrive at the most infimal social position it is necessary to travel the beaten path, to go through all the stages, to obtain all the guarantees, to conquer all the diplomas; he knows, now, that to please the crowd and dominate them, it is necessary to have the advantage of youth, beauty, activity or power. Why did he break the links to his past? Why did he throw overboard the advantages that resulted from his personal efforts and social complicities? Who can return him the gifts that no mortal receives twice and what will become of his work, now that he has lost the absolute confidence that gives audacity, the physical vigor that permits dogged work, the assurance of a living that procures the insouciance of material needs? What are intelligence and genius worth without that?

If, at least, the love he has always had for the wretched could sustain him—but his altruism has not emerged unscathed from the struggle for existence; although he always excuses the weak and the stupid, he no longer has the strength to tolerate them; although injustice revolts him, stupidity irritates him and although he pities the victims, their resignation disgusts him, he cannot help despising them.

Is he going to allow himself to be beaten by so many disillusionments and ordeals?

A thousand times no! He will make superhuman efforts. Too bad if his reason totters.

He works day and night, puts all his notes in order, rewrites the enormous treatise that will destroy the work of Dr. Albin, and sets out in quest of a publisher.

Those who once humbly solicited the favor of putting him in print sent him away with ironic smiles or insolent forthrightness. Others demand the twenty-five or thirty thousand francs necessary for the publication of the work. Only one asks him to leave his manuscript; he will have its read and appraised by competent chemists and will publish the work if it has the value he claims.

That proposal, although perfectly logical, does not satisfy him at all; he knows the competent chemists in question only too well. They are enemies or rivals; they will rob him shamelessly or suppress the work; he is not sufficiently naïve to hand them the key to his decisive experiments.

He has recourse to the Press again, publishing without flagrant proofs combative articles in which acrimony and bitterness play too large a part. Audacious denials, mordant criticisms, cruel ironies and acerbic sentiments of justice drawn from past miseries and tribulations are mingle therein, and give his polemics subversive appearances that make him profoundly hated by all those who eat tranquilly at the well-garnished trough. The inexplicable information drawn from mysterious sources give his articles a redoubtable range. If his blows are not bruising, they sting and flagellate in the most sensitive spots; the foreigner is denounced, threatened with expulsion: the mouth must be closed that dares brazenly to vomit the truth; the pen must be broken that spatters with ink the national glory of Dr. Albin!

He stops, exhausted; he feels the need to draw breath, that he is not yet in a state to vanquish, and re-enters, for a few months, into silence and oblivion.

Then he is haunted once again by the memory of Mariette.

The journalist, X***, who was Rose's last lover, whose amity he has sought, glad at least to hear talk of her, confides particularities to him that stimulate his regrets.

Rose, several times surprised in tears, had never ceased to love a friend of the bad days who had abandoned her. X***, discouraged by that discovery, had made every effort to liberate her from an affection so scantly shared; perhaps that was even the reason for which the unfortunate debutante had so easily become disinterested in him.

Dr. Iblan never wearies of hearing those confidences. That love of Mariette's, recalled to him thus in fragments, astonishes him and intrigues him. In addition to the sentiment of gratitude that linked him to her, he senses that she had a secret attraction of which he can never know the cause. The perverse instincts that slumber in the depths of every individual are a very insufficient explanation, and their effusions are, in any case, generally chaste.

His imagination wandering, he dreams about anterior lives in which, centuries ago, in other forms and other milieux,

Mariette and he had met and loved one another. But it is at smiles of incredulity that those poetic metempsychoses stop.

As for the sentimental reason that it would have been meritorious to lift up a fallen woman, he knows full well that it had no great weight in his enthusiasm. On the other hand, that amour did not have the grandeur and the intensity that constitute veritable passions; otherwise, he would not have experienced the reticences, the somersaults and the awakenings followed by abandonments.

Perhaps there has only ever existed in him one sole absolute love: that of science and the truth. It is the only almost-plausible explanation that he can admit, for if the affection he felt for Mariette was real, it is also incontestable that it was incomplete and, so to speak, secondary.

The journalist X***, having become his intimate friend, found him a scientific column in a major daily newspaper, with the express condition of not attacking the doctrines of Dr. Albin. That situation, and alkaloid extractions that he made for a large central pharmacy, permitted him to neglect his aleatory clientele.

He was now waiting to accumulate to large sum that would allow him to publish his *History of Alchemy and Chemistry from the Remotest Times to the Present Day*. It was a brilliant synthesis of all known works and a critique of all anterior theories. The final volume of the encyclopedic work, *Dynamic Chemistry*, crowned it with the complete destruction of theories he had once invented. It was the final part that he wanted to give to the public first; the rest would follow thereafter.

The idea that he could soon attain that goal had brought a little clam to his soul; he was allowing himself to live and had become less aggressive when a terrifying example inflicted further tortures upon him and gave birth to serious doubts about the value of his action.

One of the journalists that he sometimes encountered in the editorial offices, an Alsatian with a Socratic head, a taciturn, bitter man whose lips only opened to distill acerbic and violent recriminations but whose pen, on the contrary, only dripped indulgent and timid appreciations, a disequilibrated mind in which dreams of revolt ended in acts of resignation, had summoned him in order to receive his care. The unfortunate, afflicted by an incurable disease, was on the brink of death. The secret sympathy that had led him to address himself to Dr. Iblan, pushed him to make him confidences.

The Alsatian, the son of a protestant pastor, exercising the priestly profession himself to begin with, in the most honorable and favorable conditions, had suddenly taken it into his head to break with a situation to which he owed his only value and, delivered to his own resources, to come to Paris to earn his living there.

The attempt, as could be judged by its denouement, had been woefully unsuccessful. From effort to effort and misery to misery, in spite of his intelligence, perseverance and determination, instead of the fortune and glory of which he had dreamed, he was going to die, a misunderstood philosopher, an obscure journalist, without even having been able to earn his bread every day. No one would accompany him to his final abode—unless, he added bitterly, someone hung a mutton-chop from his hearse in order that it might at least be followed by a dog.

The similarities that existed between his own adventure and that of the unfortunate pastor troubled the mind of Dr. Iblan profoundly. What a young and well-endowed man had attempted in vain, could he hope to accomplish at his age?

He was cursing the hazard that had just added that example to so many other objects of discouragement when he learned, a few days later, that shares and bonds worth three hundred thousand francs had been found in the dead man's lodgings.

There had, therefore, been a deep hole, a frightful lacuna, in that mind; all of his pride had consisted of wanting to live by himself, in the material sense of the phrase. If he had been thirsty for glory, if he had inspired to the intellectual life, he could have profited from that money, which would have permitted him to do his work freely and tranquilly.

That narrow logic born of the aberration of a doctrinaire mind, that pride draped in a mantle of poverty, thus had only vague similarities to his own case. All his misfortunes, on the contrary, had resulted from the loss of his money; if it had not been necessary for him to seek his daily bread; if he had those riches that the Alsatian had forbidden himself to touch, he would already have realized his projects!

He meditated then on the deadly thoughtlessness of old. How had he not thought about procuring papers and renting a domicile in the name of Jacques Liban, of depositing funds in a bank that would have paid him interest? Doubtless because no accident of that kind, however slight, had ever happened to him. It was nevertheless true that he too had had his lacuna, his hole. Was it the only one?

Had his entire project not been dubious?

Had he not been the victim of a prideful caprice?

Why could Dr. Albin not have destroyed his past work himself? Why had he allowed himself to be carried away by sentimental considerations?

And something akin to vague regrets rose up in his soul; he thought about the life of glory, fortunate and honor, magnificent prey that he had left for the shadows. The past—which until then, although precise, had seemed, like dreams, to be born of the unreal—came closer to him and became more tangible.

Chapter XXXI

It was in that state of mind that he read an advertisement one day for a fête for the benefit of morally abandoned children. Several society ladies, among them Madame Larmezan, were to lend their collaboration to it.

Love of music had been the point of contact that had once united them; it was on hearing her sing that he had thought of making her his wife, a marriage advantageous in every fashion.

Since the day of his funeral comedy, he had carefully avoided encountering her; the few rare appearances in which he had glimpsed her vaguely had always been produced independently of his will. That extreme delicacy, pure of all coarse sentiment of curiosity, had never abandoned him.

This time, however, because of the more frequent returns he was making to the past, an invincible desire to see and hear her again came to haunt him. The opportunity was favorable; she was appearing in public, he would be lost in the crowd; he could observe her at his ease, without fear of being indiscreet and revealing, by an involuntary expression of his gaze, that the woman had once belonged to him.

He therefore bought a ticket and went to the Hôtel Continental.

The sumptuous festival hall was beginning to fill up with aristocratic spectators. The glare of the chandeliers, the scintillation of adornments, the delicate odor of perfumes and flowers, the radiant modesty of young women, the blossoming charm of wives, the dazzling whiteness of semi-naked shoulders and marmoreal arms, the simultaneously simple and refined elegance, the tasteful dresses and the discreet tone of dinner jackets formed a distinguished and essentially Parisian ensemble.

Involuntarily, the thousand soilings to which poverty and hazard had led him presented themselves comparatively to his mind; he chased them away like bad dreams. The world that was really his own he had before his eyes, and, not being one of those that contact could stain, he felt that he was as pure, as noble and as worthy of esteem as before.

Placed in a position to have a good view of the artistes without himself being in view, he waited impatiently for the habanera arranged by Lacôme that Madame Larmezan was to sing. Was it loss of memory or the result of his past indifference? He could not retrace in an absolutely precise fashion the features of the face that he had been accustomed to seeing for such a long time.

Now that he evoked the memory, Professor Albin's widow appeared to him *en bloc*, such as she had been in her first youth, such as he had seen her on the day that he had believed that he loved her. How had he been able to rediscover that? She must be approaching forty today, but she was surely still beautiful, otherwise she would not have braved the limelight; did she not still mingle a little coquetry with her charitable works?

The orchestra played the prelude; her turn had come. She entered on the arm of her cavalier, made an amiable bow and raised her head.

He had all the difficulty in the world not to betray his emotion. Clad in Spanish style, with a short skirt and a mantilla on her head, Madame Larmezan strangely resembled Rose Gontran of the Folies Nouvelles.

Without her nobility and the discretion of her gestures, without the pure intonations of her voice, without the chaste although amorous ingenuousness of her large dark eyes, the resemblance would have been disconcerting.

He mastered himself, believing that he was the victim of a fortuitous similarity of costume, and started detailing all the features: the broad and uncovered forehead, the arched eyebrows, the slightly jutting chin, gave her, like the other, the almost masculine allure of certain daughters of Spain or Italy. Whether he liked it or not, and in spite of the shame of sorts that he felt in establishing the comparison, Madame Larmezan resembled the unfortunate Rose. The type was more refined, the expression more chaste and more distinguished, the determination less emphatic, but it was Mariette, Mariette idealized, Mariette without the corruption, without the stigmata, the Mariette he had seen in his dreams of redemption!

He told himself in vain that he was a wretch to soil by such a comparison the chaste and noble spouse of old; his reason and his delicacy could not belie the evidence of his eyes.

Frantic applause saluted the socialite artiste; the apparition had disappeared.

Is that not, he thought, the key to the inexplicable attraction that linked me to Mariette? Was I not loving, indirectly, the confused memory of the person to whom I owed all my affection? Must those two individuals, one ideal, noble and pure, the other debased, wretched and perverse, not have completed one another, to enlighten my double existence with a veritable amour?

In spite of the flagrant indelicacy of the comparison, the truth burst forth before his eyes, increasingly luminous and revelatory; the memories became precise, the points of resemblance multiplied; everything, including the sound of her voice, familiar gestures, justified the impression that had just struck his heart. Moreover, in spite of the difference in years, the face of the one, touched by time, and that of the other, marked by debauchery and distress, appeared to have the same age; the expression alone distinguished them.

He left with his head on fire, his heart full of tumult, but without regret for having come. After all, why had he been so offended by that involuntary comparison? The two women that he had loved were doubtless only separated by a social injustice. One, left to herself, without guidance and support, deprived over everything, had slid into the mud; the other, surrounded by luxury and wellbeing, had remained pure. Would not Mariette, in her place, have done the same?

Were not the natural instincts of one as worthy as those of the other? Poverty alone had created the difference and produced the evil; although Rousseau's theory of primordial equality, taken in its absolute and general sense, was false, was it not true in many individual cases?

Did he not know, fundamentally, the two individuals that the similarity had brought to light? The fortunate one had fallen to the share of Dr. Albin, whom she had cherished vaguely with the mediocre dose of love typical their milieu of circulation; the disinherited had become the companion of the unfortunate, and had loved him far more. Why should he deny that love? Was it not born of his misfortune? Perhaps it had been necessary for him to experience real suffering in order to be capable and worthy of love?

In any case, those two women were completed by one another. If Mariette, undone by hunger, had lacked nobility and chastity, the other, faded by a bourgeois education and a fortunate existence, had lacked abandonment and passion in his regard. An overly egotistical conception of life had separated them, but fundamentally, they had without any doubt been created to love one another, and if...

He stopped, sensing that he was sliding down a dangerous slope.

"Wretch, insensate," he murmured. "There were a few moments when I perceived that I loved Mariette through the memory of my wife; am I now going to regret her through the memory of Mariette? That would be stupid and vain. I have, so to speak, disdained her when I was young, rich and glorious, when it was my right and duty to love her, and now that I'm an unknown, a stranger, almost an old man; because, thanks to the other, the blindfold that covered my eyes had just fallen away, would I dare to raise my eyes toward her? That would be to run toward a lamentable and humiliating disappointment!

"By what entitlement could I reclaim and affection that I have voluntarily and legitimately lost?"

But all these arguments did not succeed in chasing away the memories and regrets to which that transfiguration of sorts gave birth.

A circumstance fortunate for his repose put him in the presence of Madame Larmezan again, a few weeks later.

That day, the day of the dead, the crowds in mourning heading toward the cemeteries reminded him of his dead daughter, his Jeanne, whom he had loved so much but the memory of whom had almost been effaced in his heart.

He reproached himself for that incomprehensible forget-fulness and resolved to take a few flowers to her grave.

As he got closer to Père-Lachaise, the increasingly com-pact multitude took on a silent and meditative sect that moved him involuntarily. From the anxious expressions of some and the hope-illuminated eyes of others he could deduce various beliefs, what curbed all those heads, the sentiment compound of respect and fear that dominated those countless living indi-viduals, was the religion of death.

An instinctive terror chilled his heart. His action ap-peared to him in all its criminal horror: he had offended the pitiless Goddess, he had toyed with her power, he had mocked her worship. And to arrive at what pitiful result?

He almost regretted having thought of the duty whose accomplishment was occasioning him discouraging thoughts. He hastened his steps, penetrated into the cemetery and fol-lowed the narrow path that led to the Albin family crypt. A woman in full mourning, whom he recognized from afar, was coming toward him with slow steps.

His heart started to beat violently; what part had he had in her prayers and her tears? Quickly, he hid behind a stele and was thus able to study her at close range. This time, the face had an unhealthy pallor and was marked by nascent wrinkles; her expression was full of reserve and tenderness.

The resemblance that he had thought so striking now ap-peared to him more uncertain and vague. Had he, then, been the victim of an illusion of costume and make-up, perhaps a hallucination? His overexcited imagination alone was culpa-ble!

It was the first time since the day of the funeral solemni-ties that he had seen the place where, by virtue of his cunning

315

will, his first existence, so favored by destiny, had come to an end. He was no longer thinking of laughing. The funereal monument, which he perceived in the distance, appeared to him as an ironic reproach. He advanced almost regretfully.

He went nevertheless to deposit on the tomb the bouquet of hyacinths that he was holding in his hand, and gazed for a long time, plunged in a profound sadness compounded of disillusion and remorse and the iron door that had closed on his wellbeing, and reread several times the epitaph that celebrated the glory of Professor Albin. Then, fleeing the location that reminded him of his overly audacious lie, he made appeal to his pride, which was the only thing still sustaining his wounded hope.

What is death? A change of state; he had not, therefore, deceived anyone; was he not the master of his existence? He had committed civil suicide. That was his right; the error, the crime would rather be to believe that he was mistaken, to abandon the task he had undertaken, to want to resume his original personality; but if he had vaguely thought of that in a moment of weakness, he was not so cowardly, above all now that that amorous whim had suddenly vanished.

He left the cemetery, astonished to have almost recovered calm and forgetfulness.

Soon, a strange impression took possession of his heart.

It seemed to him that, like Mariette, his wife was dead forever, and that, thus confounded, he loved them both with an effaced and distant amour.

Chapter XXXII

A messenger had been waiting for him at his home for a short while; the editor of the newspaper requested that he come to the office immediately.

"Herr Doctor," he said—they had an irritating mania in the editorial offices of making him understand that they considered him to be a shameful German—"it's an opportunity to distinguish yourself forever. A talented young sculptor, in the intelligent hope that the State might make the acquisition, had just completed a very fine statue of the illustrious Dr. Albin. The director of the Beaux-Arts has exhausted his budget—the directors of the Beaux-Arts never have any money, that's taken for granted—but he has applauded the idea and advised a public appeal and had promised formally to support it. A committee, the cream of the crop, has been formed, the paper has been chosen to launch the subscription and I have orders to set out on campaign immediately.

"As it's a patriotic endeavor and, at the same time, excellent publicity for us, you're going to write me an article quickly, for tomorrow: you know, one of those uplifting, decisive articles overflowing with enthusiasm; in brief, something to whip up excitement. Above all, don't forget the chauvinistic aspect. The patriotic couplet in confections of that sort is as necessary as it is in café concert songs; one battles on scientific terrain as on others; it's necessary to prove to foreign science that we're not prepared to let ourselves be overtaken. You can see the fine humanitarian tirade from here: no more fratricidal struggles, no more bloody battles, but a noble rivalry for the conquests of Science and Art, etc."

Dr. Iblan was in no hurry to reply. "It's just that," he ended up venturing, "I consider Dr. Albin's doctrine to be stained by error."

"Ha!" said the editor, in the most indifferent tone. "That's your affair; I don't care whether, privately, you approve of Dr. Albin's doctrine or not, I want you to write an enthusiastic article that will declare him perfect, that's all. The paper isn't a scholarly academy, we're not forced to take a position in a technical discussion; the excellence of Dr. Albin's theories is a matter of public notoriety and we're launching a subscription; it's a matter of ensuring its success.

"For that, the article I'm demanding from you is absolutely indispensable. That a few foreign or French scholars don't admit all of the celebrated chemist's ideas is possible, even probable; what theory doesn't have its detractors? But it's necessary for you to refrain from breathing a word of that; the slightest restriction might chill the generosity of the public, and a failed subscription is worse than a lost battle."

"I'd pass for a weather-vane—I've already voiced contrary opinions."

"Well, if you don't want to take responsibility for the article, I'll sign it myself. But it requires specialist knowledge to write it, you're my scientific reporter and it's entirely natural that I should address myself to you."

"I no longer have any prejudices," the crestfallen reporter declared, effortfully, having not succeeded in vanquishing his repugnance. "I've had to say the opposite of what I thought many a time. In this circumstance, however, I admit to you honestly that it would be impossible for me to do the work you're demanding. It would be necessary for me to proclaim loudly admirations that I no longer have, convictions whose abandonment has caused me many difficulties. Believe me, in spite of all the effort I might put into it, I couldn't arrive at the enthusiasm you think necessary."

The editor looked at him in complete surprise.

"Oh, I understand," he exclaimed, in the end. "You're not French—I'd forgotten that. That's all right, my dear Monsieur, I'll think again."

As he expected, the reporter embarrassed by so many scruples was dismissed a few days later under some pretext.

That dismissal, combined with the success of the subscription, which surpassed all expectations, threw him back into the struggle.

He had been greatly mistaken to lay down his arms; Dr. Albin's renown was an implacable enemy that would grant no mercy to any assault and prevent him edifying his own; it was necessary to make the greatest efforts to prepare its collapse.

He inundated editorial offices with violent and perfidious articles, which were, for the most part, thrown into the rubbish bin. Some, the most attenuated, appeared in rival papers and aroused the indignation of the official establishment.

Why the devil was that foreign maniac always mixing in our affairs? On behalf of what foreign government was he working? He had certainly asked for papers of naturalization, but was that better to conceal his game?

He felt that he was spied upon, followed by suspect individuals who dogged his steps and watched his slightest moves.

As long as they did not discover, beneath his mask, the bone-setter Balin and the vagabond Jacques Liban...

The United States legation had him informed confidentially that he would do better to cease his attacks; the French government had the right to expel him and would seize the first opportunity to do so. A scientific dispute was not, it is true, a sufficient reason, but the rage and acrimony that he was putting into demolishing such a well-established reputation had made him numerous and powerful enemies. Ambushes would be set for him, and he would end up compromising himself in some equivocal adventure.

He was warned, in addition, that an investigation had established the recent date of his American naturalization, and traces of him were being sought in Cuba.

That advice gave him pause for thought; he felt, once again, temporarily vanquished. After all, why should Dr. Albin not have his statue? Others less meritorious had that honor. Ought he not to be flattered, fundamentally, by an homage rendered to his original self? In what way would the statue of Dr. Albin prevent him from demonstrating the falsity of his doctrine? It would consecrate his reputation, to be sure, but what glory could resist the proofs that the *Dynamic Chemistry* would bring? An accumulation of poor reasons soothed his self-esteem in order to dissimulate and attenuate defeat.

Exhausted and discouraged by so much futile effort, he went to ground with the pride of a wounded beast. He had lost the position as a journalist that had brought him influence and profit; he no longer even had the self-respect, the good opinion of his moral value that had sustained him in difficult circumstances; he was no better than the others; his short passage in the press had sufficed to accustom him to compromises that he would once have repudiated arrogantly. He could not, however, lower himself to writing an enthusiastic eulogy of the man he was destined to combat, lick the feet of the bronze elevated to the reputation he wanted to destroy, resign himself to acts of base domesticity. That would have been to lose his self-esteem completely. And, even though he had put out his hand to beg, even though he had accepted the aid of a whore, he did not feel that he was yet sufficiently degraded to do that.

A strange situation, that obliged him to become the artisan of his own incessant disappointments.

For the moment, he had to seek new resources; the practice of medicine was too absorbing, and in any case had not succeeded; pharmaceutical work only presented itself at rare intervals. Was he about to fall back into the Bohemian ways from which he thought he had liberated himself?

He spent that day on the Boulevard des Italiens.

A carriage emerged from the Grand Hôtel, loaded with baggage. A gentleman with a bronzed complexion turned round swiftly on perceiving him and studied him with and interrogative stare. The vehicle was about to break into a trot; the foreigner stopped it and summoned the passer-by with a gesture.

"Can you, Monsieur," he asked, in English, "give me news of Monsieur Charles Balin?"

Dr. Iblan, made wary by the police surveillance of which he was the object, instinctively put on an astonished expression.

"I don't have the honor," he replied, in the most natural tone, "of knowing the person of whom you speak."

"I regret it infinitely! Excuse me, Monsieur; I mistook you for his most intimate friend." He made a sign, and the coachman urged the horses forward at a trot.

Confused, Dr. Iblan searched his memories. That face was not unfamiliar to him, and it was someone who had recognized him. He must have a very particular gift for physiognomy.

He uttered an exclamation of surprise: "Raphael!"

He leapt into a fiacre and had himself taken to the Gare St-Lazare. The London train was leaving just as he gained access to the platform.

He returned to the Grand; the list of numerous foreigners that was communicated to him furnished him with no indication.

That abortive encounter caused him a real chagrin; he had certainly lost an exceptional opportunity to arrive at his goal. Raphael, emerging from the Grand Hôtel under aristocratic appearances, had acquired some large fortune, and would have hastened to aid him. Perhaps he had even returned to Paris to find his former companion in misfortune.

While Dr. Iblan spent, in order to live, the money that he had hoped to devote to the publication of his work, the monument erected to the glory of Dr. Albin was readied for its inauguration.

He had already seen the bronze in a gallery in the Champs-Élysées; the artist had represented him with natural grandeur, clad in his professorial gown—that bronze gown must have cost a small fortune—examining with an inspired expression the retort he as holding in his hand; allegorical figures of Physics and Chemistry were extending a fraternal hand to Medicine, leaning on the pedestal. A bas-relief represented his tragic death in Tonkin, and Renown, with chubbier cheeks than usual, was playing the fanfare of his glory on a bronze trumpet. All that art has of the conventional and the pompous was assembled in the work, whose execution was not, however, devoid of merit.

The inauguration was to take place on the twentieth of July at two o'clock in the afternoon, in one of the squares of the Latin Quarter.

At first he had promised himself that he would not go to watch it, and had even sworn to take some suburban train that day, but vanity soon put an end to those vain hopes.

Since the Roman emperors, a few kings had seen, while alive, the marble or bronze that would consecrate their great deeds, sand apart from them, no mortal had ever had that honor. Ought he to avoid an opportunity to experience such a rare impression? In any case, could any event which, for good or ill, related to his goal, leave him indifferent? Had he not followed the illustrious professor's interment without flinching? He could surely witness the inauguration of his statue.

The pharmacist that employed him had an invitation, from which some other event prevented him from employing; he accepted the offer of it and when the day came, after further hesitations but yielding to the mysterious force that seemed to dominate and direct his will, he headed for the square where the monument, still covered with its white sheet, stood in the midst of a metropolitan décor. Oriflammes were fluttering on the fourteenth of July flagpoles left standing for the occasion, and escutcheons surrounded by tricolor flags representing scientific emblems, with mottos borrowed from quotations in the Latin grammar, had been nailed to them *Labor improbus omnia vincit*, etc., were resplendent there in golden letters. The setting seemed insufficient and banal; he was almost disappointed.

The platform reserved for the public was already filled with people who, for the sake of discretion, had sat down in the back seats; only the first few rows were still empty. He thus found himself, against his will, placed in plain sight facing the official platform, and the chairs occupied by the mem-

322

bers of the committee. Even though a generous wine, taken with his lunch, had given him courage, that kind of involuntary bravado embarrassed him sensibly.

Certainly, he had no fear of being recognized, but he was keenly aware of the indiscretion involved in displaying himself to all gazes. Already, journalists and colleagues had noticed the intruder; people were pointing at him and whispering. What was Dr. Albin's relentless detractor doing there, and who had had the poor taste to invite him?

Momentarily, he wanted to get up and go; an iron hand clamped him in place.

The official delegates, the entire Faculté de Médecine and numerous personalities from all parts of society came in turn to take possession of their seats. At a distance, a crowd in their Sunday clothing, maintained by a cordon of municipal guards on horseback and uniformed policemen, formed a circle around the platforms and the monument. All the youth of the schools was there, street-hawkers were selling tricolor insignia or advertising the illustrious Dr. Albin's biography. Here and there, colored umbrellas seemed to be flowering in a bed of human heads.

Finally, the band of the Republican Guard launched into the inevitable Marseillaise; the carriages of the Minister of Public Education and War, escorted by a platoon of cuirassiers, had just arrived.

Soon the Grand Master of the Universities of France, lending his arm to the widow of the celebrated deceased, came to occupy the seat of honor, sitting Madame Larmezan down to his right and the Minister of War to his left; behind them, officers decked with gold, professors in red robes, foreign representatives covered in decorations, functionaries in braided and embroidered coats, deputes and senators with a their insignia and delegates of all sorts arranged themselves on the steps of the official stage, decorated in grenadine velvet with a golden fringe, garlanded with foliage and flowers.

Dr. Larmezan, with his long thin face, black beard and Arab profile, enveloped in his scarlet robe, came to sit beside his wife. Facing him, Dr. Iblan, clearly in view, was already serving as a target for his eyes. The director of his former newspaper and the members of the committee had hastened to signal his presence. Shrugs and ironic smiles were emitted from all the ranks.

He had been humiliated by the public hostility; the official disdain struck his pride like a whiplash. Did he not have the right to be there? Who had more right than he did to witness the ceremony? He raised his head and paraded his gaze over all the spectators.

In any other circumstances he would have avoided pausing it on Madame Larmezan, but today once again, by an unfortunate fatality, the indelicate comparison he had made at the Hôtel Continental, awakening an unconscious curiosity, took possession of his mind again. He saw Dr. Larmezan lean toward his wife and say a few words to her in a low voice. The window of the glorious deceased looked straight at the foreign chemist, blushed suddenly, made an abrupt movement of anger and struck him with a thunderous glare. He was both pained and delighted. She had loved Dr. Albin, then, since she was spitting in the face of his detractor—for, he had sensed, the gesture was sincere and the anger real.

How pretentious and stupid I am, he immediately thought. *She's defending the glory that reflects on her and nothing else. If she had loved Dr. Albin, she would have noticed, divined, that I resemble him.*

Behind the fan that served her as a veil he sensed a gaze imprinted with profound astonishment fixed upon him.

The band had fallen silent; the minister saluted the widow of the illustrious professor with a few amiable words, and the official dithyrambs commenced. Apart from a few periods and epithets adapted for the circumstances, they were no different from those pronounced before his tomb.

It was the turn of Professor R***, the old master, to speak on behalf of the Académie de Médecine. The American doctor could not help smiling. Professor R*** had once been the most determined and disloyal enemy of the author of *Bio-*

logical Chemistry. His animosity had only been disarmed on the day of the funeral, when he had remained silent. Now he was about to speak; were his honeyed and emphatic tones finally about to distil some mortal poison enveloped in eulogies?

But Dr. R*** commenced a panegyric so pompous, pronounced in a tone so convincing, that Dr. Iblan, shaken by a nervous hilarity, was unable to stifle the burst of sardonic laughter that rose to his lips.

All heads turned toward him; all curious and irritated gazes were fixed upon him. The reporters hastily took notes, the members of the audience muttered to one another. The orator, nonplussed and as if ashamed to be caught *in flagrante delicto* in a lie, stopped dead. The president of the committee said a few words to him in a low voice; he turned toward the impudent interrupter.

"I know," he cried, crimson with wrath, "that there are vagabonds devoid of name and fatherland, false scholars, envious unknowns, brazen charlatans, who want to contest and sully the glory of my friend of genius. I have read their odious attacks, and disgust has sickened me. These scornful individuals do not exist, they do not warrant the honor of an indignant response, but I am rightly astonished that one of them, after having had the indelicate audacity to insinuate himself among us, should permit himself to disturb my speech in a vulgar manner. Does he not understand that his presence here is a lack of respect for the illustrious audience and the supreme authority that presides over it, and insult to the dead man that we venerate, and a challenge to his family and his admirers— which is to say, to us?"

Unanimous cries of assent and frantic applause saluted the oratory outburst. Policemen in plain dress had approached the foreigner and demanded to see his invitation. It was not in his name, and they asked him to quit the place that he was occupying illicitly.

He stood up to obey the instruction, and a volley of insults and threats flagellated him from all directions. Before the outrage and the sarcasms, the pariah lost all his composure; anger and pride disturbed his reason. Should he allow himself to be expelled like a stupid intruder from a ceremony that, in reality, was being held in his honor? Certainly not. He would not go without serving them the truths that had been incessantly rising to his lips for an hour.

"That statue," he roared, "it is not to Dr. Albin, either to his person or to his merit, it is to you, to your social organization, to your official science, to your mediocrity, that you have erected it!"

The protestations and epithets redoubled in fury, the rumor of the crowd added its instinctive growl; the word "foreigner" had been pronounced.

"Down with the spy! Down with the German!" cried students and bourgeois, at random. People coming down the steps surrounded him on all sides; agents of the Sûreté had seized him by the collar. The official personages were alarmed by the scandal. Professor R*** and Dr. Larmezan were bombarding him with gestures; the disorder reached its peak. The American chemist struggled and tried to continue to make himself heard...

"Shut up!" was shouted at him from all sides. "Get out! You have no right to speak!"

Then Dr. Iblan lost his head completely; mad with rage, he shoved away the people who were trying to drag him away.

"More than anyone here, I have the right to speak," he howled, with all his might. "I'm Dr. Albin!"

A sudden relaxation was produced in all the ranks. The anger of the audience and the crowd changed into an enormous burst of laughter.

"He's a madman! To Bicêtre! To Charenton!" cried all the voices.

He disappeared, dragged away by representatives of the public force, laughter and jeers saluting his departure. But one woman—Dr. Albin's widow—had vanished.

Chapter XXXIII

In his narrow cell at Bicêtre, Dr. Albin thinks about the enormous imprudence that he had just committed.

First of all, he had been taken to a police station, where his qualities as an American journalist and physician had earned him a certain respect. In order not to be arrested for causing a scandal and insulting the foremost French authorities, he simulated stupidity and maintained an obstinate silence. Physicians have examined him in haste and sent him to Bicêtre. He has committed the act of a madman; therefore he is mad, or officially considered as such—which is, from the viewpoint of results, exactly the same thing.

That's better, he thinks, *than passing for a rational individual. I really don't want the law to examine me too closely, I fear that more than science. But how am I going to get out of this?*

He knows, in his capacity as a physician, that it is easier that it is easier to get in here than to get out. It is necessary, for the moment, that he resigns himself to being here for some time. Everything is so quickly forgotten in Paris! In a few weeks, no one will any longer remember the scandal he has caused; the longer he waits, the more chance he has of not being pursued.

He continues, therefore, to play his bewildered role, and then, little by little, pronounces a few words, manifests signs of intelligence, and is permitted to walk in the courtyard.

The majority of the lunatics who surround him scarcely interest him. He knows them; he studied them once; but a few among them impress him particularly because, in their obscure language, which he once found denuded of sense, he now glimpses profound ideas.

One of them, as soon as he saw him, has run toward him.

"Dr. Albin!" he cries. "How is the dear doctor?"

"You recognize me, then?" he replies.

"How could I not recognize one of the illustrious jokers that had me locked up here?"

"In what epoch, on what occasion?"

"About ten years ago. I wanted to get rid of a vampiric person who had stolen all my luck and whose glory was based on my discoveries."

"And it's Dr. Albin, you say, who had you interned here?"

"You know that very well, since it was you."

"You're mistaken, my friend. The illustrious joker, to use your expression, has been dead and buried for more than seven years. Perhaps I have some resemblance to him, but that's all."

The madman bursts out laughing. "If it's me that you want to swallow such a lie, you're wasting your time. Dr. Albin is you, unless"—he suddenly becomes serious and suspicious—"you're his larva; but larva or objective being, you're Dr. Albin."

He could not help making an ironic reflection: only one person consents to recognize him, and that man is mad!

"What is your name?" he asked.

"Marcotte."

He searched his memory and recalled that he once gave his advice in the case of a young astronomer culpable of an attempted murder. He judged it pointless to disabuse him.

"Well, yes," he confessed, "I'm Dr. Albin, and you can see that I have no luck; after having had others locked up, now I'm locked up in my turn."

"Bah! Might you, perhaps, have made some discovery of genius? I thought you had the means. Between ourselves, your biological chemistry brought nothing new; it's a transposition. You transformed a mathematical operation, an algebraic operation, that's all. You didn't even suspect the radiant state of gases."

"Genius, mediocre or stupid," he replied, with a certain ill humor, "I'm your companion now."

"Oh, I'm not mad; I'm submitting to the punishment of the bestial vice called anger, and that's justice; I should have

328

been able to master fatality by will. The stars incline, but don't necessitate."

"One can see that you're an astronomer."

"Astronomer, mathematician and astrologer, and it's so universally admitted that astrologers ought to fall into a well that, when they don't fall, they're pushed."

The poor devil recounted his story. He believed himself to be a victim of official vampirism.

If, taken individually, false scholars are impotent, the force that results from their association is considerable. It is an aggregate that attracts all individuals of value, absorbs them, fashions them, and pours them into a mold of mediocrity. If a mind of genius resists them, they gang up against him; the collectivity is fattened at the expense of the individual, in order to take away his means.

It was to avenge himself on a man of renown, who was profiting from his work without wanting to acknowledge his merit, that, in a moment of exasperation, he had had recourse to crime.

The dialectic of the hermetic philosopher was tightly bound; furthermore, the new perceptions that he had in the sciences and the arts rendered his conversation infinitely interesting.

He had written a treatise on harmony based on the Pythagorean theory of numbers and a meteorography full of precious indications on the art of producing and directing atmospheric phenomena. Like the ancient thaumaturges, he manipulated the thunder and unleashed the tempest. In chemistry he admitted a mineral scale analogous to Darwin's animal scale. He had obscure aphorisms whose revelation gave rise to profound thought, and it was not without profit that Dr. Iblan heard him announce that "Quaternary chemistry is Tertiary chemistry returned to unity by the radiant state."

Another poor fellow, an erotomaniac, a former professor of Mathematics, whose companions in misfortune had nicknamed him Père Absolu, claimed to have discovered the Absolute.

"And I don't sell it, like that rogue Wrinski,"[29] he exclaimed. "I don't make a secret of it; I unveil it to anyone who cares to listen to me. The mistake of science," he declared, "is to have decreed that there are inferior organs and others that are superior; hence the error of philosophers and idealist scholars; they've always sought the absolute here"—he tapped his forehead—"but once again, the brain is a simple recorder, it only centralizes the complex acts of the organism. It's a kind of bureaucracy; it's necessary not to give it an importance it doesn't have; it ought to administrate and not govern; to want address yourself to it alone in order to know the secret of creation is to want to be the victim of error infinitely. It's thus that humans have created a God in their own image and an absolute at the height of their comprehension—which is to say, a relativity; and yet it exists, the Absolute, and is manifest. But it's not here"—he struck his forehead again—"that it's necessary to seek it, for I've found it, the Absolute, and it's for that reason they've locked me up here."

With a kind of fury, the unfortunate old man repeated: "I've found it. Everything is in everything; to know the secret of an organ is to know the Absolute, and that's where it is, nowhere but here; it's by this means alone that we can arrive at an understanding of it."

---

[29] I have left this name as it appears in the original, as the error might be deliberate, but the reference is certainly to Józef-Maria Hoëne-Wronski (1776-1853), a Polish mathematician and mystic philosopher whose aspiration was to revolutionize human knowledge with a theory of absolute (or ultimate) matter. Like the previous theorist encountered in Bicêtre by Dr. Iblan he was a great enthusiast for Pythagorean number theory. He worked in France for the last thirty years of his life attempting, among other projects, to build a perpetual motion machine and a machine for predicting the future. Most people thought he was a crackpot, the principal exception being the occultist who called himself Éliphas Lévi.

The vulgar gesture that accompanied these final words and the laughter of the inmates, anticipating the amazement of the newcomers, interrupted the conversation.

A third, a meek and literate individual, the victim of poetic visions, thought he had lived for thousands of years, and recounted the marvels of his metempsychoses. He transported his listener to Egypt to Greece and from Chaldea to Rome, fought in the back-streets of Florence and groaned in the Piombi of Venice, with an extraordinary richness of imagery, a luxury of detail, local color and the picturesque.

On various occasions, people had tried to get him to write down his dreams; then, they were no more than incoherent and inconsequential words; an intern struck by the beauty of his tales had wanted to write them down, but the eloquent lips had immediately closed. Interrogated on that mutism he had replied, full of sorrow: "What I recount must not be written; it's for having wanted to violate that order that I'm here."

The neighborhood of these poor castaways, victims of their noble pursuits, saddened Dr. Iblan profoundly. The sojourn at Bicêtre became intolerable to him; he was afraid of submitted to contagion and sinking in his turn. He resolved to get out.

"Monsieur," he said to the chief of service, who, in the capacity of a colleague, treated him with sympathetic regard. "I ought to make you a confession. You've been able to convince yourself by my words and actions that I'm entire sound of mind. This is the explanation of the scandal that bought me here. I have the bad habit, acquired abroad, of smoking a mixture of Indian hemp and opium. My friends had told me many a time, by way of a joke, that I resembled the illustrious Dr. Albin, whose scientific doctrines I have perhaps opposed a little too energetically. On the eve of the inauguration I have yielded to my baneful passion. There's no need, is there, to explain to you the effects of hashish. It is, therefore, the cause of the temporary morbid state that procure me the honor of your acquaintance. I did not give you that explanation immediately, fearing pursuit and wanting to give the interested parties time to forget my ridiculous fit."

The specialist, having, indeed observed no sign of mental alienation, referred the matter to the court. Several noted alienists were charged with examining him again. A new theory saw the light of day in his honor.

"All madmen are simulators," affirmed the celebrated Z***, with reason. "Dr. Iblan has committed an undeniable act of madness; he is simulating reason, therefore he is mad."

His smiling colleagues did not admire the syllogism, and concluded in favor of the foreigner. He thought that his ticket of release would be rapidly signed, but days and weeks passed and the chief of service always engaged him to be patient, making him understand by implication that a higher will than his own had intervened to oppose his liberation.

Dr. Iblan conceived an ever-increasing irritation. He feared than an order might suddenly arrive to transfer him to a provincial asylum, which would lead, in a short time, to definitive forgetfulness and then real madness and death.

The powerful man who was bolting the doors of the horrible gehenna where his mind would end up succumbing with so much obstinacy could not be anyone but Dr. Larmezan, Dr. Albin's successor, the representative of the honor and interests of his family. He asked to make him a communication of the greatest importance. What was he risking? Clarify or conforming the doubts of his former pupil? Perhaps—but Dr. Larmezan was less disposed than anyone else to recognize him. He would keep to himself the suppositions that would result from their conversation, and the fear of seeing the specter of Dr. Albin reappear would submit him to the desire of Dr. Iblan.

The professor of biology, very intrigued, came to Bicêtre the next day and considered the author of the scandal with an anxious curiosity.

"It can't be denied," he murmured, striving to laugh, "that there's a certain resemblance between you and my master. What do you have to say to me?"

The American repeated the explanation that he had already given, and told him the conclusion of the experts and the physician caring for him.

"I know all that," he professor repeated. "Let's get to the point. What do you want to confide to me, or what do you want from me?"

"For you to give the order to let me out of here."

"Let you out of here!" exclaimed the professor, disappointed. "That's not in my power, Monsieur. You ought, in any case, to reckon yourself fortunate to be here. The court, based on your declaration of smoking opium, wanted to send you to the petty sessions court; it's to your quality as a physician that you owe the benefit of madness." Doubtless making allusion to private conversations, he added: "Perhaps also, a little, to the bizarre resemblance that, in spite of your appearance of a Spanish-American, one can't help noticing."

"If the court had charged me as a responsible individual, I would get away with two or three months in prison or an expulsion order, whereas I'm here in the quality of a madman, which is far from being a benefit in my eyes. As it's impossible for me to support the imprisonment and promiscuity to which I'm subjected any longer, it's necessary, *at any cost*, that I get out. Please weigh the value of those words: *at any cost*."

"I don't understand," declared Dr. Larmezan.

"Between us, any categorical explanation is impossible; I can and ought only to make myself understood in an uncertain fashion. If I spoke to you clearly, you would refuse energetically to understand me."

"Ha ha!" sniggered Dr. Albin's successor. "I knew full well that you weren't cured."

"Don't oblige me to prove, in a definitive fashion, that I am not, and never have been, a madman. In spite of my repugnance, rather than suffer the slow agony of incarceration, I'd be capable of telling the truth."

"Calm down, my poor friend, calm down," exclaimed the professor, "and above all, shut up, because you're about to claim once again that you're Dr. Albin."

"I shall refrain very carefully from doing that, or, if I emitted a similar pretention it would be with evidence to support it. But it's not in that fashion that I shall justify the exclamation that brought me here. It would be by summoning the intervention of the man who permitted me to speak in his name: Dr. Albin himself."

Dr. Larmezan's hesitant laughter rang false. "Insensate words," he proclaimed. "My illustrious master is dead and buried."

"Are you certain that his veritable remains were taken to Père-Lachaise?"

"Alas."

"Don't pretend regrets that you've never had," said the mysterious individual, "and don't assert either a certainty that you have not had since the moment you measured scientifically the head that was sent to you from Tonkin."

Dr. Larmezan was no longer laughing; he had gone strangely pale, and was considering fearfully the possessor of a secret that he had never revealed. He tried very rapidly to get a grip on himself. "And it's with assertions of that sort that you intend to prove your cure?" he said.

"I can't hold those words against you, for you alone can understand them; I shall therefore keep them to myself...if I get out of here; but it's *necessary* that I get out of here."

"I'm not the cause of the delay that has been placed on your release," affirmed the official representative. "I'm even astonished by it, since the report of the experts concluded the cure. I shall, therefore, try to disarm the enemies you've created by combating the illustrious deceased with so much violence. I fear, nevertheless, that you won't be able to avoid an expulsion order."

"Anything is preferable to this sojourn," murmured the inmate of Bicêtre.

The preoccupied professor of biology was visibly trying to return to the subject that has just disturbed him. The pretended madman interrupted him as soon as he spoke.

"Insensate words," he sniggered in his turn, "which you were wrong to take to heart. He put his index finger on his lips and added: "This mouth will be forever as mute as the tomb. I no longer have any desire to be interned as a lunatic. Forget what I said."

"So be it," said Dr. Albin's former pupil, who moved toward the door.

He changed his mind. "It seems to result from our conversation that you knew my illustrious master well. Why, then attack him with such great bitterness?"

"I long admired the *Biological Chemistry*," the unknown responded. "Then, one day, I made discoveries in flagrant contradiction with his theories. It's therefore necessary that I demolish the reputation of the author in order to establish mine."

Professor Larmezan went out, shaking his head.

Two days later, Dr. Iblan was told that he was free to leave Bicêtre, but that he was to cross the frontier within three days. Scarcely time to sell the little furniture that remained to him!

In fact, that concern was to be spared him; his creditors, informed of the scandal, had hastened to seize it; his landlord, fortunately for him, had got in first; he was thus able to save his personal effects and his manuscripts from the debacle.

He had a moment of terrible anxiety; he was almost penniless, and the journalist X***, the only friend who had not abandoned him, was not in a situation to assist him; they had all the difficulty in the world scraping together a hundred francs. It was with those meager resources that he was taking the road of exile!

He would have preferred to go to Spain or Italy, where his failing health would have found a more favorable climate, but his poverty and the hope of earning his bread more easily obliged him to leave for London.

He quit France with a frightful heartache. Would he ever return? Exile, at his age and in those conditions of poverty, was almost equivalent to a death warrant.

Sitting on a heap of ropes, he watched sadly as the Norman coast disappeared from view. Soon, it was no more than an indecisive line that was lost in the autumn mist.

He had bought a newspaper before leaving; he opened it mechanically, doubtless hoping to change the course of his ideas. The name Mariette suddenly struck his gaze and he read the relevant article.

What can one not find in the Seine? Divers exploring the bed of the river between the Châtelet and the Louvre have brought out various objects—a long list followed, which he skipped in order to arrive at his find: *A woman's handbag in Russian leather containing a thousand francs in gold, forty francs in silver coin, a small mirror with the initials R.G., a box of rice-powder, keys and a modest gold bracelet with the inscription* Mariette, 18**, *doubtless a desperate woman whom amorous chagrins had driven to suicide. Anyone who can supply any information is invited to contact the Prefecture of Police.*

A cloud passed before his eyes. For a long time he had no longer doubted the fatal verity, but the complete absence of indications had sometimes been a badly jointed door that had let through feeble rays of hope. He had told himself that perhaps Rose Gontran was abroad. Now he had absolute certainty that the poor woman was dead. That mirror with the initials R.G.; that bracelet, his first gift, which she regarded as a talisman and from which she was never separated; the name and date that he had had engraved on it, were irrefutable proofs.

"Poor Mariette," he murmured, remembering that last letter, the only memory of her that he was carrying. "Poor Mariette!"

It was at that moment of supreme melancholy, on the ferry that was carrying him toward a somber unknown, that the confirmation of his suspicions, the complete annihilation of his vague hopes had fallen, as if by chance, before his eyes!

Chance! Why was he obstinate in speaking of chance? There was too much logic, precision and cruelty in all the blows that had struck him for him to refuse, any longer, to deny the mysterious power that was relentless in his pursuit!

Passengers were chatting nearby.

"Here we are, in sight of the English coast," said one of them.

He looked, and saw nothing before him but a horizon of thick mists, an intense and yellow fog rising from the turbulent sea.

Chapter XXXIV

Oh, those first weeks of exile! Sharp and penetrating rain, thick shrouds of fog. Muddy marshes of slippery streets, flagellations of cold winds, icy blizzards of blinding snow, earth and sky distilling spleen, despairs without a mirage; the bleak solitudes of crowds, contact with individuals whose elbows are brutalizing, nights in which imprecise dreams are formless and repugnant possessions, days spent wandering, groping searches, prodigal disappointments, disgust for the present, regrets for the past, fear of tomorrows...

The idiot torpor that paralyzed his debut in poverty has let its lid fall once again on his thoughts and will. The same darkness envelops him; his cranium is a child's rattle in which ridiculous beads agitate; fragments of sentences devoid of meaning obsess him day and night: "That is certain," "It is evident," he mumbles continually, without that certainty responding to any precise question. He makes enormous efforts to follow a train of thought or make a practical resolution, but a glancing collision, the racket of an omnibus or a whistling passer-by is sufficient to break the thread.

The only clear and precise impression that remains in his head is the memory of shameful jeers and past suffering, the incessant recall of which multiplies his fear and distress tenfold.

Once again he exhausts the strength to act therein, but it disconcerts and paralyzes him. He wanders aimlessly, and in the London fog, where the décor of crossroads and edifices takes on fantastic proportions and lugubrious aspects, he seems to be moving, a predestined victim, through an implacable drama whose unknown denouement fills him with tragic terror.

Certainly, the poverty suffered on native soil is cruel and harsh, but there, a little pity still seems to be disengaged from people and things; the sky has smiles, the street-corners memories, the passers-by a discreet indifference—but poverty abroad, the abandonment of exile, the glacial inclemency of harsh climates, the scornful insensibility of another race, do not take long to engender the worst despair: the one that no longer fears death. Death would be repose, deliverance; but a banal and cowardly death, obscure death, is unworthy of his pride, the only piece of wreckage that is sustaining him and to which, as he drifts, he clings on desperately. Who, then, will accomplish his work?

Thus far, he has lived on the little money he brought from Paris, and then sold his watch, a few minor objects, and the surplus of his garments. He has nothing left now but a dozen shillings with which to lodge himself sordidly and not to die of hunger for a few more days. If he has found nothing by then, he will simulate an illness and try to get into a hospital. After that, come what may!

A vendor of French newspapers has indicated to him, in one of the most sinister districts of London, a sleazy inn kept by a compatriot, and it is there that he proposes to go to hide his destitution.

He goes into the Dauphin Tavern and first orders a slice of salted piece. Several individuals at table before pots of beer seem to be plotting in a corner. His arrival has interrupted all conversations; he is being examined with a suspicion that no one takes the trouble to dissimulate. A few words of French are exchanged in low voices. He has not understood the conventional meaning, but he senses that he is being watched. He looks at the strangers with a sad smile, supposing that he is in the presence of political refugees, and feels the need to speak French to them; he does not want them to mistake him for a police spy.

"If you have something private to say to one another," he declares, "don't speak the French language, or else I'll be obliged to understand you."

"You've arrived from Paris?" says one of them.

"Expelled," he replies. "The newspapers have doubtless informed you of my adventure. I'm Dr. Iblan."

"The author of the scandal," exclaims a voice. "The energetic protester who launched harsh words at the official world?"

"The same."

"Weren't you locked up as a madman?"

"I have, in fact, emerged from Bicêtre."

The ice seems to be broken; the strangers ask him for permission to sit down at his table and bombard him with the most various questions.

"The papers don't always reflect public opinion," one of them asked "What are Parisians saying about anarchists?"

"Those I know think that isolated acts of violence are futile and criminal. It's by means of the Idea that it's necessary to fight."

A pale, thin young man with white hair and blazing eyes laughs bitterly. "But to fight by means of ideas," he exclaims, "it's necessary that the fighter can make himself heard. He needs a stage, a tribune, a pulpit, a newspaper or a book. Now, I don't admit for a moment that the power won't stifle the voice that dares to proclaim the Truth. Who is there, among the combatants of ideas, who hasn't sensed his faith totter as soon as he finds himself in a position to make himself heard? As long as he's at the bottom of the ladder, his energetic demands launch a challenge, but scarcely has he climbed a few rungs than his words change complexion. His affirmations of the day before take on question marks, justice becomes the law, love is transformed into commiseration and pity. He no longer demands his rights imperiously; he begs for them as if he were soliciting favors; he no longer threatens, he warns. His satisfied egotism and pride find that that life is good and that Society or Suffrage can recognize merit. He hasn't yet forgotten his principles, but he always finds that the moment to apply them isn't yet opportune—and in the meantime, the lamentable herd of the wretched continues, as before, to die of hunger!"

"I know, in fact," Dr. Iblan replies, "that present society is a corrupting milieu, and too often closes the mouth it is afraid to hear roar with honors and money. I know too that the most ardent convictions are disarmed by wellbeing and the satisfactions of self-esteem. But aren't those inherent weaknesses of our incomplete nature? Do they legitimate violent means? In my humble opinion, I think that the slightest scientific progress—the discovery of the transmission belt, the importation of the potato, the discovery of vaccines, and a thousand others—has done more for humankind than all political, religious or social revolutions."

"Don't exaggerate the value of your discoveries," retorts the old revolutionary. "First of all, without the revolutions you dismiss, it's probable that you wouldn't have been permitted to make them. Secondly, what you call progress is a tree of which the powerful take possession for their own profit; the people water it with their blood, science by its sweat, so that the masters can devour the good fruits, and scarcely leave us the worm-ridden ones.

"Capital has grown monstrously, but wages haven't followed the proportion. Works has become easier; they have it done by women and children and pay them less; machines have led to overproduction, which is to say to people being out of work; competition has produced the lowering of wages; the means of preserving human life have improved, it prolongs the agony of the poor—it would be better to attenuate their suffering!

"Go ask those who have nothing to eat whether they have any great consideration for Parmentier. Believe me, your humanitarian who cures all the evils of the future thinks too little about immediate distress; your propaganda by the Idea has had its trial; for too long it's been lulling us, putting us to sleep, duping us, promising everything and delivering nothing. Since there are still people dying every day of hunger; since an entire class, the most numerous, the sanest, the most valiant, can't succeed in obtaining the price of its crushing labor; since..."

The man stopped dead and lowered his head; three individuals had just entered quietly and sat down at a neighboring table. The whispers that had greeted his own arrival immediately recommenced. Then, one by one, his companions disappeared from the table without saying a word.

"Don't stay here," the last of them said to him in a low voice. "Come with me."

They moved at a rapid pace through narrow and stinking streets, went into a narrow passage, took a kind of long corridor, found themselves in another street and doubled back. Night was beginning to fall.

"Our three policeman should have lost the trail," said the unknown man, breaking the silence. "Flanked by two English detectives, that was a police spy from Paris who wouldn't be sorry to know where I live. For more security, I'll be off." He added: "Perhaps we'll never see one another again. May your exile be light, Monsieur, and adieu."

"Thank you for your good wishes," replied Dr. Iblan, "and excuse the liberty I'm taking. Do you know of a means by which I might get out of embarrassment? I have no resources and no work."

"Perhaps. What kind of work are you looking for?"

"Anything."

"If you're content to be a teacher of music and French at an institution near London, present yourself in the afternoon, the day after tomorrow; the place will be vacant." The unknown wrote a few words in pencil on a page of a notebook, left him the address and disappeared.

For want of anything better, Dr. Iblan has taken up the ruler again. The memories he retains of the Béguinard school are not such as to inspire him with enthusiasm for the profession, but there, his special functions at least save him from the imbecilic teasing of the children.

Part of his day is spent preventing the young Englishmen from mangling the French language too much, and holding the most exasperating conversations with them. He goes to the market, buys all sorts of vegetables, meat and fish; he enquires about the time and health, discusses the weather and asks for directions; he changes money, buys socks, rents hotel rooms, buys tickets in railway stations, debates prices with cab-drivers and guides, produces model letters, etc., etc.

The rest of his time is devoted to teaching them an infinity of instruments that he scarcely knows and listening to them massacre on the piano "God Save the Queen," "My Jenny," "The Last Rose of Summer" and rapid jigs.

Months go by. It is no longer black poverty, but it is still poverty. He allows himself to live in a kind of neurasthenic resignation in which revolts become increasingly rare. Fortunately, the sight of his completed manuscripts, ready for publication, is still an aliment that reanimates the vacillating flame of his energy. Will he continue to vegetate so pitifully? He has learned, by showing others, to play the cornet and the clarinet passably. Has he abandoned so many honors and so much glory to play the roles of an obscure buffoon?

He makes new efforts to seek employment with a manufacturer of chemical products. He has visited nearly all of them in his hours of liberty, with no result.

A conversation overheard in the course of his last attempt inspires an audacity that borders on expediency. An individual whose jovial and well-to-do appearance denotes a successful businessman has just ordered a hundred liters of oxygenated water[30] and is complaining about the high price demanded by the previous manufacturer.

"What do you expect?" replies the merchant of chemical products. "The manufacturing process is in the hands of German chemists; we're their tributaries, they skin us as we please."

"In your place, I'd try to discover their secret; oxygenated water has bleaching properties that render it precious to a number of industries. Someone who could manufacture it cheaply would make a colossal fortune in a short time. Look, for myself, if the price permitted me to bleach all my cod that

---

[30] i.e., hydrogen peroxide.

are too old or damaged, I'd have a net benefit of several thousand pounds a year."

"Thief!" murmurs the eavesdropping petitioner—but an idea suddenly occurs to him. He runs after the ship-owner and catches up with him as he is about to climb into his cab.

"How much do you pay for your oxygenated water, Monsieur?" he asks him, point-blank. "I'm doubtless in a position to be useful to you."

"A pound a liter," replies the businessman, who looks him up and down. "Why do you ask?"

"I can manufacture it for half that," he affirms, without batting an eyelid. "What am I saying, half…a quarter, and still make a tidy profit."

The ship-owner becomes perfectly amiable. "To whom do I have the honor of speaking?"

"Dr. Iblan of the Faculté de Paris, who has made a specialty of chemical studies."

"Well, Monsieur, come to find me at five o'clock this evening. Here's my address. Perhaps we can come to some arrangement."

Dr. Iblan only knows one very costly laboratory procedure, but the dazzling vision of a rapid fortune that caused him to make that risky declaration, the belief that he can achieve what others have done, causes him to renew the lie before a competent person that Sir Arthur Frey, a great owner of fishing-boats, has judged it appropriate to ally himself.

Of the method, of course, he has not breathed a word; the presence of the other chemist explains that reserve; but the unknown gives proof of knowledge so vast and so conclusive that no doubt can be born in the minds of his listeners. A few days later, the businessman, a rich and adventurous man, signs a contract of partnership with him, and, as the inventor relates that, because he has been expelled from France for political reasons, he is a schoolteacher and does not have the money necessary to equip a laboratory, he receives two hundred pounds in advance.

The precise and immediate objective that he is required to attain if he is not to pass to the rank of a vulgar crook, returns all his lucidity to him in an instant; he struggles with the energy of a man who has thrown himself into a gulf in order to learn to swim. He only emerges from his laboratory to eat in haste and sleep for a few hours. His trials multiply; discouragement succeeds hope; then enthusiasm burst forth; success crowns his enterprise. His oxygenated water can be produced for less than a shilling.

That is a fortune, in a short time. This time, he glimpses the final goal with a delirious joy. Destiny is disarmed; misfortune releases its quivering prey; a glorious glimmer of dawn rises over the horizon of France.

Feverish impatience comes to assail him. The glacial wind that sometimes passes over his forehead warns him that Death is hovering close by; his heart, worn out by so much anguish, might suddenly cease beating; his bronchi, corroded by the pestilential fog, need to breathe his native air; he is in haste to return to Paris; exile weighs so heavily upon the soul of the banished.

Sir Arthur Frey, glimpsing millions, talks about establishing a vast factory; thousands of liters have already been ordered and he has not yet undertaken any advertising.

"It's necessary that I return to France immediately. I'll sell you my share of the partnership," proposes Dr. Iblan.

"How much?"

"Two thousand pounds and ten per cent of the future profits."

The bargain is too advantageous not to be accepted.

The dissociation agreement, drafted without delay, is signed by the interested parties. Sir Arthur, an excellent fellow at heart, even though his commercial conscience permits him to sell damaged merchandise as first rate produce, experiences a real solicitude for such a competent and disinterested auxiliary, and urges him to shorten his absence as much as possible; the factory needs his enlightenment, the direction will be his as soon as he returns.

Dr. Iblan thanks him, takes his check and hastens to cash it; then he runs of the Monks Agency, reintroduces himself, and asks for authentic French identity documents.

Chapter XXXV

Mr. Monks' little eyes blink, and his face, the color of cooks crab, lights up in keen satisfaction.

"We have a dozen, you can take your choice. What age are you? At first sight one would estimate fifty-five or fifty-six."

"That almost exactly right."

"A few years more or less are no obstacle," says the book-dealer. "Edgar! Go to the reserve; bring me the French identity papers between fifty and sixty." He turns back to his client. "Please wait for a few moments; as you might suppose, I keep my papers in a safe place. People can come and search here as much as they please; they wouldn't find a single dubious document among all these papers."

The sales clerk came back half an hour later and handed two files to his employer.

"Only two," says Mr. Monks, a trifle disappointed. "I thought I had more."

Dr. Iblan scans the files that the businessman hands to him after having examined them rapidly himself. One is that of a mariner, a native of Paimpol, the other that of a Dauphinois, a small manufacturer of braid. He cannot dissimulate a slight grimace; the two identities offered to him are not at all seductive.

It would be strange, to say the least, if a former Breton mariner or an obscure braid-maker were the author of *Dynamic Chemistry*.

"That's all I have between fifty and sixty, but I can guarantee the honorability of the two individuals."

"How do you procure these documents?" he hazards, not without anxiety.

"Oh, that's my secret, Monsieur," replies Mr. Monks, sharply, "and the question is indiscreet."

"I don't want to be accused later of having stolen them, or seeing the man whose name and titles I've usurped appearing before me."

"Nothing of that sort is to be feared, Monsieur. I can't tell you our method of procedure, but I can guarantee that my dossiers are authentic and that they belonged to honest men, dead today without anyone ever having worried about them, and buried under other names. The latter of the two you opened is that of a French refugee who came here after the Commune, who created resources here and because of that, did not want to take advantage of the amnesty. It's among political refugees, I must confess, that we have the best chance of encountering relatively honest individuals. The other Frenchmen who come to London are far from offering the same guarantees. You could assume the skin of a thief or murderer, but that wouldn't be in your interest or mine. Although all our precautions are taken, we don't want the name of the Monks Agency pronounced in the court of assizes, and it never has been. You must have noticed that I sometimes speak in the plural; that's to admit to you that I'm simply a representative, and that there are people behind me who have the greatest interest in not being compromised. It's therefore important for the prosperity of the agency and our security that I don't deceive my clients, and as they—present company excepted, of course—are almost always flawed individuals, it's necessary that I dissimulate them under the mask of an honest man."

An individual came in, with a clean-shaven face like the blade of a knife, a turned-up nose, anxious eyes, severe but dirty attire and the obsequious manners of a sacristan.

"You have news, Mr. Box?"

The man made a sign of the head indicating the stranger.

"You can talk, he's a French client."

The newcomer looked at the client with a grimace that he probably believed to be a smile. "It's a French civil estate that I've brought," he hastened to announce, with a kind of ironic unction. "I believe I've arrived at an opportune moment; not only is the gentleman almost the same age, but he even resembles the honorable gentleman." He passed a wad of papers to Mr. Monks. "I've had my eye on them for three weeks," he added. "The worthy fellow didn't want to resign himself to dying."

"When did he die?" interrogated the fake bookseller.

"Yesterday. He's in the process of being buried; I'll wager that the grave isn't yet filled in."

"All the formalities have been completed?"

"All of them; the devil himself would only see smoke."

"That's good. Leave us, Mr. Box."

Mr. Monks immediately set about examining the documents that had just been brought to him. Grunts of satisfaction escaped him after reading each one.

"Here's something that will suit you admirably if you care to pay the price. "It's a civil estate in the names of Jacques Bilan."

"Jacques Bilan!" exclaimed the stranger, utterly amazed. "An anagram of Albin! That's the one I need—that's the one I want!"

He took the file. The documents were numerous and presented the most serious characteristic of authenticity: a birth certificate establishing, by a strange coincidence, that Jacques Bilan had been born in Perpignan on the twenty-eighth of December 18**,[31] very day when Louis Albin had been born in Paris; certificates of baptism and first communion; documents establishing that the deceased had received first orders in a seminary in his native city, a bachelor's diploma from the University of Toulouse, four inscriptions in the École de Médecine in Paris.

They had studied together, then?

He recalled his memories, vaguely evoking the silhouette of an excitable Pyrenean whose Republican opinions had impressed him. The pile also contained an appointment as Chief

---

[31] The year in question must be 1836, counting back from the spring of 1883, when Dr. Albin was forty-six.

of a Battalion of the Commune, awarded by Flourens, and several testimonials by merchants of heads of institutions, one of which related that Jacques Bilan had shown a great deal of intelligence, activity and rectitude in the employment confided to him but that he had sometimes given evidence of an independence not in accordance with his subordinate position. That description was far from displeasing the exile; it proved that Jacques Bilan had not lived without dignity.

"This Jacques Bilan died yesterday?" he asked.

"Dead and buried under an assumed name—which is to say, alive, if you buy these documents from me; but I won't press you, seek information. Although I have every confidence in the marvelous flair of Mr. Box, it's prudent for you to take account for yourself that, outside of his political condemnations, no defect has tarnished the reputation of the deceased."

"He wasn't an anarchist, at least?"

"Anarchist! An amnestied Communard!" exclaimed Mr. Monks, laughing. "It's the first time that I'd have seen that: reactionary, mitigated, reformed, re-entered the fold, rosewater socialist, perhaps, but anarchist, never. Name me one of them who's in the public eye! Then again, the anarchists are of all nationalities; nine out of ten of them are agents provocateurs charged with discovering their projects."

"And what's the price of this dossier?"

Certain that the client had made his decision, Mr. Monks made elevated demands. That title of Chief of a Battalion of the Commune appeared to have considerable importance in his eyes; thanks to that, an adroit man could not fail to have himself elected as a député or bag a prefecture. After long haggling, he consented to sell it for six hundred pounds, and the exile, who was sighing after Paris, accepted the bargain, subject to enquiries.

The duplicate of the birth certificate, which arrived a week later from Perpignan, the favorable testimony of English businessmen to whom he addressed himself and the affirmations of Mr. Box, who said he was a friend of the deceased and had known him for twenty years, convinced him to conclude the bargain definitively.

Impatient to leave, he returned to the agency, paid the agreed sum and emerged on to Holborn Hill under the fateful name of Jacques Bilan.

He immediately proceeded with the transformation that the new identity required. It was necessary that Jacques Bilan did not resemble the American doctor too closely. The indications given by Mr. Box facilitated the metamorphosis. He wore his hair short, a moustache, a goatee, and, pale, thin and dressed modestly, but with the characteristic good taste of the French, no longer had any but a distant resemblance to the exotic Dr. Iblan. It was, in any case, a year since the latter had quit Paris; no one would be thinking about him any longer.

How should he proceed? The obtaining of the official titles that he had believed so necessary had not been of any great utility; he ought, above all, now that he was able to do so, publish his work, and then launch himself body and soul into the combat that the scientific event would unleash. Great as the power of his contradictors was, they could not rest the evidence cited, the experiments carried out. Admitting, at the worst, that he was recognized as Dr. Iblan and was obliged to resume the road of exile, his glory would be no less definitively established and he would think later about the fashion in which, at the opportune moment, he would unveil his true identity.

He went to bid farewell to Sir Arthur Frey, who strove to retain him once again.

"Would it be indiscreet to ask you the reason for such a hasty departure?"

"The necessity of rapidly publishing a history of Alchemy and Chemistry that will place me in the first rank."

"Why can't you publish it here?"

"I could, if necessary, but various reasons push me toward Paris. It's there, and nowhere but there, that I must go. And then, this air stifles me, this climate is killing me, and homesickness is tormenting me." In a voice tremulous with

351

emotion or anger, he added: "Perhaps there's also a motive that it's almost shameful to admit. Hatred has entered my heart; there are brows that I want to see furrowed with anxiety and eyes that I want to see shedding tears. I'm no longer the benevolent and indulgent being I once was, the individual who had only known the suffering of others. Today, I've been hungry, I've been cold, I've wept, I've descended into all the hells of poverty; prison cells and lunatic asylums have delivered me to vindictive thoughts. I've asked myself—how many times!—whether honest, noble and delicate sentiments aren't primarily the results of environment and education.

"Wretched, I didn't judge men and things in the fashion that I'd appreciated them in times of wellbeing and glory; I pitied those I had scorned, I forgave those I had condemned, and, on the other hand, I began to hate those I had admired and loved. Even though the disinherited and the humble, in recompense for my sympathy, have brought me some help in the accomplishment of my projects, contact with them has humiliated and soiled me, after the mediocrity if the powerful, the stupidity of the crowd have ridiculed my genius.

"The necessity of living has forced me to resort to lying. A prostitute gave me bread and I was obliged to give her in exchange all the gratitude and nobility that remained in my heart, a part of my blood and years of my life. Now, Sir Arthur, if you knew the man that I was before all that, you would wonder in amazement how it is possible that I can still be alive. It is therefore necessary that my triumph bursts forth in the place where I have suffered so much. That will be my sole vengeance, but it will strike in the heart the legion of those who have persecuted me. Then, all my dolors, all my bitterness will be forgotten forever, and I shall be able to die content. I shall have crowned with glory a double life, one of extraordinary wellbeing, the other of inconceivable suffering. No mortal will be able to equal me; I shall be illustrious among the illustrious, and when I lift the thick veil that covers me, cries of admiration raised from all the corners of the globe will bear my name to the clouds!"

Jacques Bilan had raised himself up to his full height; his voice was vibrant, his eyes flashing. Did he not believe that he was finally going to accomplish the work of Truth?

Chapter XXXVI

The train is engulfed in the Gare St-Lazare; an impatient man gets down, his manner assured, his head held high, his stride feverish. The fiacre he hails takes him rapidly to a hotel on the Boulevard St-Germain, where he registers in the name of Jacques Bilan, selects a room, sets down a heavy suitcase, tidies himself up a little and then goes downstairs again in haste. He mingles with the crowds of students going up and down the Boulevard St-Michel.

The autumn sky is gray, but the air is still mild.

It is about midday; the traveler goes into a restaurant and has lunch with the appetite to which a fortunate event and the joy of homecoming give birth, and then goes back into the crowd and heads for the Jardin du Luxembourg.

The last leaves are littering the ground. The Fontaine des Médicis evokes charming memories of a distant youth and distant amours. Clumps of chrysanthemums open, as of old, their ragged corollas. On the terraces surrounded by balustrades, the queens of France still have the noble attitudes of yore, Pigeons and sparrows still come to feed from childish hands. Amorous couples are still seeking deserted pathways.

Oh, how good it is to live in that elegant and majestic landscape! How sweet it is to breathe that natal air! Jacques Bilan inhales it delightedly; it seems to him that life is entering his lungs, poisoned by the cold mists of English soil.

He goes to the galleries of the Odéon, leafs through new books and periodicals. What delightful moments those shelves enabled him to pass when he as a student!

He goes down toward the École de Médecine; floods of young men, their books and notebooks under their arms, are going to lectures. The temple of blissful routine still maintains its appearance of a Greek monument erected to the glory of Aesculapius, Hippocrates and Galen. It seems that the world is eternally condemned to live on the ill-digested acquisitions of past centuries. If his eyes do not launch a challenging gaze, it is because victory renders him magnanimous and the hour of triumph will not be long in chiming.

He resumes his stroll at a slow pace and pauses, curiously, before the publishers of scientific books. The names of his former pupils are already mingled with those of old masters. If the Sacred Arch incarnates the past, these window displays inform him that thought and toil have not lost their rights and that the efforts of new generations still produce their fruits.

A stout volume surrounded by a strip bearing the legend *Just Published* attracts his attention. It is written in German, recently arrived from Dusseldorf, is entitled *Principles of Thermodynamic Chemistry* and is signed Ludwig Keller.

New publications of that sort are always disquieting, but this one, more than any other, causes him to experience an instinctive contraction of the heart. The near similarity of title astonishes him. The name of Ludwig Keller, which he is seeing for the first time on the cover of a book, seems nevertheless not to be entirely unfamiliar to him.

He goes into the shop, buys the octavo volume and immediately starts to read it. The introduction throws him into an extreme disturbance; he skips pages with a kind of rage, arrives at the final pages, utters a cry of despair and falls over.

Another man, a foreigner, has just published the conclusive experiments that destroy Dr. Albin's theory.

The sales clerks hasten to help the invalid; a physician who happens to be there lavishes cares upon hm. The unknown man slowly recovers consciousness. Uniformed policemen who have been summoned arrive to take him back to his hotel. He murmurs his name and address, but the malaise has disappeared; he refuses the fiacre and the aid that they offer him, takes the volume that has caused him so much distress, and goes back to his room in haste. Perhaps he has misread, has misunderstood, mistaken his fears for realities?

He locks himself in, reads the volume from beginning to end. Everything, down to the last detail, is there.

His work, if he published it now, would be nothing but a heap of bibliographical research crowned by a flagrant plagiarism.

Anger and rage are mingled with his despair. He takes his manuscripts, useless henceforth, piles them up in the fireplace, sets the alight and watches them burn with cries of hatred and malediction. He remembers now the article that once appeared in the *Revue des Sciences*. Another, alerted by his polemics, has stolen his glory. And it is poverty, pitiless society, that has robbed him of the just price of his labor. The truth, to be sure, will radiate over the scientific world, but he is not the one who will hold up the torch, even though that honor was due to him.

If he had deposited the results of his labor at the Académie des Sciences, under seal, he would be able to claim the priority, but he did not even think of doing that; his pride prevented him from believing that another was capable of equaling him, and his disdain for officialdom caused him to neglect that elementary precaution.

Someone knocks loudly. Perhaps he has not hard? The door is opened with the aid of a duplicate key. Several people, the manager of the hotel at their head, invade his room.

"What is the significance of these madman's roars," complains the hotelier, "and why that violent fire? You've frightened all the guests."

He looks at him with haggard eyes, and then stammers apologies. The visitors withdraw, not without making unkind remarks.

He reflects for a few minutes; the tone in which the manager has just spoken to him causes him to suppose that he is not looked upon kindly. He goes down to the office, says that he does not want to inconvenience anyone, pays for his room and asks that they keep his suitcase; he will have it collected by the bellboy of another hotel.

Night is beginning to fall. He wanders mechanically hither and yon. The sight of a newspaper kiosk makes him think of his friend X***. He recalls that he owes him a hundred francs, goes into a café, puts his remaining banknotes into an envelope and posts them to him. An adieu, almost illegible, to which he does not attach any determined meaning, escapes his pen.

He resumes his aimless wandering. His head is empty; incoherent words emerge from his mouth. Passers-by into whom he bumps turn around, calling him drunkard or madman. Uniformed policemen speak sharply to him. He changes direction, goes into a square, and suddenly finds himself face to face with the monument erected to the memory of Professor Albin.

The moonlight, filtered by the mist, envelops it with a vague light; the man of bronze is still examining his retort with an inspired expression, and Renown is still inflating her cheeks immeasurably.

He stops, as if petrified, and passes his hand over his brow.

A flash of light traverses his intelligence. Nothing will remain of all that glory, to which, as an obscure pioneer, he administered the first blow of the pick-ax, and that work of destruction, which he was only able to consent to do on condition of at least reaping the glory of it, another has just accomplished. Past glory and future glory: everything has just collapsed. The efforts and sufferings of his second life have only served to annihilate his original personality.

Would it not have been better, then, tranquilly to enjoy his wealth and his honors? If love of truth alone had possessed him, there would have been no need of a mask to overturn his doctrine. It was, therefore, a folly of pride that was the principle motive for his action, and that action, without the sanction of glory, is no more now than a criminal imposture.

A warden taps him on the shoulder.

"We're closing, Monsieur. It's a little late for visiting monuments; come back tomorrow. Come on, didn't you hear me—move along!"

That phrase reminds him of the injection of the policemen when he had collapsed, dying, on a bench on the boulevards. All his hatred revives; it is poverty that has sterilized his genius and society that has refused him bread, which has placed him in debasing conditions, broken his pen and gagged his mouth!

He resumes walking, wandering for entire hours. From time to time, an ardent thirst dries out his throat. Then he goes into the first wine merchant's shop he encounters, orders a drink, downs it in a single draught, throws a coin on the counter and flees without waiting for the change.

The streets are empty, the boulevards deserted. The despairing individual walks on, suppressing his exclamations of anger, hastening his march for brief intervals, and then suddenly stopping.

It is two o'clock in the morning. He finds himself, by chance, on a bridge. The river, swollen by rain, is flowing with a muffled roar. The flames of the gas-lamps, refracted by the fog, extend obliquely in luminous lances that seem to be held upraised by a line of invisible cavaliers, menacingly. He imagines, in his hallucination, that they are forbidding him to pass on.

Then the memory of Mariette suddenly returns to his mind and makes his intentions, latent until then, precise. That is where she is; he knows it; he feels it; that is where he must go to rejoin her.

What remains for him to do on earth? Why should he live? Has he not suffered enough? Will he have less courage than poor Mariette? Will he remain deaf to her appeal?

"Companion Bilan," murmurs a voice behind him. He turns round; men throw themselves upon him brutally, tie him up rapidly, He is dragged under a gas-lamp.

"It's definitely the man in question," affirms the hotel manager, who examines him.

"We recognize him," say the two policemen called to assist the man who fainted. The joy of agents of the Sûreté bursts forth noisily.

"We've got him," exclaims one of them. "It's not too soon."

"Don't give us any trouble," adds another, addressing the prisoner. "Dead or alive, we're taking you in."

Jacques Bilan has not made any movement of self-defense or pronounced a single word. He is taken to the prefecture. He is harassed by fatigue, inert, annihilated; a heavy slumber nails him to his iron-framed bunk. He does not even take the trouble to undress. It is the sleep of a man who has resigned himself to death.

"Is your name Jacques Bilan?" the examining magistrate asks him, in haste to open the investigation in honor of an important prisoner.

"If you wish," says the accused, determined not to defend himself. "It's all the same to me."

"It's not what I wish; all the papers seized with your suitcase and on your person prove it. I must admit that it's rare to find so much evidence of identity on a man who has every interest in hiding it. So you really are Jacques Bilan?"

The accused shrugs his shoulders.

"The police reports tell us that you were in London last week. With what purpose have you returned to Paris?"

"To occupy myself with chemistry."

"If that's an allusion to your criminal projects, I find the joke sinister."

"I don't understand."

"You burned a large quantity of papers in the fireplace of your room. You were doubtless afraid of compromising accomplices."

"Tell me straight out, then, of what I'm accused; that will be simpler, and I can reply to you if I think it appropriate. Know, first of all, that I'm not an idiot; if I had known that I had an interest in hiding, I wouldn't have furnished myself with those proofs of identity whose multiplicity astonishes you, and if I had feared compromising accomplices, I wouldn't have embarrassed myself with compromising papers. It would have been easy to leave them in London or throw them in the sea. But once again, of what am I accused?"

"You know full well! You've already been subjected to two condemnations, one under the name of Jacques Liban and the other under that of Charles Balin."

"Yes, involuntary fraud and the illicit practice of medicine."

"Ah! You admit that."

"Why not?"

"You're right, all the more so as it would be futile to claim the contrary."

"Then why ask me?"

"One can't have too much evidence. You had a registered prostitute for a mistress, Mariette Gantron. What became of her?"

"I'd be most obliged if you could tell me."

"You're wrong to be insolent. Let's get to the facts: on the eighteenth of December last, almost a year ago, accompanied by your friend Blandon, you went into the Café Mansard and you placed a bomb there."

"It's the first I've heard of it. I admit, though, that if I had had a bomb to deposit in a café, I would have chosen that one rather than another."

"So it's that one that you chose. Futile to deny it; Blandon has admitted everything."

"That's quite possible. I don't know Blandon, of course."

"You're affecting a strange cynicism. In any case, the act of which you've rendered yourself culpable doesn't surprise us. We knew that you were an anarchist of the most dangerous kind, that you profess propaganda by action, and Blandon's revelations have only confirmed our suspicions. Your crime has had terrible consequences; the manager was unhurt, but a customer was killed and three others more or less seriously wounded."

"I regret it."

"Finally, you admit it!"

"No, I limit myself to regretting that poor devils who went into a café to have a glass of beer have been victims of an anarchist crime committed, quite possibly, by Jacques Bilan and his friend Blandon."

"But Jacques Bilan is you! You admitted that at the beginning of my interrogation."

"Wrong! To your question 'Is your name Jacques Bilan,' I replied: 'If you wish; it's all the same to me.' That doesn't mean that I'm Jacques Bilan; it signifies, in good French, that it's profoundly indifferent to me whether you take me for Jacques Bilan and that I have no fear of the consequences of that misapprehension. To cut your questions short, this is the part of the truth that it's permissible for me to tell you: I'm neither Jacques Bilan, nor Charles Balin, nor Jacques Liban. They're borrowed names that conceal my true identity, and although it's true that I've been condemned twice under false names, I'm innocent of the crime of which I'm accused, since it was committed a year ago and I only took the name Jacques Bilan a week ago. Now, for reasons that it's needless to explain to you, having decided to die, and even envisaging the scaffold with a certain pride, I repeat to you that being the victim of a judiciary error is a matter of indifference to me."

"If death on the scaffold appears to you so desirable, you could simply admit that you were Blandon's companion, the author of the odious crime committed on the eighteenth of December."

"I refuse to do so, firstly out of respect for the truth, and secondly because of the imbecility of the anarchist act; if I had had the intention of committing such an act I would have chosen a better place. My defense will be limited to affirmations and I shall not offer any proof because, although I have nothing with which to reproach myself in regard to the crime of which I'm accused, I nevertheless deserve to die, and the scaffold appears to me to be the logical, necessary and inevitable result of my actions."

"So you claim that you are not Jacques Bilan. It's evident that you've been informed of Blandon's death; you don't fear that he will contradict you. In any case, assuming that you're not the author of the crime, who are you?"

"I don't judge it appropriate to satisfy your curiosity."

"Say rather that it's impossible for you to do so. If you weren't Jacques Bilan, you'd be eager to tell us who you are; you cannot tell us, therefore you are Jacques Bilan, and everything proves it: the documents seized, the papers burned, the antisocial vociferations, including the work of chemistry that you've just purchased. Once again, if you're not the anarchist Bilan, knowing that your head is at stake, you'd tell us immediately who you are and how Jacques Bilan's papers come to be in your possession."

"I bought them in London."

"Prove it."

"There's no need. I shan't make any effort to save my head. I'll tell the truth when it pleases me to tell it, that's all."

The examining magistrate changes tack then. He becomes tender, sympathetic, unctuous, full of forbearance. He adopts an innocent expression, retracts his claws and purrs.

"Come on, my friend," he insinuates.

"Am I your friend, then?"

"It's a manner of speaking," the magistrate replies, swiftly. "I beg you, if you're not the criminal of the Café Mansard, if you can prove that to us, speak. Look, I'm assuming that you're not the incriminated anarchist, I'm even respecting your incognito, you can see that I'm a good prince and I'm not trying to set ambushes for you. Tell me frankly..."

The accused interrupts him with an ironic smile. "You're going to ask me where I was on the day of the crime, aren't you? Having not committed the crime and not having had, in consequence, any interest in creating an alibi, I don't know, any more than you probably know where you were and what you were doing on that day. Look, let's leave it there, and believe me, Monsieur, I'm sorry to have to give the lie to your reputation as an impeccable interrogator. I swear to you that if reasons above all other considerations didn't oblige me to keep quiet, I'd have a veritable pleasure in making the revelations that would be earn you, be sure of it, the congratulations

362

of all your colleagues. Now, I warn you, I shall no longer reply to any of your questions."

The accused keeps his promise and the investigation is necessarily closed after a relatively short time.

Such a trial being a trampoline for establishing or confirming a reputation, several advocates solicit the favor of defending the enigmatic individual; he refuses them all; he is given a young official advocate.

The enthusiasm of the defender is quickly cooled by the indifference and silence of his client.

"I'm going to plead insanity," he exclaims, discouraged, "since you don't want to furnish me with any other means of defense."

"Refrain from doing that, Monsieur," he instructs him. "It's a means that is veritably worn out and unworthy of your talent. Moreover, I shall be obliged to give you the lie on that terrain; believe me, you won't be able to compete with me."

"How do you expect me to defend you? The evidence and testimony are overwhelming."

"I don't want to be defended."

"But my duty as an official advocate is to defend you. My professional honor and my reputation are at stake. Can I limit myself to pleasing extenuating circumstances? It's very little."

"If I didn't pity your embarrassment, I'd reply that your reputation and your professional honor are of no importance to me. But since you insist—for which I understand and forgive you—permit me to give you an idea."

The young man opens his eyes wide.

"Plead for the scaffold," the man envelope by mystery goes on, gravely. "Tell them that you have a duty, after all, to satisfy your client and that a condemnation to death would be the solution most satisfactory to him. It's the first time that argument has been presented—tomorrow, you'll be famous!"

The advocate tries to laugh, but is in reality impressed by the sincerity with which those unexpected words have been spoken.

"How can you expect me to plead for the death penalty," he objected, "since you claim, and in my capacity as your defender, I'm obliged to believe you, that you're not Jacques Bilan and that you haven't committed the crime of which you're accused?"

"I've committed, against Society and perhaps against myself, a crime a thousand times greater than the one of which I'm accused. Hundreds of human beings have paid with their lives for a whim of my pride. Although it is a sin, that act is outside the scope of the law; it has never been foreseen by it and perhaps could not be; it has no weapon with which to strike it; it is doubtless for that reason that Destiny, having condemned me to die with a sinister renown, caused me to assume the identity and the crime of an anarchist.

"I was about to throw myself in the river when the pitiless but logical fatality of the chain of events to which I have given birth came to inform me that the punishment in question would neither be worthy of me nor sufficient for it. It's the scaffold or the pedestal that people of my species require. My pride, which could not be content with the one, must inexorably expiate its error on the other. It's even fortunate that the crime of which I'm accused, although stupid, is only an anarchist atrocity. I might have taken on the identity of a murderer soiled by theft! There is, therefore, in the supreme Will that is punishing me, something akin to a pity for my genius, a species of regard for what I once was!

"That is why, if you consider my interests and not yours, you ought not to defend me. If you snatched me from death—which is, in any case, fatefully impossible for you—that absurd crime of which I am accused and which I did not commit, I would now be capable of committing. Furthermore, mortally wounded in my pride, embittered by inconceivable misfortunes, if shame and debauchery did not drown me in the mud, I would put all the intelligence and life that remained to me in the implacable service of the revolutionary cause, and on the day when I did throw a bomb, believe me, it would be in other conditions and in another milieu."

The advocate looks at him, terrified.

"Jacques Bilan," he murmurs, as if talking to himself. "Jacques Bilan, the imbecile of the Café Mansard. Let's go, then! Let them only set me free for a week, and they'll see whether I won't blow up one of their Bastilles!"

The ferocity that he senses gives birth within him to furious sniggers, floods of hatred that that rise to his lips. He has turned to the young defender.

"If, by chance, you saved my head," he cries, "you'd be committing a crime against Society!"

Chapter XXXVII

It is a gala day at the assize court. Although the drama is not a crime of passion and the accused is neither young nor handsome, numerous ladies in elegant dresses are fighting over the entrance tickets. Advocates in robes grouped in all the corners of the courtroom, political men and ambassadors occupy the best seats and the journalists bench is fully packed.

The pale winter sunlight that passes through the white curtain comes to die on the dark green back wall of the room, where the Christ, in whom indifferent eyes indifferent eyes no longer see the tragic symbolism, is dying in vain on his cross.

Animated conversations fill the sanctuary of the law; the composition of the jury is examined, predictions are made on the verdict, bets are laid.

On a table, among the pieces of evidence, the debris of a bomb, bloody garment, etc., are the identity papers of Jacques Bilan and Ludwig Keller's *Principles of Thermodynamic Chemistry*.

"Messieurs, the Court is here; silence please!" cries the usher.

The Court makes its solemn entrance; the accused is introduced, and a vivid movement of curiosity takes possession of the spectators. People cry: "Sit down!" One might think that they were in a theater.

The clerk immediately reads the charge sheet. Everyone knows the facts, no one listens; all gazes are fixed on the accused. His attire is modest but correct and proper; his goatee, his moustache and his short hair are all white. His forehead is broad, his face very thin; in his profound ringed eyes a dark gleam vacillates. A first sight, one might believe oneself to be in the presence of a retired subaltern officer, but the intellectual expression of the gaze impresses and quickly deflects the veritable observers.

The clerk finishes his litany and the President proceeds with the interrogation. The facts already known return to the floor. The accused, with more deference for the Court than he showed the examining magistrate, nevertheless gives analogous answers. All the honorable magistrate's efforts to trap him in contradiction are devoid of result. The accused, while refusing to clarify the mystery that envelops him, limits himself to telling the exact truth, only pointing out that certain implausibilities are too flagrant, and it is merely in a spirit amorous of rectitude that he does so.

"You admit to having used various names?" the President asks him.

"Yes, Monsieur," he relies.

"You had in that epoch an important reason for hiding your identity. Jacques Bilan, condemned to death by a court martial in 1871, did not want to return to Paris under his true name."

"An infantile precaution that the veritable Jacques Bilan, the author of the crime, were he not dead, would not have failed to make if he had taken it into his head to return to Paris."

"There is, indeed, a lacuna in your intelligence that it is difficult to explain, but criminals are subject to such absences; we have evidence of that every day. You were also unaware that the law knew the authors of the crime."

"I was unaware of the crime itself."

"Naturally. You didn't even know that anarchists existed."

"Oh, that Monsieur President I learned and understood one night when I was about to die of hunger and desired to live."

"So you are an anarchist?"

"I might well become one if Monsieur Deibler[32] does not do his job," he sniggers.

A shiver runs through the auditorium.

"You have a macabre sense of humor," observes the President.

"It's a product of circumstance, Monsieur. Forgive me—it's me who will bear all the expenses."

"The reports of the expert chemists inform us that the bomb in the Café Mansard was loaded with an unknown and very powerful explosive; it was not one of those primitive devices fabricated by inexperienced hands. You are very occupied with chemistry."

"Almost all my life."

"Did you not play a certain role in an explosion that took place in 18**?"

"A very active role; I was experimenting with a powder of my own invention."

A murmur rises in the hall.

"Admit, then that you are Jacque Bilan. Everything proves it."

"I have only been using that name for three months."

"Once again, that system of defense does not hold up, Messieurs the jurors will have immediate proof of it. If you are not Jacques Bilan, who are you?"

"I cannot reply to you."

"It would be very easy, if you are neither Jacques Liban, nor Charles Balin, nor Jacques Bilan, to tell us who you are, with supporting evidence. The accusation would fail of its own accord and you would not be pursuit fir the usurpation of titles. You have no response? Thus, you are Companion Bilan, and if you are not the author of the abominable crime of the eighteenth of December, you are someone worse, since, in that case, you would be judging the identity of the murderer to be

---

[32] Anatole Deibler was the public executioner from 1885-1939, having inherited the job from his father at the age of twenty-one.

preferable to yours. A mysterious and singularly accusatory letter found on you ten years ago seems to prove that."

"The reasoning has appearances of logic," observes the accused, imperturbably—a further rumor rises up in the audience—but adds immediately: "but it is false. Apart from one fact, which is not in your competence because you would consider it an act of madness, I am a very honest man—in the relative sense of the word, of course."

"If you were an honest man you would prove it to us, but the evidence and the accusation demonstrate to us that you are the anarchist Jacques Bilan and that a sentiment of vengeance moved you to accomplish the deadly work of the Café Mansard."

They pass on to the hearing of experts and witnesses.

The manager of the Café Mansard recounts the incident of the fifth of May 18**. He has seen the accused twice under different appearances; the first time he had a check suit and blond hair; the second time, he came in the appearance of a petty employee or tradesman to settle the bill of seventeen francs that he had owed for two years. That fact had seemed extraordinary to him.

Laughter bursts out in the hall; the President calls for order.

"All the more extraordinary," the witness goes on, "because he had already served three months in prison for it. There was, in consequence, something shady about that action; perhaps he was already meditating his revenge and wanted to allay suspicions?"

Unfortunately, he had not seen the man who was carrying the bomb, but he had no doubt that it must have been him.

"Why don't you doubt it?" asks the defender.

"Because I had him arrested."

"Is he the only client you've had sent to the police station for reasons of that sort?"

The manager replies, bitterly, that crooks have never inspired tenderness in him.

The waiters and regular of the café contradict one another. Some recognize the accused, other hesitate; the anarchist had a full white beard.

It is the same with the agents charged with surveillance of foreigners. One of them affirms categorically that he has seen the accused in the company of an anarchist in an ill-famed tavern in London. There were two men of a certain age in the group, one of whom was Jacques Bilan; unfortunately, the English agents charged with guiding him only had a vague description based on the age of the companion.

"You took your meals at the Dauphin Tavern?" asks the President.

"I went there once."

The other agents are unanimous in saying that they have rarely had the opportunity to glimpse Jacques Bilan, that he gave them the slip every time they pursued him, and that he disguised himself with surprising skill.

"You have often changed names, appearances and costumes?" the magistrate interrogates.

"Yes, Monsieur," the accused replied, tranquilly.

The manager and guests of the Hôtel St-Germain recount the cries of rage and hatred that they heard through the walls.

"You burned a quantity of papers and pronounced the words that the witnesses heard?"

"Yes, Monsieur."

"And you say that you are not Jacques Bilan?"

"No, Monsieur, I am not Jacques Bilan."

A few exclamations and bursts of immediately-stifled laughter are heard.

"Messieurs the jurors will decide," adds the judge.

The hearing of the witnesses continues.

A police commissaire testifies to his insolence; he arrested the accused for fraudulent misdemeanor, and the accused had insulted the authority.

Monsieur Béguinard, the director of an education institution, hastened to throw him out after a fortnight.

Maître Lampe, entrepreneur of copies, whose establishment he entered in the capacity of an honest retired customs officer, recounts that Monsieur Balin accused him of exploiting his staff and wanted to commit acts of violence on his person. He had for a companion a certain Raphael, whose shameful mores were publicly notorious.

A concierge in the Rue Vavin certifies that he came back late at night every evening.

An agent of the Sûreté, who has made enquiries several times, gives the most detestable information about his antecedents. His mistress, who maintained him, has disappeared. He has never been able to find any trace of her.

For the first time, the accused shivers and emerges from him impassivity. "Wretch!" he shouts, forcefully. "You're the one who killed her!"

The policeman, momentarily disconcerted, emphasizes his accusations. He was so convinced that the man was a murderer that he had not investigated a single crime without first making enquiries in his direction.

"Which permitted the veritable guilty parties to escape the law," sniggers the defender.

Several registered prostitutes vaguely recognize him as the man who collapsed one night on a bench, and whom they helped. One of them, Eugénie Bourette, alias Nini Nichon, whose appearance at the bar obtains a great success, affirms that he lived off the earnings of Mariette Gantron, who thought her lover was a curé. She saw him one evening distributing louis on the boulevard; doubtless he had pulled off some good coup.

"What do you respond to all that?" the President asks him.

"That the majority of those accusations are stupid, and the rest despicable," replies the accused, having become utterly calm again

"That's not a response."

"It's sufficient for me, Monsieur Président."

"It will doubtless not be sufficient for Messieurs the jurors."

"I've made the sacrifice of my life; there is no longer any judge but one that I care about, and that is myself," declares the accused, whose imperious voice impresses the audience.

Other witnesses report a series of facts doubtless relating to the real Jacques Bilan, and which, distantly or closely, represent him as soiled by all shames and capable of all crimes. He makes the decision not to reply any longer.

Three witnesses for the defense appear. The first, a merchant of liquids on whose account Charles Balin manipulated explosives, comes to declare that the envisaged goal was the fabrication of a new powder which they intended to present to the Ministry of War. The President makes the severe remark that before any dangerous experiment and to avoid all suspicion, he ought to have made a declaration to the Prefecture of Police.

The second, an obese second-hand clothes dealer of morbid aspect recounts that Charles Balin treated him and cured him while he was a stationer in Bellevue, and that he greatly regretted his departure.

The entire audience writhes with laughter. The President dismisses him and reminds him that, having already had two convictions for receiving, his testimony is more harmful than helpful to the accused.

The third, a former federate under the orders of Jacques Bilan, summoned by the prosecution to recognize his battalion leader, initially swore that the accused was not Jacques Bilan. In a spirit of justice, he was summoned as a witness for the defense, but the Communard, perhaps influenced by the milieu, is much less categorical; previously, he had affirmed; now, he limits himself to emitting doubts.

"When was the last time you saw Jacques Bilan?" the President asks him.

"On the last day of the Commune we separated at the Porte de Romainville; he headed for Lilas, I went to the Prés Saint-Gervais."

The advocate general stands up. His speech for the prosecution, a kind of biography decorated by oratorical movements, can be summarized as follows;

"Jacques Bilan," he says, pointing at the accused, "for the man you see before you is not an cannot be anyone by Companion Bilan, as I shall prove, is the accomplished type specimen of the individual come down in the world whom Pride, disappointments and bad conduct have fatally pushed him to anarchism.

"The son of a cobbler, raised with the aid of the clergy, was single out for his keen intelligence; endowed, it seems, with an exceptional memory, he won a number of initial successes that his relatives and friends must have made the mistake of exaggerating, and entered a small seminary in his native town

"We are in 1851; the coup d'état has just erupted. This time, the people take to the streets to defend legality. Jacques Bilan, a fifteen year old insurgent, takes up the rifle.[33] Certainly, Messieurs, our opinions are known; we are Republicans and like him, we would have been defenders of the law."

Sniggers depart from the group of young advocates, whom the President regards with a severe expression. The advocate general has turned toward them.

"Yes, Messieurs, we would have defended the law. However," he resumes, "what we would have one in the name of true principles, he, as his precocity and his entire life prove, determines to do purely for love of trouble and disorder. The young revolutionary is taken prisoner. A powerful compatriot and the director of the seminary intervene; his recklessness is attributed to his youth; the victors are content to send him to a

---

[33] Given the date recorded on his birth certificate and the previous deduction that the year must have been 1836, Jacques Bilan was still a fortnight short of his fifteenth birthday in early December 1851, when Louis Napoléon carried out his coup, but the public prosecutor can surely be forgiven the slight inaccuracy.

house of correction, from which the same influences, moreover, soon obtain his release.

"He resumes his studies. Anyone else would be grateful to his protector for the services they have just rendered him. He, driven by pride, scorning the sacred habit for which he is destined, believing himself destined to play a great role one day, obtains his baccalaureate, comes to Paris, which attracts him, and begins medical studies.

"Note that particularity well, Messieurs the jurors, it will explain to you why the accused subsequently became a medical orderly and a bone-setter; and if the anthropometric service does not have of Jacques Bilan, it has that of Charles Balin and Jacques Liban, two anagrams under which the identity of Jacques Balin is concealed.

"The indomitable nature of the medical student does not take long to get the upper hand. Serious incidents occur at the school. An illustrious professor is jeered, insulted, even struck in his pulpit, and who is at the head of the young rebels? Jacques Bilan. The police try to arrest him, but the young student has sensed that he is menaced by an exemplary punishment and that his past ingratitude will receive a striking lesson. He avoids all research and succeeds in reaching Brussels.

"Here we lose sight of him for a considerable lapse of time. Where did he spend the next fifteen years? What did he do to earn a living? He alone could tell us. Doubtless he wanders from city to city, country to country, poverty to poverty, for we only find him again at the end of the Empire, irreconcilable, embittered, cited among the most restless agitators. The majority found honorable and even fortunate positions in exile; Jacques Bilan comes back to us poorer than ever.

"The war breaks out, the Prussians surround Paris; others run to the front and die gloriously at the hands of the enemy; he is in the first rank of the fanatics who invade the Hôtel-de-Ville. The Commune, as was fatal, could not have a more enthusiastic defender; he it is who instigates the massacres of the Rue Haxo. He is the leader of the Bilan battalion, which, from the heights of Belleville, resists the defenders of order to the

374

end. Luck favors him again; he escapes and disappears; but Jacques Bilan of sinister memory has left memories too bloody for the law to forget him; a court martial puts him on trial in his absence and condemns him to death.

"A few years pass; he changes his name and face, and we would lose track of him again if the taverns of London did not resound with his diatribes full of bile. There again, while many others, having become wiser with experience and age, have reformed, the irreducible revolutionary, grouping around him all the international scum, stimulates rancor and preaches conflict.

"Political passions having eased, the vanquished of yesteryear begin to raise their heads again. He experiences the need to see France again, to judge for himself the state of minds, and as he cannot return to France under his real name, he borrows a mask His name is Jacques Bilan; a simple inversion of syllables appears to him to be sufficient, so he calls himself Jacques Liban. Note well, Messieurs the jurors, that correlation of names; it is characteristic; it is called an anagram.

"What does he do in that epoch? What abominable and mysterious crime has he committed? The law has not been able to discover it. What we know is that he collected a sum of five hundred thousand francs in a financial establishment in May 18**, that he entered the Café Mansard immediately afterwards, spent seventeen francs there and refused to pay the bill, claiming that he had been robbed

"The manager had him sent to the police station; the Commissaire de Police interrogated him; he was searched and this damning letter was found on him."

The prosecutor reads and comments on the letter found on the legionnaire.

"Although the examining magistrate was unable to clarify the mystery," the prosecutor resumes, "this letter proves, at least, that Jacques Bilan, under an assumed name, and after committing a nameless crime that alone might legitimate your verdict, enlisted in the Foreign Legion and was then sent to Tonkin, thus playing the comedy of despair and remorse.

"Thousands of heroes fell out there for the Fatherland; an illustrious surgeon left honors and wealth to water that distant earth with his noble blood. He, instead of dying, deserted at the height of the struggle, comes back to Paris and is arrested, thanks to the manager of the Café Mansard—you will not have forgotten, Messieurs the jurors, that it was the manager of the Café Mansard who had him arrested. He is taken to the police cells; the anthropometric service did not exist at the time of his first arrests; he is not recognized, and is only sentenced to three months in prison.

"He comes out. Here, witnesses to whom I cannot attach any real moral value, represent him playing the comedy of hunger, then having himself maintained by a registered prostitute; I only cite them for the sake of memory; you will make of the circumstance what you please. As for the deposition of the entrepreneur of copies whom the accused reproached or the odious exploitation of his personnel, the reproach is so well-merited that I am far from wanting to make a weapon of it If the majority of employers, I must confess, resembled Monsieur Lampe, we would all be socialists."

A burst of ironic laughter ripples through the hall; the President, with a pained expression, recalls the auditorium to order. "I am astonished," he observes, gravely, "that you have the courage to laugh when the life of a man is at stake."

The public minister continues. "There are, however, among the scantly recommendable depositions that I just mentioned, two particularities that I ought to pint out: he accused is described as a former priest, and his alter ego is one of those vile creatures whose name modesty forbids me to pronounce. The man who wants to reform his fellows is prey to the most shameful passions!

"We find him again, a year later, at the hospital, which he has entered initially as a patient, and has stayed on in the capacity of an orderly; but here, it is no longer the name Liban that he uses to conceal his identity, but that of Balin, and

376

Balin, Messieurs the jurors, I nothing but a new anagram of Bilan. Now, you will confess that if the first might, if necessary be put to the count of coincidence, but it is at least strange that the coincidence is repeated twice.

"Acts of insubordination and a lack of propriety with regard to his superiors oblige the honorable director to dismiss the orderly Balin. The former medical student imagines that he can and ought to remonstrate with his masters. A few well-made dressings and a successful operation succeed in turning his head. His conceit no longer knows any bounds; he openly makes money with the difficult and delicate profession of medicine, and on that account is condemned to a further three months in prison.

"Here occurs an event whose import will not escape you; a terrible detonation frightens all the inhabitants of a suburb; the police mount an investigation, and who is the manufacturer of the explosive that casts terror into a peaceful locality? The guilty party is sitting in the dock.

"His recent condemnation and his previous misadventure have occasioned difficulties; Paris, which seems to have divine him, refuses him the fortune and position coveted; he returns abroad. Months pass; the audacity of the anarchist sect has taken on frightful proportions; the law redoubles its vigilance. London, where all the crimes are perpetrated, is inundated by agents. Jacques Bilan hides under a thousand ingenious forms, but we find him again, calling attention to himself by the violence of his theories, publicly preaching propaganda by action, glorying in his past crimes, anathematizing the lukewarm, arming the excited, becoming the chemist of the sect, fabricating terrible and blind engine of destruction that never strike the chosen victim.

"We arrive at the crime of the eighteenth of December; that evening, two men stop outside the Café Mansard. Paris is terrorized by previous crimes, but the hall is nevertheless packed with customers. Who could imagine that an imbecile hatred might afflict inoffensive employees or tradesmen relaxing after the day's hard labor? Two wretches are there, however, who are preparing to sow terror and death. And why have they chosen that establishment, frequented above all by the humble, rather than a thousand others more luxurious, where their so-called social crime might attain capitalists and employers? Because a sentiment of personal vengeance drives them; because one of those men is Jacques Liban."

The designated accused makes a simple sign of negation.

"Companion Blandon stands watch; the other, the bearer of a package wrapped in newspaper, enters the hall, sits down near the door, deposits his device under the bench, orders a drink, for which he pays immediately, ostentatiously lights a cigarette, drops it, bends down as if to pick it up, and leaves.

"That other is Jacques Bilan.

"You know the frightful consequences of that abominable crime. One man dead, three others seriously wounded, one widow, orphans, three unfortunates incapable henceforth of earning a living And it is in the name of humanity that fanatics have dared to commit that crime!

"The guilty parties have profited from the general confusion to flee. The law has grave suspicions, but it cannot find complete certainty. A providential hazard soon informs them of the whole truth. Companion Blandon, put under suspicion, is drawn into a trap and stabbed several times. The unfortunate, left for dead, is still breathing; the approach of death drives him to repent; he declares himself guilty and surrenders the name of the accomplice who conceived the plan, directed it and execute it; and that accomplice is the wretch you are about to condemn, Jacques Bilan.

"Agents immediately set out in search of him; they find traces of him in Brussels, The Hague and Amsterdam, but the anarchist—has he not just admitted it himself?—is a Proteus who changes form at will; the finest sleuths cannot catch him.

"Almost a year passes. The companion does not know that we are aware of his culpability; he thinks that the moment to carry out a new crime has come. He arrives in Paris, and books a room at the Hôtel St-Germain."

"Registering there under the name of Jacques Bilan," the accused interjects, ironically.

"That scarcely accords with his renowned skill," observes the defender.

"Yes," replies the accuser, "he imprudently registers under his own name, because he does not know about Blandon's confession, and because he has, in any case, only gone there to burn incriminating papers, to get rid of his suitcase and leave quickly, never to return.

"There is a kind of bravado in that, a challenge thrown down to the police, to Society. But the law is on the alert; it is informed that the audacious criminal is in Paris; he is found; he is arrested, and here he is before you.

"Now, what is the inconceivable system of defense that he has chosen? He is not Jacques Bilan, he says; the numerous papers that prove it are not his; he ought them in London to hide his true identity; the other facts that overwhelm him are unfortunate coincidences, etc. That's very easy to say—but then, why, on two different occasions, choose anagrams of Bilan to dissimulate himself?

"Who is he? What is the dishonor, the infamy, the crime that he wants to hide under all these names? An honest man does not hide. Who among you, Messieurs the jurors, a victim of a similar situation, before the prospect of the scaffold, would hesitate for a single instant to cry: 'My name, my birthplace, my family, my friends, my actions: here they are; I am not the man who committed the odious action of which I am accused.' But the accused refrains from breaking his silence; he does not respond; he will not respond."

"He does not want to respond!" exclaims the defending advocate.

"He cannot respond," replies the public prosecutor, "because he really is Companion Bilan, the bitter enemy of all social estate, the murderer who has not hesitate to strike the innocent, the humble, the workers in the name of his infamous doctrines."

And with a vehement peroration, the orator demands the pitiless application of the law.

The audience and the judges whisper, exchanging their impressions. All eyes turn toward the dock. The pseudo-Jacques Bilan remains impassive.

A juror requests to ask a question.

If Bilan, Liban and Balin are, as the accused claims, borrowed names that hide his true identity, they denote a mania for anagrams that might assist the law to raise his mask. Has a search been made for anagrams of Bilan?"

The accused looks at the questioner with a singularly troubled expression. The man is on the right track.

The President intervenes. "Monsieur, the law does in deal in puerilities; we do not play the diviner here. Address yourself to the illustrated papers!"

"The public prosecution has, however, made a weapon of those puerilities," observes the stubborn juror.

"I do not have to appreciate the fashion in which the public prosecutor judges it appropriate to establish the accusation."

"The arguments that are apparently the most futile," replies the advocate general, who sees a scarcely-dissimulated criticism in the honorable president's words, "are sometimes of capital importance; I am ready nevertheless to abandon that one if you judge it unworthy of the law. Is this man Jacques Bilan, as all the evidence, all the facts and all the documents demonstrate that he is? If he is not Companion Bilan, it is easy for him to tell us who he is and why he is hiding. One again, who is he? If he continues to remain silent, it is because he is the anarchist Bilan, it is because he cannot be anyone but him. That is all I ask you to remember, Monsieur juror."

"Is that all you had to ask?" adds the President, to the juror, who is still standing. The nonplussed bourgeois sits down without breathing another word.

The defender gets up in his turn. He is a very young blond man, almost beardless, whose debut is awaited with curiosity. The official advocate, conscious of the heavy task that is incumbent upon him, appears very troubled by it.

"Messieurs the judges, Messieurs the jurors," he said, in substance, "you find yourselves in the presence of an intriguing mystery, and inextricable and unprecedented situation that troubles your conscience and disrupts your logical thinking. Certainly, it is not the first time that an accused has hidden his identity under an assumed name; you have not forgotten the Campi affair;[34] but there, the accused really had committed the murder with which he was charged; it was an admitted murderer that was hiding behind an assumed name, whereas here, the case is absolutely opposite; it is an honest man who is hiding under the name of a criminal.

"Can you admit for a single instant that if this man really were Jacques Bilan, the anarchist of the Café Mansard, that he would have registered at a hotel under that name, furnished with all the documents that were found in his suitcase? But in that case, the man would be mad, and no longer responsible for his action! No, Messieurs, the accused is not the author of the abominable crime or which he is reproached.

---

[34] The case in question was a murder committed in August 1882, when an old man named Ducros du Sixte was stabbed to death in his home. The murderer, arrested at the scene, who initially gave his name as Michel Campi but subsequently admitted it to be false, was extremely selective in answering the examining magistrate's questions and refused to disclose his true identity. His trial, long delayed while the police attempted to discover who he was and why he had committed the murder, eventually went ahead without that information, and he was convicted and sentenced to death anyway. His defending advocate claimed that the accused had confessed his true identity to him, on condition that he had sworn not to reveal it, and it remained a mystery forever. The sensation caused by the case might well have played a part in suggesting the present plot, or at least its climax, to the author.

"There exist in London, and perhaps elsewhere, shady agencies that make a commerce out of various documents and civil estates; these establishments take infinite precautions and it is almost impossible to catch them in the act of committing fraud. It is there, you can be certain, that my unfortunate client procure the compromising papers of which his valise was full. The veritable guilty party is dead, or if he is not, has disposed of his own free will of a dangerous identity. Perhaps he is tranquilly following these debates; his incontestable reputation of cleverness gives me the right to make the suggestion.

"But if this man, as common sense proves, is not Jacques Bilan, you ask me, along with the public prosecutor, who is he? What reasons does he have for hiding? Here, Messieurs, I cannot and ought not to respond to that legitimate question. Respectful of his individual right, I ought not to tell you the near-certainty that has taken possession of my mind. He alone ought to lift the veil that covers him. Considerations beyond all human laws, causes so great that looking death in the face cannot shake his resolution, prevent him from doing so.

"Not only does he not want to be defended, not only has he made no effort to point out the absurdities of the witness statements and the contradictions that are to be found in the eloquent speech of Monsieur the advocate general, but to all my remonstrations, to all my supplications, he has responded with a single assertion that had profoundly troubled me and convinced me of his innocence.

"'I am not Jacques Bilan,' he has said to me. 'I have not committed any action that can fall under the lash of your law; nevertheless, for an action as audacious as it was insensate, which has put me outside humankind, destiny has condemned me to death; it is necessary that I die. I was about to throw myself in the river at the very moment when I was arrested; the supreme power that is punishing me found that the punishment would be unworthy of me and insufficient for it; my pride, not being content with a pedestal, must fatally mount the tragic platform; blood is required to wash away the outrage that I have done to society: plead for the scaffold.'"

A dull rumor of astonishment runs around the room.

"Are those," the defender resumes, veritably emotional, "words that Companion Jacques Bilan would have pronounced? No, Messieurs, the anarchist would have proclaimed his doctrines, thrown down challenges to the law, cursed the scaffold that is the instrument of social vengeance. Perhaps he would have put on a brave face before death, but he would not have wanted it, he would not have summoned it.

"You are therefore in the presence of a man in great despair, a man who feels very guilty, but guilty of a sin that human law does not recognize, and it is because his forehead, over which an aureole must once have been resplendent, is today surrounded by dense shadow, it is absolutely necessary that you plumb the depths of this mystery, which must certainly affect you intensely, and that, forgetting his recommendations and his pleas, disobedient to his desire, I demand and I beg you not to confound him with the author of the stupid crime committed at the Café Mansard, and not to condemn him to death."

The same juror requests again to ask a question.

"You have, Monsieur Defender, spoken of a quasi-certainty with regard to the identity of the accused; is it not your duty to make us party to it?"

"I cannot," the young advocate replies. "One of two things must be true: either my supposition, as strange as it is improbable, is false, and it would be wounding an illustrious family; or it is true, and then it would only have weight with the assent of my client, since he alone can provide the proof, and a simple negation would suffice to destroy all its value. Now, until this moment, he has persisted in remaining silent."

"This is melodrama," jeers the advocate general.

"It is drama," the defender ripostes, sharply. "A drama in which tragedy is intervening, as in the ancient tragedies."

The young defender's sincere emotion seems to have produced a good effect. The advocate general thinks that he ought to add a few words.

"If such a precedent is established," he observes, without emphasis, "the application of laws will soon become a dead letter. It will be sufficient for the accused to claim that an evil fate has caused him to take the name of the guilty party and that he has special reasons for hiding his true identity, in order to find mercy before his judges. That really would be too convenient. You affirm, Monsieur the defender, that a mystery envelops this man. He has only one word to say, and I wish with all my heart that he would pronounce it, in order to clear our conscience. If he is not Jacques Bilan, who is he?"

"Once again," says the President, obsessed by an anxiety, to whom the face of the accused did not seem unfamiliar, "Who are you?"

The accused remains silent. His left hand, raised in an enigmatic pose, seems nevertheless to affirm an irreducible resolution to keep quiet.

The President comes to the rescue. "Before passing into the deliberation room, accused, I will grant you five minutes of reflection."

A great silence reigns in the auditorium; one would think that no one wants to trouble that ultimate meditation. All gazes converge on the dock, where the man, prey to an internal combat, his head bowed and his eyes haggard, seems to be appealing for help with all the energy of his soul.

Bated breath is audible.

"The Garden of Olives," murmurs a poet.

The five minutes have elapsed; the President speaks again.

"Stand up, accused; the moment is grave; your life might perhaps depend on your words. One last time, if you are not Jacques Bilan, who are you?"

"I cannot tell you Monsieur le Président," he replies, with a movement that betrays a moment of weakness. He rapidly recovers his composure. "If I told you," he added, with a bitter smile, "you would not believe me."

"Why not?" observes the President, in a veritable tone of good will.

"If I told you that a man who was illustrious among the illustrious, a man whose bronze stands in one of your public squares and whose renown has resounded all over the world, a man who has been dead and buried for years, stands before you today, what would you respond?"

"I would demand a name and proofs!" exclaims the magistrate, who suspects a simulation of madness and frowns.

The accused hesitates for a few seconds. Now that nothing any longer attaches him to life, is he going to make honorable amends to the society that has deceived him unworthily? Is he going to evade the just punishment, humiliate himself, beg its pardon? Is he going to crown the abortion of his adventure with cowardice? Is it Pride or Destiny that is sealing his lips?

"You remain silent," the President resumes, in an angry voice. "You prove to us thus that you are combining imposture with cynicism, that you are simulating madness, that you are trying to gain time."

"*Sic fatum*," murmurs the accused, in a low voice, sitting down again.

The jury's deliberation is brief. The court returns after half an hour. A sinister silence hangs over the assembly. To the questions "Is the accused Jacques Bilan" and "Has Jacques Bilan committed the atrocity at the Café Mansard?" the majority has responded: "Yes."

Are there any extenuating circumstances? It has responded: "No?"

Jacques Bilan is condemned to death.

Chapter XXXVIII

In spite of the insistences of his advocate, Jacques Bilan has refused his right to appeal or to sign a petition for mercy.

"Convict prison! Exile under the whip of brutal guards!" he cried, finally irritated by the persistence and pleas of the young defender. "That would be a torture a thousand times worse than death! Do you think that I have not reflected maturely before taking the definitive decision to remain silent? If I had told them who I am they would not have wanted, and they would not have been able, to believe me. There is only one man who could demonstrate the truth scientifically. That man occupies my place, possesses my wife and enjoys my fortune, and I do not want to put him to such a rude proof. Once, allowing myself to be carried away by an absurd fit of anger, I shouted my name to them: the padded cell immediately came to bid me to be silent. I could, if necessary, have arrived at that result again, but I have preferred the scaffold. Would you want me now to accept the ignominy of deportation, the ignominy of contact, the ignominy of chains? For whom do you take me? Have you not divined that I really was someone? Was your speech nothing but oratory art?"

Confronted by the young man's expression, however, he quickly suppressed that surge of indignation.

"Excuse me, my dear Monsieur," he went on. "You are yielding to very natural sentiments of pity and I'm wrong to receive the proposition you're making to me so poorly, but I beg you not to persist any longer. My resolution is unbreakable, my life is intolerable to me now, futile and purposeless, and my madness is too responsible not to be punished. The law, in suppressing me, is, in fact, making an instinctive act of prudence. The certitude of death has extinguished all the hatred in my heart, but if fatality threw me back into society, I sense that I would no longer have the strength to pardon it for the misfortunes of which I am nevertheless the first cause, since I have placed myself outside it of my own will. It is in memory of the unusual favors that it lavished upon me when I was still under its tutelage that I forgive it the disappointments with which it has overwhelmed me when I wanted only to owe my elevation to my own merit, that I consent not to harm it, and that I want to die."

With a sad smile he added: "I'm still speaking as if I were in command of my destiny! A man is, however, not the absolute master of his fate. It is for having forgotten that verity, for having believed in the omnipotence of the human Will, that I am going to climb the scaffold. Never forget, Monsieur, that the man really is mad who, born in the official routine, spoiled by the success that he owes to a relative superiority, takes it into his head one day, out of pride, to break the bonds that attach him to the collective mediocrity! Energy, the love of the truth, genius, if they are not accompanied by wealth and power, are broken like glass by any social organization. Every collectivity seeks instinctively to elevate its average of wellbeing or intelligence to the detriment of the individual; it consents to protect him on condition that he concedes to it the best part of his merit and his dignity. Woe to the man who does not accept the bargain; all will be in league against him, and the stupidity of the petty will add to the injustice of the great.

"Believe me, it is not an anarchist—a companion, in the present sense of the word—who is speaking to you; the disasters of my last years have only compensated for the undeserved fortune of the first; I have no right to recriminate, I had my large share of wellbeing. But having benefited from all the advantages, all the privileges that present society can procure, and then having suffered, myself or by contact, all the miseries that it engenders—and always will engender, alas, so long as humans are not physically and intellectually equal—I have been able to make comparisons and differentiations that have made me pass into the camp of the revolutionaries: which is to say, the weak, the oppressed; for revolt is fatally born of oppression.

"I have observed thus that, In spite of the generosity of his heart and the elevation of his soul, the fortunate man cannot veritably sympathize with the sufferings of the poor and understand them; and, on the other hand, the disinherited cannot judge without envy and bitterness those whom a superiority has placed above them. The inevitable consequence is the wellspring of tears and blood, the antagonism, that it will be very difficult to eradicate. Inequality, inherent or acquired, is always the social evil that eats us away; it is for that reason that the blind but instinctive crowd ridicules genius.

"The weak will only admit individual efforts toward improvement if you at least offer them material compensations. It is therefore logical that the initiative of an entente should come from intellectuals and the powerful. Would it not at least be just, for example, to give labor the value and the wage that it merits? Every human being has a right to work—which is to say, to live—and all work ought to have just retribution; but I have learned, by suddenly finding myself in poverty, that things do not happen like that. If, as in Voltaire's time, abuses no longer serve the laws, the laws too often still serve abuses.

"Look, this is my testament: you're young, a long and brilliant career is opening before you; doubtless you will soon be a magistrate. Always have pity on the unfortunate that you have been called upon to judge. Never forget that collective crime often has a large part of the responsibility in the individual fault. All is not for the best, believe me, in the best of societies. It is time to hear the clamors of those who are dying of hunger every day.

"There is in mechanics an absolute principle known as the resistance of materials: superimposed materials can only support a certain force without being disorganized. If you allow too many injustices and miseries to be heaped one atop another, your social edifice will not take long to crumble. Already, a sinister cracking is making itself heard. Don't continue to remain deaf to it, or you'll be buried under the rubble.

"One final plea: will you take charge of conveying to the Minister of Public Education, in order that he might confer with is colleague in Justice, the letter that I'm going to dictate to you.

"*Monsieur the Minister of Public Education.*

"*A man, who has been condemned to death, has committed a social crime far greater than the one of which he has been accused. He would like to redeem it by rendering humankind an exceptional and inappreciable service. Human vivisection being, so to speak, impractical in our present organization, the psychology of the brain is groping in the dark; pathological hazard has scarcely cast a few rare glimmers of light therein—it is thus that Broca was able to find the location of speech in the third circumvolution. It is, however, of primordial necessity that that localization of cerebral function should at least be entirely known and demonstrated. How many scientific, and even philosophical, issues could then be elucidated; what giant steps might be taken in biological and psychological studies; what points of support might be provided to mental pathology?*

"*Condemned to die futilely on a scaffold, a vestige without authority of barbaric epochs, he solicits the honor of lending himself to these experiments of the highest importance. He will experience cruel suffering, but his energy and determination will enable him to endure them. It is urgent that you make a rapid decision; the preparation and preliminaries of that vivisection require a fairly long lapse of time.*

"*With the hope that French science will not lose the precious and perhaps unique opportunity that he offers benevolently, he has the honor, Monsieur the Minister, to be our humble and obedient servant,*

"*X, known as Jacques Bilan.*"

A fortnight later, the governor of La Roquette received the following response, which he comes to read to his prisoner.

"*Monsieur the Governor,*

"*The condemned Jacques Bilan has solicited the favor of serving in experiments in human vivisection; please will you tell him that his request has not been greeted favorably. In*

addition to the humanitarian sentiments opposed to its ac-
ceptance, it would be require, to organize a circumstance of
that order, a special law to modify the penalty in vigor. Never-
theless, the Minister not being indifferent to the good will of
the guilty party, authorizes you to engage him to sign a peti-
tion for clemency.

    "On behalf of the Minister of Public Education,
    "R."

The governor adds: "You have heard what I have just read. It's certain clemency that is being announced to you; hasten to sign the recourse."

"No, Monsieur Governor," he replies. "If I had wanted to live, I wouldn't be here. The fatality that is pursuing me will not even permit me, it seems, to die usefully. So much the worse for my fellows, and so much the worse for me, for such a death would have been more glorious."

"You're wrong to refuse the favor that is being offered to you," says the governor, amazed.

"The only favor that it will be agreeable for me to obtain would be the removal of this straitjacket that I have been wearing since my condemnation."

"I'm sorry not to be able to comply with your desire; the regulations formally oppose it; it would be necessary for an order to come from higher up."

"Well, let's not talk about it anymore."

During the long days he has been sighing for eternal repose, the wait has begun to weigh upon him heavily. For fear that a regret might attach him to existence, he has not wanted to read any book, he has avoided distractions and the conversations that the guards have attempted to strike up with him; he has refused charitable or curious visits and has not accepted the anonymous assistances that have reached him. The days are spent in long meditations. The approach of death has further extinguished his hatred and disarmed his vengeance; he regrets the threats that wounded pride caused to rise to his lips.

"Forget," he says to his defender, who has come to see him for the last time, "the insensate words that you once heard. Anger renders us stupid and causes us to go astray; it is not human beings, immediately replaced by others just as mediocre, egotistical and unjust, that it is necessary to destroy; it is institutions and ideas that it is necessary to change. It is very rare, in any case, that a violent means arrives at the right time—which is to say, at the moment when the reaction that it inevitably provokes is not fatal to the cause it wants to serve. The theoreticians of anarchism, those whose words suggest action, would do well to meditate that truth. I wonder, now, why those ideas of vengeance invaded me. Perhaps I needed really to become an anarchist in order to accept without weakness the punishment that has been inflicted upon me as such...

"And yet," he murmurs, "the crime that I have committed is far more antisocial, far more worthy of me than the infantile conceptions of those such minds! Collective revolt produces transitory results, but individual revolt..."

After a silence he adds: "Adieu! May all your desires be accomplished! Don't come to see me again; it's necessary that the slightest sympathy should not slip into my heart. I need all my courage; waiting is a thousand times more cruel than death."

Only the memory of Mariette, rendered pure of all mixture, aids him to support the long anguish of his agony. It is no longer Rose Gontran, however, but the prostitute Mariette, the streetwalker, who appears to him and consoles him. She alone seems worthy of pity, admiration and regret. It is the alms of love that the registered prostitute gave to the old pauper, and the unforgettable night when, savage and unchained, she entered forcefully into his heart, that come to haunt his solitude and causes tears to rise to his eyes. Why did he abandon her? She merited being redeemed. Poor Mariette!

The dream he has that night announces to him that the hour is near. The man he saw one day in a London tavern, the dead man whose name he has taken suddenly surges forth before him.

"Why have you denied me?" the veritable Jacques Bilan murmurs. "Why, having substituted my identity for yours, did you not have the courage to accept responsibility for my actions?

"You do not foresee, then, as you emerged from the Monks Agency under my remains that our two past lives would henceforth form a single social entity? You did not know that we had once been conceived at the same fleeting instant, that the same influences presided over our creation, that the same share was conditionally attributed to us, the same gifts accorded to us? Fortune alone created the difference; born in your opulence, I would have shone with your glory; and you, born in my poverty, would have been the revolutionary that I was.

"Why did you not divine the architect of your ruin? When the truth was revealed to you, you ought to have prostrated yourself at its feet, chased away the error of your life, chased away the error of your work. Instead of that, you wanted to benefit from an impure glory; you only adored the goddess in order to compel her to become the servant of your pride; an insane idea germinated in your head; you committed the sacrilegious imprudence of mocking the Death that had not summoned you and the Destiny that, to my detriment, had already allowed you to take more than your share; you underestimated their power; you wanted to impose your will upon them.

"Insensate! In transgressing the decrees of Providence, which ceased to protect you, in placing yourself outside the social conditions that had been your only safeguard, in wanting to avoid the sacred laws that regulate the forms of human existence, you forged for their avenging arm the flaming double-edged sword. In that civil and social death, you lost the best part of your value; your incomplete and defenseless self was henceforth the prey of errant forces; you became the empty house by the roadside whose walls are soiled by vagabonds and in which beasts lurk.

"The names that you took at hazard created vague identities for you, but the day when you took mine, everything that survived me, acts and thoughts like, was fatally bound to take possession of your being. Your fate, from that moment on, became exactly similar to mine, and, as you bore within you the crime that I have committed, the crime that your past forbade you to carry out, it was necessary, in order for you to be justly punished, that you also take my place."

He wakes up with a start. Dull rumors seem to reach him.

No regret agitates him, but a nervous anxiety torments him. He fears that his courage and his pride might abandon him; he is afraid of showing the slightest sign of weakness.

A noise of bolts; the door grates and opens; eyes full of pity gaze at him, surprising him still in bed.

A brief moment of anguish grips him. He makes an energetic effort, sits up, and then stands up, having mastered himself completely

"The time has come, hasn't it?" he says, anticipating the customary words.

He puts on his civilian clothing while the representatives of the law accomplish the formalities. A magistrate asks him whether he has any revelation to make or any last wishes to express.

"I want my cadaver to be delivered as quickly as possible to the Faculté," he replies. "The simulacrum of inhumation is an unnecessary legal hypocrisy." Then he manifests the desire not to be tied too tightly and to escape the brutality of his aides; he will place his head on the bascule himself and put his neck into the inferiors semicircle of the lunette.

"My body will serve for physiological experiments," he adds. "It is vital that the separation be made quickly. With the system of the bascule, the strangulation of the lunette and the jostling of the aides, one arrives at oblique sections that spoil a head."

A painful shudder takes possession of the assistants, even though they are accustomed to these supreme conversations. Even the executioner looks with an amazement mingled with respect at a condemned man giving proof of competence and the concern for being guillotined properly.

"Yes, yes," he murmurs. "We'll be careful; I'll take personal charge of the oper..." The word sticks in his mouth.

"The operation of social surgery," the condemned man continues, with an imperceptible smile. "I'm counting on you, and I thank you in advance—all the more so," he adds, with the same smile, "as it will be difficult for me to thank you afterwards."

The strange condemned man goes on: "The first time I was decapitated, the section was perfect and I couldn't help thinking about the deplorable results obtained by the blade of the guillotine... Don't be too astonished by my words; I'm not mad; I'm speaking figuratively."

The priest keeps discreetly to the rear; he fears that Companion Bilan might receive his offers with a few coarse rebukes.

Divining his embarrassment, he says: "Excuse me, Monsieur l'Abbé; I have nothing in particular to confess to you. If we professed the same religious ideas, I'd be honored to have recourse to your ministry."

"I will pray for you, Monsieur," the priest replied, quietly. "Only permit me to accompany you."

"If you wish. Nevertheless, I recommend you not to hide the guillotine from me; I need to look it in the face."

He is taken to the registry; he transfer of the prisoner to the executor takes place; the aides proceed with the toilette; cold scissors cut into the shirt, freeing the nape of the neck. He shivers involuntarily.

"Don't go so quickly," he murmurs. "You're doing me more harm than the blade is going to do."

Monsieur de Paris scolds his employee.

His hands and feet are tied.

"At least give me enough slack to let me walk," he requests. "You can see that I have no desire to flee. That march with short, jerky steps, has always produced a painful impression in me."

A cord is passed around his waist. That detail intrigues him; he interrogates. Monsieur Deibler simulates the action of taking a cadaver and throwing it into the basket.

In the square, dawn has just broken; the guillotine confusedly outlines its banal silhouette of a great frame on the bare gray walls of the old prison; the plane trees exhale a scent of spring buds. The privileged seated around the funereal instrument of justice are chatting discreetly among themselves.

In the distance, the Rue de La Roquette is swarming with people; the keepers of order have difficulty containing the lovers of capital executions outside the barriers. Clusters of human heads fill the window-frames and groups of enlaced human beings are clinging to the chimneys on the roofs. Late diners in suits and girls in bright dresses emerge from the first rows, standing on fiacres or ladders. All those people are almost certain of seeing nothing; perhaps it is the odor of blood that attracts them.

The squadrons of mounted police, fearing some anarchist manifestation, charge at the slightest pretext, driving back men in working clothes into the adjacent streets. Rumors and cries are born of the collisions.

The doors of the somber vault have suddenly opened wide; a command rings out, followed by shrill shrieks of steel; the gleam of sabers surges forth in the pallid down; the journalists and the curious remove their hats; the tumultuous rumbling from the distant crowd is immediately followed by a great silence. The cortege has just appeared.

Jacques Bilan is pale, but his gait and his gaze are assured. The sight of the guillotine seems to stimulate him; his eyes shine; he walks toward it, fascinated; he seems glad to be finally going to die.

A few anxious moments of expectation go by. The blade slides in the grooves and falls heavily upon the flesh. A long exclamation of horror rises from the turbulent populace.

The law is satisfied, and society avenged.

Chapter XXXIX

In a corner of the nave that Danton, Marat and so many others once filled with their tumultuous eloquence, the laboratory of the practical school, more numerous than usual, the physicians and their pupils proceed actively with the preparations for the usual experiments. The piles, the electrical apparatus, and the instruments of transfusion are carefully checked, the defibrinated and oxygenated blood is maintained at the required temperature. They await with impatience the head and the body of the executed man, which the delegates of the Faculté will not take long to bring them.[35]

Everything is finished. Clad in their white aprons, bareheaded or ornamented with black velvet skullcaps, leaning on the walls or sitting on the corners of tables, they smoke their cigarettes and chat familiarly among themselves.

"What a pity," exclaims Professor Larmezan, the head of the laboratory, "that the Ministry didn't think it ought to accept the anarchist's proposal! Think, Messieurs, of the immense advantages we might have obtained from a human vivisection; my illustrious predecessor and master would have been shivering with joy in his tomb. He always dreamed of

---

[35] The author of the present text would, of course, have been aware of numerous previous literary dramas that conclude with the guillotining of the protagonist, often after harrowing tribulations and frequently with flagrant injustice, in the interests of making philosophical condemnations similar to his own. In adding this coda, he was doubtless aware of the fact that one of the most striking of those previous mordant dramas, Jules Janin's *L'Âne mort et la Femme guillotinée* (1829; tr. as *The Dead Donkey and the Guillotined Woman*) had prompted the author's friend, Honoré de Balzac, to add an extra chapter following the poor woman's body into the dissecting room.

finding an intelligent condemned man who would lend himself to it."

"And this one was of superior intelligence," a young physiologist adds. "His proposal proves it; he would have been admirably submissive to all our experiments; today would have been a memorable date in the history of science."

"The Minister of Education," affirms a surgeon, "wasn't hostile to the idea, but his colleague in Justice laughed in his face, and the entire Council asked whether he was insane."

"Routine on one side and sentimentalism on the other," observes a professor of the Collège de France. "What would the Anti-Vivisection League say?"

"And the politicians? The government would have been hauled over the coals the next day. What fine speeches about the sacred laws of humanity! The religious sects would come together in a touching chorus. The Ministry wouldn't survive for twenty-four hours."

"The same individuals who criticize us for ignorance," the surgeon continues, "haggle over the means of instruction. They want to be delivered of all their ills, they demand that we spirit away their pains, and they reproach as a crime the death of a few rabbits that we sacrifice in order to cure them."

"Which doesn't prevent them," an intern remarks, "from killing the same rabbits themselves and devouring them without remorse."

"Let it be said between us," puts in Dr. R***, a member of the Society for the Protection of Animals, "that some physiologists indulge in unnecessary and overly numerous vivisections; come on, Messieurs, when an experiment is conclusive, a definitive demonstration made, it isn't necessary to repeat it hundreds and thousands of times."

"I'll wager," ripostes the Professor of the Collège de France, sharply, who believes that he is being criticized "that you've shot more birds hunting than I've killed guinea-pigs in my laboratory."

"I kill game in order to eat it."

"And I kill animals to instruct my pupils; on your side, the stomach to which you refuse nothing, on mine, the brain that you want to submit to the congruent portion. You're going to object that you expedite your victims without making them suffer and I torture mine, but what about the crustaceans that you boil alive, the quails and capons you blind in order to cram them? As long as you don't become a vegetarian, I won't believe in the sincerity of your tenderness."

"People protest against useful vivisections," adds a Limousin student, rolling his *r*s, "and cast fire and flames against bullfights, but no one seems to care that geese are plucked alive to make eiderdowns."

"And the hundreds of workers devoured by the manipulation of chemical products, the victims of phosphorus, mercury, acid, sulfur, carbon..."

"You can say all that in the Chambre when you're a député," says Dr. Larmezan, smiling.

"A human vivisection!" says the young physiologist. "But an immense clamor would rise up from all corners of the world. That men die uselessly on the scaffold, fine, but that a condemned man has the audacity to want to redeem his crime by a service that will do a thousand times more good than the evil he's committed—stop there!"

"Society is logical," replies old Master L***. "It wants to punish a guilty man; it wants him to die on the shameful platform; it wants the example to impress the crowd. I don't affirm that it's right, but that is its goal. If it permitted its victim to serve for such experiments, that goal would not be attained; it would not be to shame that the guilty man would be led but to glory. Think of the renown of the man who would permit the penetration of the complex arcana of human thought. Imagine the right he would have to the gratitude of future generations—especially a man whose murder could pass for a political crime. His murder would be immediately pardoned! A century would not go by before his statue would be erected in a public square; streets would bear his name; cities would dispute the honor of having given birth to him."

"People prefer to reserve that glory to conquerors!" exclaims a pupil.

"Don't speak ill of conquerors, young man," replies the old professor. "War is a just and necessary thing."

"Still a partisan of bleeding," sniggers Dr. Gérot, a professor in the École de Pharmacie.

"We'll come back to it, my lad, we'll come back to it; bleeding is preferable to the dirty drugs with which you teach students the art of poisoning their clients."

The conversation risks taking on a bitter tone; one member of the audience hastens to change the subject.

"By the way, do you know who he is, the companion whose remains are about to be brought to us?"

"Did you know him?"

"No, but I read the debates. He's the famous orderly at the hospital who made the femoral ligature that put poor G***'s nose out of joint."

Everyone bursts out laughing at the memory of that adventure.

"Bah! That orderly who resembled Dr. Albin?"

"The same."

Involuntarily, Dr. Larmezan frowns

"It appears, too, that he was a former medical student."

"Hence the request for vivisection and the scientific terminology of his explanatory letter."

"Personally, if I'd been on the jury, I wouldn't have condemned him to death. The man was surely a general paralytic[36] with delusions of grandeur; his obstinacy in claiming that he wasn't Jacques Bilan and that an illustrious individual was concealed beneath that borrowed identity was clear proof of it."

"Not so clearly as that. Perhaps he wasn't Jacques Bilan. All the witness evidence was valueless, without exception. There was only one sole piece of evidence against him: the

---

[36] "General paralysis of the insane" was a label invented to describe the neuropsychological effects of tertiary syphilis.

papers found in his possession. Now it's quite possible, as he claimed, that he had bought them in London. Agencies exist that deal in that commerce; I know, pertinently, that more than one charlatan has passed his doctorate that way."

"And what about the anagrams? Was the advocate general mocked sufficiently on that subject?"

"There was good reason," declares the old master. "The law ought to be above such childishness. You can see from here the court of assizes condemning my friend Gérot to death because a vagabond named Goret cut an old lady to pieces after subjecting her to the utmost outrages."

The assembly guffaws loudly.

"That would perhaps be less absurd than being obstinate in killing people by bleeding them!" exclaims Dr, Gérot, red with anger.

"Come on, Messieurs, we're not at the Académie," remarks Professor Larmezan. "No vulgar words; preserve your forces—there's a session tomorrow."

"It wasn't me who started it," murmurs the old master.

"A mania of the sixteenth century, anagrams," adds Dr. Larmezan. "This Jacques Bilan must be erudite."

"The question asked by a member of the jury wasn't as negligible as the President declared, since the anarchist had a mania for anagrams and claimed to be hiding under a pseudonym, it would have been interesting to research all the anagrams of Bilan."

"That's quite easy," proposes an intern, picking up a pencil and a piece of paper. "Bilan, you say? Let's see: Nibal, Linan. Balin. Inbal, Iblan..."

"Iblan, the American doctor!" voices exclaim on all sides. "What if it were him? It's quite possible. The articles he published were anarchist."

"Hang on, I'll continue: Linab, Blain, Lanib, Labin, Albin..."

Professor Larmezan has great difficulty repressing a start of anger and fear.

"Enough, Messieurs! No jokes in bad taste; let's respect the memory of our illustrious deceased and not let his name by mingled with such infamies. Leave the anagrams alone. It's already enough that that question of resemblance—which was real, I admit—has come into the discussion."

"So that orderly really did resemble my friend Albin?" asks Dr. R***, who is perhaps not sorry to annoy Larmezan.

"Yes," the latter replies. "Dr. Albin had a distinctive physiognomy, and yet, on three different occasions I've encountered people who resembled him closely. First that orderly…"

"Who was jolly good at surgical operations."

"Well, Messieurs, physical resemblance is sometimes accompanied by similar mental and intellectual aptitudes. Then, on the day of my marriage, an unknown with the appearance of a petty clerk who watched us come out of the church."

"Banquo's ghost!" murmurs the old master between his teeth.

"And finally, the famous flashy foreigner whose name has just been cited, the author of the scandal on the day of the inauguration, that lunatic Dr. Iblan."

"Oh, that one didn't resemble him at all."

"Make no mistake, Messieurs; beneath that Spanish-American appearance, he was the one who resembled him most closely. I saw him at close range at Bicêtre, and I'm not alone in having perceived that bizarre particularity. The ferocious enemy and stubborn detractor of *Biological Chemistry*, bore an astonishing resemblance to the author of that work of genius, and it was that singularity that had done him the bad turn of sending him to Bicêtre. He'd eaten hashish, and our savant friend Gérot will tell you that the effect of Indian hemp is to exaggerate ideas."

"Gérot has never eaten it, then," declares the old partisan of bleeding, pursuing his friend like a dog after a rat. Dr. Gérot shrugs his shoulders.

"And sometimes deforming them," the professor of biology adds. "Dr. Iblan, who was aware of that resemblance, imagined himself to be Dr. Albin."

"Cases of resemblance are excessively common," adds the old master, in a detached tone that announces nothing benevolent. "The human species can be divided into a small umber of characteristic types to which numerous categories of individuals are attached more or less closely. Without being a determined partisan of transformism, one can divine merely from the appearance of an individual the animal type to which his physiology attaches him. To cite only one example, it would be necessary to be blind not to recognize at first glance a perfect representation of the so-called equine type in the nobly accentuated features of my excellent comrade and fried Gérot."

A burst of laugher salutes the new gibe.

"*Asinus asinum fricat,*[37] you old gorilla," replies the colleague, advancing menacingly.

"Come on, Messieurs," Dr. Larmezan interjects. "Get ready; I can hear noises on the stairs; the decapitated man is arriving."

The door opens; two physicians, followed by an amphitheater assistant, who is carrying a large basket, come in.

"Here's the head first," says one of them. "The body's downstairs."

"You're very late."

"Is that our fault? It's always the same rigmarole, as you know full well; they never finish with their formalities."

The head is brought out of the basket. It is enveloped in compresses, stained with blood and sawdust. It is wiped in haste, and placed on the table. The face is bloodless; the wide open eyes have conserved, as if staring, an energetic gaze; the corners of the lightly curled lips have a bitter smile.

---

[37] Literally, "the ass rubs the ass"—referring metaphorically to mutual flattery.

Everyone considers it with an astonishment mingled with stupor. No one dares say a word.

"I recognize him!" cries Dr. R*** suddenly. "That's the head of Dr. Iblan. The fellow was well worthy of such an end!"

Professor Larmezan opens frightened eyes. "That's quite possible," he murmurs, after a moment of painful silence. He quickly recovers his composure. "Come on, Messieurs," he says, "we're wasting precious time. The identity of the corpse scarcely matters; let's get to work."

The habitual experiments are rapidly executed. An intern armed with scalpels and a saw prepares to make the cranial section in order to determine whether the brain is undamaged and to what extent the guillotine can be considered as responsible.

"Stop!" cries the professor of biology. "We'll do the autopsy of the brain this afternoon. I'm late for my visits."

He hastens to send everyone away and he makes a false exit himself.

Soon afterwards, however, the laboratory door opens noisily; the eminent professor, prey to the most vivid agitation, runs to his anthropometric instruments and makes minute measurements of the diameters and the facial angle of the severed head.

As the operation progresses, incoherent words emerge from his mouth; emotion renders him breathless; a cold sweat pearls on his forehead.

Then, thinking that no one can see him or hear him, the truth finally escapes from his trembling and blanched lips:

"The head of Dr. Albin!"